Dr

Leila popped the cork with a theatrical flourish and poured three glasses. 'And you, Ginny? Are you pleased?'

Ginny, glowing with the adrenalin rush of performing in front of an appreciative audience, threw her arms round Leila and kissed her. 'I'm not only pleased, Leila. I can't tell you. I loved it. It was like being someone else. Like being a film star.'

Leila picked up one of the glasses and raised it in salute. 'I'm absolutely thrilled, Ginny. Thrilled to bits. And just wait till you hear what you're going to do next!'

Gilda O'Neill was born in the East End of London and now lives in Essex with her husband and two grown-up children. Her grandmother owned a pie and mash shop, her grandfather was a tug skipper on the Thames and her great uncle was a minder in a Chinese gambling den in Limehouse. Her other books include five novels and *Pull No More Bines: An Oral History of East London Hop Pickers*. She has just completed her new novel *The Lights of London* and is currently researching a book on the history of East London.

GILDA O'NEILL

Dream On

— For Pat —
with every best wish
to you, love from
Gilda O'Neill

ARROW

XXX

Published in the United Kingdom in 1998 by
Arrow Books

3 5 7 9 10 8 6 4 2

First published in the United Kingdom in 1997
by William Heinemann

Arrow Books
Random House UK Ltd
20 Vauxhall Bridge Road, London SW1V 2SA

Random House Australia (Pty) Limited
20 Alfred Street, Milsons Point, Sydney,
New South Wales 2061, Australia

Random House New Zealand Limited
18 Poland Road, Glenfield
Auckland 10, New Zealand

Random House South Africa (Pty) Limited
Endulini, 5a Jubilee Road, Parktown 2193, South Africa

Random House UK Limited Reg. No. 954009

A CIP catalogue record for this book
is available from the British Library

Papers used by Random House UK Limited
are natural, recyclable products made from wood grown in
sustainable forests. The manufacturing processes conform to
the environmental regulations of the country of origin

Printed and bound in the United Kingdom by
Cox & Wyman Ltd, Reading, Berkshire

ISBN 0 749 2172 5

For Tanja Howarth

As with all my previous novels, *Dream On*
is set in a real place during a real time,
but I have created the characters and some
of the street names especially for the story.

Book One

Chapter 1

1945

'Ginny? Gin? It's only me.'

Dilys Chivers was shouting at the top of her voice as she barged, uninvited, through the open street door and along the narrow passageway of number 18 Bailey Street.

'Come on, you lot,' she went on, throwing her coat over the end of the banisters, 'if you don't get a move on, you know what'll happen. That greedy mare from number 20 will have stuffed all the grub. She'll be dancing with all the fellers. And you'll all still be—'

As she stuck her head round the kitchen doorway, Dilys quite uncharacteristically shut her mouth and stood stock still in puzzled silence.

Sitting in the kitchen, hunched over the little scrubbed table, nursing a cup of tea, was a miserable-looking middle-aged woman. 'All right, Dilys?' she muttered.

'Whatever's the matter, Nellie?' Dilys, recovering her composure, pulled out a chair and sat herself down opposite the woman. It looked as though there might be a story to glean here and, young and pretty as she was, Dilys was as partial to a bit of gossip as any of the elderly battleaxes of Bailey Street.

'Honest, Nell,' she went on, pulling off her hat and tossing it on to the table between them, 'you look just like you wanna go for a' – she flashed her eyebrows – '*you know*. But you've gone and lost the key to the lavatory door.'

'It's this party, ain't it?' Nellie answered, her lips pursing in self-pitying anger. 'I can't go, can I?' She tilted

3

her head to one side and stared sorrowfully into the middle distance over Dilys's shoulder. 'And after surviving all them years of war an' all. Putting up with the Blitz, and what with the doodlebugs . . .'

Dilys might have relished a bit of scandal, but putting up with Nellie Martin's tale of woe was a price she wasn't prepared to pay. Dilys had never been a patient sort of person, and while she wanted the full story, she didn't fancy the boring moaning bits that looked like going with it.

'You just forget all about them bad memories, Nell,' Dilys said briskly, slapping her palms on the table. 'You just tell me what this is all about.' She paused, then added firmly: 'Briefly, like.'

Nellie's lips twitched. 'It's her, ain't it?'

It took Dilys a moment. 'D'you mean Ginny?'

'Yeah,' spat Nellie, unable even to speak her daughter-in-law's name.

'What on earth's she done to get you into this state?' Dilys's forehead pleated into a frown; this was getting really confusing.

While there wasn't exactly any great love lost between Nellie and Ginny, they usually managed to rub along well enough together. With Ginny keeping her mouth shut and doing as she was told by her husband – Nellie's son – and with Nellie not giving a bugger about anyone but herself, in its way, the household functioned. So all this upset, especially on a day like today, well, it just didn't make sense.

'If you must know, she's shut herself in the bloody front bedroom and won't come down, that's what.' Nellie spread her hands in wretched supplication. 'How am I meant to go to the party by myself, Dilys, eh? You tell me that. I'll be a laughing stock. Everyone'll have their

4

families with them – except me. And I can just see that Florrie Robins . . .'

Nellie paused for a moment, visualising the woman who was her oldest friend and, therefore, her oldest rival. 'I know her. She'll be sitting round there at her daughter's street party in St Stephen's Road, with all her grand-children round her, acting like flaming Lady Muck, while they all wait on her, and fuss over her, and make sure the old cow's got everything she wants.'

Nellie's face puckered in on itself until she looked exactly as though she was sucking a lemon. 'And you know what everyone'll be saying, don't you? I can just hear 'em. But I swear on my life, Dilys, he never so much as touched—'

'Hang on, Nell,' Dilys interrupted, 'why're you so worried about Ginny not going with you? You can go with your Ted, can't you?'

'Him!' sneered Nellie, astonishing Dilys by showering her son's name with almost as much venom as she would probably have trowelled on to her daughter-in-law's – had she allowed her name to pass her lips. 'You wanna ask *her* about *him*.'

Nellie lifted her chin and stabbed her thumb ceiling-wards. It was a gesture reminiscent of the one that the minister from the local evangelical hall used when he admonished the sinners, telling them they should be list-ening with their hearts to the Lord of Heaven, and not with their throats to the landlord of the Prince Albert. But it would have been obvious, even to the unbeliever, that Nellie's reference was not exactly reverential.

'Go on,' she hissed, 'you go up and see if you can get any sense outta the snivelling little mare, 'cos I'll be buggered if I can.'

'Gin. Gin, it's only me, babe.' Dilys's voice was tender

5

and wheedling as she tapped gently on the door. 'Come on, girl, let me in, eh?'

A muffled sob came from inside the bedroom.

Dilys stuck her ear to the door. 'What was that?'

There was another low whimper.

'What?' Dilys knelt down and squinted through the keyhole, as though it would help her hear more clearly. 'Speak up, Gin. I mean, I can't help you if I can't hear you, now can I?'

Ginny blew her nose loudly, then croaked in a tear-sodden voice: 'Leave me alone, Dil, please. Just leave me.'

'As if I'd do that, you dopey cow.' Discarding the softly-softly approach, Dilys gave the doorknob a good rattle. 'Now you either open this door, Ginny Martin, or I'm gonna go along to Tommy Fowler's and borrow his ladders. And then I'll stick 'em up against your front wall and I'll climb in through the bloody bedroom window. How'd you fancy that!'

She paused, listening for a response. 'I mean it, Ginny. You know me.'

Ginny did indeed know Dilys – for as long as either of them could remember, in fact – and Ginny also knew that once Dilys Chivers had made up her mind about something, there was no stopping her. And Ginny didn't much relish the idea of having her clambering up the outside of the house and messing up all her VE-Day decorations. Especially not in full view of the neighbours, who had all been out in the drizzle-slicked cobbled street getting the party ready since first light.

With weary resignation, Ginny decided she had no choice. 'Hang on, Dil,' she sniffled, 'I'm coming.'

'I knew you would.' Dilys grinned in self-satisfied triumph as she straightened up from the keyhole. She smoothed the silky fabric of her new dress down over her thighs, tossed her head and patted her dark, shiny, permanently waved hair back into place with a little sigh of contentment.

The bedroom door opened and Ginny stood there, her head bowed and her arms dangling loosely by her sides.

'Blimey, Gin, will you just look at yourself,' chirped Dilys without a trace of compassion in her voice. 'You look worse than Nellie and that's saying something. Whatever's got into the pair of you?'

Without even pausing for a reply Dilys executed a neat little pirouette on the tiny lino-covered landing, flung out her arms in best pin-up style, dropped her chin and peered seductively through her lashes. 'Well?' she demanded. 'Ain't you gonna say nothing about me new frock, then?'

Before Ginny had the chance even to wonder how Dilys had managed to get something as expensive-looking as that – when they both knew she'd used up all her clothing coupons ages ago – Dilys was shoving her back into the bedroom.

'So,' she whispered conspiratorially, rolling her eyes and jerking her head towards the door in the general direction of the stairs, where Dilys presumed Nellie would be standing earwigging – just as she would have been doing in her position – 'what's been going on with her down there, then?'

Ginny slumped on to the double bed she shared with her husband and started picking at a loose quilting stitch on the pink satin eiderdown.

'Come on, Gin, you know you can tell me.'

Ginny shrugged. 'I dunno, Dil, do I.' She shook her head, making her soft blonde curls bounce around her face. 'I really don't.'

'For Gawd's sake, Ginny, pull yourself together girl. You're like looking at a bleed'n' wet weekend. Even

Violet Varney's making more effort than you.' Dilys gestured dramatically towards the window and the street beyond. 'That woman was out there last night till all hours doing up her front with a bit o' bunting.'

'So was I.'

Dilys huffed dismissively. 'Yeah, but her old man's in a bloody prisoner of war camp.'

Ginny looked up at her pitifully. 'At least she knows her Bert'll be home soon.'

'Whatever you on about now?'

Ginny turned her head so that Dilys couldn't see her tears. 'Look, Dilys, I know how much Nellie's looking forward to the party and I really hate letting her down, 'cos I know it ain't her fault, it's mine. And I feel terrible. But I can't go out there. I just can't.'

'Why not?'

A sob shuddered through her body. 'It's Ted. He's not been home.'

'He's *what*?' Dilys sprang up from the bed and stuck her fists into her waist. 'The rotten, stinking, swivel-eyed, no-good cowson of a . . .' Her fury got the better of her tongue and Dilys ran out of insults.

Ginny covered her face with her hands. 'Don't say them things, Dil. Like I said, it's my fault. No one else's. I must have upset him somehow. But I've been sitting here racking me brains—'

'I'll kill him,' Dilys fumed. 'I'll bloody well kill him.'

Ginny dropped her hands and looked up at her friend. 'You're a good mate, but it's down to me to sort it out.'

She turned her head away again and said in a voice so small that Dilys could only just make out the words: 'You and your mum are really important to me, Dilys, you know that, but since losing my own mum and dad . . .' Her shoulders shook as she rubbed the tears roughly from her cheeks with the back of her hand. '. . . Ted and

8

Nellie are all the family I've got. And I just don't know what I'd do if Ted left me. I do try to make him happy, but sometimes I just seem to get on his nerves. He gets so wild with me. Now he's started staying out all night. What am I gonna do?'

'That's it. I've heard enough.' Dilys took Ginny firmly by the arm and pulled her over to the polished walnut dressing-table, which took up almost the whole wall beneath the window of the cramped front bedroom in the little terraced house.

'Now you listen to me, Ginny Martin. You sit yourself down on that stool. Go on. Do as you're told. And you get your war-paint on. You're going to this sodding party whether you want to or not. We'll show bloody Ted Martin that he can't get away with this; he'd better start watching his step or he's gonna be in for a nasty surprise, a very nasty surprise indeed. 'Cos if he ain't careful, the bastard's gonna have me to deal with.'

As Ginny reluctantly stepped out of number 18, with the help of a push from Nellie and a shove from Dilys, she actually found herself smiling – she would have had a hard heart not to – because, just like every other ordinary little turning in the East End, Bailey Street in Bow had resolved to put on its finest for its VE-Day party. And, in the watery afternoon sunshine, despite the debris left from the bomb damage where the rocket had fallen in nearby Grove Road, and the houses that were boarded up, and the tarpaulin-covered roofs, Ginny saw a street where the residents had done themselves proud.

Each one of the remaining terraced houses was festooned in every conceivable shade of red, white and blue. They were draped with swags of home-made bunting; handwritten banners declaring Britain's greatness and the East End's allegiance to the King; and strung up

9

high, right across the street, on cords stretched between upstairs windows, were tattered but loyal Union Jacks, flapping in the still damp, but now warmer, afternoon breeze.

Along the middle of the road stood a line of ill-matched kitchen tables, transformed by a covering of assorted patched and darned bedsheets into a single long dining-table. Although letting your neighbours have a close-up look at your repaired sheets certainly wasn't what most people in Bailey Street would have considered proper behaviour, it didn't matter today, because it was a day unlike any other. All that was important was the mountain of food piled on top of them; food which despite the rationing had been victoriously, if rather mysteriously, procured for the great event.

There were plates of sandwiches – none, it had been agreed by common consent, made with the usually unavoidable tinned pilchards – trays of pies and tarts, bowls of trifle, dishes of jellied eels, mounds of winkles and cockles, jugs of orange and lemon squash and, stacked next to a gleaming urn that someone had managed to 'borrow' from the church hall, tottering stacks of cups and saucers.

As if all that wasn't enough, outside the Prince Albert, the pub on the corner of the street, there was a row of beer barrels, topped with a double layer of crates of light and brown ale, ready and waiting for the festivities to begin. And there was certainly plenty to feel festive about.

There would be no more bombs and no more rockets; dragging yourself out of bed and down to the shelter was a thing of the past; and, with a bit of luck, rationing would soon be nothing but another bad memory – just like the Blitz and Utility underwear. The East End was ready to celebrate all right and no one would be able to accuse the families who lived in Bailey Street of not doing their best to show everyone how it should be done.

'Over here!' Pearl Chivers shouted from across the street, waving both arms at Nellie, Ginny and Dilys.

Pearl, Dilys's mum, was standing outside her house, number 11, supervising her husband, George, and her two teenaged sons, Sid and Micky, as they battled with her beloved piano, trying to manoeuvre it out of the house, over the doorstep and into the street without damaging it.

'Come and help me organise this idle mob, will you? Just look at 'em.'

She turned to point at the impromptu removal crew. 'Oi! Watch my walls, you dozy lot. That passage was only decorated last year.'

'I know, sweetheart. Sorry,' replied George good-naturedly. He knew better than to try and argue with his wife. He loved Pearl with all his heart, and everyone knew she was a genuinely good woman – as Ginny would have been the first to testify – but she was also the possessor of what George described as a 'strong type of personality' and had more energy than a dozen normal people. Like her daughter, Dilys, Pearl Chivers wasn't one to be messed around with.

'I was the one what painted and papered the flaming thing,' George added under his breath.

'Oi! I heard that!' Pearl grinned. 'Tell you what, girls, let's leave the fellers to it and go and help with the food instead. By the looks of it, they need some sorting out up there or it'll never get finished. Just look at 'em. You'd think they was doing it for a guv'nor instead of for 'emselves.'

She turned back to her husband and sons. 'And no

slacking, you three, I've got eyes in the back of this head of mine, remember.'

'As if we could forget,' Sid muttered.

'And I've got ears like a bat.' She chuckled, nudging her son in the side. 'So you wanna watch it, my lad. You might be nearly six foot in your stockinged feet, but you're still not too big for a wallop with the copper stick.'

Pearl didn't wait for Sid to reply, she just linked arms with Nellie and guided Dilys and Ginny forward in front of them towards the knot of women milling about at the business end of the tables, where yet more sandwiches were being made.

When he judged the women, or more specifically Pearl, to be out of earshot, George gave up the unequal contest and surrendered to the piano, leaving it perched on the street doorstep, hanging half in and half out of number 11 like an indecisive visitor.

Nodding for his sons to do likewise, George relaxed back against the door jamb, took a packet of Capstan Full Strength from his waistcoat pocket and offered them to the boys.

'And for Gawd's sake don't let your mother see,' he said, striking a match for them.

Micky inhaled deeply, his eyes narrowing against the smoke. 'Sixteen years old and she still treats me like I was a little kid,' he complained.

'Less of the "she", thank you, Micky.'

'Sorry, Dad.'

'You can talk,' sneered Sid. 'How d'you think I feel? If this war hadn't have ended just before I was old enough to bloody join up, she'd have *had* to have started treating me like an adult.'

'Pipe down, will you? I'm sick of the pair of you sulking and moping about. You don't know you're sodding born, either of you. You should have had the life I had, when I was your age.'

George took a long drag on his cigarette, then lifted his chin towards Ginny. She was standing to one side of the other women with a sad, far-away look in her eyes.

'Or the worries that poor little cow's got; then you'd know what trouble was all about. Look at her. Left all alone with Nellie again while he's out and about, and up to Gawd alone knows what.'

Sid shook his head in wonder. 'Honest, Dad, I reckon Ted Martin's gotta be off his head. I mean, you'd have to be mad wouldn't you, leaving a lovely bit of stuff like Ginny at a loose end?'

Micky snorted, his youthful imagination painting glorious visions of Ginny in his mind. 'I wouldn't leave her at any sort of end. I'd—'

Sid punched his younger brother in the shoulder. 'Shut up you, you little squirt.' He rolled his eyes at his dad in a gesture of mature male solidarity, to demonstrate that he was obviously above such smut. 'Typical of him though. I reckon he gets away with murder, that Ted Martin.'

'You're right there,' agreed George with a sigh. 'Must be one of the fittest young fellers in the street. And what is he, twenty-five, twenty-six? But did he do the decent thing and join up? Do me a favour. Bad chest, he reckoned. I've never heard so much old fanny. If he's got a bad chest, then I'm—'

'Here we go,' murmured Micky.

Sid punched him in the arm again. 'Shut up, mouthy.'

'Come on.' George flicked his half-smoked cigarette into the gutter and straightened his cap. 'You've had your break. Let's get this finished before the foreman catches us.'

*

'Least the weather's cleared up, eh, Ginny love,' Pearl said gently. 'You know, I was surprised our bedroom ceiling never come down on top of us when that thunderbolt dropped last night. Right overhead it was. I thought we was back in the Blitz for a minute.'

She put down her butter-knife and smiled at Ginny, trying to encourage her to join in. Pearl knew it was no use leaving it to Nellie to look after the poor little thing, it wouldn't even occur to her. She might, on a very rare occasion, consider her son, Ted, whom, Pearl was sure, Nellie loved in her own peculiar way; but it would be very seldom that she would put even his needs before her own. And apart from that, well, she had no mind for anyone but herself; even on that terrible night in 1941, which Pearl supposed the inconsiderate old trout probably wouldn't even remember.

But Pearl would never forget that night.

Ted and Ginny had been together, on and off, for almost two years by then; far more off than on, as anyone but the starry-eyed Ginny would have admitted, but a kid as innocent and trusting as her had stood no chance against the smooth ways of a handsome charmer like Ted Martin. After spotting the newly blossoming, pretty little blonde going into number 11 to see Dilys, Ted had homed in on her like a rocket launcher.

The night that stuck in Pearl's mind was one of the occasions when Ted had actually turned up to take Ginny out as he had promised, and after an evening spent up West, he was taking her back to her house in Antill Road.

They were later than they'd said they'd be and Ginny was expecting a right rucking, but, instead of finding her mum and dad sitting up waiting for them in the back kitchen, all they had found was a pile of bombed-out rubble.

It was strange, the sort of thing that made the hairs

stand up on the back of Pearl's neck just to think about it, but Ginny had said afterwards that before she and Ted had even turned out of Grove Road and into her street, she had known there was something wrong. She could feel it somewhere deep inside, as surely as if someone was speaking to her.

Ginny had let go of Ted's arm and stumbled along in the black-out, tripping and sliding on the debris and the sand spilling from the ripped and shredded sacking bags, ignoring the firemen, policemen and wardens who tried to stop her. She cared nothing for their shouts and warnings, nothing for her own safety, all she wanted to do was reach her house and her family. She had to get to them.

As she finally skidded to halt on the pavement, her heart was racing and her blood pounding in her ears.

But she was too late.

Her mum, her dad, and her five little brothers and sisters – all seven members of her family – were dead. Gone together in a single hit.

Ted had held her to him, stroking her back and rocking her as if she were a child with a grazed knee that he could make better with a kiss. He'd breathed into her hair, telling her not to cry, soothing her. But there was no need. Ginny couldn't cry, she was too numb; tears had no purpose or meaning.

Ted had walked her back to his house in Bailey Street, whispering gently to her that everything would be all right; she would stay with him and his mum for the night, and he would sort everything out in the morning.

But when they reached his house, they couldn't get in. Nellie had locked up the place hours ago, having cleared off to the shelter in the cellar of the Drum and Monkey, a pub on the corner of nearby Darnfield Street. She had paused, it had to be said, for a brief moment to think

15

about her son as she had locked the door against potential looters; but had then blithely presumed that, being like her – a twenty-four-carat survivor – her boy Ted would have made his own arrangements and had proceeded to untie the key from its string behind the letterbox and pop it into her pocket.

And so it was, with the flash and the flare of bombs and shells lighting up the black, moonless sky, and with the stink of fires and explosives souring the night air, that Pearl had taken the pair of them into her home.

They were lucky to have found her in. Pearl and her husband had intended taking the children down to the underground station at Mile End to shelter, but at the last minute their plans had changed. George had been asked to cover a fire-watching shift for a sick mate and Pearl hadn't fancied packing up all the gear and organising the kids by herself – the boys were at the age when they would start a row if one of them even thought that his brother was looking at him a bit sideways – so she'd decided to stay home instead.

She and the children had spent an uncomfortable and chilly night crammed under the kitchen table; not that a few inches of scrubbed deal would have made any difference if a bomb had fallen on them, but Pearl was a home-loving woman and her kitchen, and its table, made her feel safe.

Ted Martin was also lucky on another count: ordinarily, Pearl would never have let him across her doorstep. Unusually for a woman as generous and loving as her, she'd always found it difficult to take to him. She'd watched him grow up in the house right across the street and had seen a spiteful, selfish streak in him even as a little boy – probably not surprising with a mother like his – and she had been happy to avoid having anything to do with him. But when she'd opened her front door that night and had seen him with his arm folded round Ginny's shoulders, Pearl couldn't turn him away. She wouldn't have seen a dog left out on a night like that. And then later, when he'd told her what had happened, Pearl had actually been quite impressed by how well he was handling young Ginny's terrible shock. She resolved to try to see the good in him from then on and Ted had pleasantly surprised her – for a while.

But the occasions on which Ted Martin showed his decent side were becoming rarer and rarer and, try as she might for Ginny's sake, Pearl found it harder and harder to find excuses for his behaviour. It broke her heart to see the way Ted was turning out, and as for the way that Nellie was treating her daughter-in-law, sometimes it beggared belief that Ginny could put up with it. Maybe if she hadn't been put through so much, if she hadn't been left feeling so completely alone, maybe then she might not have been so quick to marry into such a family. But although Pearl had come to have feelings for Ginny that were almost as special as those she had for her own children, Pearl wasn't an interfering woman and it was really none of her business what went on behind the street door of number 18. She'd leave meddling to the likes of Florrie Robins. It would be an entirely different matter, of course, if Ginny ever came asking for help, then Pearl would be over there like a shot; or even if it was her Dilys who'd got herself hiked up to the no-good so-and-so. But her daughter wasn't even married. More was the pity. With so many young men lost, whatever would happen to girls like Dilys?

Pearl sighed and shook her head at the thought of it, but common sense, past experience and bloody awful, grinding necessity told her that it was no good fretting about things like that. She wasn't the sort to dream, she was the sort who pulled herself together and got on with

17

the job at hand, no matter what it was. And, right there and then, Pearl's job was spreading marge.

'Dilys, you and Ginny take these ones what I've done on the trays and start dishing them out on to them dinner-plates.' Pearl waved her knife to show where she meant.

The two young women did as they were told, Ginny silently and Dilys with eyes rolling and tongue clucking in complaint. Dilys would much rather have been helping the men. Especially the couple in uniform, who were staying along the street in the Albert with their Aunt Martha and Uncle Bob. Dilys had been dying to talk to them since she'd first set eyes on them that morning. It was driving her mad having to waste her time hanging around with all the old girls.

'That's that done, thank Gawd,' said Dilys, shoving the pile of empty trays under the table.

'Don't leave them there, Dil.' Ginny bent down to retrieve them from beneath the layers of sheeting. 'Someone might hurt themselves.'

Dilys made no effort to help her. 'Fancy going along to the Albert to see if we can do anything for Martha?'

'You go, I'll just take these trays back to Pearl.'

'Suit yourself.' Dilys shrugged, then flicked back her thick dark hair and wiggled her way along the street towards the pub, targeting the two young servicemen as surely as a darts player eyeing up the bull.

The party turned out to be a real success. Everyone was in just the mood to celebrate: looking forward to the dawning of the wonderful new world where families would be reunited, where there would be plenty of every-thing for everyone and, as soon as Japan was sorted out, fighting would be at an end for ever.

18

Everyone was in the mood, that is, except Ginny.

As she leaned back against the soot-blackened wall of the terrace, watching the now drunken dancers whirl around outside the pub in the flickering light of the bonfire burning on the bomb-site opposite, Ginny had none of their optimism. All she could feel was disappointment.

Plenty of others had had their own share of disappointment, of course: loved ones still abroad and fighting in the East; husbands and sons still being held in camps; or, worst of all, no loved ones left, just black-crêpe-swathed photographs on the sideboard that would have to take their place for ever.

But Ginny's disappointment was different. She had married Ted Martin and that didn't get her sympathy so much as pity. After all, her husband was not abroad fighting and he was still, as far as she knew, very much alive – or at least he had been when he'd left home yesterday morning on 'a bit of business', whatever that was supposed to mean. But with the pain he was causing, he might as well have been amongst the missing. Ted Martin had let her down yet again. Increasingly, he made his own rules, deciding what was or wasn't important and, unfortunately, Ginny seemed to come very low down on his list of priorities lately. But even though he thought only about himself and did exactly as he wanted, the trouble was, Ginny still loved him, loved him with all her heart. He was all she had, he was her life. That's why it was so hard for her to bear. She had had so many hopes for their future together; now it began to seem as though they were nothing more than a handful of girlish dreams. But they were dreams she had to hold on to. What else was there?

'Come and have a dance with us, Gin,' slurred Dilys, weaving towards her, a half-empty glass of something slopping about tipsily in her hand. 'I'd rather dance with a feller.' She grinned as she flopped back against the wall next to her. 'But there ain't too many of them about here tonight, are there?'

She waved her glass in the direction of the pub. 'There's a flipping queue up there for them two soldier boys. And when you start talking to 'em, you know what? You realise that's all they are: bloody boys. Give me a man every time, I say. Fellers more in their sort of mid-twenties. Like your Ted. They're more my cuppa tea. Men with a bit of experience.'

Ginny said nothing.

'There'll be plenty of 'em around soon enough though, won't there?' Dilys went on, oblivious of the tears that had started to spill slowly down Ginny's cheeks. 'Soon as they get this demob lark sorted out, there'll be plenty for everyone. And add in a few of them GIs for good measure and it'll be flipping paradise.'

She nudged Ginny in the side and giggled. 'Till then, Gin, I'll have to make do with you for me partner. Come on.'

'Leave me alone, Dilys.'

'What's up with you this time, humpy? Even bloody Nellie's smiling.' Dilys sniggered wickedly. 'Reckon she's forgot all about seeing something nasty in the black-out, eh, Gin?'

Ginny couldn't help herself; she turned on Dilys. 'It's not funny, Dilys. I know everyone's having a good time and I don't wanna spoil it or nothing, but how can I join in, while he's off Gawd knows where? Look at me, I'm only twenty-two years of age, a married woman, but I might as well be an old maid.'

'You ain't gonna start going on about Ted again, are you? Why don't you give it a bloody rest?'

Ginny shrugged wretchedly. 'How can I?'

'Leave off, Gin. You know what blokes are like when they get going.' Dilys waved her arms about expansively as though the street were packed full of men, all standing there just waiting to illustrate her theory. 'The silly buggers have about ten pints too many and wind up drunk in a gutter somewhere.'

'Some blokes, maybe.'

'Well, to be honest, Gin, if you can't let a feller celebrate tonight, then when can you, eh? I mean, who wants a man what's tied to your apron strings? You wait and see, he'll sober up and be back home before you know it, with a head on him like a sore bear and not the foggiest about what happened to him.'

Satisfied that her words of wisdom had had the desired effect, Dilys grabbed Ginny by the arm and began hauling her along towards the pub. 'Come on, we'll get a few drinks inside you, we'll have a bit of a dance and then, you trust your Auntie Dilys, you won't know yourself.'

Just as they reached the pale pool of light coming from the street's single lamp-post, with three doors still between them and the tantalising draw of the Albert, Ginny pulled away from her friend. 'No, Dilys, I can't. I'm going back indoors.'

'You're *what*?'

'I wanna be there when Ted gets back.'

'Eh?'

'Look, I don't wanna upset him again by being out here at the party, all right? And we've gotta get up for work tomorrow, remember.'

'Work? Work?' Dilys looked horrified. 'I do not know what gets into you half the time, Ginny Martin. You must be mad, it's the only answer. You wanna be like me, girl. Start living for today. Forget tomorrow, forget yesterday. Just live for today.'

'It's not as easy as that.'

'It could be if you bloody well tried.' Dilys's knees wobbled and she grabbed at the lamp-post for support, shaking her head in despair at her friend's obvious insanity. 'Know the trouble with you? I'll tell you. You're always sodding mooning about. It's like you and that bloody old film.' She paused for a moment, doing her best to gather her drink-befuddled thoughts into something approximating sense. 'You know. That load of old rubbish.'

'Dilys . . .'

'Gone With the Wind.' She sneered with distaste as she remembered. 'That's the one. You go on and on about that Scarlett tart, or whatever her name is. I wouldn't mind, but anyone with any brain in their head could tell you it's that other dopey mare what you're a dead ringer for. That bleed'n' goody-goody.'

'Melanie.'

'That's her!'

'I thought you said it was a bloody old film and to forget the past. But you seem to know enough about it.'

'Are you surprised?' Dilys let go of the lamp-post, swallowed the rest of her drink and took a long moment to balance the empty glass on the window-ledge behind Ginny. 'We might have seen the flipping thing right at the beginning of the bloody war – flaming years ago – but you've gone on about it so much, I know the bleeder off by heart.'

Ginny was on the defensive. 'Well, it's a good story. And I like the clothes, and the house, and . . .' She paused. 'I know Scarlett's everything I'm not, but—'

'Who but you would care about old-fashioned toot like that?' Dilys butted in. 'And anyway she didn't even get the bloke.'

'You don't know that. Not for sure. It's like at the end she's still kept her dream, and—'

Dilys poked her finger close to Ginny's nose, her aim as shaky as her inebriated logic. 'I tell you, you wanna be like me and stick with the modern stuff. *Brief Encounter*. Now *that's* a film. None of that old fanny you go on about. Just a proper good story about fancying having a bit of how's your father when your old man ain't about.'

Dilys tried to wink, but the drink had not only loosened her tongue and ruined her aim, it had also made her eye co-ordination a bit haphazard, so she contented herself with a lopsided grin instead.

'Mind you,' she continued, her face suddenly serious, 'when you think about it, she didn't get the bloke either in the end. I don't understand that, Gin.' She shook her head in bewilderment. 'I'd have left my old man like a shot and gone off and, you know, *done it*, with me fancy piece. Bugger all that being noble lark. Gimme a bit of adventure every time.'

Ted stretched back on the pillows, yawned and released a rumbling, smelly fart.

'Oi, Ted, d'you mind?' she wailed. 'D'you have to be so rude?'

Ted rolled over, trapping her beneath his muscled forearm. 'I'll show you rude.'

'You're a dirty pig,' she said, pushing him away with an unconvincing shove.

He flopped on to his back and grinned drunkenly up at the ceiling, still half cut despite the pubs having closed hours ago. 'That's me all right, darling. *Dirty*.' Then, smacking the sagging mattress, he sat up and rubbed his face, drawing his fingers slowly down his stubble-covered cheeks. 'Better be off, I s'pose.'

She sat up next to him. 'But Ted, you promised you'd stay with me all night. You said we'd celebrate together.'

Leaning back and taking his weight on his elbows, Ted considered her prettily pouting mouth. 'Maybe I could stay just a bit longer,' he drawled, in a passable imitation of Clark Gable, which immediately had her giggling. 'But you'd have to be extra nice to me, of course. I was meant to be taking me old woman to a party tonight, so when I say extra nice—'

The podgy young redhead, who, for the life of him, Ted couldn't remember taking back to this room wherever it was, didn't let him finish speaking; instead, she threw herself at him and began covering his face with kisses. She wasn't going to let him get away that easily, not after the amount of money she'd seen him pull out of his back pocket while they were in the boozer. He must be good for at least another fiver.

A couple of hours later, Ted lifted the gently snoring girl's plump arm from across his chest, threw back the blankets and carefully swung his legs out of the bed and on to the grubby rug.

'What is it?' the girl mumbled in her sleep.

'Ssssh, it's all right,' he soothed her, as he scrabbled round in the darkness for his clothes. The room was so gloomy it was almost as though the black-out was still on, but it wasn't a few yards of cloth that was obscuring the light from the gas lamp in the street outside, it was the layers of grime and soot which caked the unwashed window-panes.

He had been in some bugholes in his time, but this was something special. The place didn't want fumigating, it wanted burning down. It made him sick to the stomach to see how some of these toms lived and he didn't exactly

24

feel proud of himself for winding up in such a dump. He must have had a real skinful.

Finally dressed, and with the two pounds he had given the girl earlier tucked safely back in his pocket with the rest of his money, Ted started for the door, creeping away from the bed with the practised guile of a stray dog nicking sausages from the butcher's shop.

But this time he just wasn't careful enough. As he reached for the handle, a floor-board creaked and a wail went up from behind him. 'Ted! Where you going? You promised me you'd stay.'

Slowly, he turned round to face her. 'Shut your noise,' he said calmly, his face creased with disgust.

'But Ted, you did, you said—'

'I said, shut it.'

'Yeah but—'

He moved so fast that she didn't even see him raise his fist; the first thing she knew was the pain of her front teeth shattering beneath the full force of his punch and the metallic taste of blood filling her mouth.

Dilys sat up in bed with a start. It sounded just as though someone was rattling the letter-box. But who'd be doing that in the early hours of the morning? Definitely neither of the soldier boys; they'd cleared off with two sorts she'd never even laid eyes on before. But they weren't much of a loss, they were a right pair of drips.

Maybe it was the wind, or she'd been dreaming. She dropped back on to her pillow and pulled the covers up to her chin.

It could have been a drunk. There were still plenty of those left sitting outside on the kerb when she'd come in to bed and that was the sort of prank that would probably amuse them. But that was hours ago. Surely they'd all have gone home to sleep it off by now?

Dilys closed her eyes.

There it was again.

It was definitely the letter-box. And it was getting on her nerves.

She slipped out of bed, pulled on her dressing-gown and tiptoed across the room, so as not to disturb the rest of the house.

Lifting the corner of the curtain, she peered down into the street.

Hardly able to believe what she was seeing, Dilys dragged back the rest of the curtain, raised the window as quietly as she could, leaned out and waved her arms frantically at the person below. 'Stop it, for Christ's sake!' she spluttered. 'You'll have the whole flaming street awake!'

'Well, come down and let me in, then.'

Dilys flew down the stairs with barely a sound, wrenched open the street door and dragged Ted inside. Looking up to the landing to make sure no one had heard them, she closed the door gently behind him.

'What the hell d'you think you're up to?' she whispered.

Ted grinned and grabbed roughly at her breast. 'Quite a lot, I hope, darling.'

'Ssssh!' she warned him, brushing away his hand. 'You'll have them all out of bed. You *know* you're meant to tell me when you're coming over. If anyone hears you—'

Quite suddenly, she stopped speaking and shrank back against the wall. 'Whatever's that you've got on you?'

Her mouth dropped open like a trapdoor as she realised what it was. 'Ted,' she gasped. 'It's blood. There's blood all over your hands. And on your shirt. Look at you.'

'You know me, Dilys.' Ted waggled his eyebrows and

pulled her back to him. 'I can't help it if I'm irresistible. I have a few drinks in a pub and wind up fighting, don't I? Blokes get jealous of the way their girlfriends look at me and start having a pop. What am I meant to do? Ignore 'em?'

He touched his lips gently to hers. 'You can't blame them, can you? Handsome bloke like me goes in a place. I drive women wild, don't I?' He kissed her again, harder this time.

'I know you drive me wild, Ted,' Dilys breathed, her hand sliding down his chest, over his taut belly and coming to rest on his groin, where she began opening his fly buttons with practised ease.

Ted jerked his head towards the stairs. 'We going up then, or what?'

Dilys didn't answer straight away. She stopped fondling him and ran her hands through her hair, watching his eyes staring into hers. It was always exciting smuggling Ted up to her room in the early hours when everyone else in the street was in bed – including her own family upstairs – it made what they did even better. But Dilys was still annoyed with him for spending most of the night somewhere else; he'd promised her he'd be at the street party. If he was playing away from home, then Dilys wanted it to be with her, and only her, not with some little tart, or worse still with some glamorous sort he'd met up West in one of the clubs he was so fond of.

'You do love me, Ted, don't you?'

'Course I do.'

'I wore the frock you got me for the party. And I was right disappointed that you weren't there to see me in it. You said—'

'Look, Dilys, do us both a favour, just shut your noise

and get up them stairs, there's a good girl. Or I might get bored and have to go over home to Ginny instead.'

Chapter 2

Ted flapped his hand in her face, trying to brush her off, as she kissed him tenderly on the forehead.

'Leave off, Dilys, for Christ's sake. You know I hate all that sloppy stuff of a morning.'

'Sorry, Ted. I wanted to wake you up nice and gentle, that's all.'

He rubbed his knuckles into his eyes and stifled a yawn. 'What time is it?'

'Nearly a quarter to six. Dad'll be getting up in about ten minutes, so I—'

'It's what?' Ted just stopped himself from shouting. That would have been all he needed, having her dad and brothers bursting in to give him a working over.

As he threw back the covers and started pulling on his clothes, Ted felt as if he'd gone ten rounds with Joe Louis. He was worn out. What he wouldn't have given just to have rolled over and gone back to sleep, but he knew he had to get a move on. He might have been getting pretty good at dishing out the kicks and punches, but Ted was definitely against the idea of anyone laying so much as a single finger on him. And in the sober morning light, he didn't have an ounce of the courage left that his drunken self had had, when he'd thrown his weight about under the coward's cover of darkness.

Ducking his head to look in the mirror that stood on Dilys's chest of drawers, Ted ran his fingers through his hair and barked his orders. 'Go and see if the coast's clear.'

Dilys did as she was told: clambering across the narrow single bed and poking her head out of the door of her little box-room, which stood at the top of the stairs.

From there she could see that the two other doors – the one to her parents' room and the one to the room shared by her brothers – were both still closed. It was a routine to which she was accustomed.

'You're all right. There's no sign of them.'

Ted snatched up his jacket, tucked his shoes under his arm and then, pushing past her with a conspiratorial wink and a grin, took the stairs two at a time in his stockinged feet.

Dilys stood on the landing and watched until he disappeared through the street door, then rushed back inside her room, scrambled across the bed and over to the window and looked out at him as he made the short journey across the cobbled street to the house he shared with his wife and mother.

Even though the Chivers' street door was on the jar, Ginny waited politely for someone to answer her knock.

George, Dilys's dad, welcomed her with a baffled smile. 'I'm sure I shut that door last night,' he said, scratching at his head so that his greying hair, which had until then been oiled into flattened submission, stood up in an untidy fan. He was wearing his usual outfit for that time of the morning: collarless shirt, open and showing his vest; shiny trousers resting on his increasingly round pot-belly; and braces dangling to his knees.

'Must have had more to drink last night than I realised. That or I'm going a bit doolally.' George chuckled to himself as he stood aside to let Ginny in. 'Go through, love.'

'Dilys still in bed then, Mr Chivers?' she enquired

matter-of-factly as she walked along the passage towards the back kitchen.

Although Ginny was in front, George Chivers shook his head as though she could see him – he was used to women having eyes in the back of their heads; he was married to Pearl, after all. 'No girl, she ain't. Believe it or not, our Dilys was up and about this morning, singing like a flipping skylark, before her mum or me was even dressed.'

Now it was Ginny's turn to be baffled. She stood in the kitchen doorway and gawped. Dilys was indeed up and about; there she was, admiring herself in the flower-etched mirror on the chimney-breast, fiddling about with her compact, tipping her head this way and that, as she considered the effect of the finishing touches she was adding to her make-up.

George stepped round Ginny, took the couple of steps it needed to cross the little kitchen, and let himself out of the back door and into the yard without another word. Three women chattering away nineteen to the dozen was more than he could take at that time of the morning, especially after the amount of ale he had sunk at the VE do the night before. A visit to the sanctuary of the outside lav was just what the doctor ordered.

'Morning, Gin.' Dilys greeted Ginny's bewildered reflection with a cheery wave of her powder-puff. 'I was right, wasn't I? Told you he'd be back.'

'Eh?' was all Ginny could manage in reply. She was genuinely confused by this strange turn of events. It was part of their regular morning routine – always – that Ginny came over half an hour before they actually needed to leave. She then spent a frustrating twenty-five minutes coaxing and persuading her friend to get a move on, so that they could get to the clothing factory off the

31

Whitechapel Road where they worked, without being too outrageously late for clocking in.

Dilys never, ever, got up without a fight, yet here she was, looking as though being out of bed was a pleasure she wouldn't have missed for the world.

'Blimey, Gin, pull yourself together girl, for Gawd's sake,' Dilys said, snapping the lid off her lipstick. 'I'm talking about Ted. I said he'd be back, didn't I?'

'Cup o' tea, Ginny?' Pearl asked, flashing a warning look at her daughter to both mind her manners and to keep off the subject of Ted Martin. 'I think the boys left some in the pot.'

Dilys finished painting her mouth and then sat herself down at the table to straighten the seams of her stockings. 'They looked as gormless as you, Gin, when they went out just now. You should have seen 'em. Talk about wreck of the flaming Hesperus! But at least they had an excuse, they must have drunk that Albert dry between the pair of 'em.'

'I didn't get much sleep last night,' Ginny said quietly. 'I tried to keep awake for Ted.'

'It bloody shows.'

'We all got to bed late last night,' Pearl said sternly, narrowing her eyes at her daughter. Then, turning to Ginny she held up the teapot. 'You having one then, sweetheart?'

'I'd love a cup, please, Pearl.' Ginny sat down opposite Dilys. 'How d'you know he was back then?'

'Nosy, ain't I?' chirped Dilys. 'I woke up early see, and I heard a noise down in the street. So I looked out and I saw him going indoors. Lovely bright morning it was,' she added with, for her, unusually sweet wistfulness. 'Really lovely.'

Ginny nodded at Dilys's explanation, as she took the cup that Pearl was shoving towards her across the oilcloth-covered table. 'You was right about where he was and all, you know, Dil. He hadn't stayed out 'cos he had the hump with me at all. It was like you said, he'd just had a few drinks too many. He met these fellers in some pub over Bethnal Green way and, before he knew what was happening, he was out cold in one of their mum's armchairs. I dunno if you noticed,' she added with a sheepish, almost guilty, glimmer of a smile, 'but he'd had a bit of a fight and all by the look of him. His shirt's got all sorts on it. I dunno how I'm gonna get it white again.'

'Can't say as I did notice, actually,' Dilys said hurriedly. 'I mean, I was only looking out of me bedroom window. I didn't say I had flaming binoculars, now did I?'

She reached behind her and picked up her handbag off the green-painted dresser. 'Come on,' she said, taking the still half-full cup from Ginny's hand. 'We don't wanna be late, do we?'

Pearl frowned as she watched her daughter almost skip out of the kitchen. What on earth had got into the girl? Whatever it was, Pearl wasn't sure she liked it. In her experience of her daughter's moods, this was probably just the lull before a very nasty storm.

As they stepped out of the house, Dilys linked her arm through Ginny's and took a deep breath of morning air. 'What a smashing day,' she sighed.

'Yeah, you're right, Dilys, it is a smashing day.'

Ginny looked up and down the street and smiled, a smile which came more easily this time, as she took in the signs of last night's party, still evident all around them. From the empty bottles and crushed paper hats littering the gutter, to the now slightly drooping swags of flags and ribbons draped across the soot-ingrained

33

terraced houses, anyone could see that Bailey Street had had a good time.

'I know I get a bit down now and then, Dilys, but you know how it is. No one said being married was easy, did they? Still, I should have listened to you, shouldn't I? Ted came home, and he came home to me.' She squeezed Dilys's arm. 'And on mornings like this I'm counting me blessings, 'cos I don't half love him, you know, despite our little ups and downs. And he was so sweet when he got in. Right sorry he was that he'd got himself tanked up and missed the party and everything. I've promised meself I'm gonna be extra nice to him to show him I understand and that it's all all right.'

Ginny lowered her chin and added quietly. ''Cos if he ever did get fed up with me, I dunno what I'd do without him, Dilys, d'you know that? Soon as I was old enough to realise what fancying a bloke was all about, I started thinking what it'd be like to be Ted's wife. What it'd be like to set up home together. And then, when me mum and dad—'

'All right. Leave off, can't you?' Dilys snapped, pulling her arm away from Ginny's. 'There's no need to go on. Just leave it, will you?'

Ginny shut up immediately and automatically. She had been married to Ted for three years now and, despite keeping hold of her romantic dreams, she was also learning the self-protective habit of doing as she was told.

'Well, come on, if you're coming.' Dilys straightened the collar of her jacket and began walking along towards the end of the street with Ginny following obediently behind.

As they came to the Varneys' house, the last one before the pub on the corner, they saw Violet balancing on the top of a set of steps, unhooking the bunting from the upstairs window-ledge.

When Ginny stopped to talk to her, Dilys folded her arms and tutted with impatience. 'You've got one minute!' she said to Ginny without further explanation.

'Don't take them down yet, Vi. Leave them up a bit longer,' Ginny urged her.

'No,' said Violet flatly without looking at her. 'I'm taking them down now.'

'Go on, be a devil. Everyone else is. Makes the street look right cheerful.'

'I said, no.' Violet pulled out a drawing-pin from the window-ledge and dropped it into the pocket of her cross-over apron.

'But why d'you—'

'I've had a telegram. This morning. It's my Bert. He's dead.'

Carefully and slowly, Violet wound the bunting round her arm as though it were a skein of wool.

'Funny, ain't it?' she said, as much to herself as to Ginny. 'I was celebrating yesterday 'cos the war's meant to be over. And my Bert goes and cops it. And I never knew. Dancing and drinking I was, like I didn't have a care in the world. Don't make no sense, does it? Don't make no sense at all.'

She let the flags drop on to the pavement and buried her face in her hands. 'The kids don't know yet. I couldn't bring myself to tell the poor little sods.' Her shoulders shook as she began to sob.

'Violet, I'm so sorry. Is there anything I can do?'

Dilys, with a look of contemptuous distaste at such a public display of grief, tugged at Ginny's sleeve. 'Come on, Gin.'

'Hang on, Dilys.'

'She don't want us. And we can't do nothing anyway.'

'But—'

'Look, me mum'll be popping out for her errands in a minute. She'll see to her. You know what Mum's like.'

Ginny might have learned not to put up a fight, but she still felt ashamed of herself as she allowed Dilys to drag her away. In fact, she felt so guilty at her own weakness that as they came to the corner of Bailey Street she twisted round and called to Violet, 'I'll pop in after work, Vi. I promise.'

Violet didn't reply.

Ginny and Dilys turned into Grove Road and headed for the busy junction with the Mile End Road, walking past the debris left by the rocket attack on the railway bridge that, like bomb-sites all over London, was now blooming with all kinds of gloriously colourful wild flowers.

As usual, the sight of the pinks and mauves and yellows bursting triumphantly through the rubble brought a smile to Ginny's face, but they could have been rare orchids and Dilys still wouldn't have given a damn. 'D'you know what, Gin,' she said as they dodged across the broad thoroughfare to the bus-stop by the tube station, 'you've right got on my nerves, you have. I was in a proper good mood this morning and now you've gone and upset me. First you keep going on about Ted, then you wanna hang around with bloody Violet Varney and make us late for work. What's up with you?'

'I'm sorry,' Ginny apologised, steering her friend carefully to the back of the queue to prevent her from trying her usual embarrassing trick of pushing to the front. 'But that poor woman, she must be—'

'For Christ's sake, Ginny! No wonder Ted stayed out all night. The way you go on, it's a wonder he bothered to come home at all.'

They completed their journey to work in silence, with

Ginny wondering how she could find ways of being nicer to Ted so that he would spend more time with her, and Dilys thinking exactly the same.

By the time they were ready for their midday break, Dilys had at last calmed down. Even though all the girls in the workroom, except Ginny, had been at parties till the early hours, they had all worked flat out on their sewing machines. They were on piece work and if they wanted a decent wage packet on Friday they knew they had no choice but to get stuck in.

But nobody really minded, especially today. The war was over and boyfriends, husbands and brothers would soon be home; everything would be wonderful again. And the nurses' uniforms they were making were definitely a lot easier on the fingers than the greatcoats and battledresses they had been sewing for the last few years. The money wasn't quite so good with the medical clothing, but it was certainly quicker and more pleasant working with the lighter-weight fabrics.

'Where we going, then?' Dilys shouted over the whine of the machines and the blaring of the wireless, as she tossed another completed tunic on to the pile by her chair. 'Canteen? Or down the Lane?'

Ginny allowed herself a little smile of relief; it wasn't in her nature to like being in anyone's bad books, but she particularly hated upsetting Ted or Dilys. Along with Pearl, they were the people who mattered most in her life and it really worried Ginny when either of them was wild with her. Sometimes she didn't even know why they were angry, they just were; it must have been something about her she supposed. She had that effect on Nellie as well at times. She only wished she could figure out what it was that set them off.

'I don't mind, Dil,' she hollered back. 'Wherever you fancy.'

'Down the Lane,' Dilys decided for them. 'I could do with buying a few bits to cheer myself up.'

'That's good,' Ginny agreed happily. 'I'll be able to pick up some veg and that'll save Nellie having to lug it home from the Roman Road tomorrow.'

Dilys said nothing, she just rolled her eyes at Ginny's totally aggravating saintliness.

After walking through the grim, bomb-damaged streets, with their high-walled, soot-impregnated warehouses and sweatshops, stepping into Petticoat Lane – the local name for the market area around Middlesex Street and Wentworth Street – was like entering a fairground. Stall after colourful stall lined the roadsides of the shop-filled streets, their owners calling a running commentary of jokes and invitations to passers-by to come and look at their wares, be they dark-green, curly-leafed cabbages, or enormous salmon-pink satin corsets.

Competing with their shouts were the street-corner beigel and herring sellers. Draped from neck to foot in swathes of stained white cotton aprons, their feet in big rubber boots and their sleeves rolled up to show their reddened arms, they dipped into their brine-filled barrels and held up the pickled fish for the customers' inspection. Then, their sale made, they slapped them into a cone of paper with a couple of the shiny, sweet bread rolls they'd hooked off the tall wooden pegs balanced precariously against the kerb.

Then there were the less vocal vendors: the sharp-suited men with goods that had somehow been liberated from locked and guarded warehouses, and from the backs of tarpaulin-sheeted lorries. A nudge and a whispered offer to examine their wares was a temptation that few resisted. Even the supposedly upright citizens, those who worked for respectable companies in the nearby City offices and banks, crowded round eagerly to bargain for the illicit contents of the spivs' battered suitcases and from inside the depths of their lairy jackets.

But none of these attracted Dilys; she was more interested in a stall selling sewing notions: the ribbons, bows and buttons of the haberdasher.

'What d'you think of these then, Gin? Big enough to go on the front of me new cream swagger jacket, d'you reckon? I don't like them bone ones on it, they're too dull.' She shoved a card of silver-coloured button backs in Ginny's face for inspection. 'I could take them in to the Ugly Sisters and get them made up, if I can find a bit of black velvet,' she said, jerking her head towards the little shop behind the stall. 'That'll look the business that will. Black and cream.'

'Don't be rotten,' Ginny scolded her, as she visualised the two elderly spinsters who spent their days covering buttons for the steady stream of customers, most of whom were just as uncomplimentary about their looks as Dilys.

The Ugly Sisters might have been skilled and inexpensive workers, but they were certainly no beauties and had earned their unfortunate nicknames when they had been little more than plain, skinny girls learning their trade at the knee of their surprisingly pretty mother.

'You're such a bloody hypocrite, Ginny. You know they're ugly.' Dilys threw down the buttons, bored with the thought of having to go to the trouble of finding material suitable for covering them.

'Yeah, but it don't mean you have to be nasty about them.'

'I don't *have* to be nasty about no one,' Dilys said

casually, as she strolled along to the next stall, 'I just like to be.'

'Morning, Mum,' Ted yawned. He rubbed his hands over his unshaven face, sat himself down at the kitchen table and opened the paper. 'What's for breakfast then?' he asked without moving his eyes from the story on the inside page about the intensifying official outrage over the black market.

'Breakfast?' sniffed Nellie. She was standing at the butler sink, up to her elbows in an enamel basin of soapy water. 'More like sodding dinner, you lazy bugger.'

'What time's it then?'

'Gone half past twelve, ain't it.'

'It's *what*?' Ted leapt to his feet, sending his chair skidding across the lino-covered floor. He might have been only twenty-five but sometimes he thought he was getting too old for all this carrying on with birds lark. He must have gone out like a light when he eventually got into bed with Ginny.

He ignored the now overturned chair, reached round Nellie and tipped her bowl of sudsy water straight down the plughole.

'Oi you, that was me hand washing I was putting in to soak.'

'Ne'mind your bloody laundry, Mum. I'm late and I need a shave.'

Ted was washed, dressed and out of the house within minutes; with his hair freshly oiled and his gleaming white collar held neatly in place with a discreetly striped tie, his hat in his hand and his overcoat slung over his arm, Ted Martin looked a picture of well-presented prosperity. And within less than an hour, he was sitting in a pub not five minutes' walk from the market where Ginny was doing her best not to aggravate Dilys by taking too long over buying her vegetables.

'So, what's your best price then, Joe?' Ted asked, pushing a pint along the bar to the middle-aged man by his side.

Joe half emptied his glass in a single swallow, brushed the foam from his moustache with a delicate flick of his forefinger and thought for a moment. 'It's a lovely little runner, Ted. Whoever owned it took good care of it. Very good care.'

'I didn't ask that.' It really got on Ted's nerves when someone he was trying to do business with jerked him around like some bloody mug punter. If he hadn't wanted to do this deal with Joe he'd have told him where he could stick it. But although Ted had a temper, he wasn't stupid; he knew that Joe had the cheapest cars anywhere north of the river, which wasn't surprising, considering his finely tuned system for acquiring them.

Joe would nick the motor, get it back to his workshop under the arches in Bow Common Lane, have the numbers changed and any distinguishing marks wiped out, all within a couple of hours; then come up to this discreet little City pub to flog it off to the so-called respectable types – the respectable types with a few quid in their pockets, that is – the ones who made their living pushing pieces of paper back and forward across their big, polished desks, the same ones who flocked around the spivs in the Lane.

He was a real craftsman, was Joe; Ted admired that.

Joe knocked back the rest of his pint and stared down at the empty glass. 'Now let's see.' He screwed up his face and scratched the side of his head. 'Got a fag?'

Ted tossed his cigarettes on to the bar. 'Stop pissing about, Joe. You ain't dealing with a know-nothing knob of a shipping clerk. This is me, Ted Martin. The bloke what's seen you right for the last few years.' He lowered his voice. 'The one what's got you all them lovely petrol coupons. Remember?'

Joe stuck one cigarette in his mouth and another behind his ear. 'Buy us another pint; get us another couple of bottles of that Scotch. The good stuff mind, you can keep the old shit for the mugs. And it's yours for a oner.'

A flicker of a smile passed across Ted's lips as he slapped palms with Joe. An almost brand-new Talbot for a hundred quid! 'You've got a deal, my son.'

Ted walked out of the pub with his chin in the air and a swagger in his step, every trace of tiredness forgotten. Now he had a decent motor he'd be well away.

He'd been doing all right up until now, of course, but now there'd be no stopping him. Things were really going to look up. Ted Martin had plans, big plans.

He was going to be a face to be reckoned with.

Chapter 3

During the next few months there were many changes for families in the East End and those who lived in the area around Bailey Street were no exception.

They experienced home-comings, as husbands, fathers and sons returned from abroad and were demobbed; and departures, as young women married boyfriends newly back from the war and went to live in what were, to them, alien neighbourhoods. The girls were, in reality, moving just a few streets away, but might as well have been going to try their luck at surviving in the depths of the Amazon jungle, such were the ties that cockneys had with their own tight-knit communities.

Most of the home-comings were, of course, joyful: moments to be photographed, treasured and remembered, but it wasn't the same for everyone. After the exhilaration of the victory in Europe and then in Japan, the longed-for pleasures of being back home and returning to what had once been normality, had more than their share of pressures and frustrations. Six years of war had changed people. Women had learned to control their own lives, to be the bosses in their own homes; they had earned wages and made decisions and now their men – who, to their children, were sometimes little more than a vague memory and a faded, sepia-toned snap on the mantelpiece – were expecting to take charge again and the women didn't always appreciate it.

It wasn't always easy for the men either. While they weren't exactly sorry to be away from the danger and the dying, they certainly missed their mates, the routine, the excitement even, and, as they were beginning to realise, they were missing out on a lot of other things as well. The land fit for heroes that they had been promised now all seemed to be a bit of a con. Instead of getting what they had all looked forward to: good homes, decent food and sharing a few pints down the local with the lads, they had come home instead to bomb-sites, queuing and ration books, and wives who seemed more interested in going out to work than in fetching them a cup of tea while they toasted their toes in front of the fire and listened to the Light Programme on the wireless.

Some of the older residents of Bailey Street weren't at all surprised by the younger men's disillusionment and were only too keen to say so, adding dire warnings about the newly elected Labour government for good measure. It wasn't so much that they didn't approve of what they were being offered by this Labour lot – who but a fool would refuse the promise of a bright new Britain for all, and most had actually voted for them – it was just that they couldn't help but think how it was all so reminiscent of what had happened to them after the Great War.

Promises had been made then too. And they had all been broken, dissolving in front of their eyes like the foam in a wet beer glass. The so-called boom had quickly turned to dust and the brave new world had sunk into the horrors of the 1930s and the Depression. How could they not be wary when their dreams were still haunted by nightmare visions of the workhouse and the shame of being visited by the despised Relieving Officer?

Sometimes, when Ginny stopped to pass the time of day with one or other of her elderly neighbours, she found herself sympathising all too readily with their fears about the way the world seemed to be heading, especially when Ted was being difficult – as he seemed to be more and more lately. But she knew that no matter how down she felt at times, it was always best to try and put on a brave face, to keep her chin up and to look cheerful. That way she didn't upset things even more and it also helped her convince herself that everything would turn out all right in the end. Although it wasn't always easy to be positive, especially when Dilys was working herself up into a mood.

'I just don't see why you ain't bloody furious like I am,' Dilys fumed, as they waited at the bus-stop on the corner by Aldgate East station. 'Anyone'd think you'd had a win on the dogs instead of getting the flaming sack.'

'But we've not had the sack, Dil, have we? Not really. It's more like we've lost our jobs.' Ginny stamped her feet to warm them against the damp autumn chill. 'I mean, you can't blame old Mr Bloom for retiring, now can you? He must be eighty if he's a day. And what with the last of the uniform work going . . .'

'Can't blame him?' Dilys shook her head in amazement.

'Anyway, this might be just the chance we could both do with. You've always said you fancied going on the buses.'

Dilys's mood, always unpredictable, took a swing away from gloom and touched on almost optimistic interest. She pouted and swung her shoulders, as she visualised herself in a conductress's uniform being chatted up by a bus stuffed full of men, all eager to show her a good time.

Ginny dropped her chin and continued shyly, 'And what with Ted doing so well, it's probably as good a time as any for me to start thinking about staying at home and having a baby. I've—'

Shocked back to reality by such treacherous talk, Dilys almost exploded. 'You wanna get *pregnant*? By *Ted*?'

A large, middle-aged woman standing in front of them in the queue looked over her shoulder at Dilys and stared in scandalised reproach. 'That's nice talk for a young girl, I don't think. In my day, we didn't even know the meaning of the word.'

In reply, Dilys poked out her tongue and the woman looked away with a loud huff.

'Of course by Ted,' Ginny hissed, her fair cheeks flushing as pink as a stick of candy-floss. 'Who d'you think I wanna do it with, the bloody coalman?'

'You take my word for it, Al, I'm telling you, if you can show her you've got plenty o' dough, then any bird you fancy, she's yours for the taking. You don't even have to spend that much on 'em. Just flash it about a bit. They ain't got a lot of brains see, birds ain't.' Ted tossed back the last of his drink and weighed his empty glass in his hand.

'Like another one in there?' asked Al, rising from his chair.

'Why not? And you can get us a chaser an' all this time.'

At barely eighteen years of age, and not usually much of a drinker, Al was not exactly sure what sort of a drink a chaser was, but he would find out and Ted would have one if that was what he wanted. Al was determined to impress this new-found friend of his, because while he might not have known much about boozing, Al knew something very clearly: he definitely did not like the idea of being conscripted, especially now there wasn't even a war to fight. And Ted, whom Al had met only a couple of hours ago – when he had tipped him the wink that he had better put his suitcase full of nylons back in his boot

46

as a copper was heading his way – had been telling him all sorts of fascinating things.

Ted had told him, for instance, that there were plenty of ways to avoid being called up and had even gone so far as to slip him a piece of paper with a doctor's address on it, with the promise that it would come in more than useful when the dreaded buff envelope arrived. He'd told him, as easy as that, and just to repay him for his help in avoiding being collared by the law!

After a few rounds of drinks, all paid for by Al, Ted had gone on to tell him that he too could earn enough money to have a flash motor and sharp-looking suits. But probably most important of all for a reluctant virgin such as Al, Ted had been generous enough to share with him the benefit of his experience with women.

Ted had said, quite matter-of-factly, that after the cheapest of nights out, he should definitely expect a whole lot more than a quick fumble inside their blouses.

This was music to Al's ears. He wouldn't have admitted it to someone as sophisticated as Ted, of course, but he had often spent the best part of the week's wages he earned at his clerking job and had not even got as far as a serious kind of kiss, let alone a real bit of how's your father.

But then, according to Ted, the way that Al earned his living showed what a mug he was. In Ted's book, anyone who worked for a governor was no better than a fool.

Al put down the three drinks, his own half pint, Ted's pint and a tot of whisky – the barmaid had been very helpful in explaining chasers, especially after Al had bought her a drink as well – and sat himself down next to Ted. 'So, Ted,' he said, raising his glass in salutation, 'you was saying about this, what was it, working the tweedle? How does it go again?'

Ted grinned; it was a while since he'd met a kid as

innocent-looking and as trusting as this one. He was a real one-off. Particularly around the East End. He must have been brought up wrapped in cotton wool.

Ted studied him across the rim of his glass. Maybe he could be of further service some time. All right, so he wasn't exactly Brains Trust material, but a look-out with an honest face was always useful when you were on the creep around a warehouse. And anyway, it amused Ted to see the kid hanging on to his every word. He enjoyed a bit of respect.

Patiently Ted explained the con one more time.

'I get it!' A flash of understanding at last lit up Al's baby face. 'You have *two* rings. A real one and a fake one. And when you go back, you sell the jeweller the schneid!'

'Right. That's it.' Ted winked at the lad, then asked his usual question whenever he met anyone under the age of thirty. 'Now, tell me about yourself; you got any sisters, son?'

'No, only brothers.'

Ted paused. No sisters. Well, you couldn't have everything. Then another thought struck him. 'So how old's your mum then?'

'Dunno.' Al grimaced. 'Just old, I suppose, like all mums.'

Ted didn't let his disappointment show. 'Where's this office o' your'n? Up the City?'

'No, down the docks. I do the paperwork for the bonded warehouses.'

Ted could feel the happiness spreading through his body like warm treacle dribbling over a spotted dick.

When their bus finally arrived, Ginny was, for once, delighted to see that it was really crowded and that she

48

had to sit by herself. She had been shown up quite enough for one day by Dilys and her big mouth.

Dilys, on the other hand, wasn't very happy at all, though her increased displeasure had nothing to do with losing her job or how many people were on the bus. It was the idea that Ginny was thinking about having a baby that had *really* upset her. That was the last thing she wanted to happen, because Dilys had been thinking very seriously about her future with Ted. Despite all the servicemen being demobbed, good-looking blokes with a few bob in their pockets were still very thin on the ground and Dilys wasn't getting any younger. She was nearly twenty-three, for goodness sake, and Ted was getting to be a bit of a last resort. All right, he was already married, but the papers were full of stories about people getting divorced. Once it had been something only the rich and famous could do, but nowadays it seemed as though every Tom, Dick and Harry could get shot of his wife if he wanted to. All you had to do was spend a couple of days down in Brighton with some willing tart or other, have a quick snapshot taken leaving your love nest, and Bob appeared to be your uncle. So why not Ted? Well, maybe it was a bit more complicated than that, but if Ginny went and got herself up the duff, it probably wouldn't matter anyway, as Dilys had seen how funny blokes could get when their wives got pregnant.

They came over all stupid and loyal, and started staying in and holding their old women's hands and talking about whether it would be a boy or a girl, and if they should name it after Auntie Flo or Uncle Harold. No, Ginny getting herself pregnant was definitely not a very good idea, not a very good idea at all. Dilys had to get the thought right out of Ginny's stupid, curly blonde head, and she had to do it soon, before it got out of hand and Ted got to like the idea of becoming a daddy. And a little thing like the three rows of people sitting between her and Ginny certainly wasn't going to deter Dilys from putting her plan into action.

To Ginny's alarmed embarrassment – but to the obvious interest of the press of passengers surrounding them – the moment she sat down, Dilys started firing a barrage of questions at her. 'Oi, Ginny! So what's Ted got to say about all this baby lark then?'

Ginny took a deep breath, twisted round in her seat and mouthed very quietly, 'I haven't mentioned it to him yet, Dilys.'

That wasn't exactly true; she had tried to raise the subject once or twice, but Ted wouldn't even discuss it. In fact, he had forbidden her to talk about it. But now she had no job and the war was over, maybe he'd feel differently. She would have to be careful how she brought it up, of course, as she didn't want to aggravate him, and Dilys opening her big gob certainly wouldn't help matters.

'And I'd appreciate you not mentioning it either, Dilys.'

Dilys could have kissed the silly cow. She hadn't even talked to him about it. Perfect!

Suppressing the urge to burst into laughter, Dilys carried on – her face now arranged into a concerned frown. 'Well, he won't like it, you know.'

'I don't agree.'

'I'm telling you.'

'Dilys, please, d'you mind?' Ginny pulled her coat collar tighter around her throat and tried to shrink down into her seat.

'And how about Nellie? What's she gonna say?'

'I'm sure Nellie would love a grandchild.'

'What, Nellie? Are you sure? With all that screaming and crying keeping her awake all night? Clothes-horses full of wet nappies all over the place. She'd go barmy.

And you know Ted can't stand fat birds,' she added with a sudden flash of inspiration. 'And with your legs and figure, you'd blow up like a barrage balloon. You do know that, don't you, Ginny? You'd be like a right flipping elephant. Stuck in a chair, day in day out, with just Nellie for company. You'd hate it. I'm telling you.'

'That's what happened to me,' chipped in a sharp-nosed woman in a peculiar brown felt hat, who was sitting across the aisle from Ginny. 'Didn't it, Charlie?'

Charlie nodded. 'It did. Just like an elephant she was. And her legs . . . You've never seen nothing like 'em.' He winced at the memory. 'Went all veiny and horrible, they did. And her ankles! Swollen up like a pair o' prize marrows they was. Months she was like that. Couldn't get a pair o' slippers near her feet, let alone a decent pair o' shoes on her. And as for her guts . . .' He shuddered. 'Talk about taking over the Bile Beans factory. She must have swallowed a hundred boxes of the bloody things. But nothing worked her. Bunged up like a bottle with a cork, she was.'

Dilys was triumphant. 'See! Can you just imagine what Ted would have to say if he had to put up with all that for nine months?'

That was enough for Ginny. *She knew* Ted could be difficult and that Nellie wasn't exactly a loving mother-in-law, but Dilys didn't have to let the whole bloody bus know. She stood up and jerked the string above her head to ring the bell.

'Excuse me,' she muttered to the woman next to her, 'I wanna get off.'

'Where you going?' Dilys bellowed, as Ginny shuffled sideways along the aisle towards the back of the bus.

'Home. But I've decided to walk. All right?'

Dilys raised her eyebrows in surprise, then turned to

face the steamed-up window. 'Suit yourself. But you must be garrety, it's started pouring down out there.'

By the time Ginny eventually got back to Bailey Street she was cold, wet through and thoroughly miserable; but even though all she felt like doing was going indoors, slipping into a warm dressing-gown and sitting in front of the fire with a nice, hot cup of tea, she couldn't bring herself to walk past Violet Varney's without at least knocking on her door to see how she was getting on.

In the four months since the poor woman had heard of her husband's death, Ginny had called on her most evenings, although Violet usually found a reason not to let her over the street doorstep. It was obvious, even from the brief glimpses Ginny had of her, that she was not doing very well.

Ginny rapped on the glass panel in the door. 'Violet? You there?'

Violet's youngest, a skinny, hollow-eyed child of about ten, opened the door just wide enough to peer through the crack. 'Who is it?'

'It's me, babe. Ginny, from over the road.'

The little girl opened the door wider. 'Me mum's in the kitchen,' she said, nodding along the passage.

'You sure it's all right if I come in? Mummy usually talks to me out here.'

'Mum only said I was to say she wasn't in if it was the rent man, or the bloke for the tally money. She never said nothing about you.'

Ginny nodded, but she wasn't actually listening to what the child was saying, she was far too preoccupied with the look of her. There had been talk that Violet was neglecting the kids, giving them a beating even – something that nobody would ever have thought of accusing her of before – and here, right in front of Ginny seemed to be proof that the gossips were right for once. The child's cheek had a series of wounds across it that certainly hadn't come from any playground rough and tumble; she had been cut with something a lot sharper than a stone or a hopscotch marker.

As soon as she noticed Ginny looking at the red, angry slashes, the little girl instinctively raised her hand to her face and dropped her chin, making Ginny flinch at her victim's shame.

'She's in the scullery,' the child muttered, then turned on her heel and fled.

It tore at Ginny's heart as she watched the poor, scrawny mite disappear up the unlit stairway. She felt as though she could cry out loud with pain, but not only for the desperate youngster.

Ginny had seen herself reflected in the look that had clouded the child's pale, careworn little features. It was a look that Ginny sometimes glimpsed lately, when she sat in front of the mirror. No matter how she tried to deny it – to brush it away, refuse to acknowledge it – it was a look that had stained, and that told anyone who chose to see that Ginny was a woman who knew what it was like to have her dreams shattered.

When Ginny eventually went home she found Ted sitting at the kitchen table eating his tea, with the evening paper propped up in front of him against the sugar bowl.

'Where d'you think you've been?' he asked, flicking over the page.

Ginny took off her sopping wet coat, draped it over the back of one of the chairs and stood it in front of the gas stove to dry. 'I popped in to see Violet Varney, on me way back from work,' she said shaking out her hat and combing back her damp hair with her fingers. 'She wasn't very happy at first that her little one had let me in.'

Ted looked up at her with disgust. 'Well, while you was over there chatting, me mum had to do me tea for me. And now she's so whacked out, she's had to go up and have a lay down. Satisfied, are you?'

Ginny thought about her spoilt, idle mother-in-law snoring her head off upstairs, and she thought about how exhausted Violet Varney looked and how skinny and unhealthy the child had been.

She would have liked to have gone up and dragged Nellie out of bed and across the street to see what being whacked out really meant. She'd have liked to have rubbed her self-regarding nose in it, and she'd have liked to have told the lazy old bugger – and Ted – exactly how she felt.

Instead, Ginny said nothing. She knew there were lines she shouldn't cross, so, as always, she acted the appeaser. 'I wasn't chatting, Ted,' she said defensively, as she filled the kettle at the sink. 'And I only meant to go in for a couple of minutes. You know, to see if there was anything I could do. But when I saw the state she was in—'

'What state d'you expect her to be in?' Ted interrupted. He tore a chunk of bread from the loaf, mopped up the gravy from his plate and shoved it in his mouth.

Ginny didn't reply immediately. She lit the gas and sat down at the table to wait for the water to boil. Ted liked to have a cup of tea after he had finished his meal. She herself had no appetite after what she had seen across the road, but even if she had, she knew it would have been pointless to ask if Nellie had made anything for her to eat.

'I didn't expect her to be as bad as she is, to tell you the truth, Ted,' she said eventually. 'She was going on about all sorts. Kind of rambling. She was talking about this place, Southern Rhodesia, wherever that is. A welfare lady went round to see her the other day and said they was offering places at some college over there. And parents who ain't managing very well can send their kids. Their older ones like. It's because they need more people in their country or something. I didn't really understand what Violet was going on about, but she reckoned it sounded like a good thing.' Ginny sighed loudly. 'Can you imagine being that desperate that you'd let some stranger take your child?'

She waited a moment to see if Ted had anything to say about such a terrible decision for someone to make. When he said nothing, she continued with her story. 'You see, this welfare lady turned up because of the school.' Ginny got up and warmed the pot and began slowly spooning in measures of tea. 'They was worried Violet's been beating the kids. Not giving them a smack, I don't mean, but really hurting them. She's been driven off her head I reckon, since she heard about her Bert.'

Ginny filled the pot with the boiling water and carried it back to the table. 'I think she's gonna do it, you know, Ted. See, she's really in trouble.'

Ted snorted derisively and forked in another mouthful. 'What, one of her punters put her in the club, has he?'

Ginny almost dropped the teapot. 'You *know* what she's been up to?'

'Don't everyone? She's been hanging around outside the billiard hall down Chris Street for months now, waiting for customers.'

Ginny shook her head. 'I never knew. In fact, I didn't even know whether to believe her when she was telling me just now. It's not like her to say much at all, especially about personal things. So when all that came pouring out, well . . . I didn't know what to say. But she said it was a relief to have someone to talk to about it.'

She poured Ted's tea, added sugar and milk and automatically stirred it for him, before setting it down next to his plate.

'And d'you know what else she told me?' she continued in a low voice. 'She thinks she's got a dose.' Ginny shuddered. 'VD. Can you imagine? Said she's been going with all sorts of men, just to get a few bob for the kids. She was so scared they'd put them in a home if she wasn't feeding them right and dressing them decent. But the poor little devils was more at risk in their own flipping house. She was so upset when she saw how one of the blokes she brought home the other night looked at her youngest that she went sort of barmy.'

Ginny took a gulp of her scalding hot tea as Violet's horrific words replayed in her head. 'She held her down and cut her little face. With the bread knife. Said she was trying to make her look ugly.'

'Silly whore.' Ted threw down his knife and fork, and shoved his plate away from him.

'I don't understand it either, Ted. I can't imagine how desperate you'd have to be to go and do something like that. How anyone could sell their body . . .' Ginny shuddered again. 'But at least she's gonna try and do her best for the kids. She's gonna send the oldest two to this Rhodesia place. And the others are gonna live with her sister. Until she can find a way to get herself straight. She feels so guilty about what's been happening. But I said to her, it's not your fault, I said. Well, what else could I say? But honestly, Ted, fancy doing that. It's horrible. If only she'd have said something. If only she'd have let people help her.'

Ginny picked up Ted's plate and carried it to the sink. She turned on the tap and looked over her shoulder. 'I suppose it'll be easier to understand when we've got kids of our own.'

Ginny winced as she realised, too late, that she'd gone

and blurted it out. Instead of preparing him gently as she had intended, of speaking to him about her dreams of them having a baby, a proper family of their own, and getting him used to the idea, she'd just gone and said it. She could have bitten her tongue off. She'd mucked it up. She was *so* stupid.

Ted picked up the paper and folded it neatly. 'What did you say?'

'I never meant—'

'Look. You've got on me nerves enough tonight already. Now what did I tell you?'

'I'm sorry, Ted, I—'

'Don't sorry me.' Slowly, he rose to his feet and walked over to her. 'I asked you a question. What did I tell you?'

Her mouth was so dry she could barely get the words out and the cold, hard edge of the sink was digging into her back. 'Not to talk about having kids.'

'And what did you just do?'

'I didn't mean—'

'You didn't *what*?' Ted grabbed hold of a handful of her hair and jerked her head back.

'I didn't mean anything,' she gasped through the pain, desperate not to let the plate slip between her fingers and drop to the floor. That would only make him angrier.

Ted drew back his fist and slammed it full into her cheek. 'I told you last time. Why don't you just keep that mouth o' your'n shut? That's another black eye you've made me give you.' He stared at her already swelling face and blinked rapidly as though he couldn't quite believe what he was seeing. 'Look what you've made me do, you stupid cow.'

Ginny opened her mouth to apologise, but said nothing when he yanked her hair even harder.

'Now, you ain't gonna start making no noise and wake me mother up an' all, are you?'

Ginny gave a tiny shake of her head. Why *was* she so stupid? She felt so ashamed of herself. She'd done it again. Why did she have to go upsetting him all the time?

Careful not to pull away from him, she stretched her arm behind her and put the plate gently on to the wooden draining board. Then, biting her lip to stop herself screaming out in agony, she let him drag her out of the room and up the stairs by her hair.

Chapter 4

1946

'Ted . . .'

'Yeah?' He sounded bored. He could never see the point in talking after sex.

'Have you read about them GI brides?' Her voice was soft and cajoling.

'What about 'em?' Ted stretched his arms above his head and drummed his knuckles rhythmically on the headboard. Here we go.

'They're going to special camps to learn about what it's gonna be like in America. Before they leave to go over to be with their new husbands.' She sighed longingly. 'Can you imagine what it must be like? Fancy having to learn about a whole new way of life because it's so different from this rotten hole. They've got everything over there. Just like you see in the films. It must be smashing.'

'You got something to complain about, then?'

She gasped at the stupidity of his question. 'Are you kidding? With this new rationing lark it's as bad as it was during the sodding war. It's freezing cold out; there's no coal; and I'm telling you, I'm sick and tired of bloody queuing for every single thing I want. And at least when the war was on there was a bit of fun.'

A slow smile spread over Ted's face. 'I thought we just had a bit of fun.'

Dilys snuggled up to him. 'We did, but . . .'

'But you want some more little presents?'

'Well . . .'

Ted threw off the covers and, unselfconsciously naked, he walked over to the wardrobe he shared with Ginny and pulled open the door.

'There's no rationing when you're with me, darling. Help yourself.'

He picked up his jacket from the floor and patted the pockets to find his cigarettes and matches. 'But don't be too greedy, eh?'

Ted hadn't even finished speaking when Dilys, also naked, was beside him on her knees, raking through the pile of things that had been half hidden by the hems of her supposedly best friend's dresses.

'These are lovely, Ted,' murmured Dilys, tearing open a packet of stockings and draping the shiny lengths of nylon over her arm. 'Really lovely.'

Carefully she put them to one side and dived back into the treasure store.

Her face was glowing with covetousness as she reappeared with a square-shouldered bottle of scent. 'Is this really the proper gear?' she breathed.

'What else would you expect me to have?' he asked, flopping back on to the tangle of bedclothes. 'Dig a bit deeper, there's some chocolates in there and all.'

Dilys was in heaven. Sitting there, rooting through the packets and cartons, she was the picture of a spoilt child on Christmas morning, unwilling to share her booty with her less pushy brothers and sisters.

'Oi, Dilys! Watch how you handle them boxes,' Ted warned her, his eyes narrowed against the smoke from his cigarete. 'I've gotta sell that lot.'

She flashed a worried look at him over her shoulder. 'Not all of it?'

He laughed, recognising his own greed in hers. 'No. But don't go too mad. I've got a living to make, remember.'

Dilys held up the nylons again, admiring their sheen against the pale March sunlight that was filtering through the freshly laundered lace curtains – the same lace curtains that, only a few days before, she had stood on her street doorstep watching Ginny rehang after she had washed them and cleaned the windows.

She touched the nylon to her cheek and gave a little moan. She loved nice things. She deserved them. And she would have them, no matter what the price.

With her lids half lowered and her lips pressed into a sultry pout, Dilys crawled over to the bed on all fours. She then slinked her way across the bed until her naked body was draped across Ted's. Slowly she ran her fingertips up and down the inside of his thigh. 'Ted,' she murmured into his ear, 'will you take me to a club tonight? So's I can wear me new stockings and that lovely scent?'

Ted rolled her off him, propped himself up on his elbows and looked down at her flushed, eager face. He reached across her and ground out the stub of his cigarette in the pink cut-glass pin tray that had pride of place on Ginny's dressing-table. 'D'you think I'm made of money?'

'Well, ain't you?'

'No.' He dropped back on to the pillows. 'Anyway, how about you earning some money for a change? You ain't done a day's work since you lost your job last year.'

'What? D'you really want me to go out all day like Ginny?' She sounded horrified.

'At least Ginny's bringing home wages.' He clasped his hands behind his head. 'That girl's done all kinds of jobs since Bloom's closed.'

Dilys was having trouble keeping up with this new turn of events. 'But, Ted, who'd keep you company?'

He grinned up at the ceiling. 'There's that to it, I suppose.'

This was more like it. He was obviously having a joke with her. 'This is my job now.' She giggled, crawling back on top of him and grabbing him between the legs.

'That's enough of that, Dilys,' he said, lifting her hand away.

'But, Ted—'

'You've gotta go, I've got business to see to.'

'But—'

'Don't start whining, Dilys. Anyway, Ginny'll be back from work soon.'

'She'll think I've been over here helping Nellie for you, like she always does. And Nellie won't give us away. You know she likes me better than Ginny. We have a laugh. And I don't walk around the place with a face like a kite and keep tidying up round her all the time.'

'Ginny don't bribe her with a bottle of the hard stuff every couple of days you mean.'

'You give me the bloody stuff to give her!' Dilys fumed.

'Look, Dilys, I reckon even Ginny'd be suspicious if she finds us both up here stark bollock naked. Now come on.'

'But why d'you even bother with her, Ted? Why—'

'Look, don't give me earache about it again, Dilys. She's me old woman. Right? And while it suits me to have her live here, have me shirts washed, the place kept nice and be looked after—'

'But if you got rid of Ginny, I'd look after you.'

'Yeah. Right. Course you would.' Ted snorted in contemptuous disbelief. 'You can't even look after yourself. Now, come on, Dilys. Play the game, girl. Get yourself dressed and get moving.'

What Ted didn't add was that he wanted her out of there before her brothers got in from work. Sid and Micky might have been a good ten years younger than Ted, but they had earned themselves reputations for being a tough pair of bastards and Ted wasn't about to start messing with them.

They now both worked in the docks, with George, their dad, who had managed to wangle them in there. And the boys couldn't have been happier. The physical work suited the pair of them well; not only were they built like a pair of muscled-up oxen, but doing dock work had meant that they could avoid the threat of conscription – something that preoccupied most young men and their families now that the war was over and joining up all seemed such a complete waste of time.

No, Ted definitely wasn't interested in upsetting those two. He always liked the odds to be very much in his favour whenever he got a bit rough with someone. So he wasn't going to start advertising the fact that he was knocking off their big sister. Especially as the arrangement suited him so very well just the way it was.

Ted was a man who had developed quite a need for women. Not a liking for them, definitely not that, but a real need to have them do as he said, a need to have them submit to him. He was only interested in women who kept very much in their place – and that could be the bedroom, or the kitchen, he didn't mind which – and Dilys popping over of an afternoon suited him very nicely. For the moment at least. He got his end away whenever he fancied it – which was most of the time – and his old mum got a bit of help round the house. Not much help, it had to be said, but enough to keep her quiet until Ginny got in of a night.

Ted reached out for his jacket again and fumbled around until he had found his wallet. He slipped two pounds from a fat wad of notes and handed them to Dilys, who took them without protest. 'Now will you

shut up and get dressed? And take *one* pair of stockings
and *one* bottle of scent. And then get your arse down
them stairs and peel the spuds for me mum, or whatever
it was you was meant to have been doing all afternoon.
And then bugger off and be indoors when your family
gets in like a good little girl.'

Dilys scowled sulkily. Peeling spuds! She'd have to
get things better organised than this or he'd have her
scrubbing the bloody floors next.

As Ginny turned into Bailey Street, the sight she always
dreaded confronted her. There, in a pool of light from
the gas lamp, she saw Ted, all booted and suited and
rubbing the early evening dampness off his windscreen.
He was going out again. And it was Friday. She'd be
lucky if she saw him again before Monday morning. And
that was being optimistic. If only she could handle him
a bit better. Make him care more for her. Make him less
angry with her. Try and get him to share her dreams . . .

She pinned on a smile and broke into a trot. He hated
her to be miserable and was likely to accuse her of
nagging if she wasn't grinning from ear to ear whenever
he saw her. If she could at least have a quick word with
him, maybe he'd stay in.

Maybe.

'Ted!' she called with a cheery wave.

'All right?' he said, straightening up. He tossed the
cloth he had been using into the passenger side of the car
and wiped his hands on his handkerchief.

'Sorry I'm a bit late,' she puffed, 'but I've been doing
that bit of overtime, because I know Nellie's had her
heart set on a new wireless. So I went and put a deposit
on one. For her birthday.'

Ted looked at her for a long moment. Sometimes he
really wondered if she was taking the piss with all her

kind little thoughts and all her concern for Nellie. Surely she must have known that his mum now felt nothing more than contempt for the pathetic doormat she had let herself become.

But who cared, so long as she kept the place nice and did as she was told? And, it had to be said, she wasn't too bad at the other, considering she was his wife. Good little figure. Pretty face. And a lovely pair of pins. If he wasn't in such a hurry . . .

'Ted? Is something wrong? You're staring.'

'Eh?'

She looked into his eyes and lifted her gloved hand to her cheek as though she was using him as a looking-glass to reflect the blemish she was sure he was staring at. 'Have I got a smudge or something?'

'No.' Ted walked round to the driver's side and got in. 'Don't wait up,' he said, then slammed the door and drove off.

Ted whistled softly, a short, high note followed by a lower, longer one – the prearranged signal for Al to let him in.

'Hurry up, Al,' he grumbled, as the young man fiddled around with the locked gate. 'It's brass monkeys out here.'

'I'm sorry, Ted. You know me. I'm nervous,' was all that Al could offer by way of defence.

'You're what?' Ted tutted irritably. 'We've been doing this for how many months now? And you're still acting like some bloody big girl.' Ted reached through the bars of the gate and held out his hand. 'Give it here. Come on. Or we'll have the sodding dock coppers on our backs.'

With practised ease, Ted held the torch in his mouth and slipped the key into the lock, then switched off the torch and swung the gate open without a sound, just enough to let him edge through.

The experience Ted had gained going on the creep during the war – breaking and entering houses and shops that might, or might not, be occupied – had stood him in good stead, and not just for sliding into Dilys's bedroom without disturbing her mum and dad. Ted's skills had equipped him to manage in all sorts of delicate situations.

He shoved Al in the direction of the deserted office. 'Move yourself, for Gawd's sake.'

Inside, Al pulled down the old black-out blinds that nobody had bothered to remove, checked that the door was locked securely, then turned on the green-shaded clerk's lamp on his desk.

Ted sat himself down in the battered, high-backed leather chair and leaned back with his fingers linked across his taut, muscled stomach. 'What you got for me tonight then, Al? Something tasty?'

Al went over to the window and lifted the edge of the blind, a nervous checking that the dock police hadn't suddenly taken it into their minds to alter their nightly routine patrol.

Ted was losing patience. 'Look, Al, I don't need all this. This ain't the only dock office with a bit of bent gear to sell. I'm flaming freezing, I want a drink and I ain't got all night. Okay? So are you gonna show me what you've got or shall I take myself off down the road and see what's on offer down there?'

'Sorry, Ted. It's all that stuff they've had in the papers about the black market. They've been having all these checks.'

Ted sat up straight. 'When?'

'Earlier.'

'They catch anyone?'

'Yeah, Arthur Waters.'

'What, red-headed Arthur?'

Al nodded miserably.

'Don't look so worried, Al. That's good news.'

'Is it?' Al didn't sound very convinced.

'Course it is.' Ted broke into a broad grin and tapped his temple with his forefinger. 'Use your loaf, Al. They won't be looking for any thieves tonight, now will they? They'll think that everyone'll have the wind up and'll be lying low. I mean, who'd be stupid enough to go nicking when someone's just had his collar felt?'

Disarmed by such logic and bolstered by Ted's apparent lack of concern, Al did his best to impress him with his own confidence. 'I was only being cautious, Ted, I wasn't really worried.'

Ted stood up and slapped him matily on the back. 'Course you wasn't, son. Course you wasn't. Now, let's see what you've got for me, shall we?'

When they had finished ferrying the final cartons of illicit goods through the dock gates, and round to a dimly lit street where the Talbot was parked in the shadows of a tall, bomb-damaged warehouse, Ted slipped Al a tight roll of notes. 'Good work, son,' he said with a wink. 'Now, how about a little celebration?'

Al nodded readily. He savoured the excitement of going for a drink with Ted Martin after their deals almost more than he enjoyed the money Ted gave him. Being a clerk might have brought him the kind of respect that his mum and dad approved of, but Al craved respect of a different sort: the sort that had birds ready to jump into bed with you and blokes wanting to shake your hand and be your mate. And going into a pub with Ted Martin gave Al a much-savoured glimpse of what that felt like. He scared him a bit too, if he was honest, but that was part of the thrill.

Al waited for Ted to get in the car and then did the same. He sat there, silently watching in the shadows as Ted checked the angle of his hat in the rear-view mirror.

'Tell you what,' said Ted, turning and flashing him one of his devastating smiles as he fired the engine into life, 'I know of a couple of right dirty sorts who'd just love to keep us company tonight. Fancy having a few drinks with them and then . . .' Another one of his smiles. 'Well, who knows?'

Al nodded again. He hadn't even been with a bird when he first met Ted, but he had certainly got the taste for them since.

The 'sorts' turned out to be two flashily clothed, over-made-up girls of about twenty, who were drinking in a dodgy-looking Limehouse pub on the edges of what remained of Blitz-ravaged Chinatown. They were standing up at the bar with two tall, well-dressed men, but the moment one of the girls spotted Ted coming in with Al she nudged her friend, pointed at Ted and whispered something to her.

The other girl cast a a worried look over to where she was pointing. Her friend nudged her again, harder this time, and she immediately replaced her frown with the broadest smile she could summon up. Without another word between them, the two young women abandoned their erstwhile companions and began to push their way through the smoke-filled fug of the bar towards the door.

'Teddy!' squealed Lilly, the shapelier of the two girls, the one who had first spotted them. 'I've really missed you. I ain't seen you for weeks.' She threw her arms round his neck and, much to the amusement of all the other drinkers – barring the two men who had just been dumped – kissed Ted full on the lips.

In response, Ted ran his hand up her skirt and grabbed

68

the top of her thigh, where her stocking-top dug into her flesh.

'If you're gonna give her one, Ted, let's all watch!' hollered a big, pug-nosed man playing darts in the corner of the pub. 'I could do with a bit of a laugh!'

Lilly swung round to the man, her fists stuck into her waist. 'That's no way to talk in front of ladies!'

'We all know that,' Ted joined in, squeezing her leg even harder. 'But he wasn't talking in front of no ladies, now was he? He was talking in front of you and Marge.'

To Al's surprise, rather than being offended by Ted's lack of gallantry, Lilly gave every impression of being really pleased with such treatment and, with only the merest hint of a glance at her friend Marge, she gave him another full-on-the-mouth smacker by way of reward. She then linked her arm through his and nodded at a table at the far end of the room. 'Let's go over there and sit down,' she suggested, without so much as a glance back at the two men who were still standing, tight-lipped with hostility, at the bar.

'Come on, Marge,' she prompted her friend, flashing her eyes for emphasis, 'come and sit with us. And bring that little cutie-pie with you. He's a real little smasher, ain't he? Where d'you find him then, Ted?'

As Lilly sashayed over to the table with Ted's hand clamped firmly over her buttock, Al felt his neck and then his face flame red, but it wasn't Ted's crude behaviour, or even Lilly's teasing that was making him blush, it was the strangeness of the situation. While Ted might have been happy to go and sit down in the corner, Al definitely wasn't. In fact, he didn't want to be in the pub at all. He couldn't see the sense in staying in a place where you'd just taken two women away from a pair of blokes who had probably been buying them drinks all night. Novice as Al was at this sort of thing, it seemed to be asking for trouble.

As Al followed Ted across the room to the table, he leaned forward and spoke to him in a tone so low that it was just about audible. 'Don't you feel a bit awkward?'

Ted looked round at him in surprise. 'No. Why should I?'

Al jerked his head over to the bar where the two men were watching them with unmistakable resentment. 'How about them?'

Ted threw his head back and laughed loudly. 'Here, you ain't one of them nancy-boys, are you, Al? You don't fancy them instead of the girls, do you?'

'Blimey, I hope he don't!' Marge shrieked in a voice so shrill it sounded more like that of a puppet than a fully grown woman.

'But if he *is*,' Lilly screeched back at her, 'you'll soon be able to show him better ways, won't you, Marge?'

'Course I will! You know me, Lilly, always glad to oblige!'

'So I can see,' muttered one of the two disgruntled men. 'Drink up, Johnno, and we'll be on our way. I don't like the stink what's come up in here.'

With that, both men drained their glasses, snatched up their hats and topcoats from their bar-stools and barged their way out of the pub, followed by hoots of derisive glee from Ted. 'I think you've upset your friends, girls,' he hollered after them.

'They ain't no friends of ours,' Marge said, wriggling her body closer to Al's. 'We ain't never set eyes on 'em before, have we, Lil?'

Lil shook her head dismissively. 'No, never.'

When the door was slammed firmly shut behind them, Ted turned to the darts player in the corner. 'So who were the pair of charmers then, Puggy?' he called.

'Dunno mate. I'm as much in the dark as the girls.'

That was good enough for Ted. They weren't locals, just visitors. And it wasn't as though he'd enticed the girls away, they had come over to him by choice. And anyway, blokes didn't get into fights over birds like Lilly and Marge. They were disposable, interchangeable, the sort you used and then dumped. Within Ted's logic, everything was just fine.

He banished the two men from his mind and set about really enjoying the rest of the evening. And he had every reason to celebrate: he'd done a good deal down at the docks – more than a good deal, actually, as Al was still wet behind the ears when it came to asking a fair price for the knocked-off gear he passed on to him – and now he had a pint in his hand and a warm and willing woman pressing herself against him, just asking for those chubby thighs of hers to be groped. Yes, Ted had every reason to be a happy man.

Marge watched Ted and Lilly fondling and kissing one another with growing nervousness. She was doing her best to get Al in the mood, but he didn't seem to want to know, and she was worried that, being Ted's mate, Ted would get angry with her for failing to get the kid's interest. She knew Ted. The trouble was, Al seemed less concerned with putting his tongue down Marge's throat than in pouring booze down his own gullet. And he kept looking over at the door as though he was waiting for the other two blokes to come back. Maybe it wasn't a joke after all, maybe he was a bit the other way. Marge hoped not. That was all she needed. Still, she could only do her best . . .

When the four of them eventually staggered out of the pub – Lilly clinging gingerly to Ted as though he were an over-inflated life jacket that was liable to explode in

71

her face at any moment and Marge with the now para-
lytic Al draped round her like a fur stole – the cold night
air hit them like a wall.

'Bloody hell, Ted,' gasped Lilly, pulling her thin
woollen coat tighter around her neck, 'I'm gonna freeze
me tits off if we don't get inside soon.'

'I've got the motor, ain't I?' Ted grinned, towing her
across the street towards the Talbot. 'We'll soon warm
up, with the four of us all going at it at once in there.'

'What? All in there together? That'll be cosy, won't it,
Al?' giggled Marge, rolling her eyes suggestively at him,
in what, she promised herself, was her final attempt to
arouse his interest.

It should have been clear, even to Marge, that Al was
now so drunk, a whole harem of girls, hand-picked to
suit every taste and with fairy lights hanging from every
digit, would have been hard pressed to have gained even
a glimmer of appreciation or response from his semi-
conscious form.

Being about as used to drink as he was to women, Al,
in his efforts to make himself feel better about the two
men, had drunk himself almost senseless. If he hadn't
had quite so much to drink he would have realised what
Ted had in mind and wouldn't even have contemplated
letting Marge drag him over to the car. Al was only just
getting used to the idea that he could engage in the
straightforward type of liaisons with women. In any
other, even slightly more sober, circumstances, the
thought of all four of them being together in the car
would have terrified the life out of him and he would
have had it away on his toes, back to his mum's and
dad's place as though the dock coppers themselves were
after him. But Al was not only drunk, he was now what
could only be described as totally rat-arsed.

Marge looked at him with resigned weariness and frustration. She just hoped he'd liven his ideas up a bit before they got down to it, or she was really going to have to put on some sort of act so that Ted wouldn't realise what was going on. If that was the case, she could only keep her fingers crossed that Lilly was in good enough form to keep his interest from straying to what she and Al were supposedly up to.

She pulled Al's arm more firmly round her shoulder and hauled him over to the car, where Lilly was pawing Ted in a show of increasingly revved-up anticipation. 'Hurry up, Ted,' she was urging him in a breathy little voice.

'All right, all right,' Ted snapped. 'I know you can't keep your hands off me, Lil, but let me find the bloody keys, will you? And stop pulling at me coat.'

The pulling stopped, but was immediately replaced by a hand gripping Ted's shoulder. It felt like a vice being tightened against his collar-bone.

'What the fuck?' Ted demanded and spun round to confront her for daring to do such a thing. His face was contorted with anger at her presumption. But it wasn't Lilly who had grabbed him.

The next thing Ted knew was a knee slamming into his groin. As he crumpled to the frosty cobbled ground, cupping his testicles in an effort to protect himself from further agony, he squinted up through his pain to see one of the men who had been drinking with the girls at the bar.

'Billy Saunders,' said the man, raising his hat in a parody of polite introduction. 'Don't forget the name, will you. You'll be hearing it a lot round here. I've decided Limehouse might just be the place to start up a little business.'

He turned, raised his hat once more and smiled magnificently at the two now ashen-faced girls. He pointed at Lilly and jerked his head towards where Ted was still squirming on the damp ground. 'What's his name?'

She didn't answer, but Billy noted that the girl shot an urgent, warning look at her friend.

'Scared of him, eh?' said Billy with a disgusted shake of his head. 'I wondered why you both went running over to the flash little bleeder.'

Billy took a cigarette out of his case and waited for the other slightly taller man to light it for him, then he strolled the few steps over to Ted. 'You fucking coward,' he said simply, gave him another vicious kick and turned back to Lilly and Marge. He raised his hat again. 'Ladies. Let me wish you both a very good night.' With that, the man and his companion strode off into the shadows.

The girls exchanged a terrified glance. What the hell were they meant to do? It was bad enough being stuck with a nutter like Ted Martin when he wasn't even upset, but now . . .

Lilly took a deep breath, put her handbag on the kerb and linked her arm through Ted's. It was just a shame he wasn't as pissed as the stupid kid he'd brought with him, then she and Marge could have cleared off and left them both to the dippers and cosh gangs from Chinatown and neither of them would have been any the wiser that the girls had abandoned them. Still, it was no good wishing; good things just didn't seem to happen to the likes of Lilly. 'Help us then, Marge,' she gasped.

Between them, the girls somehow managed to haul Ted to his feet. He staggered backwards and slumped against the car.

'Billy Saunders,' Ted panted. 'I won't forget you, you bastard.'

Al dropped down on to the kerb next to Lilly's handbag and stared at the three people in front of him. Even with all the alcohol fuddling his brain he was able

74

to see that the girls were as scared of Ted as he suddenly realised himself to be.

There was something in Ted's expression, a strange, distant look in his eyes as though he were seeing something that was only visible to him. Something that Al felt genuinely relieved he couldn't see, or even begin to understand.

He had seen Ted turn to violence before, going berserk over the merest slight; smashing his fist into a woman's face for just looking at him the wrong way; or giving a real whacking to an old night-watchman at one of the bonded warehouses, who had simply asked him what he wanted. In fact, in the months since Al had first met him, Ted Martin had proved himself to be a really vicious sort of bloke, especially where women were concerned, but Al had never seen that look before. And it really frightened him. Drunk as he was, Al knew that he was well out of his depth.

He picked up Lilly's handbag, clasped it to him like a comforter and vomited all over it.

Chapter 5

When Ginny woke up the next morning she was saddened, but not surprised, to find that the covers on Ted's side of the bed were undisturbed and that his pillow had not been slept on again. She might have become accustomed to him staying out all night, sometimes for days on end, but she would never feel happy about it.

Sleeping alone and being scared to open her mouth when Ted actually deigned to be there: it wasn't how Ginny had expected things to turn out.

Early on in their marriage, Ted had been nothing like he was now, or so she had thought. Maybe love, or grief for the loss of her family, had blinded her to the truth, but even though she had heard rumours about Ted she had put them down to jealous gossip; there was always plenty of that in the neighbourhood for those who chose to listen. All right, she knew he had a reputation for having a bit of a temper, so did a lot of blokes his age, but Ted himself had never given her any reason to believe that they wouldn't be leading a happy, ordinary married life together. She had pictured it so many times: the war would be over – she was right about that, at least – and Ted would be going off to work every morning, doing a normal sort of job. Something like Dilys's dad and brothers did down at the docks maybe, where he would graft hard, but honestly, not ducking and diving and pulling the Lord alone knew what sort of strokes. And he would come home every evening and greet her and their children with hugs and kisses, scooping them high into the air, making them giggle and shriek with happy laughter that would ring around their picture-book, perfect home. Then she would put on a pretty flowery apron to keep her dress nice and dish up their tea, and afterwards Ted would help her put the little ones to bed, and . . .

She rubbed her hands roughly over her eyes, refusing to cry at the cruelly taunting images in her mind.

Children. Would they only ever be a dream?

She rolled on to her side and slapped angrily at Ted's untouched pillowslip. Dreams *did* sometimes come true and her dreams were the one thing she wouldn't ever let anyone take away from her.

She *would* dream about having children; about Ted changing into the sort of man she'd believed she'd married; and – her latest fantasy – about Nellie vanishing from number 18 and leaving her and Ted alone in the house for ever. Ginny didn't know why, but her mother-in-law was treating her more and more like an unwanted lodger lately and Ginny honestly, if guiltily, wished her gone.

She had a glorious vision of her disappearing in a puff of red smoke, just like the wicked witch in the films, leaving behind only a pair of steaming carpet slippers and a smouldering cigarette end dangling in mid-air like the smile of the Cheshire cat.

Ginny too was smiling – at the picture she had conjured – although she felt no happiness. What she felt was a desperate, intense, gut-wrenching loneliness: a woman imprisoned by her own girlish dreams.

But if anyone had seen her, on that bright but chilly mid-March morning, as she drew back the curtains and looked down on to Bailey Street from her bedroom window, they would never have been able to guess at her sadness. Instead of weeping and wailing and making a fuss, as many others would have done, Ginny simply took Nellie her morning cup of tea and got on with the chores. Just as she did every weekend.

Nellie could, of course, have done a lot of the jobs during the week while Ginny was out at work and, up until about a year ago, she had at least made some pretence at helping. But that was all in the past. Now Nellie did nothing, except for the odd times when she cooked something for Ted.

The only time Ginny had been foolish enough to ask her to lend a hand more recently, Nellie had looked at her as though she had taken leave of her senses and had gone straight to Ted, accusing Ginny of being a slave driver. She had ranted and raved like a mad thing, screaming and shouting about the hard time her lazy good-for-nothing daughter-in-law was giving her. Her, a woman in her fifties! And why she should be expected to work her fingers to the bone while Ginny, a bit of a girl, sat around doing nothing, she couldn't imagine.

Ted had been furious with Ginny and given her such a slap that one of her back teeth had come loose. She had been in agony for days.

Ginny had not made that mistake twice. She held her tongue and got on with things, just as she was doing that Saturday morning. At least since Dilys had been out of work, she had taken to popping over to do a few bits and pieces to help Ginny out, peeling a few spuds or chopping a cabbage. But it made very little dent in her workload; there was still so much to do.

Before Nellie had even shifted herself from her bed that morning, Ginny had scrubbed and whitened the street doorstep; she had stripped the linen from her and Ted's bed; had put the washing in to soak, while the copper heated up ready for the weekly boil; and had gone on to sweep and dust, and mangle and peg, and scour and rub, and wax and polish, until she was all but exhausted.

By then Nellie had roused herself and had found her way down to the kitchen. That was the cue for Ginny to take a break from the housework; not to sit down, but to make a pot of tea and a plate of toast and dripping: a rushed lunch for her and a leisurely breakfast for Nellie.

After downing a quick cup of tea and swallowing a few mouthfuls of bread, Ginny went out to the backyard to bring in the still damp washing for ironing and airing. Although it was a fine, early-spring morning, the air still had the damp feel of winter about it and the laundry would get no drier hanging outside.

While Ginny stood at the table ironing, Nellie sat by the blazing kitchen fire scorching her legs to a mottled, corned-beef red and finishing off the rest of the tea and toast, actually shifting herself at one point to shoot another shovel of coal on the fire.

Ginny had it on the tip of her tongue to ask her mother-in-law to be a bit more careful with their precious fuel, because although Ted usually turned up with a few sacks he had managed to get from somewhere – rationing seemed to have no meaning for him – Ginny knew she couldn't depend on him remembering. And if they ran out of coal and they had another cold snap like last week, Nellie would really get her moaning hat on. Ginny had enough on her plate without the thought of her leading off about her poor old frozen feet and the agonies she was suffering with her chilblains.

But Ginny had seen Nellie in action too many times of late to dare comment about being wasteful. Her mother-in-law had changed so much. She could now take it into her head, for no reason other than causing mischief it seemed, deliberately to misinterpret the most innocuous of Ginny's remarks as being the most cutting criticism.

And she would throw even more coal on the fire just for spite.

Tired, anxious and fed up as she felt, Ginny had no choice but to try and keep Nellie in a good mood. 'I'm really glad I've got this new job, you know, Nell. But who'd have thought I'd be working in an electrics factory, eh?' Ginny allowed herself a little smile as she thought about the deposit she had taken from her week's wages to put on the wireless the day before. With her staff discount she had chosen a model that was really top of the range. Even Nellie couldn't help but be pleased when she saw it.

'I'd prefer to be doing machining still, of course, but at least I'm earning until something more suitable comes up. And I can get plenty of overtime at this place.'

'Overtime? Is that what you call it? Well I call it staying out all hours. You're never sodding here when I need you.'

Ginny flinched at Nellie's tone. 'You've got Dilys to help you,' she replied cautiously.

She draped the final shirt over the clothes-horse and put the iron outside the back door to cool down. 'She told me she's been doing all sorts over here,' she said, straightening up and kneading her knuckles into the small of her aching back.

'You could say that,' Nellie snorted.

Ginny refilled the kettle at the sink. Nellie put away more tea than anyone Ginny had ever known; and Ginny was expected to keep her well supplied. 'So,' she said, lighting the gas stove, 'what gossip have you got for me then, Nell? I haven't had much of a chance to catch up, what with all the extra hours I'm putting in.'

Nellie paused for a moment, torn between pointedly ignoring Ginny's attempts at pleasantness on the one hand and, on the other, the pleasure she would gain in passing on a story that would wind up the silly little cow like a watch spring.

Nellie's new-found fondness for malice against her dozy daughter-in-law won. But it was her own fault, Nellie reasoned; if only the girl had shown some spirit, Nellie would probably have left her alone – she might even have tried discouraging Dilys a bit – but Ginny was just too easy a target to resist.

At one time, she had tolerated Ginny – just – but over the years she had started wearing down her patience more and more, and Nellie was beginning to wonder whether she should really start working on her and perhaps she'd bugger off and let Dilys move in. Not that Nellie was that struck with Dilys. But at least she made her laugh. Plus she was generous with the booze; and Nellie seemed to get through the hard stuff faster and faster these days. She'd have hated that little source of pleasure to dry up.

'You heard what happened to that stupid mare over the road yesterday, I suppose?'

'What, Dilys?' Ginny asked over her shoulder as she rinsed out the teapot.

Nellie was sorely tempted to say yes, that's right, Dilys. She's been over here schtupping your old man while you've been grafting all the hours God sends. That'd wipe the stupid smile off her face. It would do her good to hear a few home truths. But she didn't. Not because she cared for her daughter-in-law's feelings, of course, but because Ted wouldn't have liked it if she'd grassed on him. Nellie had never really figured out why, but her boy seemed to like keeping her around the place, flapping about with her bloody dusters and irons. The more Ted had a pop at the soppy tart, the more she tried to keep the house looking like a flaming palace. It drove Nellie to distraction.

Nellie looked her up and down as she walked back to the table, folded the ironing blanket and stuck it away in the bottom of the dresser. At least she had a decent figure, Nellie supposed, and her Ted liked that in a woman. So maybe she was good for something.

'I was talking to Pearl earlier,' Ginny said amiably, 'while we was both out scrubbing the street doorsteps. And she never said nothing about Dilys.'

Nellie sighed theatrically. Huh! Pearl Chivers. Dilys's flaming perfect mother and Ginny's *special friend, who was always there if Ginny needed her*. She made Nellie sick. She was another one always cleaning and polishing. But at least Pearl could have a row and had a mouth on her like a docker when she let go. Nellie had to hand that to her: she wasn't a mouse. Not like Dolly Day-dream, who didn't seem to know what day of the week it was half the time, let alone how to stand up for herself.

'I don't mean Dilys, do I?' Nellie rolled her eyes and tutted. 'And if you'd just keep your trap shut for a couple o' minutes, and let me get a flaming word in edgeways, I'd bloody well be able to tell you who I mean.'

'Sorry, Nellie.'

'I should think so.'

'Well?' Ginny asked, her voice small and coaxing.

'I was talking about Violet Varney.'

'What, she's turned up, has she?' Ginny asked hopefully, as she returned to the sink and filled a blue-rimmed white enamel bowl ready to peel the potatoes for teatime.

'Yeah. She's turned up all right.'

'Thank Gawd for that.' Ginny bent down and took a string bag full of potatoes and some old newspapers from under the sink, and carried them and the basin of water over to the table. 'You know, Nellie, I reckon it broke Violet's heart having to send them kids away.

When she went amongst the missing last week, I really thought, that's it, she's gone off her head, she's had it away 'cos she can't stand it no more.'

Nellie folded her arms triumphantly across her aproned bosom. This was going to shock the dopey little madam. 'If you must know, you was right. She did go off her head.'

'How d'you mean?' Ginny let a long thin curl of peel drop on to the paper she had spread out on the table.

'The stupid tart's gone and topped herself.'

'She's *what*?' The knife and the half-peeled potato fell from Ginny's hands into the bowl with a messy splash.

Nellie stared critically at the spilt water. 'Left this really miserable note, didn't she? Her Bert found it propped up on the front room mantelpiece. Went screaming along the street to Bobby and Martha at the Prince Albert, just like a man possessed. I'm surprised Pearl never mentioned it to you. She must have heard him. And what with you two being so *friendly*.'

She said the last word as though it were a nasty, contagious affliction that might infect the incautious at any moment.

Ginny could only stare, as Nellie paused to search the pockets of her cross-over apron for her Woodbines. Having found them, she stuck one in the corner of her mouth, lit it and tossed the spent match carelessly into the hearth.

Picking a stray strand of tobacco from her lip, Nellie continued as casually as if she had been discussing nothing more interesting than the price of cod. 'That kettle's boiling,' she said with a lift of her chin. She made no attempt to get up.

Automatically, Ginny went over and switched off the gas. She twisted round to face Nellie with a puzzled frown. 'Look, Nellie, am I missing something here? You did say Bert, didn't you? Bert Varney? How could Bert find the note? He's dead.'

'No he ain't. It's Violet what's dead. Mind you, when he finds out Violet was on the sodding game, I bet he'll wish he was a goner.' Nellie screwed up her nose and shuddered with revulsion. 'And wait till he finds out about her getting a dose ... What a show-up! A right win double!'

Ginny dropped down on to her chair and rubbed her hands over her face, trying to make sense of it all. 'I know I must sound stupid, Nell, but start again, will you? You're saying Violet's dead, but Bert Varney ain't?'

'Blimey, you got cloth ears or something?' She puffed irritably on her cigarette. '*Yes*, Violet's Uncle Ned. And *no*, Bert ain't. Got it? It was all a mistake. He was in a camp, wasn't he. In Japan or somewhere.'

Ginny could hardly take it in. 'But that Japan business was all over more than six months ago. How could he—'

Nellie threw up her hands in exasperation. 'I *know*, but he was sick or something, wasn't he. Got transferred to some hospital. With some nuns ...'

'How d'you mean?'

Nellie shrugged nonchalantly. 'I dunno, do I. He had this fever thing. Didn't know his arse from his elbow, let alone who he was, or what his name was. But when he got better they sent him home.' She shook her head contemptuously. 'Bet they were glad to get rid of him, with all his moaning. You know what he's like.'

'So how did—'

'And *then*,' she continued, not best pleased at being interrupted – conversations were always more monologues than dialogues as far as Nellie was concerned – 'when he found out that Violet had mullered herself and she'd sent his oldest kids to the other side of the world to that Africa place, and that his youngest had gone to live with Vi's sister down in Yalding. Well, he led off alarming, didn't he. Bobby got him straight out of the pub and on to the first train down to Kent. Best place for him, if you ask me: surrounded by hop gardens and sheep, and with a bunch of bloody carrot crunchers for neighbours. They won't know no better if he goes dool-ally, will they? 'Cos they're all a bit funny down there anyway.'

Nellie shifted her bosom with the back of her hand. 'Must be all that fresh air.' She wrinkled her nose with distaste. 'Can't do you no good, can it?'

'Nobody should have to sink as low as she did.' Ginny dropped her chin and stared down at the floor. 'I should have done more to help her. But you know what she was like. She was so private—'

'Private?' Nellie spluttered. 'She was bloody ashamed! Filthy trollop.'

Ginny shook her head in disbelief that so much tragedy could visit just one family. 'That poor feller.'

'Who's a poor feller?' someone asked.

Ginny looked up to see Ted standing in the kitchen doorway, leaning against the jamb.

'Ted!' Ginny leapt up from the table and ran across the kitchen to him, but he held up his hands to make sure she kept her distance.

'Mind off, you dozy cow. Can't you see I'm in pain?'

She winced, not at his harsh words, but at the unmis-takable, if faint, whiff of scent. She swallowed hard, determined to keep her voice steady, then asked softly, 'What's wrong, Ted?'

'I slipped, didn't I? Last night. On the wet stones down the docks. While I was having a trade. I hurt me leg.'

She frowned as she watched Ted hobble over to the table and carefully lower himself on to one of the hard kitchen chairs. It didn't look as though it was his leg that was hurting.

Carelessly, he shoved the bowl, potatoes and peelings to one side and rested his elbows in their place. 'I couldn't drive, could I. So I had to stay the night with a bloke I was doing the bit of business with.'

She felt relief flood through her. He had stayed at a friend's house. The scent must have been from his wife. Ginny was a past master at convincing herself of anything where Ted was concerned.

'And have you brought anything home from the docks for your poor old mum?' Nellie asked pathetically.

Gingerly, Ted, shifted his weight and eased his hand into his trouser pocket. He held out his car keys to Ginny. 'Go out to the car. There's some bananas on the back seat.'

'Bananas!' Ginny ran out to the car to fetch them.

Nellie wasn't so impressed. 'I'd rather have a few quid. Or a nice leg o' pork.'

Ted snorted at his mother's ingratitude. 'I bring you the first bananas this country's seen since bloody 1939 and you don't even say thank you.'

'Well, can you sodding well blame me?' Nellie no longer sounded pathetic, she sounded put out, very put out, and very loud. 'D'you know what they had in the paper yesterday?'

Ted didn't answer.

'Oi! I'm talking to you. A bloody recipe for Squirrel Pie. That's what. That's what the sodding government's telling us to eat.' Nellie was getting into her stride – it didn't take much. 'We're going to have a lovely time, ain't we? Squirrels and pissing bananas. I'm not getting no younger, Ted. I need a bit of comfort in me old age.'

Ginny had heard her mother-in-law's hollering from outside in the street, but she was determined not to let

Nellie upset her. Ted was home and that was all that mattered.

She came back into the kitchen and took the bananas from under her apron – although she was sure that all the neighbours knew what Ted was up to, she didn't like to advertise the fact – and, with a careful smile, put them on the table in front of Ted.

Ted ripped one off the bunch and tossed it to Nellie.

Grudgingly she peeled off the skin.

'Don't get a gob on you, Mum,' he sighed. 'What sort of a son do you think I am? You know you won't have to go eating no squirrels while I'm around.'

Nellie shrugged, unable to speak with all the fruit she had crammed in her mouth.

'We've got plenty.' Ted jerked his head at Ginny. 'Go up and get some of them boxes down, Gin. Show the old girl what I've got up there. When I flog that little lot, we'll be rolling in it. And there's plenty more where they come from an' all.'

As Ginny knelt in front of the wardrobe, she heard someone come into the room behind her.

She looked warily over her shoulder – she would never get used to Ted's 'business' – but it was all right, it was Ted.

He limped slowly towards her. 'Leave that for now,' he said, his lips stretched with pain. 'I wanna bit of peace. I'm going to bed.'

Ginny stood up. 'Shall I get in with you?' she whispered.

'Leave off.' Ted climbed on to the bed and rolled over on to his side, clutching himself in agony. Billy Saunders, he fumed to himself. I swear, I'll find you, and I'll have you, you bastard . . .

*

It was Saturday morning, two weeks after Ted had been attacked, and Ginny hadn't seen hide nor hair of him since the night before.

He could now walk around without clasping himself in agony, but his improved health hadn't done anything to improve his mood. Whenever he did condescend to come home – which wasn't very often – he always seemed to be angry with Ginny about something or other. Anything could get him going: from the food on his plate suddenly not being to his liking, to Ginny singing quietly to herself as she washed up after him. It was like living with a time bomb that was ticking away, just waiting to go off in her face.

Any other Saturday, Ginny might have kidded herself that she was pleased Ted wasn't there to get in her way while she did the housework, but today was 30 March, Nellie's birthday and she had expected her son to be there with her. So Nellie wasn't very happy.

She had carried on at Ginny as though it was all her fault that he had stayed out all night again, and instead of being grateful, or even pleased, with the wireless that Ginny had bought her, Nellie looked at it with about as much interest as if she'd been given a pair of size fifteen football boots without any laces.

It wasn't that Nellie didn't like Ginny's gift – she loved it, although it would have killed her to say so – no, it was the fact that she wanted her Ted there, fussing over her, giving her presents, treating her like the queen she believed herself to be. Her son had gained himself quite a reputation around the East End for being a black marketeer, a real spiv, and Nellie basked in his notoriety as the bloke who could get you anything. It gave her a feeling of superiority to know that people were beholden to her boy for all the little things that were so difficult to get unless you had 'contacts'.

No matter how they pretended to be good, law-abiding citizens, it seemed that nearly everyone was involved in some sort of fiddle: buying a bit of this and a bit of that from any source they could find. And it wasn't only luxuries that were hard to come by. Everyday food items were still in short supply and anything that could help stretch the rations – that were now even meaner than during the worst of the war years – could be sold for a good profit. As to where the stuff actually came from . . . Well, that didn't seem to be much of a cause for concern for all the eager customers.

Nellie had longed to see her Ted walk through the kitchen door with his arms full of gear that her neighbours could only dream about and say, 'Here you are, Mum, happy birthday.' But he hadn't, and she had gone on and on about it. She went on so much, in fact, that when Pearl and George came over to take Nellie down to the Albert for a lunch-time celebration port and lemon – Pearl's all-seeing eyes hadn't missed Ginny's predicament – Ginny put her hands together in gratitude. It seemed almost like a treat to be left in peace to get on with the housework.

Ginny had just finished scouring the wooden draining board when the back door flew back on its hinges and Ted burst into the kitchen. 'Get upstairs,' he snapped. 'Now.'

Ginny's heart leapt: Ted might not have expressed himself very romantically, but she was so relieved that he was still interested in her, she treasured his words as though they'd come written on a card with a dozen long-stemmed roses.

It had been two weeks since they'd last been to bed together and she'd been seriously worried that he'd finally gone off her. And she couldn't have stood that.

Despite everything, Ginny just couldn't contemplate life without him; couldn't stand the thought of being completely alone. The past fortnight had been terrible. Whenever Ted had been home, he'd made her sleep downstairs on the armchair in the front room. She knew it was because he was in so much pain, but she would have happily slept on the bedroom floor – if he would have let her.

'I've missed you, Ted. I've really—' she began, walking towards him.

'You can get that idea right out of your head,' he sneered, barging past her and out into the passage. 'Now come on. Move yourself. We've gotta get all that gear out of the wardrobe.'

'What, have you got a customer for the whole lot?' she asked, running up the stairs after him. Someone must have a few bob to spare. That should put him in a good mood.

'Just help me shift it out to the motor.'

'The motor?'

He spun round on the landing and glared at her. 'What are you? A fucking parrot?' he snarled. 'Just do it. Unless you wanna get me nicked.'

Ted jumped into his car with a muttered warning that, if Ginny knew what was good for her, she was to keep her trap well and truly shut, except for what he had told her she could say. He was going to lie low for a while and he didn't want her blabbing her big mouth off to anyone. Not to Nellie, Dilys, Pearl, no one. Then, with his car full of gear, Ted disappeared out of Bailey Street with a screech of rubber.

Less than ten minutes later there was a loud rapping on the front door of number 18. Ginny took a deep breath, nervously patted her hair into place and walked slowly along the passage. Ted had told her what to say; all she had to do was remember it. She could only pray that she got it right. Thank Gawd Nellie was down the Albert. She would just have got herself hysterical and made matters worse.

Pinning a neat smile on her face, Ginny opened the door.

As she had expected, it was the police. There was a black squad car parked outside and in the driver's seat sat a uniformed officer. But what she hadn't expected were the two smartly dressed men confronting her on her doorstep. From the little she knew about coppers, Ginny assumed they were detectives of some kind. And if they were, then this was no casual warning about selling bent gear, this was serious.

She licked her lips. Her mouth was so dry, it felt as though she had been eating uncooked porridge. 'Can I help you, gentlemen?' she eventually managed to say.

'Mrs Martin?' asked the taller of the two men, taking off his trilby.

She nodded.

'Perhaps we could step inside for a moment?'

Ginny nodded again and stood back to let them in, ushering them towards the front room. 'Won't you sit down?'

As she stepped inside the room and gestured towards the matching over-stuffed armchairs standing either side of the fireplace, Ginny hoped they didn't notice her hand was trembling.

'We'll be all right standing, thank you,' said the man who had spoken before.

'Cup o' tea?'

'No thanks.'

Ginny blinked slowly. She felt as though she were watching a film. Take deep breaths, she told herself.

You've got nothing to worry about. Ted's shifted everything.

Before anyone had the chance to say anything else, the street door was sent crashing back on its hinges and Nellie came hurtling into the room like a lunatic. 'What's happened?' she yelled, grabbing the smaller of the two men by the lapels. 'Has my boy been hurt?'

The taller man spoke. 'Mrs Martin senior?'

Nellie ignored him. 'I asked you a question!' She spat the words into the shorter man's face. 'Someone runs into the Albert and tells me there's a law car outside my house and you stand there asking me my sodding name!'

Surprisingly delicately, the man unpeeled Nellie's fingers from his coat and brushed her hand away. 'No, Mrs Martin, your son hasn't been hurt.' He paused and exchanged a brief, smug grin with his colleague. 'Not yet. But someone's got it in for him. I think you ought to know that, so you can pass that little message on to him. And whoever it was didn't mess about. They went straight to the top. Tipped off the Ministry of Food.'

The other man nodded at him to indicate that he would take it from there. 'I'm sure you've heard about the Ministry's campaign against the black market. Well, we're co-operating with them. There's road blocks going up all around London. We're searching lorries, vans, cars. You name it. Shops and restaurants, they're all being raided.' He flashed another look at his associate. 'Aw yeah, I forgot. And houses. They're being searched too. So if you don't mind, Mrs Martin – either Mrs Martin will do – I'd like you to show us around the place.'

Two hours later the house was in a shambles and the two men were putting on their hats ready to leave.

'Satisfied now you've upset an old lady?' wailed Nellie.

92

'Not really,' said the tall one casually. Then, turning to Ginny, he added, 'You will remember to tell your husband that someone's got it in for him, won't you, Mrs Martin? The word is that he's upset one of the big boys. And I reckon they're right. So I'd watch out if I was you. See, they're not too fussy how they go about paying someone back, especially when it's just a little two-bob spiv they've got the hump with. They'll pick on wives, mothers . . . Anyone.'

With that, he raised his hat and treated both Ginny and Nellie to a bright, sunny smile. 'Cheerio then, ladies. I'm sure the Detective Constable and myself will be seeing you again soon.'

At thirty-eight years of age, Billy Saunders was a man in the prime of his life. He was tall, dark, powerfully built, and had a self-assured manner that convinced everyone he was handsome, despite the fact that, on closer inspection, he was more striking, in a rough, almost threatening sort of way, rather than conventionally good-looking.

He and Johnno, the minder who had been with him on the night he had given Ted a kicking as a reward for his bad manners, were paying an afternoon call on the same dodgy Limehouse pub where it had happened.

As they walked through the door, a few people looked up, but most of the customers got on with what they were doing: drinking, playing cards, or just staring into their beer. People in that area, so close to the docks and what remained of the bomb-damaged but still secretive world of Chinatown, knew to mind their own business.

That attitude – as well as the possibility of buying up cheap property – was one of the reasons Saunders was interested in the area.

Two of the people who did take notice of Saunders and his sidekick were Lilly and Marge, the girls who had inadvertently been the cause of Saunders giving Ted the beating.

The pair exchanged a nervous glance and hurriedly grabbed their handbags from the bar. The last thing they wanted was trouble; it was hard enough finding pubs that weren't complete bugholes, where they'd tolerate girls plying their trade. As it was they had to give the landlord his cut. Causing fights could only put his price up even more.

Billy Saunders, with his most charming smile, took off his hat and walked over to them. 'Not leaving already, are you, ladies?'

'Er, yeah, we've gotta be going, ain't we, Marge?'

'That's right. We've got an appointment,' she agreed.

'Shame,' Saunders said. 'I was going to make you both a nice little offer and all, wasn't I, Johnno?'

Johnno stretched his lips tight across his teeth in regret. 'He was.'

Marge immediately put her handbag back on the beer-stained counter. She wasn't going to let a chance like this slip by. These two looked much cleaner and better off than their usual punters and they might even take them to a decent hotel, instead of expecting to have a quick knee-trembler under one of the slimy, dripping railway arches. She grabbed Lilly's arm, holding her back. 'What sort of offer would that be then, darling?'

'I was going to offer you a job.'

Marge's face dropped. A job! What was he, barmy?

Lilly looked relieved. 'Come on, Marge.'

'I don't think you understand.' Saunders turned to Johnno. 'Fetch a round of drinks and bring them over to that table,' he said, walking over to the corner of the pub.

The girls followed him. They weren't stupid, they knew when they had to do as they were told; there was no one in the pub who would take a tom's side in the general run of things, never mind against these two big buggers, and especially not after what they'd done to Ted.

There were two men already sitting at the table that Saunders had chosen. 'You don't mind chaps, do you? Only me and the ladies want a bit of privacy.' He winked and slipped a ten-shilling note into the nearest man's hand.

Without a word, the men moved.

Saunders sat down on the bench seat that ran along the wall and gestured for the two girls to sit opposite on the rickety, splintered little stools.

He shrugged out of his camel coat and folded it carefully, setting it beside him as though it were a pampered pet cat being bedded down for the night.

He looked across at the girls, fixing them with his unusually pale blue eyes. 'I'm expanding my interests.'

'Aw yeah,' said Marge warily. 'What sort of interests would they be then? Painting and decorating?'

He laughed at her cheek. People didn't usually give him that sort of backchat, nervously or otherwise. 'Business interests. Property. Clubs. Mostly clubs at the minute.'

He paused while Johnno put down a tray of drinks. Beer and chasers for him and Saunders, and gin and orange for the girls.

'Up West, they are,' Saunders went on. 'But I fancy setting up one or two out this way, and in a few other spots round the East End. Shoreditch maybe. From the sort of deals I've heard are going on round here, and with all the money I've seen change hands, I reckon there's plenty of people with spare dough to chuck about on having a good time. And that's where you two come in.'

Lilly and Marge sipped at their drinks, listening in watchful silence.

'I'm looking for pretty girls like you. Girls who know their way round the sort of punters you get in these parts. And that's why you're gonna work for me.'

Lilly's eyes opened wide and she mouthed something to Marge.

'If it's that twat Ted Martin you're worried about, you can forget him. He won't worry you while I'm around.' Saunders took a long swallow of beer and grinned at Johnno across the rim of his glass. 'Even a no-mark like him's got the sense to keep his head down when he knows he's in Billy Saunders's bad books.'

It wasn't even six o'clock in the evening, but as Lilly climbed, or rather stumbled, up the bleak, unlit staircase to the top floor of the grubby Stepney boarding-house where she had her miserable little room, her head was spinning as though she'd been out all night.

Billy Saunders was generous with the gin, she'd give him that. And he wasn't mean in other ways either. He had told Johnno to see them home as if they were proper ladies or something. Lilly had protested at first, not liking too many people to know where she lived. She'd never been one to work from home unless she couldn't help it, as you never knew with punters, some of them could be right nasty buggers. But, in the end, she was glad she'd given in. She could never have shifted Marge once the booze got the better of her and she'd passed out on the corner of Salmon Lane. But it was no trouble for Johnno. He'd just hoisted her up on his shoulder as though she were a bag of nutty slack and had carried her all the way home to her flat.

Lilly smiled drunkenly to herself, as she thought what Marge would say when she told her how she had been carted through the streets like a parcel. And as for the look on her landlady's face! That was something to behold.

But after the walk back from Marge's, having to persuade Johnno that she'd be just fine and then the further effort of getting to the top of her stairs, Lilly was now feeling really groggy.

She paused in the gloom for a moment, taking deep breaths of cabbage-stinking air, trying to get her balance. Pushing open the door – she never bothered locking it, she had nothing worth nicking – Lilly called huskily into the darkness, 'Ted. You awake yet?'

A groan came from the single bed that took up more than half of the mean little space.

She staggered across the room in the direction of the sound. 'Ted. Come on. You've gotta get up. It's gone tea-time.'

'So?'

'You've gotta go,' she slurred. 'You can't stay here no more.'

Ted sprang from the bed as though it were on fire and slapped her hard across the face. '*What* did you say, you dirty little whore?'

It must have been the drink that made her so brave. Swaying slightly, Lilly took aim, then stabbed her finger hard into his chest. 'I wouldn't do that again if I was you, Ted Martin. I've got someone looking out for me now.' She took another step forward. 'And his minder's downstairs waiting for me to throw you out,' she lied recklessly, half wishing that Johnno was still down there.

After a fortnight of putting up with Ted's increasingly unpredictable temper, the idea of being shot of him definitely appealed to her, although she still felt bad about chucking him out without any notice. She knew what it was like to have nowhere to go. But he *was* married –

weren't they all – let him go back to his old woman. 'I mean it Ted. You've gotta go. Now.'

Ted raised his hand. 'You stinking, little—'

Lilly lurched back towards the door, out of his reach. 'I'll do you a favour. I'll go down and say I'm giving you a couple of hours. A chance to sort yourself out. Then I'll go along to the coffee shop and wait for you to clear off. But I'm telling you, Ted, if you ain't gone by the time I get back, I won't be responsible.'

Holding on to the jamb, she paused, stared down at the faded lino and muttered that there was some grub in the cupboard and a fresh bottle of milk in the sink, then, somehow, she found her way back down the stairs.

Ginny dipped her chin and yawned loudly. She wanted to put up her hand to cover her mouth, but couldn't because she was so loaded down with shopping bags. As well as going out to work, keeping the house clean and doing all the washing, Ginny was now responsible for doing every bit of shopping as well. She felt worn out and cold. The evening sky might have been clear and bright, but there was a chill in the air that made her shiver.

When she had worked near the Lane she had often brought home a few bits and pieces during the week, but it wasn't so easy now she was working in the factory at Stratford. And getting the bags home on the bus was bloody murder. She would have made do with a sandwich but Nellie always wanted a proper dinner, which was easier said than done since Ted hadn't been around for the past few weeks, and what with all the queuing and rationing . . .

Ginny thought with longing about having a proper dinner hour when she could sit down with a cup of tea and the paper instead of standing with a bunch of women all moaning about the price of mince. Sometimes she wondered what things would've been like if Britain had lost the war instead of winning it. They couldn't have been much worse.

If only Nellie would try to help a bit, no matter how small the effort, at least it would have been a gesture. But there was less chance than ever of that now. Since Ted had gone into hiding from the police, Nellie had been even more of a pain to live with and had taken to going to bed for most of the day. She hadn't even roused herself for Violet Varney's funeral.

Ginny shuddered as she thought what had happened to Violet. How she'd wound up a disease-ridden tom, just like the women who hung around the street corners in Whitechapel. Bad as things might be, Ginny would never let her life get out of hand like that, she'd take an oath on it. She'd never give up, not like Violet.

Poor, sad Violet.

Her funeral had been a terrible affair. Martha had organised a collection in the Albert so there had at least been a few flowers, but apart from the neighbours who had turned out to show their respects for Bert's sake – the man was a war hero when all was said and done – the church was almost empty. And when the undertakers lowered the coffin into the cold, damp earth, Bert had cried silently to himself, doing his best to keep a bit of dignity, but it was obvious that he knew what people were thinking: however had Violet let herself stoop so low?

Ginny sighed. There must have been another way, surely.

Violet really must have lost her mind. There was no other explanation.

Nellie didn't even have that as an excuse. She was just a selfish, idle old trout, and her not bothering to go to the funeral hadn't surprised Ginny in the least. In fact, there wasn't much about Nellie that could surprise her any more. During the four years Ginny had been married to Ted, any illusions she had had about Nellie becoming a mother to her had slowly, but surely, worn away.

Ginny could only think herself lucky that she was fortunate enough to have someone like Pearl to go to; not that she did very often. Pearl had enough to worry about with her own family. Dilys had always been a handful, Ginny knew that, but now the boys as well – both girl mad, like any young fellers of their age – were causing Pearl aggravation of their own. She certainly didn't need Ginny bothering her as well. But it was still comforting to know that she was there. A sort of safety net, a last resort if Ginny couldn't cope any more.

At last Ginny reached the corner of Bailey Street. She turned out of Grove Road and crossed the street, heading straight for number 18. She had almost reached her front door, when she heard Dilys calling her name.

Dumping her bags on the step, Ginny turned round. 'All right, Dilys?' she greeted her.

'Come over for a minute, will you, Gin?' whined Dilys. 'There's something I've gotta ask you.'

'Dilys, I can't. Really. I've just got home and there's Nellie wanting her tea, and—'

'But, Ginny, I've been waiting for you for ages,' moaned Dilys.

'Hang on.' Wearily, Ginny reached inside the letter-box, pulled out the key on the length of string and undid the door. She put her shopping bags inside the passage and called out, 'It's only me, Nell. I'll be in to do your tea in a minute, but I've just gotta pop over the road first to see Dilys.'

She dragged herself back across the street to number

11, preferring not to wait for what she rightly suspected would be Nellie's sarcastic reply.

'D'you know how long I've been waiting for you?' Dilys demanded, pulling the door to behind her, so that nobody inside could hear them.

'Sorry, Dil, but what with Ted being away still, I'm having to do even more hours. Nellie might have the hump but it don't stop her eating like a flipping horse. And I've gotta get the money for grub from somewhere.'

Ginny didn't know how, but Dilys, as usual, had managed to make her apologise even though she had nothing to apologise for. It was one of the knacks she had.

Dilys folded her arms. 'I reckon I quite fancy a job there,' she said carelessly. 'Anything going, is there?'

'Well, they're always looking for more workers on the conveyor belt.'

Dilys looked shocked. 'Why didn't you tell me?'

'I didn't think you'd be interested.'

'I've got no choice, have I?' Dilys kicked viciously at a bit of slate, sending it spinning into the gutter. 'I've gotta be interested. Me mum and dad'll throw me out if I don't start bringing in some money soon.'

'Pearl and George wouldn't do that to you. Anyway,' Ginny grinned, shoving her supposed friend playfully in the ribs, 'how about that feller of yours you're always going on about? You said he was keeping you.'

Dilys nibbled her lip as she thought of how much she was missing Ted and, more importantly, how much she was missing the money he gave her.

'Well?' Ginny urged her.

'He's working away, ain't he?' Dilys snapped.

As Ginny lay in bed that night, she thought about Dilys's chap. He might have been working away but at least

Dilys knew where he was. She knew it was wrong to be envious, but she couldn't help thinking how fortunate Dilys was.

She wished she knew where Ted was hiding himself.

Ginny wasn't exactly angry with him for going away, she knew he had no choice, she was more worried. He'd been gone for weeks now and it was dangerous out there. The police were really after black marketeers. And, it was no good wrapping it up in any other words, that's what her husband was.

Still, he never did anyone any harm. So why did this bloke, whoever he was, have it in for him?

Something else for her to worry about. She sighed out loud and rolled on to her side, staring at the shadows cast on the wall from the street lamp outside her window.

It was bad enough being concerned about money – Nellie just wouldn't get it into her head that with Ted away there wasn't as much coming in as usual – but thinking that Ted might be in danger was far worse.

If only her mum and dad were still around, they'd know what to do. She missed them and her brothers and sisters so much.

She felt so alone.

Ginny swallowed hard, trying to sniff back the tears, but it was too late, she could already feel them gathering in the corners of her eyes. She rolled on to her back and stared up at the ceiling as they spilt down on to her cheeks, then slowly found their way into her ears.

The sound of a car turning into the street and a pattern of headlights criss-crossing on the ceiling made her turn over and stare at the curtained window.

That would be Sid from over the road. He'd just bought himself a little motor and was really proud of it. She even managed a brief smile as she thought of how Pearl had warned him over and over again to be careful, and how Sid had snapped back that he could hardly go speeding with the amount of juice the bloody government allowed you.

If only all *she* had to fret about was the petrol ration. Things were so simple when you were free and single.

Suddenly she sat up.

It was the street door.

She jumped out of bed and ran on to the landing. It wasn't Sid's car, it was Ted's! Ted was home!

Ted rolled off her, turned on to his side and closed his eyes. It was good to be back in his own bed. That tart Lilly he'd been shacked up with the past couple of weeks had really started getting on his nerves. All that old toffee about minders and him having to get out. What would minders have to do with the likes of her? Any idiot would have realised she was spinning him a line. She probably had someone waiting downstairs who was gonna slip her a few quid rent to use her bed while she was out whoring.

He only wished he'd given her a few more hidings. The mouthy cow certainly deserved them.

Ted couldn't stand lippy women like her. Mind you, he put up with Dilys's old bunny often enough, but that was only because it amused him to be having his wife's mate as his bit on the side. It added a bit of spice and he liked that. In fact, if he didn't think they'd both give him earache about it, he'd often thought it'd be nice to get them together some time . . .

A slow smile eased its way over his lips. Now there *was* a lovely thought.

It surprised him, but he'd quite missed Dilys. Come to think of it, he wouldn't mind nipping over the road to her now. She'd be as pleased to see him as Ginny had been and she always got all excited when everyone else was in the house.

But could he really be buggered getting up and going out again? He knew the answer to that: no, he couldn't.

Instead, he rolled over to face Ginny and grabbed her breast. She'd do again for now.

'Ted,' she said softly.

'What?' he grunted, annoyed at being interrupted. He hated it when women started chatting while he was doing the business.

'Please, wait just a minute, there's something worrying me. Something I've gotta tell you. When the police came—'

He levered himself up on to his elbow. 'This had better be bloody good, Ginny.'

She pulled the sheet up to her chin and nibbled nervously at her lip. How could she put it without upsetting him? 'It's something they said.'

'For Christ's sake spit it out, will you? I've been away for a fortnight and—'

'Ted, they weren't just looking for gear, there was something else. They'd come here to sort of warn you.'

'What?'

She let the sheet drop and ran her fingers distractedly through her hair. 'Well, not warn you exactly. But they said you – we – should be careful. They said someone grassed on you. Someone who's got the needle. Someone who's out to get you.'

'They *what*?'

Ted threw back the covers and grabbed his trousers.

It was that fucking Saunders! He just knew it. Everywhere he bloody turned it was fucking Saunders. Everywhere he'd been during the last few weeks, every face in the East End was talking about pissing Saunders. How he was gonna do this, and do that. Now he couldn't even be in bed with his bloody wife without the bastard haunting him. And, now he came to think about it, maybe Lilly was telling the truth. Maybe he'd even got to her . . .

'Ted, where you going?' Ginny was standing beside him, not daring to touch him, but willing him not to go.

'Shut it, Ginny.'

'Ted, please.'

'I'm going out.'

'No, Ted, please. Promise me you won't go out again. You have the bed. I'll go and sleep downstairs.'

Ted replied with his fist, hitting Ginny so hard in the stomach that she collapsed into a heap on the floor.

He stepped over her and wrenched open the bedroom door.

Lilly. He'd show her where messing about with the likes of Saunders would get her.

But not just yet. Ted wasn't stupid, he'd bide his time. For now he'd just have to take his frustrations out on Dilys.

As Ginny heard the street door slam, her tears began to flow once more. It had all been going right: Ted had come home to her, made love, even stroked her hair the way he used to, and then she'd gone and opened her big mouth.

She'd got it all wrong again.

Why didn't she ever learn?

Chapter 6

July 1946

'My Alf took me to see that new Joan Crawford picture last night, Gin.'

'No good talking to her, Mavis,' said Dilys, lounging lazily on her high-backed stool, watching the electrical circuits pass slowly by on the conveyor belt, as though they had nothing to do with her. 'You might as well try talking to the lavvy wall as trying to get any sense out of that one.'

Dilys bent forward and poked Ginny in the arm. 'In a right bloody dream lately, ain't you, Gin?'

Ginny kept her eyes firmly on her soldering iron as she guided the molten drops towards their target. 'Sorry?'

'Nothing.' Dilys flopped back in her chair and rolled her eyes in wonder at the paragon sitting between her and Mavis. 'You just keep working, girl. All the less for us to do in this bloody heatwave.'

Dilys leaned forward again and spoke to Mavis across Ginny as though she wasn't there. 'So what was it like then, Mave, her new film?'

'*Mildred Pierce* it was called.' Mavis sat up straight and arched her eyebrows Joan Crawford style. 'All about this woman and her right little tart of a daughter. What a cow! Smashing it was.'

'She's good, Joan Crawford.' Dilys folded her arms and settled back comfortably in her seat.

'Yeah, but she played a different sort in this film to what she usually does. I mean, I do a lot for my kids – I even put up with their bleed'n' father, and that's something a bloody saint'd say no to – but what she put up with from that little madam. I'd have wound up wringing her flaming neck for her, long before she—'

'Don't spoil it for me!' squealed Dilys, leaning across Ginny and slapping Mavis on the hand. 'Oops! Sorry, Gin.' Dilys pulled a mock-sorry face as she saw that she'd knocked Ginny's arm, making her spoil the fiddly bit of soldering she'd been doing so conscientiously.

Ginny shook her head. 'It's all right, it'll clean off.'

'Hark at you.' Mavis tutted. 'You sound just like Mildred flipping Pierce. Putting up with all her old fanny all the time. Have a go at her, Gin. Go on, have her!'

'She wouldn't do nothing like that to me. I'm her best mate, ain't I?' Dilys grinned, flapping her hand dismissively. 'And talk about saints; she's Saint bleed'n' Ginny of Bow, ain't you, girl?'

Ginny shrugged, but said nothing; she just got on with her work.

Dilys didn't seem at all put out or embarrassed by Ginny's silence. 'Come on, hands up,' she chirped, looking along the assembly line, 'who's going out at dinner-time then?'

A babble of replies came from either side of her.

'Count me in and all, girls.' Mavis sighed dramatically. 'My bleed'n' larder's empty again for a change.'

She leaned back and had a quick look along to the glass partition that sectioned off the foreman's tiny cubicle of an office from the rest of the workshop. Satisfied that he wasn't there, she took out her cigarettes and lit one, holding it discreetly down by her knees between puffs.

'I dunno about the papers going on about sodding bread riots in France,' she went on, somehow managing to blow smoke from her nostrils as she spoke, 'but I tell you, there's gonna be bread riots in bleed'n' Stratford if I can't get hold of a loaf this dinner-time. My old man's going mad not having nothing to take with him for his sandwiches. And he hates that canteen grub.'

She chuckled happily to herself. 'Reckons they cook even worse than me, and that's saying something.'

Mavis blew out her cheeks and stared wistfully at her work-roughened hands. 'You know, I wish the war was still on sometimes and that the ungrateful bleeder had stayed in bloody India or wherever he was. Gets right on me tits, he does. It's like having another kid around the place, getting under me feet all the time and expecting to be waited on.'

'Watch it, Mave!' someone hissed along the line. 'It's Himself!'

As the big double doors at the far end of the workshop closed, and Stan the foreman began walking slowly towards the line, Mavis made her cigarette disappear with all the cunning of a skilled prestidigitator and, like the rest of the women in the room, suddenly became fascinated by the work in front of her.

Stan came to a halt by Ginny. 'What's the chance of you staying late for me tonight, Ginny love?' he asked ingratiatingly. 'Only I'm right backed up with orders. I've been down in Dispatch and they're going barmy down there. Like raving lunatics they are. And I really wanna get off home.'

He stood there, his fingers linked across his belly, beaming down at Ginny. He was a friendly, elderly man, but he was carrying far too much weight for his height and was really suffering in the summer heat. Just the thought of spending another hour in the oppressively stifling atmosphere of the factory, when he could have been out in his backyard in Plaistow training his latest brood of young pigeons, was more than he could bear to contemplate.

He knew that if Ginny agreed to stay, he'd be able

to get away with going home at knocking-off time – something he hadn't had the opportunity to do for months now. Since the war had been over, it seemed that everyone had gone mad for buying things. Any sort of things. And what with all the rationing on clothes and food still, anything else they could get hold of was snatched up as though spending your money was in danger of going out of fashion.

Stan had been pleased at first, very pleased. It was always good to have a bit of overtime to take home to the missus, but lately it was getting out of hand, especially with the choking summer heat. And then there was the racing season. His pigeons were the first youngsters he'd been able to raise since before the war and he was already well behind with them. They wouldn't stand a chance unless he managed to get them into training really soon. But, if he went home, he needed someone to keep an eye on things at the factory, and that was where Ginny came in.

Ginny was not only a good worker, but, if Stan asked her to, she always covered for him if he wasn't around when the governor decided to come down from upstairs and stick his nose in. And also if Stan asked her, he knew he could trust her to make sure that no liberties were taken by any of the others who stayed on.

There was no doubt about it, Ginny Martin was a good kid, and pretty too, which made it all the harder to see her putting up with whoever the bastard was who gave her the regular hidings that the poor little cow was so ashamed of. She'd invented more far-fetched stories than Scheherazade to explain how she got her black eyes, fat lips and split cheeks. She was too soft for her own good, that one. She could do with standing up for herself more. But then she'd probably had all the fight knocked out of her. Stan had seen it all, in his years supervising at the factory, and had become an unlikely authority on women. But it still made him wild to see how some of them lived: girls working their fingers to the bone all week, then their old men pissing their wages straight up the wall on a Friday night and leaving nothing for their wife and babies. The thing was, it never happened to the likes of Dilys Chivers, only to good-hearted kids like young Ginny.

Still, at this particular moment, and from Stan's point of view, Ginny's good nature was something to play on, not to sympathise with.

He put on what he thought was a winning sort of smile and, just for good measure, added a conspiratorial wink. 'I'd see you all right, Gin. You know that, don't you, ducks. And I know you said you could do with the extra money.'

'I know, Stan, and I'd love to help you out—'

Stan's face dropped with disappointment. 'But?'

Ginny rubbed the back of her hand across her sweat-soaked forehead and pushed back her chair, leaving the other women on the assembly line to get on with their jobs of checking and soldering the electrical circuits that passed before them in a never-ending stream. 'You know I wouldn't let you down unless I had a good reason.'

'I know.' He looked like a big, sad baby.

'You could ask Mavis. Or Dilys.' She lifted her chin to indicate the overalled figure of her friend slumped sullenly over the conveyor belt.

Stan opened his eyes wide and let out a huff of incredulity at such an idea. 'Don't be silly, Gin. Even if I could persuade either of them two not to dash out of here the second the hooter goes, could you really imagine me trusting that pair to keep an eye on things for me? And I could just imagine what old Larkin would have to say, if he came down from upstairs and found either of them in charge.'

He put his big, beefy arm around her shoulders. 'You sure you won't change your mind, babe? Like I said, I'd make it worth your while.'

'To be truthful, Stan,' she whispered, making sure that the others couldn't hear, 'I really wanna get straight home myself. I ain't feeling very well.'

Stan released his hold on her and backed away slightly. 'Nothing catching I hope.'

Ginny smiled ruefully. 'I don't think so.'

'There's only a few minutes to go.' Stan took another step backwards. That's all he wanted, bloody head-cold germs to pass on to his birds. 'If you ain't well, Ginny, you'd better get yourself off right away.'

'I'll go with her,' volunteered Dilys almost falling over her own feet in her hurry to leave the line.

Outside the factory gates, there seemed to be even less air than there was inside. At least inside there had been the breeze blowing through the open skylights. Outside there was nothing but traffic, fumes and noise, and crowds of people making their way home from work in the sultry afternoon heat.

The prospect of having to walk up to Stratford High Street, getting on to a bus full of sweaty bodies and travelling with them all the way back to Mile End – never mind the slog along Grove Road to Bailey Street at the other end of the journey – was making Ginny feel bilious.

She leaned back against the rough brick of the factory wall, oblivious of the mass of her fellow workers now coming towards her, all as eager to leave the place as Dilys. Any moment they would come surging through the gates and whisk her along in their wake like a twig being washed along in the gutter.

'Blimey, Gin, shift yourself!' Dilys grabbed her by the arm. 'Unless you wanna get dragged along to bloody West Ham with that crew from Loading. And you know how I hate them. Shifty-looking bleeders.'

Ginny closed her eyes. 'You go on, Dil. I don't feel too good.'

'Don't you really?' Dilys sounded surprised. She peered at Ginny more closely, turning down the corners of her mouth at what she saw. 'Come to mention it, you don't look all that.'

'Why d'you think I came out early?'

'To be honest, I really thought you was swinging the lead for once. I was quite impressed. I mean, it's usually me what gives Stan the old flannel, not you.' Dilys cocked her head on one side. 'So what's up?'

Ginny sucked in a lungful of air, trying to clear her head. She immediately wished she hadn't. It tasted foul, just like the stench from the stinking clouds that wafted along from the smoking chimneys and boilers of the factories in nearby Carpenters Road.

Now her head really was swimming.

She buried her face in her hands and took little gasping breaths, as the sweat broke out on her top lip. 'D'you think we could go and get a drink somewhere?'

'Anything to get away from this mob.' Dilys wrinkled her nose in disgust at the press of bodies pouring through the gates and swirling around them.

'Oi! Watch yourself, you!' Dilys yelled, as she elbowed a tall, skinny lad who had dared to brush against her, shoving him out of the way. 'Come on, Gin.' She pouted through daintily pursed lips. 'Let's nip over the Railway away from these bloody hooligans. I could do with a nice cold shandy.'

Ginny was relieved to see that apart from a few grumpy-looking old men – dressed, despite the heat, in the regulation cockney uniform for males of their age: collarless shirt, stock, braces, waistcoat, watch chain and flat cap – the pub was almost empty. Too early for the evening crowds, she supposed, and too late for afternoon drinkers, who had better things to do than hang around pubs at tea-time.

At least that was one problem out of the way. It was going to be difficult enough as it was to make up her mind about just how much she would tell Dilys, but if the pub had been crowded with eavesdroppers, it would have been impossible to tell her anything at all. She felt so ashamed.

'You go and sit down there, Gin,' ordered Dilys, pointing to a table by the propped-open door, 'and I'll fetch the drinks over.'

Dilys wasn't feeling uncharacteristically thoughtful in taking it on herself to go to the bar, it was that, by the look of her, Ginny couldn't stand up much longer and Dilys had never really seen herself as being the nursing type. For one thing, it took far too much sympathy and understanding, and for another, Dilys didn't fancy having to scoop Ginny up off the floor if she passed out. It was far too hot for that sort of lark.

'Just a plain soda water for me thanks, Dil,' Ginny said, her voice wobbling with the effort of speaking.

Then she did as Dilys had told her and went and sat down, more than grateful for the breeze blowing through the open doorway and the opportunity to take the weight off her feet.

Although Dilys returned almost immediately with the drinks, Ginny had had enough time to decide that she was going to tell Dilys all about it. Well, not *all*, exactly, just the most immediate of her worries. Dilys was her best friend after all.

113

Ginny took a big gulp of the luke-warm, bubbly water that Dilys had handed her. The salty taste made her want to gag. But then most things seemed to have that effect on her lately.

Taking a deep breath to steady herself, Ginny closed her eyes, opened her mouth and out came the words. 'Dil,' she said, 'I'm expecting.' There, she had said it out loud. The words that made it true.

Dilys almost choked on her shandy; she felt her cheeks colour and a pulse begin to drum in her temple. 'But you *said* . . .' she spluttered. '*We* said that Ted wouldn't—'

Ginny shook her head and grabbed at Dilys's hand. 'Ted doesn't know nothing about this, Dil. And he ain't gonna know. Promise me you won't say nothing. Please.'

Dilys scraped her chair closer to the table. Her face a picture of suppressed fury as, with her forehead almost touching Ginny's, she stared across at her. 'It ain't exactly something you're gonna be able to keep a secret, now is it, you daft mare?'

'Look, Dil, you're me best mate. If I tell you something, will you promise me you won't breathe a word?'

Dilys leaned back in her chair and puffed sarcastically. 'You've already told me quite a lot, I should think. What more could there be? Someone else's, is it? Not a China-man's or nothing?'

Ginny was used to Dilys's taunts and didn't rise to them. Anyway, this was more important than that. 'You know how long I've wanted a baby.' Her voice was cracked and sad. 'It's something I've dreamed about. But I'd never really got it settled with Ted.'

Dilys shrugged non-committally as though she had little thought on the matter, but her mind was working nineteen to the dozen: Ted didn't know yet. That meant she must be quite early on. Or maybe she was mistaken. False alarms happened all the time. Dilys had had enough frights of her own to know that only too well. You got all wound up and then you woke up one morning and found you were fretting over nothing. That's what this would be. Nothing.

But even if it was a false alarm, Dilys decided, it would still be best if Ted was kept in the dark. The last thing she wanted was for him to start getting broody. She would have to play her cards very close to her chest on this one. It could go in any number of directions. And, if she wasn't careful, it might go exactly opposite to the way she wanted.

'Well, Ginny, all I can say is, I hope you're wrong, girl. I mean, I've said it often enough, Ted'd go spare if you ever did get yourself knocked up.'

'It's not that, Dil, it's . . .' Ginny turned her head slightly, her gaze flicking nervously about the dull little bar. 'I've decided . . .'

'What? What have you decided?' Dilys snapped. Although she was sure she could control the situation and was convinced that she wasn't going to let Saint bloody Ginny the martyr spoil things between her and Ted, Dilys still wasn't going to make it easy for her. Just the pathetic look on her pretty little face made Dilys want to slap her. 'Well?' she demanded.

'I've decided that now ain't the right time.'

Dilys took a gulp of her shandy. 'When would be the right time? He ain't gonna be pleased whenever you tell him. You know that, don't you? He's gonna go—'

'Dilys, I ain't talking about that. I mean it ain't the right time for me to have . . .' She lowered her chin until it was almost touching her chest. 'You know.'

'Do *what*?'

'Please, Dil. Don't shout. My head's splitting and I don't want everyone in the pub earwigging.' She sipped the soda water and shuddered. 'I've thought about it,' she went on, unable to meet her friend's gaze. 'In fact, I've thought about nothing else these last few weeks. Not only do I feel really ill, but I can't afford to give up my job.'

She paused, getting a grip on the tears that were threatening to spill down her cheeks before she could continue. 'You see,' she sniffed, 'since Ted's got himself involved—'

'Who with?' Dilys demanded. She was wide-eyed with alarm. 'Who's he involved with?'

'It's nothing like that. There's no other woman.' Ginny shook her head, dismissing the very idea. 'He's got involved in something dodgy.' Slowly she raised her eyes until she was looking at Dilys. 'You know when the law came round, a few months back?'

Dilys nodded dumbly. Silly cow, what was so new about that? Surely she realised everyone knew how Ted earned his living? He was a spiv.

'Well' – Ginny's voice was now so small it was barely audible – 'he ain't only selling bits and pieces no more. He's fencing big stuff. Expensive gear from down the docks. And he's sort of in trouble.'

'Blimey, Gin.' Dilys did her best to sound shocked, reckoning that there was no point letting on to the miserable-looking little mare. 'That's a bit of a turn-up for the book, ain't it, girl? Your Ted fencing, eh? Who'd have thought it?'

Dilys glugged down the rest of her shandy and stood up, marvelling at the close shave she'd just had. Just for the moment she had really been convinced that Ginny had either found out about her and Ted, or that the rat had gone and found himself an extra bit on the side. 'I'm gonna get another drink,' she said, holding up her empty glass to Ginny by way of invitation.

Ginny shook her head. 'No thanks, Dil,' she murmured. 'I'm fine with this.'

While Dilys was up at the bar, Ginny went over and over in her mind why she wouldn't have the child she was carrying. Why she really, honestly couldn't.

It had almost broken her, coming to that terrible decision, but she couldn't go through with it. She couldn't have a baby. Not yet. She just couldn't.

Deep in her heart, Ginny knew Ted was a violent, womanising, selfish bastard. But even when she was explaining away yet another cut or bruise, she had always told herself that he acted that way because he was worried, or had been working too hard, or, more often than not, that it was her fault, because she had irritated him through her own thoughtless stupidity.

Ginny had become an expert at lying to herself.

But there were some things even she couldn't pretend weren't happening: Ted was away more than ever and it was down to her to earn the wages. Okay, when Ted was around they might have chops, or sausages, or steak even – twice on the trot the other week – but then he'd be gone for days on end, leaving them without a word, without a penny. On the run from the latest police raids, or so he reckoned when he came back. But whatever the real reason he chose to be away, it could have occurred to him that Ginny and his mum still had to live when he wasn't there.

By the time Ginny had paid the rent man, put money in the gas, had paid her fares to work and had given Nellie enough to take her off to the Albert for her now regular nightly guzzle, the few bob that were left barely bought enough grub to satisfy Nellie's hungry guts, let alone to feed the pair of them something decent every night. It didn't bear thinking about what would happen if she had to give up her job. And if there was another mouth to feed . . .

But maybe Ted would change if they had a child.

And maybe they'd ask her to star in the next Joan Crawford film and buy her a sable coat to wear for the première in Hollywood.

Ginny knew she had no choice. And, much as she disliked her mother-in-law, it wasn't in Ginny's nature to let anyone, even Nellie, suffer. She knew what she would have thought if her own mum and dad, God rest their souls, had needed to depend on someone and they had been let down.

And then there was this bloke, whoever he was, the one the police said had it in for Ted. Even if she didn't have money worries, how could she bring a child into the world knowing that was going on?

'I *said*, so, what you gonna do then?'

'Sorry?' Ginny lifted her chin and frowned at her friend as though she was surprised to see her there.

'Blimey, Gin, you're in a right dream. I go up and get myself a drink, have a quick piddle and come back to find you've turned into a flipping zombie.'

'I'm gonna find someone to get rid of it.' Ginny said the words in a flat, conversational tone as though she was discussing something of no more significance than how she would get rid of the beer stains on the rickety little table which stood between them.

Dilys managed to suppress her smile as she reached out and took Ginny's hands in hers. 'I'll help you find someone, darling,' she cooed. ''Cos you know I'll always be there to help you, don't you, Gin?'

Although it was barely five o'clock on a bright summer's afternoon, Marge was dressed up to the nines, looking more suited to doing a turn on the stage than to wandering about in the shabby back-streets of the East End.

She stopped outside a soot-covered, derelict-looking warehouse – one of the few buildings in the grubby little turning off the Bethnal Green Road that hadn't been damaged in the Blitz – and pushed open the faded, non-descript door.

Once inside, hampered by the tightness of her skirt, the height of her heels and her bad temper, Marge tutted and wiggled her way up the narrow, uncarpeted flight of stairs that lead to the top floor of the building.

She was going in to work nearly three hours early and she wasn't very happy. If it hadn't been for one of Billy Saunders's men turning up at her flat to tell her that she was wanted, she could still have been snoring her head off in the blissful, solitary comfort of her bed.

She just hoped Saunders hadn't arranged a private party. That was all she felt like, being nice to some mug punter, with her make-up running in the heat and her drawers sticking to her with sweat.

With a bored sigh, Marge dragged her handbag up her arm and rapped her knuckles on the plain, black-painted door at the top of the stairway.

A small spyhole opened at eye level. 'Who is it?' asked a gruff voice from behind the door.

'The Old Bill. Who d'you think it is, you great daft sod? Now come on, Phil, open up.'

The door was opened immediately and Marge brushed past Phil, a huge, cauliflower-eared goon, without so much as a glance.

Phil and the other minders were useful if any of the customers started getting too friendly without coughing up enough for drinks, but other than that, Marge ignored them. She had enough trouble with the men she was paid to be nice to, so she was buggered if she'd be nice to any of them just for the sake of it.

'Mr Saunders about yet?' she asked nonchalantly, staring at herself in one of the dingy mirrored panels lining the walls.

She leaned forward and concentrated, dabbing the tip of her little finger at a streak of scarlet bleeding from her lipstick. There were definitely more lines around her mouth than there had been yesterday, she was sure of it. She would have to start getting a few decent nights' sleep a week or she'd wind up looking like the battered old bags who plied their trade along the Mile End Waste.

'Well?' she repeated impatiently, peering closely at the deepening crow's feet around her eyes. 'Is he or isn't he?'

'I'm here, Marge.'

She spun round. 'Sorry,' she stammered. 'I thought—'

'It doesn't matter.' Saunders jerked his head towards one of the spindly legged tables dotted around the room. 'Sit down.'

Marge did as she was told. What the hell was this about?

Saunders sat opposite her. He looked enormous, perched on the little chair. 'I hear your mate Lilly ain't been in to work for the last five days.'

Marge frowned. 'She ain't been feeling too well, Mr Saunders.'

Saunders leaned forward. 'If she's been working a foreigner—'

'No. No, she ain't. Honest, Mr Saunders, I'd stake my life on it. Me and Lil ain't ever been so well looked after as we have here. We love it. We'd never go behind your back. Never.'

'Do me a favour, Marge. I don't like being messed about. She might only be a brass but I still expect loyalty in my staff. And if my girls start getting the reputation for being street whores, then they know what they can do. I wanna start getting a bit o' class in my clubs. I've had it up to here with old scrubbers.'

'Honest—'

'Just listen to me, Marge, I took you two on 'cos I

wanted to start up here with girls who knew the ropes round these parts. But now there's plenty more working here I don't need you if you ain't gonna behave yourselves.' Saunders's voice was low, threatening.

Marge licked her lips nervously. She could feel the sweat trickling down her back. 'You've got it wrong, Mr Saunders. Honest. As true as I'm sitting here.'

'Look, if Lilly wants to go independent, that's fine by me. We all know you toms ain't the most reliable of workers; you come and go like sodding Christmas. But *not* on my patch. And I ain't having her coming in here and making private arrangements. Got it? You knew from the outset the cut you'd get. And you knew the rules.' Slowly he rose to his feet. He towered over her. 'Go on, Marge. Out. And don't come back.'

Marge also stood up, far more unsteadily than Saunders. 'Please, Mr Saunders, give us a chance. If I go and get her right now, you'll see.'

'See what?'

'Please, just give me a quarter of an hour.'

'Marge, I can't.' Lilly's lips were so swollen, she could hardly speak. 'Look at the state of me.'

'It don't matter what you look like,' Marge wheedled. 'Well, it does, I suppose. It's a good thing. He'll be able to see why you ain't been in.'

Lilly lifted her hand and cautiously ran her fingers along the cuts and bruises on her cheek. 'No. Not like this. I feel ashamed. Stupid.'

'You'll feel even more stupid if we wind up back down the docks, going with seaman under the arches who're too pissed or too tight-fisted to go to the dearer girls working in the case houses.'

*

'Lift your head up, Lil,' Marge urged her friend. 'Go on, show him. Show Mr Saunders why you couldn't—'

'That's enough from the gallery, thanks, darling,' Saunders snapped. 'Get yourself over to the bar and tell Phil I said to give you a drink.'

Marge went to say something, but, for once, she had the good judgement to keep her mouth shut and to do as she was told.

She flashed a look of helpless apology at Lilly. Fancy dragging her here for this. Lilly would skin her when they got outside, or rather, when they were chucked outside by one of the minders.

Nodding dumbly at Saunders, Marge slid her way along the cracked leather seat of the booth and disappeared over to the bar, leaving Lilly to learn their fate from Saunders all by herself.

Saunders took out his cigarettes and offered one to Lilly.

With a trembling hand she took one, wincing with pain as she opened her mouth to put it between her lips.

As though he had nothing else in the world on his mind, Saunders took his time and lit first Lilly's cigarette, then his own. He blew out the match and dropped it carefully into the glass ashtray he had positioned on the table between them. 'So,' he began, lifting his chin to indicate her injuries. 'What's the S.P. on all this, then?'

Lilly blew a plume of lavender smoke down her nostrils, wishing she could stop her hands from shaking. 'I fell down the steps,' she whispered. Why the hell had she let Marge talk her into doing this?

Saunders threw back his head and laughed. 'Yeah,' he said amiably, 'and you and the rest of the girls are all gonna give up the game and start working for a living.'

Lilly almost joined in with a little laugh of her own – anything to keep on his good side and to save herself another hiding – but she counted herself lucky she hadn't: in a split second his expression had changed to one of fury.

He leaned forward and smacked the table so hard the ashtray rattled around like a spun coin in a game of pitch and toss. 'Give me some credit, Lil, for fuck's sake. Now, let's have a bit of truth, shall we? Number one – Marge swears you ain't working a foreigner.'

'I ain't—'

'So it wasn't a pimp or some punter you picked up what did it?'

Lilly swallowed hard. What she wouldn't have given for a large scotch. 'It was a punter,' she said carefully. 'But one I took home from the club. He liked a bit of rough stuff.'

He held out his hand. 'So where's my cut?'

Lilly dropped her gaze and stared at the table. 'I never got no money off him.'

Saunders narrowed his eyes. He didn't appreciate being treated like a mug. 'So who was he, this bloke what gave you a slap and never even paid you for it? Never paid *you* mind, which means *I* don't get paid either.'

'I don't know his name.' Lilly's voice was barely audible, as she shrank back in her chair like a terrified child.

Saunders ground out his almost unsmoked cigarette. He was really losing patience. He had better things to do with his time than spend it arguing with toms, but he had to show that he could keep discipline or they'd all be working foreigners.

'You know the rules,' he snarled. 'No one takes home no one they don't know. Then I don't risk losing my cut 'cos you've been tucked up by some con man, now do I?'

Lilly let out a little shuddering sigh. 'I'm sorry,' she sniffed.

'Don't bother with the old flannel, Lil. Just tell me who it is. And don't bother to lie to me. I'll find out one way or another.'

'I can't. I'm too scared.'

'Look, Lil, I might be a nasty bugger at times, but you know I'd never raise a hand to a woman.'

'It ain't you I'm scared of,' she said, lying through her teeth – any tom with any sense of self-preservation learned to be scared of all men from very early on in their careers; too many men thought they could treat them like punch-bags.

'I'll protect you from whoever it is, all right? Now I can't say fairer than that, can I? But I mean it, Lil, I wanna know. 'Cos I ain't having no one taking liberties with no one who works for me. It's a piss take and I ain't having that. I ain't gonna stand for that from no one. And that includes you.'

Dropping her chin, Lilly closed her eyes and began to talk quickly. She wanted to get it over with. 'All right, I'll tell you. I did know him. He wasn't a punter. That's why I never told no one. I wasn't trying to keep your cut, Mr Saunders. I swear, on my mother's life.' She lifted her chin and looked directly into his eyes. Pleading with him to believe her. Marge was right, just the thought of going back on the streets was too much even to contemplate and maybe, with a bit of luck, Saunders wouldn't smack her one.

'It started out all right,' she went on. ''Cos I took him back to my room as a favour, see. Not to do business. His wife had chucked him out and he had nowhere else to go. She's a rotten old cow, Mr Saunders, he's had to put up with murder off her for years and—'

'Lilly.' Saunders's voice was menacingly calm. 'Would you do me a favour and stop all this old shit and just tell me the truth? Would you just explain what any of this has got to do with the state of your boat?'

She took a long drag on her cigarette, pulling the smoke deep into her lungs, then shrugged and stared down at her lap. 'I knew we was gonna do it, I suppose.' It was as though she was talking to herself. 'But there was never any question of money being involved. It weren't like that.'

'So, you've been giving it away for free, eh, Lil? That ain't very bright, now is it? At least if you was working a foreigner there'd be a bit of sense in it.' He shook his head as though unable to believe the stupidity of what he was hearing. 'Go on,' he said wearily.

'He's always been a bit on the handy side, ever since I've known him. He'd only have to get a bit upset over something and he'd give me a little slap.'

'A little slap!' Saunders's voice was incredulous.

Lilly looked up at him and began to cry. 'He just sort of went raving mad. Kicking me and punching me, and then he . . .' She shook her head, unable to go on, unable to describe the humiliating things he had put her through.

Saunders was shaking with temper, he felt ready to rip someone's head from their shoulders. Someone had had the gall to interfere with his business. To keep one of his girls off work and lose him money. To damage his property. *His* property. He'd kill the bastard slag when he got hold of him.

'Think carefully, Lil,' he warned the now sobbing woman. His voice was even, measured. 'Tell me his name, there's a good girl.'

'Ted,' she sobbed. 'Ted Martin.'

Chapter 7

It was six o'clock on a hot July afternoon, less than a week since Ginny had sat in the Railway Arms, confiding in her supposed friend, Dilys Chivers.

Jeannie Thompson was standing waiting in her kitchen doorway, picking her teeth with a broken matchstick, staring into the middle distance and thinking hateful thoughts. Jeannie couldn't bear waiting.

She was forty-one years old, but, with a good light, she could just about pass for fifty. She was what could best be described as frazzled-looking. Her mass of matted hair – bleached a startling, unnatural orangy yellow – contrasted starkly with the dark brown of her roots and of her tobacco-stained teeth. And with the red of her mottled, vein-threaded skin, she looked a more than sorry sight. Jeannie was a hardened drinker by anyone's standards and it showed. Just as the squalor in which she lived showed her not to be a student of the school of good housekeeping.

'Well,' she said to the manky ginger cat that was threading a path in and out of her bare legs, 'if the silly tart don't turn up soon, she can forget it. I've got better things to do with my time than standing about waiting.'

She bent down and picked up the mangy creature, cradling it to her well-upholstered bosom. It emitted a desultory purr.

'Mind you, if she don't turn up, Twinks, you can forget your fish supper. It'll be scraps again for you, my little pet.'

She planted a loud, wet kiss on the animal's head, which had the immediate effect of driving it into a frenzy of flat-eared, stiff-tailed anger. Escaping from her grip with a wild-eyed leap, the cat spat and hissed its way to the floor, leaving Jeannie's front smothered in ginger hairs.

It then shot out of the kitchen and, with dead-eyed accuracy, darted through the open street door, along the weed-infested path and between Dilys's splayed legs to feline freedom.

'Bloody, rotten, flea-bitten moggy!' Dilys yelled, aiming her toe at the creature's rear. 'Nearly had me off me sodding feet!'

Ginny clung to the gatepost. She had felt sick all day, but now, looking at this terrible place, she felt worse than sick, she felt completely disgusted. The house not only looked repulsive, but, even from the street, it smelt absolutely rank. Her twitching nostrils were filled with a sickly sweet stench, like the inside of a rubbish bucket that had been left to fester and moulder. There was a smell of stale cabbage about it, and something Ginny couldn't begin to describe, let alone name.

She grabbed hold of the post more urgently, anchoring herself as firmly as a barnacle stuck to a Thames barge at high tide. How could she even have considered doing this? It was madness. She would go home, tell Ted and everything would be okay.

It would just have to be.

'I can't do it, Dilys.' She shook her head determinedly. 'I can't. I can't go in there.'

Dilys gripped Ginny's arm and tugged her roughly. 'Look, Ginny,' she said through gritted teeth, 'you either do it this way, or you go home, dose yourself up with slippery elm, stick a knitting needle up your fanny and probably wind up with blood poisoning – if you don't bleed to death first. So what are you gonna do?'

Ginny screwed her eyes tight and began weeping silently.

'At least this way you know you'll be safe,' Dilys reasoned. 'Only uses best yellow soap, does Mrs Thompson. She's well known for it. Never uses none of that old—'

Realising what sort of an impression she was giving, Dilys added hurriedly: 'Not that I know anything about it, of course, but it's what everyone says. And she's got a proper rubber syringe and everything. None of that scraping and digging about.'

Ginny felt the sweat breaking out on her top lip. 'No, Dilys. Please.'

'Now you listen to me, Ginny Martin. It's a bit late to start acting up now.' Dilys was growing angrier and more desperate; surely the stupid cow wasn't going to change her mind and go through with having the bloody kid? That'd really mess things up. 'If you'd had any sense in the first place, you'd have got yourself some Rendell's—'

'Please, Dilys. Don't.'

'Well, it's you what got yourself in this state, innit?' Dilys paused as something occurred to her and then, with an even more callous lack of sympathy than usual, she actually started giggling. 'Here, d'you know old dozy-drawers in Dispatch? That Mary whatever her name is? Well, on her wedding night, she only thought she had to swallow the Rendell's, didn't she? Instead of . . .' Dilys raised an eyebrow and nodded downwards. 'Sticking 'em up her you-know-what. Must have been foaming at the mouth like a sodding mad dog. Still it worked. She went bright green from the vile taste of it and spent the night with her head down the lav. Put her old man right off his stroke, that did. Never got up the duff that night, though, did she!'

All the talk about douches and scraping and swallowing Rendell's pessaries made Ginny feel worse than ever. 'Dilys,' she wailed, 'I feel so sick. Please, I wanna go home.'

Before Dilys could reply, Jeannie Thompson threw the street door wide open and stood there, looking like a gorgon. 'What the bleed'n' hell's going on out here?' she bellowed.

'We've come to see you, Mrs Thompson,' Dilys explained sweetly, shoving Ginny in front of her. 'Sorry we're a bit late like, but me friend missed her bus, didn't she. I've been waiting for her for ages and was just giving her a right telling off for leaving me standing here on me Jack.' Dilys treated Jeannie to a charming little smile. 'Right inconsiderate some people, ain't they?'

The back kitchen of the house was worse than Ginny could possibly have imagined, and so was what Jeannie Thompson did to her.

During the next few weeks Ginny suffered. She suffered more than when Ted had beaten her; more than when she was lying awake at night, pretending to herself that he wasn't off somewhere with another woman; more even than when she had lost her family in the Blitz. This time she was experiencing a new type of pain: that of knowing she was no longer carrying the child she had dreamed for years of holding in her arms. The child she had decided she could not have.

Although Dilys had been there with her on the day, and it was Dilys who had taken her to that awful woman's house, in the end it was she, Ginny, who had made the decision that her life was in too much of a mess to bring a child into the world to share it.

And that knowledge haunted her.

The first few days after Ginny's visit to Jeannie Thompson's were a nightmare of physical pain: the result of the wild-haired woman's rough and unhygienic attentions. But she was right when she told Ginny, as she had ushered her and Dilys out of her house, that a strong young girl like her would soon recover from a *little bit of discomfort*, as she had put it. Before long, Ginny was as fit as ever, but that wasn't the end of it, it was only the beginning. The distress she had felt very quickly spiralled down into a dark, frightening despair, and she realised she would never be – or feel – the same again.

At least Ted wasn't around – which, for once, was a relief – but Nellie, unfortunately, was.

In an effort to conceal what was really wrong, Ginny pretended she'd eaten something that had upset her, made her so ill, in fact, that she could hardly get out of bed, never mind go to work. But that wasn't good enough for Nellie. Night and day she nagged her to get back to the factory, griping and groaning about her daughter-in-law's idleness and how she, an old woman, was having to go without.

Not that she actually *was* going without, Pearl had seen to that, because, unlike Nellie, Pearl guessed right away what was wrong with Ginny and her heart had gone out to her.

Like so many others, Pearl had learned, with a combination of fear, guilt and overwhelming relief, of the women who would 'help you out' if you were in trouble. During the hard times of the 1930s, having to feed and clothe the family they already had was difficult enough for most mothers and plenty found themselves paying discreet visits to their local equivalents of Jeannie Thompson. So Pearl could just imagine what young Ginny was suffering and was glad to do whatever she could to make things a bit easier for her.

But despite their neighbour's generosity, Nellie wasn't satisfied with being supplied with money for food and light. No, she wanted more. She wanted money to pour down her throat at the Albert.

When Pearl had just laughed at her request for a few extra bob for a drop of something to calm her nerves, Nellie had played her usual trump. She had gone along to the pub with her empty purse and played the old soldier, trying to mump drinks from Bobby's and Martha's more well-oiled customers. But this time it hadn't worked.

Nellie couldn't understand what was going on and said so. She wished she hadn't. It was pointed out to her, very clearly, that the reason she wasn't exactly welcome in the Albert was all down to her precious son. Using his black-market profits as a float, Ted had widened his 'business' interests to include money lending. A lot of people now owed him money, many of whom could ill afford his sort of interest rates, but they were so terrified by his growing reputation for resorting to violence over the least little thing, that they found ways, desperate ways, to meet his outrageous demands. Nellie was no longer another old moaner who wasn't particularly liked, but who was tolerated and treated to an occasional nip of the hard stuff; she had become, by association with such scum, an unwelcome ponce.

She had stormed out of the pub and back to the house, her mood fouler than ever, and even more determined to make Ginny's life a misery.

Ginny could only be grateful that she had a friend as good as Pearl to turn to.

'Ginny, love. You there?' Pearl stood in the hallway, a plate covered with a tea-towel in each hand, calling up the stairs. 'I've brought a bit of supper over for you and Nellie. How about coming down and seeing if you fancy it?' She rested her broad forearm on the banister and added, 'And don't worry, the coast's clear; I've given in and slipped Nellie a few bob to go and have a drink. Mind you, I think she's giving the Albert a miss for some reason, she was heading for the Aberdeen according to my George.'

Ginny sat at the kitchen table, picked up her knife and fork, and stared down at the boiled bacon and pease pudding. 'D'you mind if I eat it later, Pearl?'

'Course not. I'll put it in the stove with Nellie's.' Pearl covered the plate with an enamel dish and bent down to undo the cooker door. 'So, how're you feeling?' she asked over her shoulder.

Ginny stared down into her lap and began weeping softly.

'Don't upset yourself, Ginny, love.'

'You wouldn't be so kind if you knew what I've done.'

Slowly Pearl closed the oven, straightened up and said quietly. 'Don't be daft.'

'But I ain't really been ill, Pearl.' She swallowed hard. 'It was all a lie. I was expecting, and I . . .'

'I know.'

'I couldn't have it.' Ginny buried her face in her hands.

'Ssssh. There, there, darling.' Pearl wrapped her arms round Ginny and held her close. 'It's all right.'

Ginny pulled away. 'No it's not. It's not all right. Nothing's all right. Not doing that, not living here with Ted . . .' Ginny lifted her chin and looked up into Pearl's concerned, motherly face. 'And it's probably not right talking about my own husband, either, but I've gotta tell someone.' A shuddering sob ran through her body. 'Pearl, Ted's not being very good to me lately.'

Pearl bit her tongue. Not being very good? The bloke was being a first-class bastard.

'And when I found out I was ... you know, I tried to think how I could keep it. I tried so hard. I even thought about getting a divorce. But how could I bring up ... Not on me own. And I couldn't have it adopted. I couldn't give ... If I still had me mum, maybe I could've had ...'

'Ginny, listen, you musn't punish yourself like this.'

'But I—'

'But nothing. It's like poor Violet Varney—'

Ginny's eyes widened with horror. 'I've never done nothing like Violet did.'

'Ssssh. Calm down, sweetheart.' Pearl pulled out one of the chairs and sat down next to her. 'I'm not saying you did. What I'm saying is you ain't a criminal, you're a bloody victim. You've lived a life that would have driven anyone to breaking point. But you've survived, and now you've gotta start thinking about yourself for a change, not waste any more time doing what other people tell you. Throw the sodding monkeys off your back; stop letting them push you this way and then shoving you back the other. You're a grown woman, Ginny, not a servant or a kid to be ordered about.'

Ginny blew her nose noisily as her tears began to flow again. 'It's easy for you, Pearl, you're lucky, you're strong and you've got your family round you, and ... and, what have I got?'

'You've got me for what it's worth.' With surprising tenderness, Pearl took Ginny's hand in hers. 'But I dunno how you reckon I'm lucky. Look at me, I'm in me fifties and I look a right wrinkled old bat—'

'No, you don't.'

'Yes I do! I see myself in the flipping glass of a morning. But you're beautiful, Ginny. And you've got youth on your side. You've got time to be strong, but even a lorry-load of Pond's wouldn't help me. Here, know what my

133

mum used to say? If you didn't die from it, it made you stronger; whatever "it" was when it was at home.'

Ginny managed a weak smile through her tears. 'You're my "it", Pearl, you make me feel stronger.'

Pearl touched her on the cheek. 'I'm glad, but I want you to promise me you're gonna start standing up for yourself a bit more.'

Ginny swiped away her tears with the back of her hand. 'I know you're right. I mean, look where being a doormat's got me.' She twisted the soggy handkerchief around in her fingers. 'And I've gotta stop kidding myself that everything's all right. Gotta stop making excuses.'

Nellie appeared in the kitchen doorway and glared at Pearl. 'What're you still doing here at this time of night?'

Ginny stood up and answered for her. 'Pearl's been giving me some very good advice, Nell. And I've decided to go back to work.'

'About time too. I could've starved if it—'

'No, Nellie, you don't understand, I ain't going back so's I can give you more money to piss away up the pub,' Ginny told her now slack-jawed mother-in-law. 'I'm going back to the factory to get away from your moaning.'

Now Pearl was also on her feet, she was enjoying Nellie's pop-eyed reaction to the worm so suddenly turning, but there was concern in her voice as she spoke to Ginny. 'Are you sure you're strong enough to go back, love?'

'She's only had a bit of food poisoning.'

Pearl ignored her. 'Take another week off, eh?'

'No, Pearl, I've decided. You know, I'll never forget what you've done for me. One day I'll pay you back for all your kindness. I swear I will.'

Nellie rolled her eyes in disgust at such a display.

'The only paying back you'll do, Ginny love, is looking after yourself. Now you eat up that dinner I brought over and I'll see you in the morning.' Pearl turned to Nellie. 'There's a plate made up for you an' all, Nell. I stuck it in the oven.'

Nellie dropped down on to one of the kitchen chairs. 'Get it out for me, Ginny.'

'No, Nell, you get it, I'm seeing Pearl out.'

Pearl bit her lip to stop herself from laughing and followed Ginny out along the passage. 'That gave her a bit of a shock, Gin!'

Ginny pulled open the street door and stood aside to let Pearl pass. 'Yeah, but the crafty old cow knows I'll still look after her.'

'You're a good girl, Ginny, one of the best.'

'Hark who's talking. You've stood by me, Pearl, and I can't tell you how grateful I am. But I meant what I said, I'll find a way to make it up to you. I'm gonna help *you* one day.'

It wasn't long before Ginny had the opportunity to do exactly that.

'But, Dilys, you can't be.' Ginny looked from Dilys to Pearl and back again. She felt as though someone had whacked her in the guts. She'd only come over to collect Dilys for work, but instead of the usual morning performance of getting her friend moving she'd been presented with this.

'Pearl,' Ginny said, trusting her to have a sensible explanation for what her daughter had just come out with, 'has she gone mad or something?'

Pearl didn't say anything, she just sat there at the kitchen table, her hands folded in her lap and her head bowed.

'Pearl?' Ginny said again, more loudly this time. 'Tell her she can't be.'

'You're right,' Pearl eventually answered. Her voice came out low and flat, as she stared down at the scrubbed wooden table top. 'She can't be.' She gave a mirthless little laugh. 'I mean, she ain't even got a regular feller, has she?'

Ginny nodded in urgent agreement. 'That's right, Pearl. She ain't.' She turned to Dilys. 'You must have made a mistake.'

Dilys shoved the last of her toast into her mouth and shrugged. 'You can say I ain't; and you can say I can't be; and you can both say it till you're blue in the face. But I am and that's the strength of it.'

Still chewing on her breakfast, Dilys stood up and walked over to the back door. Standing sideways on to it, she squinted thoughtfully at her outline reflected in the gleaming glass panels that made up its upper half. 'Will you just look at the size of me,' she marvelled, smoothing down her skirt to reveal what the other two couldn't deny was a definitely swollen middle. 'I'm like a flaming barrage balloon.'

Pearl leapt to her feet. '*Look at the size of you? Look at the bloody size of you?* That's the least of your flaming worries,' she hollered. 'It's hard enough bringing up kids when there's two of you. However d'you think you'll manage by yourself?' Pearl threw up her hands and appealed to Ginny with tears pouring unchecked down her cheeks. 'Whatever's her dad gonna say, Gin?'

At that totally inopportune moment, George walked into the kitchen. 'Whatever am I gonna say about what?' he asked with his usual pleasant smile.

'What are you doing here?' gasped Pearl, turning away and hurriedly drying her eyes on the hem of her apron.

'Flipping charming, ain't it, girl,' George grinned,

winking at Ginny, 'when a man ain't even welcome in his own home.' He sat at the table and opened his paper.

'Why ain't you at work?'

'Blimey, Pearl, I'm sorry if I've come in and messed up your mothers' meeting for you.'

Pearl flinched at the irony of her husband's words.

Completely unaware, George closed his paper and carried on. 'Didn't get picked off the stones again today. Weren't nothing for me. Still, our Sid and Micky both got picked. That's a blessing.' He lifted his chin with pride. 'Them boys of our'n, Pearl, they're built like a couple of brick . . .' George checked himself. He was a traditional old East Ender in that way and hated it when men used bad language or off-colour talk in front of the ladies. '. . . warehouses,' he continued primly. 'Strong as lions, the pair of 'em. A ganger'd have to be mad not to pick our lads for his crew.'

To Pearl's dismay, George folded his arms across his chest and leant back in his chair. He was obviously warming to his subject and was keen to share his thoughts on it.

'You know, I reckon they think I'm a bit too long in the tooth to pick me out these days,' he continued, oblivious of the increasingly tense atmosphere in the cramped little room. 'They either have to have a mountain of work on, or be desperate, to pick an old boy like me.' He smiled good-naturedly at Ginny who tried, but failed to smile back at him.

'I'll be retiring soon, won't I. Be a gentleman of leisure. And I can't say I'll mind too much neither, especially not on a lovely August morning like this, when I could be along the road having a natter with my old mates and then popping in to see Bob for a swift one.'

He lifted the teapot and weighed it in his hand to see if there was any left. 'I dunno, girls, it don't seem like no time at all since I first started down them docks. Hardly five minutes ago, if I was truthful. Funny, ain't it, how time flies by as you get older? I was a cheeky little so-and-so then, but when I went there on that first day with me old dad, God rest his soul, terrified I was.' He shook his head. 'Seems just like yesterday. But before you know it, that'll be me, finished.'

To George's astonishment, Pearl snatched the teapot from her husband's hand. 'Well you ain't no gentleman of leisure yet, George Chivers,' she snapped. 'And if you ain't got nothing better to do with your time, you can get yourself down the Roman and get me some potatoes and greens.'

George blinked in surprise at his wife's outburst. 'Do what?'

'Potatoes and greens,' Pearl hissed through her teeth.

A look of realisation came over George's face. Thinking that his wife was trying to get him out of the house because there was something up with Ginny again – the poor kid had had so many problems with her useless waste-of-space of an old man over the years that George was used to the sight of her crying in his back kitchen – he leapt from his chair as though he'd been scalded. If there were women's problems going to be discussed, George didn't want any part of it.

He grabbed his cap and pulled it firmly on to his head; it might have been over seventy degrees outside, but George would have felt naked going out without his cheese-cutter – and he was definitely going out.

He strode hurriedly over to the kitchen door, but then paused and turned round to snatch a surreptitious look at Ginny for signs of bruises. He could see it now: she looked upset about something all right, but there were no obvious cuts or anything. Not on the poor little love's face anyway.

He switched his attention to Pearl. 'Righto then, darling,' he said, with a brief nod and the barest hint of a wink, 'I'll go and get the spuds and that for you. But don't expect me back right away. I've got a feller I've gotta see about a dog, so I'll be a while.'

The three women stood in silence as they waited for George to leave. The moment they heard him call a cheery goodbye and the sound of him pulling the street door shut behind him, the crying, recriminations and disbelief began all over again.

'You must have made a mistake, Dilys. You must have. You can't be expecting.' Pearl was shaking her head as she spoke, as though denying it would make it all go away. Then, in complete contradiction she added, 'You know when your dad finds out he'll go stark raving mad. He'll bloody well kill you.'

Ginny couldn't take it in, all she could think of was what had happened to her in Jeannie Thompson's disgusting house. And what she had let that woman do to her. And all the blood . . .

'I've decided I'm gonna keep it,' Dilys announced blithely.

Ginny's head snapped up in amazement. 'But how can you?' she gasped.

It wasn't something that she would be proud of later, but at that moment Ginny felt outraged, betrayed even, that Dilys – her best friend – could even think about keeping her child after what she had seen Ginny go through at that woman's hands.

Dilys misunderstood Ginny's question. She opened her eyes wide and stuck out her bottom lip in a casual gesture of speculation. 'The father'll have to give me money, won't he?'

'What, you mean—' Ginny shut her mouth as if it were a trapdoor. She was about to say: What, you mean the *married* feller you told me's been keeping you on and off for the last few years? But I wasn't talking about money, Dilys. I mean how can you do this *to me*? But Ginny didn't say anything of the sort. The last thing she wanted to do was hurt Pearl.

There was a long moment's silence, then Pearl, in a voice husky with tears, asked flatly, 'What feller, Dilys?'

Dilys stared brazenly at Ginny. 'I met a GI. In a club.' She was rather pleased with herself for coming up with that so quickly.

Ginny frowned. It was the first she'd heard about any GI.

'Up West it was,' Dilys offered without prompting. 'Lovely place. Makes round here look a right slum.' She sniffed haughtily. 'But then that's what it is round here, ain't it? A slum.'

'A GI.' Pearl uttered the words in a monotone.

'That's right,' said Dilys brightly, 'a GI.'

What Dilys didn't say was that although she had indeed met an American soldier, it had been only about a month ago – far too recent to account for her current condition of being almost five months pregnant. And the meeting had hardly been intimate.

It had happened one evening when Dilys had gone to meet Ted outside Leicester Square tube station. As usual, she hadn't wanted to risk Ted getting there first, becoming bored and leaving before she arrived, so she had turned up almost fifteen minutes early. As she had crossed the Charing Cross Road, she was more than surprised to see him standing there already. And that he wasn't alone.

But, for once, he wasn't chatting up another woman, he was talking to a good-looking, broad-shouldered man, made even more handsome by his stylishly cut American military uniform. Dilys was quite excited by the thought of being introduced to the man with the movie-star looks, as she'd always rather fancied the idea of going out with an American, but any such hopes were dashed. Ted was doing business.

After a brief, low-volume exchange of words, then a nod, a firm shake of hands and the passing over of a tight roll of banknotes, the serviceman flashed her a quick salute, then disappeared into the West End's Saturday evening crowds.

So, Dilys *had* met a GI and it wasn't too much of a lie for her to claim she'd met the man in a club, because Ted had taken her to a sort of club that very night. It was actually more of a drinking den, and it was a good half-hour after the soldier had left them, but she'd really enjoyed herself. Even though it wasn't much like the glamorous cocktail lounges she'd seen in the films, it was still a club. And there had been a GI. Sort of. It all suited her very nicely.

Just as being pregnant suited her; just as did taking Ginny to see Jeannie Thompson. Dilys knew what she wanted and she knew exactly how she was going to get it. If her plans continued to fall into place as neatly as they seemed to be doing up until now, then she would be very happy indeed.

Pearl heaved herself up from the table and went to the sink to fill the kettle. 'So, where is he now then? This GI?'

'He's had to go back to America. But he's promised he'll look after me. Gonna send me all the money I need, he is.'

'You know if he don't, and if your dad takes against you, you'll have to go into a mother and baby home, don't you?'

Dilys snorted with contempt. 'Don't you worry about me; I won't have to go into no home.'

141

Pearl put down the kettle on the wooden draining board. It was as though she didn't have the energy or the will to carry it over to the gas stove. 'I'll do me best for you, Dilys. But you know how your dad feels about girls getting into trouble. I'm telling you, this'll kill him. You know you've always been his baby girl.'

Gripping the side of the butler sink, Pearl started to cry again. 'But he'll wanna wring your neck for you when he finds out.'

Dilys sighed irritably. 'No he won't.'

'Maybe not,' sniffed Pearl, 'but when your brothers find out they'll bloody well wanna kill the bastard. No matter who, or where, he is.'

It was one of those miserable November days when night seemed to have fallen before it had ever really got light; rain had been bucketing down solidly for a week and Ted was just about pissed off.

A wet Wednesday night in Upton Park. Definitely not his idea of a good time. There he was with a suitcase full of gear to flog, but every pub he's been in was almost empty. At this rate, he'd be going home before closing time with less in his pockets than he'd come out with.

He leaned miserably against the polished mahogany bar of the Boleyn, nursing his almost empty glass, debating whether to have another scotch, when he felt a tap on his shoulder.

'Ted Martin?'

He stuck a smile to his lips and twisted round to see who wanted him. With a bit of luck, it might be a customer just wetting himself to buy a caseload of bent watches, or wanting a nice fat loan.

'Who wants to know, mate?' he asked, the perfect image of the chirpy spiv.

'Names don't matter, but you can call me . . . Let's see. Charlie. Yeah, you can call me Charlie.'

'Charlie' was big, very big. In all directions. He was wearing a dark-blue overcoat that was, Ted noted, of the best quality – the feller obviously had a few bob – but it was so massive it could have served as a tent for a whole boy scout troop and still have had room for the Akala. And he wasn't alone. The man standing with him was almost as big as he was. Both of them had on snap-brim trilby hats pulled down hard so that their faces were in shadow, although Ted could still see that Charlie sported a cauliflower ear that would have won first prize in any sort of contest.

Ted nodded with a grin. Very nice. It sounded like he was about to do a bit of business with Charlie and his mate. Probably not a loan, but definitely some sort of a trade.

Charlie jerked his chin towards the door. 'Let's step outside, eh?' It was an instruction rather than a question.

Charlie picked up Ted's case and started to walk away. In his great meat plate of a hand the bag looked more like a small portmanteau than a full-sized suitcase.

Ted downed the last of his drink and hurried off after his potential customers.

'Down here,' said Charlie, tipping his head towards a narrow, unlit pathway that ran alongside the pub and through to the back of the shops. 'We don't want no one to see us, now do we?'

'You're right there,' agreed Ted, stumbling his way along the pitch-dark alley. 'They all love a bit of bent gear, but only if it's them what's buying it. If some other bloke's got a few quid to spend, they come over all moral on you and wind up getting on the trumpet to the law.'

Ted tripped again, this time barking his shin against a pile of crates. 'Shit!' He sucked his teeth as he bent down and rubbed his leg. 'Here, you'll need to see what I've got. Either of you two got a torch?'

'I don't think we need a torch for what we've got in mind,' Charlie said.

'How d'you mean?'

The men moved very close to him and Ted, realising too late that he had actually been mug enough to go down an unlit alley with a pair of gorillas he had never set eyes on before, flattened himself against the slimy brick wall.

Dark as it was, Ted saw the outline of Charlie's leather-gloved fist quite clearly as it drove towards his solar plexus. 'Christ!' he gasped, doubling over with pain.

'We've been waiting quite a while for an opportunity to bump into you on our travels, Mr Martin,' Charlie sneered. 'And I mean waiting, 'cos let's face it, we didn't wanna waste our energy actually looking for someone as unimportant as you, when we knew we'd see you crawling out from under some rock sooner or later.'

Still bent forward, and with his arms shielding his head, Ted whimpered pitifully, 'I don't understand. I ain't done nothing.'

'No?' Charlie's voice dripped with sarcasm. 'I don't suppose you have, a piece o' crap like you. But think about it, you slippery little bastard. Something you done to a little lady?'

'That kid's nothing to do with me. I swear. Dilys is a fucking liar. You ask—'

'Dilys? Who the hell's Dilys?' Charlie looked at his silent mate who just shrugged. Then he grabbed hold of Ted by the collar. 'What, give a good hiding to more than one, have you?'

Ted tried a conspiratorial laugh – a man dealing with his equals. 'You chaps know how it is. You have to shut

144

their gobs for 'em sometimes, or they start taking liberties.'

When they didn't join in with his laughter, Ted shut up.

'Lilly ring any bells?' asked Charlie.

'Lilly? I ain't seen her for months.'

'Five months, actually. It was July if you recall.'

Ted shrugged. 'You don't expect me to keep tabs on all the old sorts I knock about with, do you?'

'Knock about? You said it, moosh. But she weren't yours to knock about, now was she?'

Two hours later Ted came to. He was lying in a puddle of filthy, icy cold water, on a bomb-site off the Ratcliffe Highway near St Katherine's dock, in the shadow of Tower Bridge. But with his eyes puffed up to slits from the beating he had taken, he had no idea where he was. And, with the pains in his head befuddling his thinking, he had only vague memories of how he had got there.

What he did know, as he dragged himself towards the road, was that he vowed, if it was the last thing he did, he would get his own back on Lilly, the filthy little whore who had grassed him. He'd make her suffer until she begged him to finish her off.

When he eventually got back to Bailey Street it was nearly five o'clock in the morning and still pouring with rain.

It took all his effort to bang on the street door.

Ginny was down the stairs in a matter of moments. She hardly ever slept well when Ted was away. Not that she worried about what might be happening to him any more – she was past all that. She now worried about herself, about what he might do to her if he did decide to come home in the early hours.

But when she opened the street door, instead of finding

Ted loud-mouthed, roaring with drink and ready to pick a fight as she had expected, he was soaking wet, bleeding and, by the look of him, totally exhausted.

Automatically, she reached out to steady him as he fell into the pssage. 'Ted, whatever's happened?'

He lifted his head and glared at her through cut and swollen eyelids. 'What d'you think's happened, you brainless mare? I've been to a ball and tripped over me partner's dance frock.'

Ginny stiffened. She never knew how to handle Ted at the best of times, but when he was already in a temper he was capable of anything. But despite her resolve to look out for herself she couldn't just abandon him, not in the state he was in.

'What can I do?' she asked quietly as he staggered towards the kitchen.

'Get me a drink, and a basin of hot water and a flannel to clean myself up. And then you can piss off out of it and leave me alone.'

Ginny went over to the corner cupboard and took out what was left of Nellie's scotch and a glass, which she wiped with the tea-towel before filling it. She wasn't taking any chances, something as inconsequential as a smeared glass had, in the past, been enough to get her a cracked rib.

As she took the drink over to Ted, her hand shaking, Ginny's imagination was working overtime. Thoughts and fears spun and twisted around in her mind. For Ted to have had such a beating he must have really upset someone. The man the coppers had warned her about that time maybe, the man who had it in for him. Or someone's husband.

She put the drink down carefully in front of him, went over to the sink and filled the kettle. Her heart was pounding. All she wanted to do was go back to bed, pull the covers up over her head and pray that Nellie had left enough whisky to knock Ted into oblivion before he too made it upstairs. But she wasn't banking on it. She was a woman with few illusions left and knew that things didn't work out that easily. Well, not for her they didn't.

As she searched under the sink for the disinfectant to clean Ted's wounds, Ginny was startled by a frenzied banging on the street door. She straightened up and flicked a quick look at the clock on the dresser. Ten past five. It was either the police, or – God forbid – whoever it was who had jumped Ted had decided to come round and finish the job properly.

'What shall I do?' she breathed, as the banging grew more insistent.

'Get rid of 'em,' spat Ted, stumbling to his feet and lurching towards the back door.

Ginny ran out into the hall, pulling her dressing-gown around her.

Upstairs, Nellie was yelling, 'What's all that noise down there?'

Ginny closed her eyes. Nellie starting; that was all she needed. 'It's all right, Nell,' she called up to her. 'I'm getting it. You go back to sleep.'

'Some bloody chance I've got of that.'

Ginny closed her ears to the rest of her mother-in-law's ranting, took a deep breath, swallowed hard and grasped the door handle with both hands.

When she saw who was outside she could have kissed them with relief.

Standing there in the gloom of the early morning – without coats, hats or even shirts, and with the freezing rain soaking through their vests – looking for some inexplicable reason as though they were about to pass out, were Sid and Micky, Dilys's two younger, but now enormous brothers.

'Thank Gawd you've woke up,' gasped Sid, grabbing her by the arm. 'You've gotta come over and help Mum, Gin. Please. Dad's gone for the doctor, but I think he's gonna be too late.'

All thoughts of Ted shivering and bleeding out in the lavvy in the backyard were immediately forgotten. Pearl needed her.

Pulling away from Sid's huge paw was impossible, but Ginny managed to stretch back just far enough to grab her coat off the end of the banister.

'How long's Pearl been ill?' she asked, throwing the coat over her head to protect her from the rain.

'It ain't Mum,' Micky quavered. 'It's our Dilys. She's only having the baby, ain't she.'

Ginny rushed through the Chivers' open door and took the stairs two at a time up to Dilys's back bedroom where the panic-stricken brothers had directed her.

They needn't have bothered, the sounds of Dilys screaming and hollering were signal enough for even the dimmest of wits to follow.

The brothers themselves were more than happy to have been relegated by Ginny to the kitchen to boil water – she wasn't sure they needed any, but at least it would keep them busy and away from under her and Pearl's feet.

Ginny paused on the landing. If the truth were known, she was just as scared as the boys were. This was the moment she had been dreading: Dilys having her baby. For no matter how well Ginny had managed during her waking hours to shake off any jealous or resentful thoughts about Dilys, her dreams were a different matter. Those she couldn't control. Over and over again, they came to taunt her, always the same: spiteful visions of cradling her new-born baby in her arms. Sometimes it was blonde like her, other times it was dark like Ted. But whatever it looked like, it was her baby. Hers. The images were so real that in her first waking moments she would be puzzled at not seeing her baby's crib at the end of the bed. Then she would remember, and she would weep at the unfairness of it all.

She was the one who was married – even if it was to Ted Martin – and she was the one who should be having a baby. Not Dilys. And seeing Dilys, as she bloomed with approaching motherhood, had been a daily torment for Ginny. If she hadn't gone to Jeannie Thompson's, she would be almost eight months gone by now. Ironically, almost the same as Dilys.

Almost eight months?

Ginny frowned. It hadn't occurred to her until now that there might be a problem. Babies, or rather, healthy babies, weren't meant to come into the world so soon.

Warily, she pushed open the bedroom door and focused on the scene inside.

Lit by the stark glare of the overhead light, rather than the soft glow of the bedside lamp, Dilys's bedroom was no longer the cheerful place where she and Ginny had spent so much of their girlhood gossiping and giggling, practising dance steps and trying on each other's clothes and make-up. It had been transformed into an unfamiliar place, with the smell of fear hanging thick in the air.

Pearl was kneeling down next to the bed with her back to the door, wiping Dilys's forehead with a flannel.

Dilys looked terrible. Her thick dark hair, usually her pride and joy, was plastered to her head with sweat, despite the freezing damp of the early morning, and her face was deathly pale and contorted as she thrashed about, tangling the bedclothes around her legs.

Ginny knew that Dilys had never been much of a heroine – George had always joked that whenever his daughter had said she was unwell, he never knew whether to call the doctor or a drama critic – but this time it was obvious that Dilys wasn't crying wolf. She was really suffering; the anguish on her face was, for once, genuine.

Pearl, whispering reassurances to her daughter, pulled herself up off her knees, did her best to straighten the sheets and turned round. She let out a little gasp of surprise to see Ginny standing there in the doorway.

'Hello, love,' she said, fixing an encouraging smile to her lips and doing her best to block Dilys from Ginny's view. 'What you doing over here?'

'The boys asked me to come and help,' Ginny managed to mutter.

Pearl felt like going downstairs and braining her pair of lummocking great blockheads of sons. As if she didn't have enough on her plate seeing to Dilys. How was she meant to cope with Ginny as well? The poor little thing hadn't got over her own trouble yet. Still, she sighed to herself, they weren't to know. Fellers didn't know much at the best of times, let alone at a time like this.

She put her arm round Ginny's shoulder and said gently, 'You sure you wanna stay, love? I'll understand if you'd rather go home.'

Ginny hesitated, then nodded. 'I'd like to stay if it's all right.'

'Course it is. Now you roll up those sleeves and give your hands a good scrub in that basin; then you can mop her forehead to cool her down, while I have a look at the business end of things.'

'Mum!' Dilys screamed.

'And I think I'd better be quick about it.'

As Pearl pulled back the covers she saw the look on Ginny's face. It was obvious that Dilys wasn't the only one in pain.

Pearl did her best to sound calm as she encouraged her alternately furious and then terrified daughter to push and to breathe through the final stages of her labour, but she too felt like screaming – at the complete, bloody injustice of it all. What was wrong with the world when . . .

All thoughts of unfairness were forgotten. 'Here we go!' Pearl urged her daughter. 'One last time, darling!'

Dilys grunted and heaved and yelled like a banshee, as she made her final effort, clasping Ginny's hand as though she were the last lifebelt on a sinking ship. 'I ain't never, ever,' she hollered, 'going near no bloke, not ever again.'

A few moments later Pearl straightened up and stared at her daughter. 'Dilys,' she breathed. 'You've done it.'

Ginny backed away from the bed, dropped down on to the dressing-table stool and covered her face with her hands.

For a baby born so early, Dilys's little girl was surprisingly lusty.

'Hello, darling,' cooed Pearl as she held the bawling infant in her arms. 'Today's your birthday, my sweetheart. November the twentieth, 1946. The most special day in my life.' She kissed the warm, down-covered head. 'You go to your mum, while me and your Auntie Ginny here clear up a bit.'

She bent forward to hand Dilys her child, but Dilys shook her head pathetically. 'I can't,' she wailed. 'I'm so tired and I can't stand all that noise.'

'You'll have to soon,' Pearl warned her. 'She'll need to go to your breast, love.'

Dilys shuddered with horror. 'You're having a laugh, ain't you? She can have a bottle and like it.'

Pearl turned her head away from her daughter so that

151

she wouldn't see the look of disappointment that had clouded her face. 'Good job I got some in then, eh?' she said, her voice light and comforting.

'Can I hold her?' Ginny whispered. 'If you don't mind.'

Pearl nodded. 'Course you can.'

As she placed the little bundle into Ginny's arms, Pearl saw the tears brimming in her eyes and felt fit to weep along with her. It wasn't the right thing for a mother even to think, Pearl knew that, but it would have been clear to anyone that her daughter wasn't exactly the type to take to all this, whereas Ginny looked like a natural.

Pearl watched her, stroking the baby's face with her fingertip and smiling so lovingly as its crying gradually eased, and wondered again why things hadn't turned out differently, why it hadn't been Ginny's child she had just delivered.

Pearl could only imagine what the poor kid was going through as she rocked and whispered to the baby. The thought of what that bastard had done to her, what he'd driven her to, made Pearl's usually generous heart turn to ice as far as Ted Martin was concerned. He was the one man she would gladly have seen disappear from the earth – and preferably in as unpleasant a way as possible . . .

'Mum!' Dilys wailed. 'Do something. I feel terrible.'

'You'll be all right soon, love,' Pearl said cheerfully. 'At least me and Ginny delivering the little mite saved us the six quid we'd have had to have paid the doctor.'

Pearl puffed as she bent down to parcel up the newspaper and the soiled draw sheet that she had taken off the bed. 'I've had it put by in the dressing-table for weeks now,' she explained. 'Been saving a few shillings every week, I have. From the very first day you told us you was expecting. So, I tell you what, I'll give it to you to spend on yourself. When you're up and about you can treat yourself to something nice to wear.'

'I don't think I'll ever be able to fit in nothing nice again neither.'

'You'll feel better once you've had a nice cup o' tea. I'll just sort this out first.'

'Shall I go down and make it, Pearl?' Ginny asked.

'If you don't mind, darling. Then I can get this finished up here.' Pearl wiped her hands down her apron and reached out for the baby. 'Let me take this little angel off you and I'll get her settled down next to Dilys.'

Just as Ginny was about to open the bedroom door, she pulled back in alarm at the sound of someone crashing up the stairs and coming to a skidding halt outside on the landing mat.

'Pearl?' It was George on the other side of the door; he sounded frantic. 'I found the doctor for you. But he's gonna be at least another hour. What shall I do?'

'Why don't you come in for a start?' Pearl answered him.

'You sure?' he asked warily.

'Course I am, love. All the worst is over now.'

Dilys was about to say speak for yourself, but the look on her dad's face as he stepped gingerly into the room and had his first glimpse of his grandchild was enough to silence even her mean mouth.

George, a great lumbering docker who had spent all his working life heaving weights up to shoulder height that most men would barely have been able to lift, tiptoed over to his wife and grandchild with the lightness of a gossamer-shod ballerina.

Tears streamed down his weather-beaten cheeks as he looked down at the tiny infant in his wife's arms.

'Here's your granddaughter, George. Here's Susan Elizabeth.'

The expression of love, pride and wonder on her mum's and dad's faces – never mind the sheep's eyes on Ginny – cheered up Dilys considerably. It wasn't her own maternal love and pride that was being uplifted, it was the fact that she now knew she had no worries whatsoever about being thrown out and no problems at all with having someone to mind the baby.

With a bit of luck she'd be back to normal and out on the town again with Ted before anyone even realised it, or, from the soppy look on their faces, before they even cared.

Dilys had great hopes for Susan Elizabeth: she was going to be a very useful claim on Ted Martin and a very convenient distraction.

Chapter 8

July 1948

It had been a glorious summer's day and Dilys had been sitting on a kitchen chair outside number 11 all afternoon, waiting for Pearl to come back from the Roman Road. It was now getting on for six o'clock and her mum was still not back from the market. She'd told Dilys that she was only going for a few veg and a bit of fruit and maybe to pick up something pretty for the little one, and yet she'd been gone for hours – since just before dinner-time, now she came to think about it.

Dilys was not very happy, in fact she was becoming really agitated. If her mum didn't get back soon, she wouldn't be able to get away; Ted would be left waiting for her by Mile End station, then he'd think she wasn't coming and clear off without her. Her whole evening would be ruined.

Dilys folded her arms and tutted indignantly to herself. It just wasn't good enough. Where the hell was she? It wouldn't have been so bad if her dad had been around to give her a hand with Susan, but he was off with his mates as usual. That's all he seemed to be interested in now he'd retired: hanging around talking to the other old boys about flipping football, and pigeons, and greyhounds. Everyone was so flaming selfish; it really got on Dilys's nerves.

Susan, who was now twenty months old, had also grown impatient with waiting. She liked to toddle around on the floor and play, but Dilys, not wanting to be bothered with keeping an eye on her, had had different ideas and had strapped her firmly into the big carriage-built pram that Sid and Micky had bought for her when she'd been born. With nothing more to amuse her than a crust of bread and the fringing round the hood, Susan had dropped off to sleep.

Before finally giving up and closing her eyes, she had made a feeble attempt at whining for attention, but, young as she was, Susan had already learned that it wasn't easy to get a reaction from her mummy. Her nanny and Auntie Ginny were a very different matter, they were always ready to pick her up, to talk to her and play with her, but they weren't here. So sleep had been her refuge.

It might have been better if Dilys had also had a nap, maybe then she wouldn't have been in such a foul temper. As it was, she was fuming. She was so angry that she was actually about to get off her backside and do something for herself for once. She was going to go indoors and fetch her coat, and start walking round to the Roman Road to see if she could find Pearl. But she hadn't even stood up, when her salvation appeared on the corner of the street – Ginny Martin, striding along on her way home from work, a bag of shopping swinging from each hand.

Dilys leapt to her feet and waved frantically; she would have shouted but she didn't want to wake Susan. Not that Dilys was worried about her daughter's rest being disturbed, it was just easier when she wasn't wanting attention all the time. That could wait until someone else was looking after her.

Within a matter of minutes Dilys was indoors washing and primping herself, and Ginny, delighted that her friend was going out for a few hours with her new mystery boyfriend again – the GI was still sending money over from America apparently, but that didn't stop Dilys from needing company – was only too pleased to keep an eye on Susan for her.

Ginny had popped over home first to let her mother-in-law know she was back from work and to give her the ham she had had freshly sliced off the bone for her tea. Nellie hadn't been very impressed by the idea that she was expected to boil herself a few potatoes and wash her own lettuce, and had gone on and on about her daughter-in-law's terrible behaviour. Ginny, as she usually did now, just ignored her and got on with putting away the rest of the shopping.

Being bold enough to deal firmly with Nellie wasn't the only thing about Ginny that had changed; since Susan had been born, her life had been turned around. She now felt content, complete almost, in a way she would never have imagined possible. Susan was, after all, the child of a friend, not even related to her, but the fact that Dilys was Susan's mother didn't seem to matter somehow. Ginny and Pearl spent far more time with the child than Dilys ever did and it seemed to suit them all.

Ginny smiled to herself at the thought of the happy hours and some of the unforgettable moments that she had spent with Pearl and Susan: the day the little one's first tooth had finally come through after miserable days of fretting; the first excited steps she had taken when she had tottered across the kitchen to be scooped up in her proud grandmother's outstretched arms; the wonderful feeling Ginny experienced as Susan relaxed into sleep in her arms, as she and Pearl shared a pot of tea and an afternoon's easygoing chatter about whatever came into their heads.

It was as though Ginny, who had had so much taken away from her, was being given a second chance to be part of a proper family once more. Sid and Micky often teased her, as they rushed in after work to get ready to go out with their latest girlfriends, that she spent more time in number 11 than they did and they were probably right.

Ginny almost couldn't have been happier. She no longer hungered for the crumbs of affection that Ted might let fall from his table to nourish her. She had no need of such condescension. Even the fact that he had been missing again was almost of no consequence. Maybe he was still up to his old tricks. But so what? She now had Susan to fill her time and her thoughts; a little girl she loved and who Ginny knew loved her in return.

While Dilys was indoors getting ready, Ginny sat outside the house in the fading evening light, with Susan no longer in her pram but settled comfortably on her lap, watching the children from Bailey Street and their mates from the surrounding neighbourhood playing at being in the Olympics. With all the wireless and newspaper coverage about the run-up to the great event that was to happen in August when the games were coming to London, 'playing Olympics' was all that most of the kids in the East End had been interested in for weeks.

Ginny smiled and nodded at the enthusiastic sprinters, jumpers and relay racers as they tore up and down the road. They were without the skills or the equipment of their adult idols, it had to be said, as most were dressed in ill-fitting home knits and patched and darned hand-me-downs, but they had as much passion as any internationally renowned athlete. Ginny would usually have cheered them on, willing them on towards the winning tape – a rough chalk line sketched between the pub and the bomb-site – but this evening she restricted her support to silent nods and encouraging smiles, as Susan was still fast asleep.

But the little girl's peaceful slumbers were rudely shattered as a great holler of incensed protest went up from the far end of the turning.

The older boys, using all kinds of ingenious items 'borrowed' from backyards and kitchens, had just added the triumphant finishing touches to a makeshift hurdle track, when Sid had come charging round the corner from Grove Road as if he were being chased by Old Nick himself, scattering supports, and cross bars flying in all directions.

'Oi you! You've spoilt our game, you rotten bleeder!' was one of the more polite hollers from the chorus that echoed after Sid as he skidded through the wreckage of their course.

Susan opened her eyes with a start and let out a whimper of fright at all the noise.

Sid seemed not to hear or even notice the protesters as he continued his wild flight along the street, crashing towards Ginny and Susan like an out-of-control steam engine.

Ginny stood up, hugging Susan to her shoulder, ready to give Sid a piece of her mind, but he didn't even slow down; he just ran straight past her and into the house, nearly knocking her off her feet, and Susan with her.

Clinging to the banister rail, trying to get his breath back, Sid shouted up the stairs, 'Dilys. I know you're up there. Where's Dad? I've gotta find Dad.'

'Shut your mouth, you,' Dilys yelled back at him from upstairs. 'You'll wake the bloody baby.'

Ginny was now right behind Sid. She stood on tiptoe and shouted in his ear. 'She's already awake, Dil. No thanks to this big lump. Half frightened her out of her little wits, he has.'

Sid turned around, still panting, and reached out to

ruffle his little niece's shiny dark hair. 'Sorry, sweetheart,' he breathed. 'Uncle Sid didn't mean to scare you.'

Ginny frowned disapprovingly and held Susan closer. 'I dunno what's got into you, Sid. First you go upsetting all them kids out there, and now—'

'Look, Gin, do us a favour, just tell me where me dad is.'

'No good asking me,' she said primly. 'He wasn't about when I got in from work and that must have been a good half-hour ago.'

Sid bowed his head. 'I've gotta find him, Gin. I dunno what to do.'

Ginny set Susan down on the floor. 'Go and see if your dolly's in the kitchen, babe,' she said gently, guiding the serious-faced toddler in the right direction, then she straightened up and turned back to Sid. 'Are you in trouble, Sid Chivers?'

He didn't reply, he just kept staring down at the floor.

'Dilys,' Ginny called up to her. 'Come down here. Just for a minute.'

'Leave off, Ginny. Can't you see I'm getting ready?' Dilys appeared on the landing at the top of the stairs, waving her mascara brush in the air by way of proof. She was just about to step back into her room, when Sid called after her to stop.

'You'd better come down, Dil,' he said flatly. 'It's Mum, she's been knocked down by a trolleybus in Grove Road.'

Dilys was down the stairs in a flash. 'Where is she?'

'They took her away in an ambulance.'

'They what?' Dilys rolled her eyes in enraged disbelief. 'If she's in the hospital, then who's gonna sit with the baby?'

She shoved her brother to one side so that she could see Ginny. 'You ain't gotta go home just yet, have you, Gin?' she wheedled.

Before Ginny could answer, Sid grabbed Dilys by the shoulders. 'You'd better sit down, Dil,' he said, pushing her on to the stairs. 'Mum ain't in the hospital. She's in the mortuary.'

Ginny shook her head in disbelief and pulled Sid round so that he was facing her. 'No. You're wrong. She can't be. It must be someone else. It must ...' Ginny suddenly felt unbearably cold; the blood drained from her face and, as if she were a rubber balloon being deflated, she crumpled slowly to the floor.

'He wants to watch himself,' snapped a miserable-looking old woman, as George Chivers accidently brushed her arm as he edged past her on the way back from the bar. 'He might have just buried his wife, but that ain't no excuse to go knocking people's drinks out of their hands.'

'You're right there, Florrie,' agreed Nellie, who was standing with her. 'Ignorant as shit, some people.'

If George heard the women's complaints he certainly didn't show it. He kept his eyes lowered and his head down as he made his way back to the table in the corner of the Prince Albert, the base from which he had plied backwards and forwards to and from the bar, gradually getting more and more drunk, but still feeling stone-cold sober.

He had no need to fetch his own drinks, there were more than enough of the mourners – some genuine, some, like Nellie's elderly companion Florrie Robins, only there for the free food and drink – who would have been more than willing to fetch them for him, but George hadn't listened or said a word to anyone since the funeral cars had come to the house that morning.

He plonked down onto the bench seat and knocked

back the scotch he had in one hand, then downed half of the pint of bitter he had in the other in a single swallow.

'George.' Ginny, her eyes puffy and red-rimmed from weeping, touched his arm gently. 'Can I get you a sandwich or something? You should eat just a little bit, you know.'

George said nothing, he just stared unseeingly at the floor as though watching some distant episode playing in his head.

Sid came up behind Ginny, tapped her on the shoulder and whispered quietly into her ear, asking her if she'd help him start getting people to make a move so that he could get his dad home before he drank himself into a stupor.

Ginny nodded and went to find Ted, who had actually turned up for the funeral just as she had asked him.

She found Ted at the other end of the pub. He was sitting next to Dilys. He had her child on his lap and was singing to her, a happy little nonsense ditty that he seemed to be making up as he went along. It was about a pretty canary bird called Susan, and he was smiling blissfully.

Ginny stood there watching him, not caring that she was being buffeted about by the crowds of increasingly drink-enlivened mourners.

As he continued with his song, Ted was so entranced by the beaming toddler that he was completely oblivious of Ginny's presence.

The tender intimacy she was witnessing felt like a knife in Ginny's guts. Could this sensitive, affectionate man really be the same one who had refused even to discuss having a child? The same one who had kicked her in the stomach as she lay on the floor begging him to stop just because she'd mentioned it?

'Ted.' Ginny's voice sounded strange even to her.

162

Ted looked up, the enchanted smile still on his handsome face; an expression he hadn't deigned to share with his wife in a very long time.

The moment he realised who had spoken to him his smile melted away like snow on top of a chimney pot.

'I didn't realise you even knew Dilys had a baby,' Ginny said quietly. 'Let alone that you knew her name.'

'Here, Dilys,' he said wearily. 'You take her.'

Ginny flinched as she saw how he handled the little girl: not clumsily, but in an experienced, easy sort of way, as though he cherished the very bones of her.

Ginny tried to stop herself even beginning to think it, but her thoughts were galloping ahead of reason. Ted and Dilys? Surely even Ted wouldn't do that to her?

He stood up. 'You ain't gonna start, are you, Ginny?'

'No, Ted,' she said, her voice flat. 'I'm not starting. I've just come to tell you that Sid and Micky asked if we'd all start making a move. George is getting slaughtered and they wanna get him home.'

'Shouldn't a man expect to get pissed at his wife's funeral?' someone behind her asked.

Ginny closed her eyes and groaned inwardly. It was George. She hadn't realised he was standing there.

She twisted round, ready to apologise, but George wouldn't let her. He held up his hand and shook his head. 'It's all right, Gin, I ain't blaming you,' he slurred. 'I heard what Sid said to you. But just leave me be, eh?'

With that, he shoved his way back towards the throng at the bar, leaving her standing there, red-faced and more distraught than ever.

She turned back to Ted.

He stared levelly at her. 'Me mother's not got a drink,' he said, sitting down next to Dilys again and taking Susan back on to his lap. 'You'd better go and get her one. Go on.'

Ginny said nothing. It wouldn't be right starting anything, not on a day such as this. So, as she had so often done in the past, she just did as she was told.

'All right, Nellie,' Ginny said by way of impassive greeting, as she handed her mother-in-law a glass of port and lemon.

'How about Florrie?' Nellie barked. 'How about one for her?'

Ginny didn't rise to Nellie's nastiness. Not only did she not want to row in front of everyone, but she was too distracted by the image of Ted and little Susan to bother.

'I'll get her one, Nellie, and I tell you what, I'll even fetch you a few rounds of sandwiches an' all. That do you, will it?'

'We don't want nothing hard mind,' Nellie called after her. 'Florrie's had all her teeth pulled out like me and she ain't got used to her false ones yet neither.'

Ginny was fed up with hearing about Nellie's new National Health choppers. Yes, she had agreed, over and over again, it was a wonderful thing that such luxuries could be had by anybody now, and for free, but if she'd to express her amazement at the sight of the bloody things once more she'd grab them from the old trout's mouth and dance up and down on them until they crumbled away like a stick of stale seaside rock.

And not only was she sick of Nellie's sodding teeth, if she or Flo said one more word about their made-to-measure Health Service glasses and how they beat the ones you bought lucky-dip style from the counter at Woolworths, Ginny would not be responsible for her actions.

She could feel herself coming very close to the edge and Nellie was just the person who could push her over.

Taking a deep breath, Ginny carried on towards the buffet table at the far end of the counter, keeping her chin in the air and her eyes fixed in front of her so that she didn't have to look at Ted and Dilys who were still sitting together in the corner right opposite the food.

With a weary sigh, Ginny began piling up a plate with anything and everything even vaguely soft-looking. Maybe if the old bats had their gobs full of food they'd give everyone a bit of peace for five minutes.

Ginny was just about to carry her load back to Nellie and Flo when someone rammed into her back with such force that the loaded plate was sent flying from her hand. It sailed through the air like one of the lethal tin-lid discuses the mums had barred the kids from playing with in their Bailey Street Olympics and landed with a resounding crash against the edge of the polished counter top, sending the sandwiches arcing across the bar in the direction of Martha, who had her head down pulling a pint of best.

'What the bloody hell?' yelped the landlady, as a slice of bread, butter-side first, landed with a slap on the side of her rouged and powdered cheek and slowly slipped down towards her bosom.

Ginny spun around to confront the idiot who had pushed her, her mouth open ready to ask the clumsy so-and-so what exactly he thought he was up to. But when she saw George standing there, swaying alarmingly from side to side, she was more concerned than angry.

He was jabbing his finger at Dilys and muttering furiously to himself, 'It was her what killed you, Pearl. Her. The shame of it. Bringing trouble home like some little tart.'

Dilys ignored him and carried on talking to Ted.

'Come on, George,' Ginny coaxed him, 'it's time we was all going home.'

George twisted round and tried to focus on Ginny. 'Pearl?'

Ginny swallowed hard. 'No, George, it's me. Ginny. Ginny Martin.'

'Ginny?' George stared at her as though he was trying to make sure that it really wasn't his wife.

'Yeah, that's right, George.'

George's lip trembled and his head lolled forward. 'Well maybe you can tell me what Dilys is doing with your old man. Ain't she in enough trouble with blokes?'

Ginny closed her eyes and bit back the tears that were threatening to start again. 'Come on, George,' she said, doing her best to keep her voice under control, 'let's be off, eh?'

'But look at her encouraging him,' George persisted. 'She's letting him sniff around her like a bloody bitch on heat.'

'Please, George.' Ginny grabbed his arm. 'Don't. Don't do this.'

George lifted his chin. Looking at Ginny as though he were seeing her for the first time, he nodded meekly and let her lead him through the mass of mourners towards the door.

Dilys watched their slow progress with unconcealed venom, sneering as people stopped him to pledge their promises of help and support.

'Just look at 'em,' she hissed. 'All fussing around him. They ain't got a clue how I'm suffering.'

She altered her tone to a pitiful whine. 'It's terrible indoors, Ted. Really terrible. Him and the boys sitting around with faces like fiddles, with not a thought of what I'm going through now I've got no one to help me. I hate it living there with them. Really hate it. I told Dad I should have the big bedroom now, but he wouldn't even hear of it. And you should hear the things he says to me.

166

And you can't imagine what it's like, Ted, having to push that bloody pram in and out of the passage with Dad's bike to get past.'

'You finished moaning?' Ted asked, smiling down at Susan as he chucked her under the chin, making her giggle happily.

Dilys shrugged. 'You do want me to be happy, don't you, Ted?' She sipped her drink daintily. 'Just look at him.' She jerked her thumb towards her dad, whom Ginny had propped against the wall while she opened the door. 'Fancy having to live with that. I can't stand it no more, Ted. I really can't.'

She grimaced with revulsion as Sid looped his arm affectionately round his dad's shoulders. 'Pathetic.' She dropped her chin and made miserable little sniffling noises. 'You've gotta do something, Ted. You've just gotta.'

Slowly she raised her eyes and blinked pitifully at him. 'If not for me, then for this poor little love.'

'Thanks, Gin,' Sid said, letting the pub door close with a slam behind them. 'Me and Micky'll see to him. And I'm sorry about what he said just now.'

'It's all right. I know he's had too much to drink.' Ginny stepped aside to let the two burly young men take over.

'What did he say to you then, Gin?' Micky asked, as he took George's weight against his shoulder.

Sid flashed a look of warning at his younger brother. 'Can't you keep your gob shut just for once, Micky?'

'What? I never heard what he said, that's all.'

'I didn't mean to upset you, Ginny love,' George slurred. 'I never meant nothing.'

'What you upset about then, Gin?' Micky asked.

'Micky, are you gonna belt up?'

Ginny could see the anger flaring in Sid's face. She laid her hand gently on his chest and said quietly, 'Leave him alone, Sid. I don't want no rows started on my part. Just get George off home, eh?'

'All right. Thanks.'

Sid and his brother stood one on either side of their now weeping father and gently guided him along the street, leaving Ginny in the doorway, watching them make their way back to the emptiness of number 11.

Without warning, George stopped dead in his tracks, threw back his head and a great shuddering sob shook through his body. 'It *was* her getting herself into trouble what caused all this. My Pearl wouldn't be laying in that cold ground if it wasn't for her.'

Sid squeezed his arm, encouraging him to start moving again. 'It was an accident, Dad, you know that.'

George shook his head, as he reluctantly shuffled forward between his sons. 'Your mum never said nothing to no one, but I could tell. I knew what she was thinking. She had it on her mind all the time. Every minute of the day. Day in day out. She wasn't concentrating when she crossed that road. I'm telling you, it would never have happened otherwise.'

He flicked his tongue at the trail of snot that dripped from his moustache. 'If I ever find the bastard what got that girl pregnant I'll kill him. I swear on my Pearl's grave, I will.'

Micky's chin was set with fury. One way or another, whoever it was who had made his dad cry – his dad whom he had never seen shed so much as a single tear – was going to pay. 'You don't have to worry yourself about that, Dad,' he said through gritted teeth. 'Me and Sid'll sort the whoreson out good and proper.'

If they hadn't been holding up their dad between them, Sid would have grabbed Micky by the throat and shaken the silly little sod till his teeth rattled. 'Think before you open that cakehole o' your'n for once, can't you, Micky?'

It wasn't the first time that Sid had felt like thumping his little brother. Micky was so hot-headed, Sid was sure it would land him in real schtuck one day. All right, so they'd discussed between them, plenty of times, what they'd do to the lousy no-good who'd dumped their sister – and Sid was growing more and more convinced that he knew who the bastard was, and it wasn't some American soldier – but mouthing off about it in front of their dad, especially just a couple of hours after their mum had been laid to rest, well, that was just about the last thing any of them needed.

Sid would bide his time and he just hoped that Micky would do the same.

'So it's like this see, now I'm getting this new motor, I won't be needing this one no more.' Ted patted the bonnet of the Talbot as though it were a much-loved family pet. 'And I thought, I know, it might come in handy as a runabout for Mr Roberts and his good lady. You are a married man, aren't you, Mr Roberts?'

The man in the cheap-looking brown suit rubbed his sweaty palms dry on the seat of his trousers, leaving a greasy slick on the already shiny cloth. 'I am indeed, Mr Martin. And am proud to be the father of two lovely little girls into the bargain.'

Ted smiled beatifically and slapped the man on his skinny shoulder. 'Two little girls, eh? You are a man truly blessed. And, I'm sure you have to agree, this here vehicle could only add to those blessings.'

Mr Roberts looked warily over his shoulder. They might have been standing well away from the street light, in a rain-slicked, deserted back-street in Hoxton, but a man in his position, a council officer, could not be too

169

careful. Everyone in the town hall knew that everyone else was on the make, ready to take a bung or a backhander for all sorts of little favours, it was common knowledge, but proving it was another matter and there was no point in handing it to them on a plate.

He licked his lips anxiously, his wet tongue flicking around his narrow mouth in a curiously obscene display of intimate bright-pink flesh. He knew what he had to ask next, but how to phrase it?

'What sort of cost would that entail then, Mr Martin? Buying a fine motor vehicle such as this? Probably out of my sort of price range, I shouldn't wonder. But who knows, eh? Trouble is, a chap like me might have excellent job security and a fine pension plan – a very fine pension plan, in fact – but I'm afraid the actual wages are a very different matter.'

Ted flashed him one of his specials, a real winner of a smile that made the sides of his eyes crinkle as though he really meant it. 'Look here, Mr Roberts, I am going to sell this motor, because I am now fortunate enough to own an MG.'

Mr Roberts cooed in appreciation at such bounty.

'And you know me from our previous dealings,' Ted went on. 'I like to spread me good fortune about a bit.'

Mr Roberts was practically wetting himself at the thought that he might soon be driving around in a Talbot! It would take a bit of explaining to his colleagues, of course, but maybe he could invent an aged uncle. Of Ellen's, of course, not of his. He would be called Bernard, Uncle Bernard, and he would have left the Talbot to them in his will. Perfect!

Mr Roberts couldn't resist a little smirk at his own guileful inventiveness.

'Spread your good fortune, Mr Martin? So how would that relate to this instance, then?'

'Well, Mr Roberts, let's see.' Ted clapped the man matily around the shoulder. 'You know the old saying, you scratch my back . . .'

'I do indeed.' Here it comes, thought Roberts, just about able to stop himself from drooling.

'Now, I have this friend, a young lady. Tragic story, Mr Roberts. Her fiancé, the father of her little kiddie, her only child I might add, was killed in the most terrible accident. Just two weeks before the wedding. In the RAF he was. Testing one o' them new secret bombing planes. You know, the ones what're gonna keep us all safe so we never have to have another world war again.' Ted took off his hat to show respect for the non-existent hero, shaking his head in sadness at such misfortune. 'I don't have to explain to a man such as yourself, Mr Roberts, that it was all kept very hush-hush.' Ted tapped his index finger on the side of his nose. 'Walls have ears, as they say.'

Roberts arranged his face into a suitably sombre expression. 'They have indeed.'

'Well,' Ted wrapped his arm round Roberts's shoulders, 'what I was wondering like, was how you'd be disposed to finding the little lady, this good friend of my family's, some sort of a place to live? She wouldn't be expecting no Butlin's holiday camp, just something nice. So's I can visit her privately, to offer me sympathy without anyone knowing what a charitable man I am.'

Ted winked and dangled the car key tantalisingly in front of Roberts's eyes, twirling it between his fingers so that it glittered and flashed in the light from the street lamp. 'And without getting no bugs while I'm there. If you catch me drift.'

Ginny unknotted her headscarf, stuffed it in her pocket

171

and threw her coat across the end of the banister. 'It's only me, Nell,' she called.

'Mum ain't in.'

Ginny stood in the kitchen doorway, her eyebrows raised in surprise. 'I didn't expect to see you here.'

'No?' Ted flipped the *Evening News* shut and tossed it to one side. 'Who was you expecting then? The milkman? The landlord? The coalman?'

'Leave off, Ted.' Ginny heaved her bag on to the draining board and began unpacking the shopping. 'Where's Nelly got to, then?'

'She went round Dilys's.'

Ginny twisted round to look at him, a loaf still in her hand. He was leaning back easily in his chair, with his hands linked across his firm, muscled stomach, staring at her.

She couldn't deny it, he could still make the blood thump in her ears. He was a good-looking man all right. In fact, at getting on for thirty years old Ted Martin was more handsome than ever. If she didn't know him better, she might almost be tempted to believe that he would still change . . .

With a quick swallow and a little shake of her head to clear her mind, Ginny said hurriedly, 'No, I don't think she is. There was no lights on across the street when I come along just now. And you know Dilys, she always turns 'em on full pelt, even at this time of evening.'

Ted yawned loudly, leaned forward and rested his elbows on the table. 'Dilys ain't over the road no more.'

'How d'you mean?'

'Her and the little 'un have been given a prefab. Down Stepney. The bloke come round to tell her today.'

'A prefab?'

'You ain't gonna start that bleed'n' parrot lark, are you?'

'But—'

'Now I'm here, I might as well have a bit of something for me tea. What we got then?'

Ginny turned back to the shopping bags and carried on the unpacking. 'I've got some corned beef. I was gonna make a hash.' Her voice was flat, dull with shock.

Ted opened up the paper again. 'That'll do.'

Ginny was no longer listening to him. All she could think was that Susan, her lovely little Susan, was no longer just across the street waiting with chubby, outstretched arms for Ginny to lift her high into the air and to cover her soft baby face with kisses.

What was wrong with her; what had she done that was so bad that meant every bit of happiness, every dream she ever had, was always snatched away from her?

Her family. Her hopes for her marriage to Ted. Then Pearl. Now Susan . . . How much more could she take?

It was a golden autumn evening and Ted was enjoying himself. He had the slanting rays of the last of the sun warming his back; he was being admired; and he was lapping up every single bit of attention, every envious or appreciative glance, as he drove along the busy streets with the top of his MG rolled back, showing him and his motor off in all their handsome glory.

Ted especially relished the attention from the girls, of course, many of whom seemed prepared to do everything short of throwing themselves in front of his wheels for the chance of a ride with a man like him in a car like his.

At first, however, the car hadn't proved to be such an asset. In fact, it had been a bloody millstone and Ted had seriously considered getting rid of it.

First there was the law. He had had no more trouble

from the plain-clothes mob – Saunders had obviously moved on to making someone else's life a misery and had called off his grasses – but every time Ted drove past a uniformed copper, anywhere around his usual manor, they were on him like a ton of bricks. How could he afford such a vehicle, him with no apparent means of support? They had always ignored the Talbot, but the flashy lines of the MG just seemed to get to them for some reason. But, in the end, coppers were only human and were as keen on getting their hands on a bit of steak and a few luxuries for the old woman as anyone else. And after a few weeks he had given a little sweetener to just about every Old Bill from Plaistow to the Aldgate pump. That was one problem off his back.

But then there was Dilys. Ted had just about had enough of her. Every time he went round to the prefab she wanted to go out in the car with him and would lead off alarming if he dared refuse her. If it wasn't for Susan – who, he didn't know why but he couldn't help it, had really got under his skin – he wouldn't have gone within a mile of Dilys and her bloody prefab. He wished he'd never set eyes on the silly tart.

He was on his way to Dilys's now and was dreading her starting again. He had almost not bothered, but someone he'd done a deal with the night before had quite unexpectedly presented him with the prettiest china doll he had ever seen. The bloke had meant it as a gift for Ted's wife, a little extra to thank him for his 'custom'. It was the sort of thing that birds liked to sit on their beds as a decoration, he had said. But the moment Ted had seen it he knew he had to give it to his little Susan. He could just imagine the expression on her face when she saw the dolly, almost as tall as her; and with its pretty dress and lacy bonnet she'd go mad for it.

He was just turning off the Mile End Road and into

Stepney Green when a particularly shapely backside wiggling along in the same direction caught his eye. The girl was balanced on such high heels and her dress was so tight that she could just about walk.

He slowed down to a crawl and drove along behind her, waiting for her to realise she was being followed and to turn round so he could see what sort of a boat went with such an appealing chassis. If he approved, he'd give her the full treatment: the smile, the chat, the whole bit. He could always take the dolly round another day.

It didn't take long for the woman to cotton on. She stopped, paused and slowly swivelled round.

As she did so, Ted eased on his brake.

At the moment their eyes met it would have been difficult to guess who was the most surprised.

'Lilly!'

'Ted!'

Ted was out of the car in a flash and grasping her arm. 'It is you, ain't it, you little whore?'

'Let go of me.' Lilly tried to pull away from him, but Ted was much stronger than her and had the advantage of not being balanced on top of a pair of almost four-inch heels.

'D'you know what you did to me?'

'Nothing. I ain't done nothing.'

'Nothing?' Ted's fingers pinched into the soft flesh inside her upper arm. 'Is that what you call it? That arsehole Saunders tells two of his bastards to give me a good hiding. They beat me black and blue and leave me to fucking freeze to death. But you reckon it's nothing?'

Lilly didn't even try to hide the contempt she felt. '*You* got beaten black and blue? Poor you.'

'Don't you get lippy with me, you filthy little trollop.'

'I ain't scared o' you, Ted Martin. Mr Saunders is looking after me.'

'Well you should be scared, darling. 'Cos d'you know what, because of you grassing me to that shit I had to shift me business interests away from that bastard's turf – *my* turf I should say – and I ain't very happy about it.'

'Ain't you? Aw, poor little baby.' Lilly stuck her chin defiantly in the air. She could feel her blood pumping round her body as though she'd run all the way to the West End and back, but she knew she had to try and keep some sort of control of the situation. No one was going to stop and help her if Ted started, not in an area like this where respectable families going about their business looked down on the likes of her. Even though some of the husbands were probably amongst her customers, if one of her sort got a whacking, they'd all look the other way or come over all moral and say it was what they deserved. If only she hadn't promised to come and get Marge on the way to work this would never have happened. The lazy cow would just have to get herself up and ready for the club in future.

Ted pushed his face close to hers. 'You ain't learned to shut that smart mouth of yours then?'

'Let go of me, Ted. 'Cos if you even touch me, I swear—'

He shook his head in disbelief. 'You really ain't got it, have you?'

'Got what?'

He dragged her across the pavement and threw her roughly into the car. She landed awkwardly and knocked the china doll that had been propped on the passenger seat crashing to the floor.

'You stupid bitch!' he breathed. 'Now you've really got me upset.'

*

'Hun at three o'clock!'

Young Tom Copley, a scrawny, scabby-kneed boy, with thick-lensed National Health glasses wound tightly round his ears, held both arms out wide, as he flew around the bomb-site near his house in Wapping with his best pal, Charlie Tillotson. Every shot they fired, at any German fool enough to dare invade their air space, hit home with deadly accuracy. They were the heroes of the RAF. The fad with the Olympics already forgotten, the boys, just like their comic-book favourites, had returned to their all-absorbing passion of Playing War.

'Nnnnneeeeowwww!' Tom whined down his nose as he swerved in a wide ark to confront the enemy.

Charlie, his plane imitation momentarily forgotten, pulled the pin on an invisible hand grenade and lobbed it into a German dug-out. 'Cop that, Fritzy!' he yelled, throwing himself to the ground and covering his head to protect himself from the explosion.

'Here, Charlie,' Tom called, 'come and have a look at this.' Tom held up the remains of a china doll and waved it in the air like a trophy. 'It ain't even broken or nothing. Well, not much.'

Charlie scrambled over the rubble-strewn remains of what had once been Ethel Briggs's outside lavatory to reach his friend. 'Show us here, Tom.'

'The arm's a bit cracked and one of its legs has come off, but I reckon we could fix it.'

Charlie raised his eyebrows in astonishment. 'What'd we wanna fix a doll for?'

Tom rolled his eyes and tutted at his mate's stupidity. 'So's we can sell it or something.'

'Right! Here, let's look for more treasure.'

'No,' Tom said authoritatively, 'there won't be nothing else. We've gone over this debris hundreds of times and never found it before. Someone must have dumped it last night.'

Charlie looked disappointed. 'I don't reckon you could mend it anyway.' He sulked. 'Look at the state of its hair.' Suddenly his expression changed. 'Tell you what'd be good,' he beamed, 'let's go and throw it in the river, see if it floats.'

Tom grinned back at his friend and, as if a starting pistol had just been fired, they both began running full pelt towards the lighterman's steps that led down to the Thames.

Little did the boys realise how fortunate they were not to have searched any further, or they might have found something that would have haunted them for ever: part of the left arm and the right foot of poor dead Lilly.

The rest of her, unrecognisable from the beating she had taken, was scattered about the bomb-sites of London like so much unwanted rubbish.

Book Two

Chapter 9

May 1951

'All right, Gin?' Micky Chivers called, as he closed the street door of number 11 firmly behind him.

Ginny, parking her bags on the step of number 18, looked over her shoulder and called back across the street, 'Yeah. Fine. You all right, Mick?'

Micky checked that the door was shut, stuck his hands deep into his pockets and wandered over to her, his shoulders stooped in a self-deprecating slump. Like plenty of other lads in the neighbourhood, Micky had fancied Ginny since he had been tall enough – just – to peer surreptitiously down the front of her blouse. She was a fair bit older than him of course, and she certainly wasn't like the strong-minded sort of girls he usually went for – in fact she was probably too quiet for her own good – but she was a kind, smashing-looking bird and she definitely deserved a whole lot better than the deal she got from being married to Ted Martin.

Micky had often talked to Sid about the pair of them getting hold of the no-good bastard and sorting him out once and for all, and on a couple of occasions – soon after their mum's funeral being one Micky particularly remembered – his brother had very nearly agreed. But then Sid had, as usual, calmed down and made Micky see sense, stressing what their mother had always taught them: it wasn't right to go interfering in other people's business, not unless they asked for your help and especially when it was your own sister's best mate who was involved. But with Micky's temperament, it wasn't always easy for him to bite his tongue.

'So you're doing all right then, Gin?' he said with a lift of his chin.

'Yeah, not so bad, Mick.' She shrugged. 'You know.'

Micky stood next to her, leaning back against the sooty brick wall trying to look casual. He folded his arms and crossed one leg in front of the other. 'I ain't seen much of your Ted lately. Been busy, has he?'

'Yeah. He's been out and about all over the place.' She dipped her chin, hoping to conceal her flaming red cheeks. 'You know what he's like.'

'I know.'

'How's that brother of your'n getting on with his new girlfriend then?' she asked, hurriedly changing the subject.

'Dunno, Gin. Ain't seen much of him neither. As a matter of fact I don't seem to see much of no one lately. Dad's always down the Albert, or with his pals – he ain't really got over Mum yet. I don't suppose he ever will.' He hesitated, staring down at his boots. 'Nothing's really been the same indoors since . . . You know.'

'I know.' Ginny smiled ruefully as she echoed Micky's words. 'We're a right pair o' Billy-No-mates, ain't we?'

Micky nodded in superficially amused agreement. He had plenty of mates, but Ginny, she didn't seem to have anyone except Dilys, and *she* was as selfish as they come. If only he could find the words; this could be a real opportunity. Ginny might have been in her late twenties – probably even getting on for thirty if he was honest – but she was still a terrific looker, and here she was: lonely, obviously fed up and, he would lay money on it, at a loose end on a Friday night. He liked the girl he was seeing at the minute – a feisty little redhead from down the market, just his cup of tea – but surely it wouldn't hurt to put her off for just this once . . .

'So you ain't seen Dilys neither, then?' she said, interrupting his thoughts. She ran her fingers through her mop of dark-blonde curls in an easy, yet unconsciously disturbing gesture that had Micky squirming.

'No,' was all he managed.

'I'll have to try popping round the prefab again,' she said, bending down to pick up her bags in a movement that allowed him one of the tantalising glimpses down her blouse. 'I ain't seen her for nearly a fortnight and I've got some lovely little bits I bought down the Roman for Susan and all. If I don't get the chance to give them to her soon, she'll have grown out of them.'

'I've been meaning to go round to see the little 'un myself,' Micky said in a sudden moment of inspiration. 'It ain't always easy though, what with work and that. But tell you what, I could go with you now if you like. I was only on me way to have a few jars with some of the lads from down Eric Street,' he lied. 'I'm sure they won't miss me.'

Ginny heaved the shopping further up her arm and sighed the sigh of a woman whose time was not her own. 'That'd have been smashing, Mick, but if I don't get indoors and do you-know-who's tea, there'll be murders. And I've got a few jobs to do an' all. I dunno when I could get away.'

'I heard that!' came a gruff holler from the other side of the door of number 18. 'You leave me in here starving to bloody death, while you're out there sodding gabbing about going to see your mates. What're things coming to in this house, eh? You tell me that.'

Ginny rolled her eyes. 'All right, Nell, I'm coming.'

She flashed Micky a radiant smile that had his hopes rising and his toes curling. 'I'll have to go, Mick. Even though the old trout knows I've queued up all me bloody dinner hour to get her tea for her, she still ain't grateful.' She chuckled wearily. 'But what's a girl to do, eh? If I don't look after her, who will?'

Micky shook his head in bemused admiration. 'You put up with too much I reckon, Gin.'

She shrugged. 'Not really, I just like a quiet life. Look, I'm gonna try and nip round Dilys's later on, when I've finished seeing to Nellie and that. I dunno when that'll be. But give her and Susan my love, will you, Mick? And tell them I'll be round later.'

'Look, Gin, come to think of it, I'd better not go now. It's my mates, see. They'll be expecting me, won't they?'

'You go and enjoy yourself, Mick. Go on.' She leaned forward and gave him a conspiratorial wink. 'But you know, I reckon even I deserve a bit of time off for good behaviour. So maybe you can be me gallant escort round there some other time, eh?'

Micky grinned at her like a fool. 'Yeah?'

She smiled and ruffled his hair as though he was still a little kid, completely unaware of the effect of her touch on him. 'It's a date.'

Levering himself away from the wall, Micky strode along Bailey Street towards Grove Road, whistling away as if he'd just won the coconut.

'Dilys?' Ginny shielded her eyes with her hand and peered through the prefab window, then she stretched across and rapped hard on the door frame with her knuckles.

She knew that nine o'clock in the evening wasn't the usual time that Dilys would expect her to call, but surely not even Dilys, a woman who could sleep perched on a clothes-line without so much as a dolly peg to keep her attached, would be asleep at this time of night. And Ginny was sure she could hear the wireless playing.

After what felt like a good ten minutes of calling and knocking, the door suddenly opened.

It was Susan. She stood there in her grubby little night-dress, with her hair in tangles, clutching the teddy bear that Ginny had bought her last Christmas. She looked as though she had been crying. Was that the noise Ginny had heard?

'Hello, Auntie Gin,' she said, her tone unusually wary.

'Hello, babe!' Ginny bent down and scooped the four-year-old up in her arms, trying not to sound worried. 'Let me have a good look at my best girl.'

Susan's bottom lip quivered as she peered at Ginny through tear-dampened lashes. 'Mummy said I wasn't to open the door while she was out. I didn't know what to do.'

Ginny frowned. 'Mummy's out?'

Before Susan had the chance to explain, Ginny felt someone poke her hard on the shoulder. She spun round, expecting to see Dilys standing there, holding a pint of milk she'd gone and borrowed from a neighbour, or maybe a packet of fags from the pub up by Stepney Green station, but instead she saw a stern-looking woman in her forties dressed in the housewife's uniform of cross-over apron and cotton headscarf tightly knotted into a turban.

'I've seen you round here before,' the woman said sharply. 'Friend of her'n, are you?'

Ginny simulated a smile for the hatchet-faced woman. 'I'm sorry,' she said politely, hugging Susan to her shoulder, 'do I know you?'

'I'm her neighbour, ain't I.' The woman said the word 'her' as though it were an insult of the worst kind. 'I'm Milly Barrington. She might have mentioned me.'

'No. I don't think so.'

'In my day women cared for their kiddies. They didn't only give 'em a wash when they was expecting visitors. And they certainly didn't go gallivanting around clubs in cocktail frocks every night of the bloody week.'

'Look here, Mrs Ba—' Ginny tried to interject, but the woman was in full flight.

'And all that old toffee about her old man copping it out East in the war.' She snorted disdainfully. 'I ain't never heard so much old fanny in all my life. She ain't never even had no old man, if you ask me. I know a trollop when I see one. And I know a married man when I see one an' all.'

She flashed a look over her shoulder as though checking for eavesdroppers, then nodded knowingly at Ginny, narrowing her eyes for emphasis. 'There's this one feller what comes round here at all sorts of funny hours. I've seen him. And I know his sort and all, believe you me. Dark-haired, really good-looking type of a bloke he is. Always got nice ironed shirts – that's a sure sign they're married. And drives a right flashy car an' all. If I wasn't a decent sort of a woman, I'm telling you, I'd . . .'

The woman was still droning on and on but Ginny was no longer listening. A sensation of sickness had flooded her throat. Dark-haired, she'd said. Good-looking. Flash car. No. She'd been through all this in her mind a hundred times before. It was just jealousy making her think the worst. It had to be. Ted not being around most of the time and her having to try to make ends meet and putting up with Nelly, it had driven her to thinking all sorts of crazy things. After all, there must be plenty of good-looking blokes with flashy cars. Of course it wasn't him. But if she didn't pull herself together she'd end up going round the bloody bend and winding up in Banstead.

'Look, Mrs Barrington,' Ginny broke abruptly into the woman's monologue, 'I dunno why you think any of this is your business, but I'm here to look after Susan now, so if you don't mind I'll take her inside and get her into bed.'

With that, Ginny stepped inside the prefab, with Susan held tightly against her, and shut the door firmly in Milly Barrington's flabbergasted face.

Ginny smoothed the eiderdown under Susan's chin, kissed the sleeping child gently on the forehead and tiptoed from the bedroom.

By the time she had moved the few feet along the hall and into the front room, she was trembling with rage. If Dilys had been there, she would happily have throttled her with her bare hands. Whatever had got into her, leaving Susan alone like that? And in such a state. The poor little love was filthy.

After Ginny had washed and changed her, it had taken her almost two hours to reassure her that she wasn't going to be abandoned again.

But from what she had gathered from Dilys's big-mouthed, nosy parker of a neighbour, it was no wonder she was nervous – it obviously wasn't the first time she had been shut in the prefab all alone with nothing but her teddy for company and a warning not to answer the door. Dilys was lucky no one had called the welfare people out.

Why hadn't she asked her to sit with Susan? She knew Ginny was always only too pleased to spend time with her – well, whenever she could get away she was. But then again, if that Barrington woman was telling the truth, it sounded as though Dilys was up to all sorts and probably wanted to keep her gallivanting to herself.

Guilt and anger rose up in Ginny's throat until it nearly choked her; she thought of herself back in Bailey Street, pandering to Nellie just so she could have a bit of peace and quiet from her moaning, while all the time little Susan was here, huddled up in her bed, alone and terrified. She'd have to try and find a way to see her more; Nellie would just have to lump it.

Ginny felt the tears prick her eyes. If it wasn't for her, Susan probably wouldn't know what being loved was all about.

She flopped down on to one of the burgundy uncut-moquette armchairs that one of Dilys's mysterious 'friends' had come up with – part of a three-piece suite that made Ginny's furniture look as shabby and drab as the gear they'd made do with down in the air-raid shelters – lit herself a cigarette and sat smoking in the darkness, waiting for Dilys to come home.

She stifled a yawn and reached, yet again, for her cigarettes.

At least it was a Friday night and she wouldn't have to get up for work in the morning, she thought to herself, as she watched the shadows of people walking home from the local pubs flickering past the windows. It must be chucking-out time, but there was still no sign of bloody Dilys. Where the hell was she? She was going to give her a piece of her mind when she eventually decided to show her face. Not that she'd take any notice.

Dilys never took notice of anyone; even when they'd been kids at school she'd always got her own way, and whenever she'd caused trouble it was always someone else who got blamed by the teacher. Maybe if Dilys had been brought up in number 18 Nellie would have been a match for her . . .

Nellie. Going home to face her was another bloody nightmare to look forward to. Despite the fact that Ginny now tried to ignore her as far as was humanly possible, the thought of the ear-bashing she knew she had to look forward to when she eventually got back to Bailey Street made her groan out loud. And if Ted had decided to come home for once she'd really be in for it.

From the look of things, she wouldn't be getting back there this side of midnight. That was if Dilys actually condescended to come home at all.

Ginny was shocked out of her musings by what sounded like someone trying to break in. She was immediately on the alert, her protective instincts towards Susan making her grab the poker from the companion set and stand there poised, ready to strike any intruder fool enough to try and invade the home of the child she was there to protect.

The tautness in Ginny's body relaxed, and she let out a relieved sigh, as she recognised the voice cursing the stupidity of the street doorkey and the even stupider lock.

Ginny made a dash for the hall to put a stop to all the noise before it woke Susan. 'Dilys!' Ginny hissed through the letter-box. 'That *is* you?'

'Who the fuck d'you think it is?' Dilys hissed back. 'Sodding Lady Docker?'

As Ginny straightened up she winced; while Dilys might never have had what could be called a dainty mouth, her language lately would have made a sailor blush.

There was more fumbling and rattling.

'Here, Ginny,' Dilys said, more loudly this time. 'What

you doing round here this time of night? And why ain't you got the poxy light on? I can't see a bastard—'

Ginny jumped clear as the door flew back on its hinges, the lights suddenly blazed and Dilys fell into the hall at her feet.

The combined stench of booze, stale cigarette smoke and too much expensive French perfume was stifling.

Ginny had planned to have a go at Dilys, to demand to know exactly what she thought she was up to, but she decided that could wait until later; for now, the best course of action was to humour her. Much as she wanted to bring up the subject of Susan being left alone, the last thing she wanted was for Dilys to start hollering and hooting – she had a voice on her like a foghorn in a peasouper at the best of times, never mind when she was half cut. And Susan had already had more than enough upset for one day without hearing her mother's drunken screeching.

'Your neighbour said you'd had to pop out,' Ginny said, following Dilys as she staggered her faltering way into the sitting-room.

'Neighbour?' asked Dilys, clinging to the sideboard for support as she twisted round to confront Ginny through puffy, red-rimmed eyes. 'What sodding neighbour?'

'Milly Barrington.'

'Her, the nosy bastard.' There was real venom in Dilys's voice. 'If she didn't have a face like the back of a trolleybus maybe she'd have a bit of a life of her own and stop sticking her oar in where it's not wanted.'

Dilys's attention, never having much in the way of a span at the best of times, wandered from her neighbour to the more immediate, and therefore more graspable, question of Ginny. 'Did I ask you round or something?' she asked, dropping down on to the sofa.

Ginny shook her head sheepishly and perched herself

on the edge of one of the armchairs. 'No . . .' she said slowly. 'Not exactly. See, I was just . . .'

This was ridiculous. Dilys always did this to her: *she* wasn't the one who was in the wrong, yet here she was, ready to apologise. Well, she was damned if she was going to, not this time.

'Look, Dilys, I think you've gotta start thinking about other people.' She nearly said 'thinking about Susan' but immediately thought better of it; the point of this wasn't to provoke a row. 'See, while *you* might be all right – and I'm pleased for you that you are – you probably haven't noticed, but things haven't been exactly easy for most of the rest of us.'

Dilys didn't appear to be getting the point at all, so Ginny decided to elaborate – but still without actually mentioning her worries about Susan being left alone and her fears that she was a little girl growing up without knowing a mother's love.

'Out there,' Ginny began cautiously, waving vaguely towards the window, as she stalled for time, trying to think out what she should be saying. 'In the real world like.'

Dilys nodded towards Ginny's cigarettes and wordlessly held out her hand.

Ginny took one for herself then threw the packet and her box of matches into Dilys's lap.

Dilys lit one and settled back on the sofa to study the smoke as she blew it down her nostrils.

'You see, Dil, the thing is, there's a lot of problems for everyone at the minute. What with the meat ration being cut again. And all the shortages and everything. And the terrible weather we had all winter, and the price of coal and coke. I mean, blimey, it's enough to get anyone down. And that's without all this stuff you hear on the wireless about what's going on with this Korea lark. I mean, that's enough to scare the pants off you, innit? Especially with these bombs they've got now. So it's obvious we all need a bit of fun.'

'That it? You finished?' Dilys picked a strand of tobacco from her lip, examined it, then flicked it on to the half-moon-shaped hearthrug.

'I suppose so.'

'Well, Ginny,' she said, with a loud yawn, 'I ain't got a sodding clue what you're on about, except that last bit, that bit about needing a bit of fun.' Resting her elbow on the arm of the sofa, she fluffed her fingers through her thick, dark, wavy hair and frowned from the effort of thinking straight. 'So why don't *you* shut your moaning gob, go out and have a few laughs and stop coming round here and giving me sodding earache?'

Ginny gulped. *Stop coming round here.* That's what she'd said. If Dilys had meant it, then she wouldn't be able to see Susan. And Dilys could be so pig-headed; once she'd made up her mind about something there was no shifting her. Ginny had to put it right before it was too late.

'You're right as usual, Dil,' she said, pasting on a smile. 'I always did take things too seriously. You always said so. Tell you what, I was thinking about going over the river, to see that Festival of Britain thing. Everyone's saying how good it is. Fancy coming?'

Dilys opened her eyes wide and puffed in astonishment. 'You trying to have a laugh? No thanks. I've got better things to do with me time than hanging around poxy concert halls.'

'But there's a lot more to see than that. There's—'

'You ain't got a clue, Gin.' She belched loudly. 'You understand nothing. My feller likes me always to be here.' She stabbed her finger towards the floor. 'Ready and waiting. Available like. And I ain't gonna go upsetting a bloke what keeps me so nice, now am I? I mean, look at this place. It's a little palace.' She took in the messy, but well-furnished room, with a sweep of her arm. 'So if he wants to go out, I'm here, all done up, ready to hook my arm through his and make him proud of me.'

Ginny leapt in: 'You know I'll always come round to mind the little 'un, don't you, Dil? I know how hard it must be, to be on your own with a kiddie.'

Dilys curled her lip in an unattractive snarl. 'Aw yeah? And how would you know what it's like to have a kid? You threw away your chance of being a mother. Round Jeannie Thompson's. Remember?'

Ginny lowered her chin. She took a deep breath to swallow away the pain, then said in a low monotone. 'I could take Susan to the Festival if you like. I bet she'd love the Pleasure Gardens.'

Dilys didn't answer, instead she rose shakily to her feet and stumbled across the room, her tight dress and her unsteady gait accentuating her sensuous curves. 'Fancy a drink? I've got a few bottles in the kitchen.'

Biting back what she wanted to say, Ginny said quietly, 'Just a small one. Ta.'

Dilys paused in the doorway and twisted round to face Ginny. 'Me boyfriend gets the booze for me,' she said, then added with a flash of her eyebrows and her voice heavy with innuendo, 'he gets me all sorts.'

She wobbled out of the room, intending to go to the kitchen but somehow, losing her train of thought, she wound up in the lavatory.

She pulled down her expensive imported silk knickers and sat down on the wooden seat – the novelty of having a warm, indoor, fully-plumbed-in bathroom forgotten already – and thought about Ginny's offer to look after Susan while she went out.

As far as Dilys was concerned, the more chances she had to be shot of the demanding little madam, the better; she was always wanting something. A drink, or food, or clean clothes. It drove Dilys to distraction. She was four and a half years old and was still as much of a nuisance as she'd been when she was a baby. But, despite her drunken state, Dilys could still focus on why she had to resist the temptation of having someone looking after the kid for her: Susan was getting older, she was seeing things. Noticing things. Asking questions. Dilys couldn't risk her blowing the gaff. She'd already had to threaten her not to open her whining gob to Ted about being left at home by herself, and to say that nice Auntie Milly was coming round to sit with her. What he'd have to say if he knew Susan was alone, or worse still, that she was being left alone with Ginny, Dilys could only imagine. He'd warned her enough times: if Ginny was there, Dilys had to be there too, to mind what the kid said, because he'd told her, if Susan ever let on to Ginny about him always being round at the prefab . . .

Dilys pulled the chain and sighed. If it was up to her, she would have told Ginny about her and Ted *herself*, and let her stick that in her pipe and smoke it, but she knew Ted wouldn't have it. He still wanted her around the place to look after Nellie. And if she ever did find out about Ted and her, Dilys reckoned that even a right mug like Ginny would be off like a shot.

Because that's all she was, a bloody mug. Ted didn't even bother to give her any money any more, let alone presents like he used to. She worked her fingers to the bone in that shitty factory all day, then ran round after a mother-in-law who couldn't give a toss about her. Dilys wouldn't put up with that sort of bollocks from anyone. Well, from anyone but Ted. He was different, he was worth it. He treated her all right – most of the time – but she knew just how far she could go with him; and what she'd get if she started upsetting things.

She stood up, smoothed down her skirt, belched once again, then started giggling. Living in Bailey Street with Nellie wasn't exactly the life that that dozy mare Ginny had dreamed about when they were a pair of wide-eyed, open-mouthed kids sitting in the front row of the pictures. Some flipping Scarlett O'Hara she'd turned out to be!

In the sitting-room, Ginny heard the lavatory cistern flush and, a few minutes later, she watched Dilys return with two glasses and an almost full bottle of port.

'Well, what d'you think?' Ginny asked pleasantly.

'Eh?'

'About me taking Susan to the Festival.'

Dilys shook her head. 'No. I don't think so.'

The look of disappointment on Ginny's face actually made Dilys feel a bit sorry for her. Ginny really didn't have much of a life now, not if all she had to excite her was the thought of taking a kid out for the day.

And to think Dilys had once actually been jealous of her and her pretty blonde looks. Now she was as dingy and as badly dressed as all the other idiots who didn't know how to get hold of a bit of gear, or who had no one interested enough to buy it for them.

'Why don't you ask Nellie to go with you?' she asked, more out of pity than as a genuine suggestion, as she handed Ginny the glasses and poured them both a full measure of the dark ruby wine.

Ginny stared up at Dilys as though she'd gone stark raving mad. 'Have you taken leave of your senses, Dil? I'd rather go with old Florrie's bulldog, and you know how that bugger stinks.'

Dilys threw back her head and burst into loud, drunken laughter.

Despite her earlier anger, Ginny couldn't help joining in with her. In fact her whole body shook with great sobs and gulps of laughter. It was as though she was releasing herself from all her pain, from all her loneliness and from her unspoken fear that life was rapidly passing her by.

Dilys, her moment of guilt about her supposed friend's plight forgotten as suddenly as it had arrived, smirked as Ginny wiped the tears of almost hysterical laughter from her eyes.

She chucked Ginny roughly under the chin. 'We don't have to worry about you, do we, Gin? You can go on your own. I mean, you should be used to it by now.'

Ginny turned her head; she didn't want Dilys to see the now bitter tears spilling down her cheeks.

They were right, Ginny decided: the Festival of Britain, with its pavilions and halls sparkling and gleaming on the South Bank site, where, just a short time before, a mass of Blitz-blown rubble had stuck out like an ugly scar, was indeed a miracle of achievement. A genuine, there-it-was-in-front-of-your-face miracle. Dreams really did come true.

Despite her disappointment at not having been allowed to bring Susan, Ginny was completely caught up in the wonders surrounding her. She felt just like Dorothy in *The Wizard of Oz*; as though she had left behind the black-and-white existence of the past and had entered the future, a world of glorious Technicolor. Never before had she seen anything like it.

She walked around the Festival, amongst the bustling crowds, her every sense aroused. Even the jostling was part of the fun. She smiled at other people's happy chatter, joined in with their gasps of astonishment and echoed their exclamations of delight. She marvelled with them at the Dome of Discovery; shared their appreciative laughter every time she heard the same old joke that the amazing Skylon symbol hovering high in the air was 'like Britain, because it had no visible means of support'; and even felt a genuine, if surrogate, pleasure as she watched dewy-eyed couples dancing in the open air as though they were part of a film made in a far sunnier place than England.

Although she had no partner to dance with, Ginny didn't feel so alone any longer, she was part of something big and important. It felt like being a child caught up in the wonder of Christmas and towards the end of her day at the Festival she determined that somehow, no matter what it took, she would persuade Dilys to let her bring Susan along to see it all. She had to share this with her.

Then, as she was taking one last look at her favourite part of the whole Festival, she heard someone say something so shocking, it threatened to bring it all tumbling down around her. She felt as though she'd been smacked full in the face with a wet kipper.

There she was, in the pavilion designed to show 'contemporary living created by and for the British family of today' – contemporary! that was the style she wanted, what a wonderful word! – admiring the fantastic kitchen that made even Dilys's smart little prefab look dowdy, when she overheard the most astonishing conversation.

'Honestly, Shirley, will you just look at it,' sighed a tall, slim, elegant woman who, despite the warm May afternoon was wearing a luxuriously thick fur wrap draped around the shoulders of her beautifully cut emerald-green shantung two-piece costume. 'They should be ashamed of themselves, trying to fool people into thinking that these goods are something special.'

'Well, Leila,' her similarly elegant, though slightly less

glamorous, companion sighed back in an equally bored tone, 'I suppose some people aren't used to the finer things of life.'

Ginny was furious. She hated snobs at the best of times, but ones who didn't seem to care if they spoiled what had been the best day she could remember in years were enough to raise her usually mild temperament dangerously close to boiling point.

'Excuse me,' she said as politely as her dry mouth would allow, 'but I think you're wrong. I think this kitchen's lovely. It's all right for the likes of you. You can probably have anything you want, whenever you want it. But people like me dream about having something like this one day.'

The woman who had been referred to as Leila looked Ginny up and down with an unashamedly appraising eye, taking in every inch of her from her neatly polished but shabby shoes to her naturally pretty but home-trimmed hair. 'So could you, sweetie, if you knew how to go about it,' she said with an amused lift to her smoothly cultured voice.

'Leila!' her friend hissed. 'You're not going to start, are you?'

'Don't be such a fusspot, Shirley.' Leila smiled at Ginny, showing white, even teeth. 'The name's Harvey,' she said, extending her gloved hand. 'Leila Harvey. And this miserable person is my friend, Shirley Truman. Fancy a little drink?'

Ginny, completely taken aback to be asked to accompany such stylish, well-to-do women, didn't know how to reply.

'My treat, darling,' purred Leila, 'and you can tell me all about these dreams of yours.'

Ginny was mesmerised by the woman's easy, confident manner. She thought for another moment then, almost before she realised what she was doing, replied impulsively, 'I'd really love one. In fact, I'm gasping. And as for a sit-down, well, I could murder one of them an' all. Me feet are steaming like saveloys in an urn. But I dunno what the chances are.'

Shirley's eyes rolled at the vulgar turn of phrase, but Ginny didn't notice, she was too busy trying to control the urge to ask Leila where she got her handbag from – it was real crocodile, Ginny would have laid money on it, just like the ones Ted had brought home that time, beautifully made and reeking of quality. He had unloaded them up West in no time, probably to husbands or boyfriends of women just like Leila.

She could see the bags now, as Ted stuffed them into the gloryhole under the stairs in Bailey Street. He had offered Ginny one for herself, said she *deserved* a little treat, but she had refused, thinking it far too nice for the likes of her. She could even remember the day; it was less than a month after all her family had been buried and Ted was still being really nice to her, and somehow crocodile bags had always made her feel cared for, loved. It was a feeling she missed.

She suddenly realised that Leila was staring at her in expectation. Her cheeks flamed.

'I'm not quite with you, sweetie. Would you like to join us for a drink? Or not?' Leila asked.

'Yeah, but, you see,' Ginny stammered, stabbing her thumb over her shoulder in the direction of the exotic Regency Tea Pavilion, 'I tried getting in for a cuppa just now, before I started making me way home like, thought I could do with a bit of a reviver, but there was queues like you'd never believe.'

Leila turned to Shirley and grinned broadly. 'Isn't she a poppet!'

Twisting back to face Ginny, she flashed her expertly

199

made-up eyes. 'I meant a proper drink. For God's sake, it must be six o'clock soon, I feel like I've been here for absolutely hours. So. Time for cocktails, don't you think?'

Riding in the taxi back across the river with Leila and Shirley made Ginny think again about how it had once been with Ted. He had sometimes hailed taxis for them after they'd been out for the evening, had enjoyed splashing his money about. But that was a long time ago; a time when she hadn't had to fret constantly about making ends meet. She'd never experienced quite the style of these two of course, but she certainly hadn't had to worry about things in the way she did now.

Ginny's stomach lurched and her hand went to the run in her stocking, as the taxi drew to a halt outside an impressive-looking, white stucco hotel, hidden away at the end of a quiet Mayfair side-street.

'I've never been round here before,' whispered Ginny as they sat down at a highly polished table, the feet of which were sunk deep into the thick pile of a sumptuous dark-blue carpet. She wasn't sure why she was whispering but it seemed appropriate; maybe it was because the church in Limehouse where she and Ted had been married, and the picture palace in the Commercial Road, were the only similarly opulent places she had ever visited – and in those places you had to keep your voice down.

'Haven't you, sweetie?' said Leila, dropping her wrap carelessly over the back of her chair. 'I'm thinking about buying myself a little flat near here, actually. Security for my old age.'

Deliberately ignoring Shirley's desperate signals to keep quiet, Leila took a cigarette from her handbag and screwed it into what Ginny was sure was a real gold holder.

As Ginny watched, fascinated by the poise of her every movement, she was suddenly distracted by the appearance of a dark-suited man behind Shirley's chair.

'Good evening, mesdames,' the softly spoken man said, with a bob of his head. 'May I fetch you something?'

Conscious of how dowdy she must have looked compared with the other two, Ginny screwed herself down into her seat, trying to hide her threadbare skirt and tatty stockings under the table.

'Three champagne cocktails, Richard,' Leila said without even consulting the other two. She lifted her chin, treated him to a flap of her lashes and a dazzling smile, then turned her beam on Ginny. 'How about a little bite of something?'

Ginny was in shock at the thought of champagne cocktails. How could she think about food? But she had to say something, she couldn't just sit there like a dummy in a shop window. She was scared of how her voice was going to sound. Coughing loudly into her hand to fill the silence, she nodded vigorously and peered wide-eyed at her hostess through her fingers. 'Can I have some crisps?' she eventually managed to croak. 'If that's all right.'

Leila laughed delightedly and addressed the waiter without turning to face him. 'You can arrange some crisps for the lady, can't you, Richard?'

'Of course, madam.'

'Good. And some smoked-salmon sandwiches. Enough for three.'

For some reason, no matter how Ginny wrestled with the crisp packet, the blue twist of salt would not come out of the corner of the bag, but now she had started trying to salvage the damned thing she couldn't show herself up by giving in.

'Here, let me.'

Ginny watched, horrified, as Leila dipped her flawlessly manicured finger into the contaminating grease of the fried potatoes and hooked out the little blue twist for her.

Handing the crisps back to Ginny, she wiped her fingers delicately on a lace-trimmed handkerchief, took a sip from her drink and smiled. 'So, tell me, what do you do?' She half closed her eyes and regarded Ginny closely. 'Don't tell me. You stay at home and look after some man?'

'No. Well, yes, I do.' When he's there, she thought but didn't say. Despite his neglect and cruelty, Ginny still couldn't bring herself to be disloyal to Ted. 'But I work as well.'

Leila flashed an amused eyebrow at Shirley, as much as to say, you're not the only one, dear. Shirley frowned with disapproval and gave a barely perceptible shake of her head.

Leila smiled reassuringly at her companion, pushed the plate of untouched sandwiches towards her, then returned her attention to Ginny. 'Now what sort of work do you do, I wonder.'

'I work in a factory. On the assembly line.'

Shirley rolled her eyes in boredom, lifted her glass to her lips and knocked her cocktail back in a single hit. 'Fancy another?' she asked resignedly.

Leila nodded. 'Thank you. I don't mind if I do.'

While Shirley spoke to the waiter and silently drank her way through several refills, Leila concentrated on finding out more about Ginny Martin.

It took her less than half an hour, and a few little

snippets about herself thrown in by way of reward, to gain a pretty accurate picture of Ginny's life.

She studied Ginny's flushed cheeks as she drained yet another glass.

Ginny was feeling wonderful. 'So you come here all the time then,' she chirped. 'I can't imagine what that must be like.' She shook her head in wonder.

It was a big mistake; unused to drinking very much, and definitely unused to knocking back four champagne cocktails one after the other, Ginny came over quite giddy.

Holding on to the edge of the table she levered herself to her feet. 'I've just gotta go to the lav,' she explained.

Leila pointed to a door in the corner. 'Over there, sweetie.'

As Ginny made her way across the room, Shirley leaned across the table. 'For Christ's sake, Leila, she'll get us thrown out.'

Leila sighed theatrically and took her time preparing another cigarette before replying, 'Stop going on, Shirley.'

'But why're you doing this? I know you and how bored you get, and that you like to amuse yourself, but why her? Why risk it?'

'She reminds me of me a few years ago.'

'You?'

'I'm telling you. She's one of us. She wants something more than she's got and it's killing her. You can just smell it on her.'

'Don't be ridiculous. All she is, is a quiet little drudge working in some God-awful factory, with no past, no future, no nothing. Except some old hag of a mother-in-law to torture her.'

'You're wrong. I can spot it a mile off.' Leila blew a cloud of lavender smoke above Shirley's head and watched as it curled up towards the elaborately decorated plaster-work ceiling. 'And you know the governor's always ready to pay a bonus for introducing new girls, especially if they're as pretty as her. And if they've got a brain as well, then—'

'Brain? Her? All right, I grant you, she's got a decent sort of face, but—'

Leila's face grew dark. 'Not jealous of her because she's younger than you, are you, Shirley?'

'Young? From what she said, she's got to be in her late twenties.'

'I'm sure you're right. But even you have got to admit she doesn't look it. Her skin's perfect. And with that body I'd lay money she's never had a child. And, if she works on it, she's got that sophisticated look that the foreign punters really go for. And with those big eyes. Come on, be honest, what do you really think? Am I right?'

Before Shirley could reply, Leila hissed through her teeth, 'That's enough, Shirley, there's a good girl. She's coming back.'

As Ginny slipped back into her seat Leila was all smiles again. 'Everything all right?'

'Yeah, not half. I had a bit of a wash and now I'm smashing.' She shielded her mouth with her hand and confided, 'You should see that lav. I ain't never seen nothing like it, even in the films. Imagine having a place like that to use whenever you fancied.'

'You could have a nice place, Ginny. If you wanted it badly enough.' Leila flashed a look at Shirley, warning her to keep her mouth shut.

Ginny's face puckered into a shy smile. 'You mustn't laugh, but I have this dream when I've got this really lovely place, with this great big staircase.' She dropped her chin. 'You'll think I'm daft.'

'No we won't, will we, Shirley?'

'No,' said Shirley flatly.

'It's just like Scarlett's house: Tara, from—'

'*Gone With the Wind*,' Leila finished for her.

'That's right!'

Leila acknowledged Ginny's admiration with a little shrug. 'So, where do you live now?'

Ginny turned her head away. 'You won't have heard of it.'

'Don't be so sure.' Leila giggled girlishly for Ginny's benefit, as she peered with steely resolve at Shirley across the top of her glass.

'I come', Ginny said with slow deliberation, 'from a place called Bailey Street.'

'Near the Roman eh, darling?' Leila grinned. 'Know it well.'

The difference in Leila's accent – from West End to East End in a single sentence – had Ginny boggling. 'But the way you were talking about the kitchen back at the Festival. And the way you're dressed '

'I have to admit', Leila said, her accent slipping effortlessly back to her previously haughty tones, 'I was saying those things for effect.' She lowered her voice to a breathy whisper as she leaned closer to Ginny. 'Did you notice that posh old chap standing behind Shirley? The one with the RAF moustaches? The one who was pretending to look at the electric gadgets?'

Ginny thought for a moment, then nodded.

'Well, I knew different. I knew exactly what he was looking at. In fact, I thought he was going to explode, the way his eyes were bulging as he was clocking my tits!'

Ginny suppressed a gasp. She was going mad.

Leila draped herself back into her chair. 'But I did mean what I said back there at the Festival. There are better kitchens than that to be had. Much better. That stuff's meant for the plebs. I've been in places that'd make you cry they're so beautiful. And I intend to have a place just like them.' As she spoke, Leila's eyes shone. 'The place I've got now is already quite something, but when I get *my* Swedish kitchen put in the flat I'm going to buy, it's going to be hand-made. Custom-built. Exquisite. Just for me. And as for the way I'm dressed, well, it's exactly the same. You just have to know the right places. Good shops. Good dressmakers.' She paused for effect, smoothing her hands down her emerald-silk-covered thighs. 'And you need a bit of style and a right sort of shape to go with it, of course. That's how you interest the right sort of gentlemen.'

She looked at the tiny face of her gold watch, reached out and tapped Ginny playfully on the end of the nose, then picked up her bag. 'Come on, sweetie, let's find ourselves a taxi, and while we're driving you home, I'm going to tell you a story.'

'So that's it, that's all there is to tell.' Leila ducked her head to catch a fleeting glimpse through the taxi window of the tall, shadowy buildings of the London Hospital – the hospital that could have saved her mother; the hospital that had been just around the corner from the slum where her mother had died giving birth to her, because she couldn't afford the few shillings for the local handy-woman, never mind the three quid for the quack doctor who earned his gin money 'seeing to' the local working girls. That was a part of her story, like so many others, that no one would ever know.

'The top and the bottom of it, Ginny, is that I was poor once,' she went on, 'and now I'm not. And, believe me, not is better. Don't look so shocked. What's the difference between what we do and in you being nice to the coalman for a sack of nutty slack when your old man hasn't bothered to leave you any money to heat the house again?'

Ginny's head felt fuzzy with drink. She couldn't remember telling this woman anything about Ted. But she must have done. 'I'm not shocked—'

'No?' Shirley interjected.

'No. And whatever I said about Ted I never had to be nice to no coalman.'

'I'm not saying you did. But whatever you said about Ted was the truth, wasn't it?' Leila coaxed her. 'He's left you and his mother in the lurch.'

'Well, yeah, sort of. But I've never been with no one else. Never. Not even in the war.'

'Who said anything about "going" with anybody?' Leila, quick to recover the ground she'd nearly lost, squeezed Ginny's arm reassuringly. 'Silly girl. I was simply giving an example about keeping someone company.' She laughed brightly. 'You make it sound as though we're on the game!'

Ginny clambered out of the cab on the corner of Grove Road. She was sure that was where she was, because she could make out the lights and the outline of what definitely looked like Mile End station.

'You've got the address?' Leila called to her through the open window.

Ginny nodded dumbly and, by way of proof, waved the piece of paper that Leila had given her. As she did so, she wondered at the strange, yet magical, day she had spent, but also how on earth she was going to set about cooking Nellie's tea when she could barely see straight.

She was still waving feebly as the taxi pulled away from the kerb.

Shirley fell back into her seat in a heap; her lips pursed

as though she'd been sucking lemons. 'I thought you said she was one of us.'

'She will be,' said Leila, checking her face in her compact mirror. 'As soon as she puts on a bit of slap and a bit more colour in that hair of hers. Really blondes it up – platinum would look good with her eyes. And when she learns how to speak a bit more softly in front of the clients, of course. As though she's got a bit of class rather than being just another little tart on the make.'

Shirley sighed; she felt exhausted, definitely not ready for the night's work she had in front of her. Wrapping one silk-stockinged leg over the other, she eyed her ankles with despair. She was sure they were getting thicker by the day. It wasn't fair, she didn't feel a day older than when, as an *almost* innocent seventeen-year-old, she had found herself alone and hungry in Greek Street and had let a nice man buy her dinner. Yet here she was, what felt like barely two minutes later, with a head full of grey hair that had to be tinted every single week and a body that seemed determined to give out on her. And with bloody younger women muscling in on her patch. It was a bit of luck the clubs were so dingily lit, and that she had her few special talents, or she wouldn't have stood a chance.

Leila snapped her compact shut. 'When she turns up—'

'*If* she turns up,' Shirley snarled.

'When she turns up,' Leila repeated without a blink. 'I'll talk to her about her hair and make-up.'

'It's going to take a bit more than a bottle of Hiltone to get that one working,' Shirley spat nastily.

Leila, noticing the driver ogling her in his rear-view mirror, smiled seductively. 'Don't you be too sure,' she said. Then, deliberately dropping her compact, she bent down and whispered up to Shirley from the taxi floor, 'Play our cards right, girl, and this cab ride's for free.'

Chapter 10

Ginny stared at her reflection in the little mirror over the sink. It was a long time since she'd done more than swipe a quick stroke of lipstick across her mouth and she was worried that the mascara, powder and rouge she'd put on were a bit too much.

She let out a long, slow breath and glanced at the clock – five to nine. Damn! Well, it was too late to worry about make-up now, if she didn't leave soon she probably never would, and anyway, looking on the bright side, maybe her sooty eyes and peachy pink cheeks would take the attention away from the old-fashioned floral frock that, after a thorough search of her meagre wardrobe, was the best she could come up with.

With far more determination than she actually felt, Ginny twisted round and offered Nellie a bright, confident smile – anything to stop her mother-in-law asking any more of the awkward questions she'd been firing at her all day. 'So, Nell, like I said, as it's the first time I've done this late shift, I ain't sure what time I'll be back exactly.'

Nellie stared at Ginny through narrowed eyes. 'You're a bit done up, ain't you?'

'How d'you mean?'

'For the factory. You look more like you're going on the stage.'

Ginny gave a brittle, unconvincingly carefree laugh. 'I had to make a bit of effort, Nell, didn't I? I'll be working with all new girls and I don't wanna scare 'em.'

'And how come you're on this late shift all of a sudden? You never even mentioned it till this morning.'

Ginny's patience with Nellie's cross-examination was wearing very thin and her nerve was threatening to give out. 'I told you: lates pay a lot more than the day or evening shifts. So we'll have more money to spend on ourselves.'

'How much more?'

Ginny shrugged and puffed out her cheeks as she fished around for a likely answer. 'Awwwww . . .' she finally came up with, 'plenty, I reckon.' Another false laugh. 'Enough to buy us both fags and to take you down the Albert for a few, anyway.'

Nellie digested the information in silence.

'Well, I'll better be off, or I'll be getting the push on me first night. And that wouldn't do now, would it? So I'll see you later, Nell, and don't bother to waste the electric, leaving the light on for me.'

With that, Ginny bobbed her head and kissed Nellie's crêpey cheek, grabbed her bag from the table and made a dash for the street door before her nerve really did give out and she changed her mind.

Nellie listened for her to shut the door behind her. 'That's funny, you working nights,' she said to herself, as she rubbed her face free of every trace of her daughter-in-law's kiss. 'According to Florrie's girl, they don't let women work no later than the twilight shift at your place. And that don't start at ten; that's when it finishes.' She sniffed loudly. 'Never try and kid a kidder, you stupid little cow.'

When Ginny arrived at the address Leila had given her – a place in Frith Street, a busy thoroughfare in the heart of Soho, linking Shaftesbury Avenue with Soho Square itself – she was trembling. But she wasn't cold. She was

211

shaking from the ordeal of having walked along streets where she'd been propositioned by men in doorways, had been insulted by foul-mouthed women accusing her of intruding on their pitches and alarmed by wild-eyed, tangle-haired drunks thrusting filthy hands at her, begging for spare change.

She swallowed hard. Squinting in the dim light coming from the single red bulb glowing above her head, she read the hand-written 'Members Only' notice that was attached to the black-painted door with a rusty drawing-pin.

What on earth was she doing outside a place like this? She could have kicked herself. Even someone as naive as she was should have been aware that although the address was in the West End, it was also bang in the middle of the red-light district. A place as threatening and dangerous as any of the roughest of the dock-side neighbourhoods in the East End, places where Ginny would never have dreamed of going.

Leila had seemed so plausible when she described the club: that it was a place where tired and lonely businessmen, who wanted a quiet drink and a bit of pleasant company, could go after a hard day's work. Men who were prepared to pay good money for such a haven. Okay, Leila had admitted that some of the girls made private arrangements with the customers, but that was life, wasn't it? Ginny couldn't disagree with that; you found that sort of thing going on everywhere. But Leila had assured her that the club itself was all above board, a good place to earn a good wage for not doing very much. And, also according to Leila, Ginny wouldn't be doing very much at all, just carrying a tray of cigarettes around to the customers and maybe helping out with a bit of waitressing if things got busy.

Ginny covered her face with her hands. Had she really been *that* drunk?

No. What she had been was desperate. Desperate to have just a taste of the life that she had once had, when there had always been money in her purse and a meal on the table good enough to satisfy even Nellie's demanding appetite.

'If you're not going in, get out of me way, will you.' A tall, bosomy redhead, dressed in a Persian lamb swing coat that showed her high-heeled, sheer-black-stockinged legs right up to mid-knee, shoved Ginny unceremoniously to one side, pushed open the door and teetered into the dimly lit interior.

Ginny watched the woman as she paused half-way up the flight of stairs at the end of the hall and threw up her arms in what looked to Ginny like intense indignation.

Ginny was right.

'For Christ's sake,' she hollered over her shoulder, 'the minder don't come on for at least half an hour. If you're coming in, then come in. If not, then shut that bloody door. We don't want every tramp in the flaming street walking in and pissing on the carpet.'

With that, she pulled her collar huffily up to her throat and flounced up the rest of the stairs.

Ginny hesitated for barely a moment, took a deep breath and stepped inside. Even as she heard the door slam behind her, she wasn't sure what had made her do it – maybe the realisation that the redhead's coat probably cost more than Ginny managed to earn in six whole months of eye-straining tedium at the electrics factory. Or maybe because she knew that if she didn't at least try to make a better life for herself, she would more than likely go out of her mind with the worry of it all. She had to find a way to end the scrimping and scraping, the darning of stockings and the humiliation of queuing outside the butcher's, only to be able to afford the cheapest cuts when her turn finally came, while – she was sure of it – the neighbours gloated at her downfall. She was, after all, married to Ted Martin.

As Ginny reached the top of the stairs and stood in the doorway, looking at the barn-like, shabby room before her, its every dusty corner and grimy crevice picked out in the harsh overhead lights, she almost turned on her heel and fled.

When Leila had told her about working there, Ginny hadn't had a very clear picture of what she was expecting the club to be like, but she certainly hadn't even begun to imagine that it would look quite so depressing as this.

The run-down room was empty, apart from a man who was standing behind a shabby semicircular bar with his back to her. He appeared to be engaged in an unequal struggle with one of the drinks optics and was muttering angrily to himself.

Ginny coughed politely and the man turned round to face her.

The first thing that struck Ginny about him was that he was holding a whisky bottle in mid-air, as though he were a rather bored magician who hadn't been in the least surprised to have produced it from out of a top hat, and the second was that his eyebrows had been plucked into perfect Joan Crawford half-moons.

He looked her up and down, taking in every inch of her old-fashioned outfit with conspicuous distaste. 'Mmmm? Can I help you?' he asked in a camp, slightly northern lisp.

'I'm looking for Miss Harvey.'

He sucked in his cheeks and shook his head. 'Sorry, not with you, dearie.'

'Harvey?' she repeated. 'Leila Harvey?'

'Aw, Leila. You should have said.' He returned his attention to the bottle and the disobliging optic. 'She's not here.'

'But she told me to come tonight.'

He sighed wearily and jerked his head to one side without looking round. 'Ask that lot out the back.'

'Out the back' turned out to be a dressing-room of sorts. It was a cramped, not very clean space, with a single chipped sink in one corner, a selection of mismatched chairs and a couple of mirrors propped up on rickety tables, amongst piles of cosmetics, over-spilling ashtrays and cheap, thick china teacups.

Six women, dressed in a variety of eye-poppingly low-cut dresses, were fighting for elbow-room in front of the mirrors. They were primping and preening themselves with various articles of make-up, which, by the look of their astonishingly brightly painted faces, they had plucked at random with their eyes closed from the heaps on the tables.

'Hello,' Ginny ventured, her voice tiny. 'Does anyone knew where I can find Leila?'

'Who's asking?' the tall redhead wanted to know. She was sitting in a prime position right in front of one of the mirrors, plastering yet more Panchromatic on to her already deep-orange face.

'Ginny. Ginny Martin. Leila said I was to come here tonight. To work.'

Six pairs of eyes were turned on her.

'Aw yeah, the new cigarette girl.' The redhead sniffed inelegantly and rubbed at a lipstick smudge on her teeth with a nicotine-stained finger. 'I thought you'd be older from what Shirley said.'

Ginny ignored the Shirley remark. 'Cigarette girl.

That's right,' she said politely. 'Could you tell me who's in charge, please?'

'I don't think the governor's in tonight. Well, not till much later.'

'Could you tell me what to do then?'

The redhead rolled her eyes. 'You really are fresh off the boat, ain't you, darling?'

'If you could just—'

'Look, your costume's over there in the wardrobe,' she said, flicking a scarlet-painted finger-nail towards a curtain-covered recess by the sink. 'And the cigarette tray's kept behind the bar. Gloria's in charge when the governor isn't here. She'll give it to you and explain.'

'Gloria?' Ginny looked expectantly from face to face.

'Don't look at us, darling,' one of the women said, with an amused snigger. 'Gloria's the old queen out there behind the bar. The one who probably wants to scratch your eyes out 'cos you've got better legs than he has.'

The women laughed raucously as Ginny mumbled her thanks and backed hurriedly out of the room.

With the main lights dimmed and the pink-shaded table lamps glowing, the three-piece band playing soft, easy jazz tunes in the background, and the room crowded with customers and the six girls from the dressing-room – plus about another dozen who had turned up in a giggling waft of scent and cigarette smoke – Ginny felt strangely exhilarated. The club now seemed much more like the ones she had seen on the films. While it might not have had quite the sophistication of the place where Rita Hayworth had sung and danced and twirled her long satin glove provocatively above her head – while Glen Ford's eyes stood out on stalks, poor man – it was definitely much more like it.

And the work wasn't too bad either. All she had to do

was walk around the room with the tray round her neck, selling cigarettes, chocolates and fluffy dogs. It was almost like being an usherette at the pictures, selling cartons of Kia-ora and Lyons Maid lollies during the interval. Admittedly, her uniform was a bit briefer than the cinema's regulation overalls, in fact, there wasn't much more to it than a sparkly bathing costume with a frilly skating skirt attached, but it wasn't too bad. And the men didn't bother her much either, which was a relief.

They were more interested in the girls – the hostesses, as she had to learn to call them – who were sitting staring admiringly into the men's eyes, listening to them while they paid a fortune to drink cheap booze and for the girls to sip drinks that were actually plain tonic water, so they could keep their wits about them. In fact, the men barely looked up at Ginny as they handed her crisp, unfolded fivers for items off her goody tray to impress their chosen girl for the evening. Their chosen girl who, in a few hours' time, would return the ridiculously over-priced cigarettes, toys or chocolates to the tray, on the promise of earning herself an extra pound in her wage packet every time she did so.

She also had to deliver drinks from the bar to the tables when Gloria was too busy, or overwrought – which seemed to be most of the time – but Ginny didn't mind that either. He wasn't exactly friendly, but he fascinated her with his outrageously rude manner and his camp affectation as he nagged incessantly and minced about behind his bar complaining and sighing like Bette Davis on overtime.

But although the work wasn't that hard, it was tiring. Ginny wasn't used to wearing such high heels and the effort of smiling the whole time was making the muscles in her face ache; so she was more than glad when, at ten

217

past three the next morning, Gloria said it was time to pack up for the night.

She was surprised, however, when the redhead – who had been sitting wrapped around a man in one of the darker corners of the club all night – signalled to Ginny that she should go out the back with her.

'Come on. Let's stick our feet up for five minutes before you go,' said the redhead, plonking herself down in an ungainly sprawl across one of the chairs. She offered Ginny a cigarette.

Cautiously, Ginny took it – 'Ta' – but she didn't sit down. After the way they'd laughed at her earlier, she was a bit wary of what strings might be attached to this apparent overture of friendship.

'Come on,' the redhead coaxed her. 'Keep me company while I have a smoke. I hate being by myself. I've told lover boy out there that I had to go to the little girls' room.' She lit her own cigarette, then Ginny's. 'Silly bastards. They'll believe any old rubbish.' She patted the chair next to hers. 'Come on.'

'Me feet are aching a bit.' Ginny dropped down beside her, kicked off her shoes and rubbed her calves.

'There, that's better. Now, I'm Yvette.' She grinned saucily. 'Well, that's what I call meself. I daren't tell you me real handle. You'd never stop laughing.' She sucked in a lungful of smoke and exhaled slowly. 'What was your name again?'

'Ginny.'

'So what did you make of your first night then, Ginny?'

'Interesting.'

'Interesting!' Yvette laughed, not unkindly this time, but from genuine amusement. 'That's one way to describe it, I suppose.'

'Well,' Ginny said slightly defensively, 'it's just that there are so many different people out there. It's been a while since I've been out much, so, yeah, I do find it interesting. Just watching them. And it's been a while since I've seen anyone spending that sort of money an' all.'

'You just watch yourself,' Yvette warned her. 'Don't get carried away with all their flash acting. Some of them ain't got two bob to rub together. They're just spending money they should be using to pay their bills or to give their old woman for the housekeeping.'

Ginny frowned. 'What sort of people are they, then?'

Yvette waved her cigarette in the air. 'All sorts. Black marketeers. Genuine businessmen. Playboys even – well, sometimes. Servicemen. Posh blokes out slumming. Artistic sorts. You get a lot of them round here. Painters, writers, actors and that – they've never got a ha'penny to bless 'emselves with, but they're a good laugh if you ain't busy.'

Ginny smiled. 'See. I told you it was interesting.'

Yvette returned the smile. 'You seem a genuine sort of a girl, Ginny. Make sure you stay that way. Don't let none of this get to you.' She suddenly leaned forward and stubbed out her cigarette. 'Hark at me, I'm getting sentimental in me old age. But, seriously, there are one or two things you should know.'

'Yeah? Like what?'

'There's some hard men round these parts. Men who fight over every bit of turf. The men who run the betting, the protection and most of the girls out on the streets. Men who'd think nothing of smacking a good-looking sort like you into a pulp.'

Ginny hurriedly looked away for fear that Yvette would be able to see in her eyes that she knew exactly what she was talking about.

'They're the ones,' Yvette continued, seemingly not noticing Ginny's discomfort, 'who don't have to pay for anything when they come in here. We'll make sure you know who they are.'

The two women were sitting there, both locked into their private thoughts, when two of the other hostesses came barrelling into the dressing-room like children bursting out of the school gates at home time.

'I got a fair tip but I don't reckon Leila's gonna be very pleased,' squealed one of them, a black girl with a strange accent that was a cross between a South London drawl and a musical Caribbean lilt. 'He was off like a stuck pig when I told him we could go upstairs. Stupid sod. What's he come in here for if he don't wanna do nothing?'

She inhaled deeply on a hand-rolled cigarette, holding the smoke in her lungs until she sould stand it no longer. 'How about yours, Patty?' she asked in a gasp of expelled breath, handing the cigarette to her platinum-blonde companion. 'He on for it, is he?'

'Tell you the truth, Carmen,' Patty said in a low, guarded voice with a hint of Irish brogue just audible behind her flat London vowels. 'I don't think I fancy it. See, I reckon he's pissed himself. He stunk just like the bloody men's lav.'

Carmen went cross-eyed, stuck out her tongue and made a loud, gagging sound. 'How'd you get rid of him?'

'Told him I'd just got the curse.'

'Yeah, the curse of having to have it away with ugly bastards like him!'

They both burst into loud, uncontrolled laughter.

'Ginny,' said Yvette loudly enough to interrupt their hysterics. 'Let me introduce the comedy double act – Carmen and Patty. I'm always telling these two they should go on the stage.'

As if on cue, the girls linked arms and broke into

an impromptu routine of badly co-ordinated high kicks, until, with tears of laughter streaming down their faces, they collapsed on to a pile of coats that had been dumped in the corner of the room. 'But we can't dance!' Patty screeched.

'Shut your mouth, you,' giggled Carmen, shoving her friend in the ribs. 'I'm a lovely little mover.' She puckered her lips and blew Ginny a kiss. 'Pleased to meet you, Ginny love.'

'Likewise, I'm sure,' offered Patty in a mock-posh voice that had her and Carmen spluttering and snickering all over again.

'Much as I'd love to stay and enjoy the fun . . .' Yvette said with a resigned sigh, as she stood up and smoothed the wrinkles from her short sheath dress. 'Who's left out there?'

'Only one or two,' gasped Carmen, puffing from the exertion of propping herself up on her elbows. 'The others have either disappeared upstairs, or they've gone off for the night.'

'Ah well, no peace for the wicked, eh? I'd better get out there meself before my mark gets fed up and has it away on his toes.'

'That big feller with the moustache?' Patty asked, her nose wrinkling in distaste.

Yvette nodded gloomily. 'That's the one.'

Patty flapped her hand. 'Sit down for five more minutes, Yve, he won't know the difference. He didn't even know what time o' day it was by the look of him.'

Yvette didn't take much persuading; she dropped back on to her chair without a murmur of protest. 'You wanna stay away from these two, Ginny,' she said, throwing back her head and closing her eyes. 'They're bad influences. They could lead you astray.'

'Well I reckon it's smashing to see someone enjoying themselves so much,' Ginny said.

'See,' Carmen said, thumbing her nose at Yvette. 'She loves us.' Then, suddenly serious, she said, 'Anyway, it's Shirley she wants to stay away from. Spiteful bitch.'

'You're right there,' Patty agreed with a flash of her eyebrows.

'Don't start, you two,' sighed Yvette. 'You married, Ginny?' she asked, pointedly changing the subject.

Ginny shrugged. 'Sort of.'

'He left you,' Carmen said.

'Sort of.'

'It's all *sort of* with you, ain't it?'

'I suppose it is.' Ginny shrugged. 'I've had a bit of a bad time, see, and . . .' She took a long, last drag on her cigarette before grinding it out in one of the over-spilling ashtrays. 'I can't explain it, but I always wanted more than what I seemed to wind up with. I don't mean just things, although I've always liked nice stuff, but . . .' She ran her fingers distractedly through her hair, trying to find the words to explain. 'It's different for girls now, they can get an education. Make a living with their brains. But I've got to work with what I've got. I can work here at night and do another job during the day. And I'll be able to save enough to get out of—'

'Look,' Yvette said, signalling for the other two to stop laughing, 'we all say that, darling. And we mean it. But then we all stay in bed all day.'

'I won't. I'm going to work hard. *And* I'm going to get out of the mess I've wound up being stuck in.'

'We all say that an' all, darling.'

Patty folded her arms and leaned back against the wall. 'I was talking to this bloke the other day. He reckoned he could get me in the films. Be a starlet like. I might give it a go.'

Yvette gasped in disbelief. 'You're as bloody green as Ginny. At least she's new to the game. Look, we all dream about getting out of the business and becoming models and film stars, don't we? But how could you do anything else? You need a block and tackle to get you off your arse, you lazy cow. You don't even get out of bed before four o'clock in the afternoon.'

There was a tense silence as the girls thought about their lot, then Ginny said, 'Leila reckons I've got the real makings of something.'

'Leila?'

'Yeah. That's right. She said working here would be a good start for me. That I'd meet a lot of people who'd help me get on. Give me opportunities not just to earn good money, but to change my life.'

'If it's so good,' Carmen sniffed, 'why isn't she working here?'

Ginny frowned. 'She does, doesn't she?'

The girls laughed as though she'd just cracked the funniest joke they'd ever heard.

Yvette shook her head in amused wonder. 'Leila wouldn't lower herself to actually work here, darling. She's a bit more select. And a good friend of the governor, if you get me drift. She does a bit of this and that in some of the posher clubs, and sorts out the takings here and in some of the governor's other Soho *establishments*, when he's too busy to do it himself.' She grinned wickedly. 'Mind you, that's only if she's not throwing one of the special parties the governor gets her to put on. That's her real business and she has the privilege of running that from her own flat.'

'Flat?' Patty interrupted. 'More like a bloody palace.'

Ginny was confused. 'What, she throws parties? As a business?'

'She having me on?' Yvette asked the other two. 'It's

this business she's in, dopey-drawers: getting drunks drunker and then charging 'em over the odds for a bit of how's your father. Although some of her little talents are a bit more, er, specialised.'

Patty tutted. 'She's on the game, just like the rest of us. Only Leila high and mighty Harvey gets paid a proper rate and don't have to use them poxy rooms upstairs like we do. Or go to some bloke's idea of a hotel that's more like a doss-house. All right, we ain't slags like that lot outside who hang around street corners. But we're all whores, when all's said and done.'

'Some of them treat us with a bit of respect.' Carmen pouted.

'Yeah, but they're never gonna take us home to meet mother, now are they?'

'Or the wife.'

'We're their bit of fun.'

'But it don't pay that bad. Better than flaming machining in a sweatshop.'

'Machining? You try to earn a living in a poxy hat shop where every time the owner goes out, her old man's trying to get his hand down your drawers.'

'If you're gonna let 'em have it, you might as well put a price on it,' Carmen said, then added without a trace of irony, 'and it ain't a bad way to earn a living.'

Yvette nodded her agreement. 'She's right, Ginny. You wanna get the governor to let you start working with the punters. You'll never make decent money walking around with that thing round your neck.' She stabbed her thumb at the cigarette tray that Ginny had dumped on the floor. 'All you'll get from that is a backache.'

Ginny shrugged. 'It seems decent money to me. Much better than I was earning in the factory.' She bowed her head. Her hopes of finding beauty, respectability and wealth suddenly seemed so childish.

'Yeah, but why not earn more?'

'I don't want to go with no one, Yvette. I'm not saying that what you do is—'

'Look, we all felt like that at one time.' Patty fumbled around with her bag and took another hand-rolled cigarette from a silver-coloured case. 'Wanna drag?'

When Ginny looked surprised at not being offered a whole cigarette, Patty grinned. 'It's kif.'

There was still no understanding in Ginny's eyes.

'Indian hemp?' Patty persevered. 'Reefer?'

The look of shocked realisation on Ginny's face had Carmen and Patty giggling helplessly.

Yvette stood up, slowly straightening her seams. 'Look, I've gotta get back to Mr Wonderful out there, but leave her alone, eh, Pat? We was all new girls once. And a little tip for you, Ginny, before I go: try a bit of Vaseline on them pretty teeth of your'n, it helps with all the smiling you have to do.'

Just at that moment the door to the dressing-room creaked open and there stood Leila, dressed in her trade mark emerald-green silk. Behind her stood Shirley, so plastered with make-up that, in the harsh overhead light of the dressing-room, she looked like a hideous parody of a pantomime dame.

Leila scowled angrily at Patty and Carmen, before turning a smiling face to Ginny. 'Darling! Just thought I'd come to see how you're getting on.'

'We were all telling her,' Yvette said matter-of-factly, as she threw her coat around her shoulders, 'she'll never make proper money selling fags and chocolates, she wants to—'

Leila's smile became brittle. 'Thank you, Yvette.' Then she linked her arm through Ginny's and steered her towards the door.

'I think, unfortunately, that they've come to the end of

a rather *tiring* day, if you know what I mean,' she whispered, slipping something into Ginny's hand. 'Now here's a little something on account. Get yourself a cab home and treat yourself to the hairdresser. Have that hair blonded up a bit. Platinum would look just right with your complexion.' She kissed the air next to Ginny's cheek. 'We'll see you tomorrow night, sweetie. Same time.'

With that, Leila ushered Ginny forward, out of the dressing-room and into the club, then spun round and glared at Yvette. 'I don't know what you think you're up to, but there is a very lonely man waiting for you over there, Yvette. Mind you, if you're too busy, I'm sure Shirley would oblige.'

Outside on the pavement, Ginny shivered in the early morning chill. Huddling back into the doorway beneath the dim light of the red bulb, she opened her hand to see what Leila had given her. Two five-pound notes!

She hurriedly stuffed them in her handbag, pulled her coat high around her ears and set off at a fast walk.

She would walk at least half-way and only then get a taxi. She was going to save her money, buy herself out of the mess she was in. She wasn't like those other girls.

'Oi! Mum!'

Nellie, her head bristling with metal curlers, opened a sleep-reddened eye.

Ted flicked on the bedside lamp, making her blink myopically in the glare, as she fumbled around for the glass holding her false teeth.

She smacked her lips noisily and propped herself up on one elbow. 'What do you want?'

'Where's Ginny?' Ted hissed.

226

'Aw, her. I've got some interesting things to tell you about that little whore.'

With no one of any importance to see her, Leila yawned loudly and scratched her stomach where her roll-on was cutting into her as painfully as an instrument of torture.

'Tired, dear?' Gloria sneered. 'Ain't we all.'

'Leave off, Gloria,' Leila sighed. 'It's bad enough having to cash up here, when I've already done a night's work, without you starting.'

'Aaah! Can't you manage?'

Leila was just about to tell him his fortune, when the sound of someone coming up the stairs had her jumping to her feet. 'Those stupid tarts must have left the door open. Quick, stick this under the bar.'

She shoved the cash-box towards him, grabbed a bottle off the counter, ran across the room and stood behind the door.

As a tall, powerfully built man stepped over the threshold, Leila raised the bottle above her head, ready to crown him.

Before she knew what was happening the man had grabbed her wrist and had taken it from her as easily as if he'd been picking daisies.

'It's you! You nearly gave me a heart attack.' She clutched her heaving chest. 'I wasn't expecting you in tonight.'

'You know me, full of surprises.' He grinned boyishly. 'You can go home now, Gloria.'

Gloria rolled his eyes. 'Thank fuck for that, dear. I thought I was going to be here till the sparrows started coughing. These late nights play hell with a girl's complexion.'

The man laughed easily as he threw his overcoat across the bar. 'Fancy a drink, Leila?'

'I'd love one. Thanks.' She leaned over the counter and took a bottle of the good scotch and two clean glasses from under the bar.

She handed him a triple measure. 'I started a new one on the cigarettes for you tonight.'

'Good girl.'

'I reckon I can really do something with her. She's bright, nice looking. Actually a bit sensible, if you can believe it. Like me, I suppose.'

He winked at her. 'Good.'

'She's got potential, and with Shirley looking rougher and more miserable by the day – hardly appetising – I could do with someone to take her place when we have . . .' She paused and smiled seductively up at him through her expertly mascaraed lashes. '. . . private parties to cater for,' she breathed through pouting lips.

'How about the other girls here? None of them do?'

Leila wrinkled her nose. 'I wouldn't trust any of them, not with the special clients. They'd show us up. You know the way they speak and act when they've had half a glass of champagne.'

He ran his hand up and down her silk-clad thigh, letting it linger close to her crotch. 'I'll leave it to you, Leila girl. You never let me down.'

'And I never will.' She took his hand and clamped it over her breasts that were spilling out of the top of her dress, her skin creamy against the green of the silk.

She closed her eyes and leaned forward, hoping for the kiss that she knew she could never depend on. Leila was in love, had been for years, but she wasn't kidding herself; she knew that Billy Saunders was a man who had no loyalty to anyone but himself.

After feeling the briefest brush of his mouth against her forehead, she opened her eyes to see him reaching over the bar for the cash-box.

'Come on, Leila girl, let's get this till sorted out and see how much they've earned me tonight.'

Chapter 11

'Hurry up, Dilys,' Ginny called through the letter-box, giving it a rattle for good measure. 'I'm getting soaked out here.'

Dilys, still in her dressing-gown despite it being almost half past three in the afternoon, opened the prefab door. Seeing Ginny, she narrowed her eyes suspiciously. After the business about her wanting to mind Susan, Dilys had been very firm about her never turning up without being asked – she hadn't barred her altogether, because the silly cow could usually be depended on to bring stuff round with her no matter how broke she was. 'What're you doing round here at this time of day? Why ain't you at work?'

Ginny flashed her eyebrows and grinned happily. 'If you'll let me in and make me a cup o' tea, I'll tell you.'

Dilys stood back and Ginny stepped inside.

She took off her headscarf, shook the raindrops out on to the path and ran her fingers through her damp curls.

Dilys gasped. 'You've bleached your hair!'

'Dil, I've done a lot of things and I'm just busting to tell you all about it.'

Dilys, her lips tightly pursed as she listened to Ginny's breathlessly happy description of her new work-place, made no effort to help as Ginny filled the kettle, warmed the pot, took cups and saucers from the cupboard and generally set about tidying the mess that covered every available work surface in the compact prefab kitchen. As usual, whenever there were jobs to be done or tea to be made – no matter that it was in Dilys's house – there was an unspoken understanding that, if Ginny was there, she would be left to get on with it.

But Ginny was so carried away with telling her story that she would have happily cleaned the whole prefab inside and out; in fact, she was so excited that she didn't even notice Dilys's openly hostile glare as she chattered away about her wonderful new life.

'And when I come out in the early hours of the morning,' she beamed, carrying the tea through to the front room on a brightly painted tin tray bearing the legend *Guinness is good for you*, 'the place is either still awake or getting ready for the next day. You wouldn't believe it, Dil. I know it can be lively round here, but *Soho*. You should see it. I wasn't sure about it at first, it was a bit unfamiliar like, but now I'm getting to know people I think it's smashing. Really smashing.'

Ginny didn't stop talking while she poured the tea. 'And you don't drink this stuff there, you know,' she went on, weighing the pot in her hand. 'Well not all the time. There's this place see, in Frith Street.' Her tone became reverent and a wistful look came into her eyes, as though she were describing some exotic vision. 'The Moka Bar it's called. And they make this frothy coffee with a special machine. You should try it, Dil. It's great.'

While this newly vivacious, platinum-haired Ginny perched herself on the edge of one of the armchairs and continued to talk nineteen to the dozen, Dilys sat in the armchair opposite, sipping mechanically at her tea, not saying a word.

'So what I was thinking,' Ginny went on, 'as this is my night off, I've got a bit of time on my hands, so, if it's all right with you, as soon as Sue gets in from playing with her little friends I'll take her down Burdett Road to

Mandor's. I saw this beautiful little coat and hat in their window that I want her to try on. Bright-red wool it is, with little cords with brown fur bobbles on the end to tie under her chin. And you should have seen the little hat that went with it. Talk about cute. She'd look a real sweetie in it!' Ginny dipped her chin and blushed. 'Hark at me! *Sweetie*! That's what Leila calls everyone. She's the one who got me the job, the one I told you about. Mind you, I could only put a deposit on it for now. But I'll pay it off weekly, then as soon as I get myself straight, I'll pay off the rest and get it for her. It'll do her just nice when she starts school. And that'll be here before you know it.' Ginny looked at her watch. 'I hope she gets in soon. What time did you tell her to be back?'

Still Dilys didn't say a word.

Rather than provoking Dilys by pressing her about Susan – she would probably be having tea with one of her little friends – Ginny carried on talking. 'Anyway, I could get her some of them lovely little Cherub vests and matching knickers, and some of them pretty petticoats an' all. She'll like them better than them scratchy old-fashioned liberty bodices, I'll bet.'

Dilys plonked down her cup and saucer on the arm of her chair and let out a long, slow breath. 'There's nothing wrong with Susan's liberty bodices.'

'Yeah, but they're what Florrie passed down to her from her daughter's kids. I was talking about getting her some nice new things. Not going mad or nothing, 'cos like I say, I've gotta get myself straight first and I'm gonna try saving a few bob an' all. But I definitely reckon I can afford to treat her to a few bits and pieces.'

So carried away was Ginny with this new dream world she had entered, a world where Susan would be dressed up like a real little doll and would have all the toys she could ever wish for – a Fairy Cycle even! – that she didn't notice the look darkening Dilys's already irritated expression into one of pure, murderous hate.

As Dilys turned her head away to avoid having to look Ginny in the face for a moment longer, her eye was caught by the matching vases on her sideboard, a gift from one of her recently acquired American 'friends'. And, as she stared at the heavily engraved glass, she thought how easy it would be to snatch up one of them and to bring it crashing down across Ginny's pretty blonded skull.

Had Ginny realised just how close she was to being crowned with a couple of pounds of cut lead crystal she would soon have shut her mouth, but it was the sound of the street door opening, as Susan let herself in with the key she wore on a string around her neck, that saved her.

As always, the moment Susan spotted Ginny she launched herself across the room, with a delighted whoop of 'Auntie Ginny!'

After a hasty brushing of her lips on her mother's cheek, Susan struggled out of her wet, oversized coat – another legacy from Florrie's grandchildren – and let the heavy, dull-brown garment drop in a heap on the floor; an action that Ginny noticed drew not the slightest reaction from Dilys.

'And where have you been, my little angel? You're soaked.'

Susan looked warily at her grim-faced mother. 'Out playing.'

'You dopey thing!' exclaimed Ginny, reaching out to ruffle the child's damp hair. 'You should have come home when it started raining. Go and fetch me something to dry you off.'

Susan ran out of the room and returned immediately

233

with a dingy-looking towel, clambered on to her 'auntie's' lap and gazed up adoringly at her.

'You could have fetched a clean one,' Ginny teased.

Susan managed a thin smile and snuggled closer.

'Like I was saying,' Ginny continued. 'I meant what I said about good money, Dil. Honest, I'm earning plenty. I've even given up me job at the factory.'

She leaned forward and dropped her voice to a conspiratorial whisper, mindful that Susan was sitting with her. 'D'you know, the girls earn at least a tenner a night. Their basic's quite low, but what with the commission on all the drinks that the customers have to order,' Ginny winked at Dilys behind her hand, 'by way of payment for their company, if you catch me drift; plus all these tips they get. And even their cocktail dresses are supplied by the governor. I've never met him, but apparently he likes to keep the tone of the club just right. Likes a bit of class about the place. But I'm not a fool. I know that some of the girls', she looked down at Susan and then mouthed, '*go* with the blokes. But you should see the presents they get from the fellers when they do take them upstairs for a bit of you-know-what. I'm not saying I agree with it, but like Leila says, even—'

Dilys leapt to her feet, her dressing-gown flapping open. 'You *what*! You come round here looking like a two-bob tom with your bleached hair and your nylon stockings—'

Ginny's hand went automatically, defensively, to her legs, as her bright smile closed – snap! – on her face.

'—talking filth in front of my baby!'

'Your baby?' Ginny said quietly, hugging Susan protectively. 'What, the one who was out in the rain, Gawd knows where, and had to let herself in, while you was sitting here not even dressed?'

Dilys pulled Susan away from Ginny. 'D'you really

think I'd let you buy my kid anything out of whoring money?'

Now Ginny was also on her feet, but she kept her voice low, as she didn't want to scare Susan. 'Dilys, I told you, I ain't got nothing to do with that side of things. I sell cigarettes. That's all.'

'Cigarettes, my Aunt Fanny. Pull the other one, *sweetie*, it's got sodding bells on it.' Dilys jabbed a furious finger in Ginny's face. 'I'm disgusted with you, Ginny Martin, really disgusted.'

Susan picked up her coat, stuck her thumb in her mouth and made resignedly for the haven of her bedroom and her teddy. She knew when it was best to keep out of the way.

Dilys was now in full flight; her venom at seeing Ginny looking so good and so happy, and her own dissatisfaction with the joys of motherhood, triggering off every kind of nastiness and wild accusation.

'Just look at the way you're done up,' she finished triumphantly.

Ginny blinked back the tears that threatened to spill on to her cheeks, determined not to let Dilys see how much she was hurting her, knowing that her friend's temper would subside as easily as it flared. 'I thought you'd be pleased to see me looking smart again,' she said reasonably.

'Smart! You call dressing like a brass smart? And Christ knows what you think you're up to, hanging around clubs.'

'I thought you liked clubs.' Ginny could have added: 'Well, according to Milly Barrington, your nosy neighbour, you do,' but she didn't want things to degenerate any further, certainly not with Susan in the next room.

'I ain't a bloody married woman, am I? But you are.'

A married woman? A punch-bag more like. Ginny

swallowed hard, as the memories of the kicks and beatings, and the humiliation, flooded her mind. She rubbed her hands over her face. She wouldn't let the memories stay there, she wouldn't let Ted have that power over her. But then, as clearly as if it were happening right in front of her eyes, Ginny saw Pearl's funeral and Ted sitting with Susan on his lap . . .

She had to stop letting these stupid ideas taunt her, or she'd make herself ill.

'Are you listening to me?' Dilys demanded.

'What?'

'I said, you should know better. And Gawd knows what Ted's poor mother's got to say about all this.'

'Nellie don't know nothing about what I'm doing.' Ginny drew her breath in sharply, as she saw the look of triumph on Dilys's face. 'But it wouldn't matter if she did,' she added hurriedly. 'You know her. She wouldn't give a toss what I'm doing so long as there's money coming in.'

'Well, I reckon you're wrong there, 'cos even Nellie's got standards.'

There was a moment's uneasy silence, as Ginny bit back the question as to what on earth Dilys knew about standards. She couldn't risk not being allowed to see Susan for a few weeks, just to score an easy point in a row that would, as usual, be forgotten as soon as Dilys grew bored with it.

Ginny had to be the appeaser. With all the dignity she could muster she fixed on a smile and said cheerfully, 'Well, if we're gonna get there before the shop shuts, me and the little 'un had better get going.'

'Better get going?' echoed Dilys incredulously. 'I'll give you better get going. You just get out of here, Ginny Martin. Go on. You go back to your Yvette and your Carmen and your Leila and all the rest of them. And don't bother coming back. I ain't having no kid of mine mixing with no whores.'

As Dilys shoved Ginny towards the street door, she seemed genuinely unaware of the irony of her words.

While Ginny was waiting at the bus-stop in the pouring rain, not caring, or even really noticing, that she was getting drenched to the skin, so angry was she with herself at not handling Dilys better, Ted was pulling his car into the kerb outside a scruffy-looking terraced house in Plaistow.

Ted hated his new car, a tiny Austin that looked as though it should have a family squashed into the back seat, complete with picnic hamper and tartan travelling rug, singing 'Ten Green Bottles' at the tops of their voices. But he had to have something to drive after he sold the MG.

It had almost physically hurt when he'd had to let his open-topped bird-puller of a car go, even though he'd made a more than good price on it. He'd always enjoyed displaying that he had money to spend, and what sort of impression did selling the MG and driving a bloody Austin give to people? That he was having hard times, that was what. And the impression was just about right: times weren't so good for Ted Martin any more.

It seemed that no matter what he tried lately, it all went wrong. Everything was so difficult, there were barriers no matter which way he turned and it was sending him round the sodding bend. In the past he'd always been able to make a living, a very good living, ducking and diving, doing a bit of this and a bit of that – he had been well on the way to becoming what he'd always wanted to be, a face to be reckoned with – but then it had all started going wrong. And Ted was convinced he knew why.

Saunders. That was all you heard nowadays. It had been bad enough when they'd had that ruck over that stupid bitch Lilly, but that was nothing like what was happening now. Since the bastard had started expanding his business into the East End it seemed like the no-good cowson was everywhere. No matter what scams and schemes Ted tried setting up, all he got was: 'No mate, not without clearing it with Saunders first.' And Ted knew exactly what Saunders's reaction would be if he did turn up with a deal.

Even the money-lending had gone wrong on him. His loans had been 'bought up', and he'd been paid off – nothing compared with what he should have earned out of it – by a pair of goons who would have terrified even the likes of Freddie Mills. They'd told him that someone else was running the debts now, and that if he knew what was good for him, he'd sling his hook like a good little boy and keep his head down and his nose clean.

The trouble with arseholes like Saunders was they were powerful enough to do exactly what they felt like and to hold a grudge for a very long time. They didn't have to be beholden to anyone, but they still knew they had to show that they held all the cards, all the power, in their hands, or someone else was standing there, ready to step right into their shoes.

Jamming his trilby on his head, Ted shut the car door with an angry slam. Poxy rain! He could happily have murdered Saunders. He was earning a fortune and what was Ted doing? He was back to having birds doing tuppenny ha'penny hoisting for him; lifting bits and pieces to sell off in pubs for fucking peanuts. Pubs that weren't even on his own manor. Not that he had a manor any more.

And it was all Saunders's fault.

He smacked at the street door with the flat of his hand.

The silly whore had better be in. He didn't have a penny to bless himself with and he was getting bloody soaked.

'Are you telling me this is all you've got?' Ted snorted heavily, as though he had been running, but his panting was more to do with anger than exertion. He held up the striped hand-towels with a scowl of disbelief. 'You're a lazy bastard, Irene.'

'*Me* a lazy bastard?' Irene, a girl of barely nineteen, stuck her fists into her waist and threw back her head. 'If what I've nicked ain't good enough for you, then do something about it. You take the bloody risks. I've had enough of this lark anyway, and I've had enough of you thinking you can stay here whenever you fancy it. Well, you've got a shock coming, mate, 'cos I'm getting out of here. The place has been bought up by some businessman. He's paid me and all the other tenants in the street to move out. So I'm going. I've got plans.'

'What did you say?'

'You heard.'

As she continued to talk, telling him exactly what she thought of him and what she was going to do about it, Ted rose slowly to his feet.

Young Irene no longer had her prettily dimpled chin stuck arrogantly in the air, she had it tucked down close to her chest, as she cowered against the wall with her arms folded over her head, trying to protect herself.

A few hours later, Ginny was sitting alone in the front room of Bailey Street, listening to the wireless she had bought for Nellie's birthday, with the paper, unread, in her lap. She felt really miserable and instead of making the most of her first night off from the club, she was dreading spending the rest of the evening alone.

It wasn't really the row – Dilys always had been one

for making dramatic gestures – it was something else and it wasn' so easy to deal with. Ginny hadn't realised just how lonely she had become before she had met Leila.

Knowing she was going to be with the girls each evening had given her something to look forward to. Hearing their constant chatter, their joking around, sharing in their laughter, was like a bright light shining into her life. And even if their jokes were sometimes a bit close to the knuckle, at least there was no pretence with them.

Not like Dilys and her sudden moral conversion.

Ginny sighed loudly. All her adult life she had had to give in or make allowances for someone or other. And it got her down at times, but she knew that she would soon be round the prefab, knocking on the door, smiling like a fool as though nothing had happened, hoping that Dilys either wanted something off her, or was in a more reasonable mood, so that she would at least let her in and allow her to apologise. And, if she wanted to see Susan, that's what Ginny knew she would have to do.

She looked up at the clock. It was only ten to eight – although it felt more like midnight – and she didn't know what to do with herself. She had finished all the clearing up and there wasn't a single handkerchief left unironed. There wasn't even anybody to talk to, not even Nellie and her moaning, as she'd taken herself off to Florrie's to play cards and to put the world to rights.

Ginny sighed again. Things were in a bad way when she found herself wishing she had Nellie for company.

She was as bored as hell, but she was damned if she was going up to bed.

She'd make a cup of tea. That's what she'd do. There was nothing else to bloody do . . .

'Hello, gorgeous. Enough left in the pot for me?'

Ginny spun round and let out a little gasp of surprise, nearly dropping the teapot. 'Ted! I didn't hear you come in.'

He winked lazily and lifted his foot, displaying a heavily buckled, crêpe-soled, black suede shoe. 'Brothel creepers. Silent but deadly. Got 'em off this bloke in a pub. Latest thing from the States, they are. You see, they'll all be wearing 'em soon.' He laughed easily as he pulled a chair out from under the kitchen table and straddled it as though he were riding a horse. 'Swapped 'em for a set of poxy hand-towels, if you can believe it. Told him they was best Turkish quality, as found in all the big hotels up West. What a mug!'

Ginny joined in with his laughter. He was in a good mood and he hadn't been drinking. *This* was the Ted she had fallen for: the one who made her smile, made her feel good about herself. The one she loved. It was over a month since she'd even set eyes on him and that had only been for a few minutes when he'd come to collect some clean clothes in the middle of the night; and she had missed him. Well, she had missed this particular Ted.

As she looked at his handsome, smiling face, while he sat there at the table as though he had just finished his supper and was telling her little stories about his day, her old optimism bubbled up around her like water from a spring. With her earning decent money, maybe she could help him start a different sort of life, just as she had done. One they could share. A proper life. With children . . .

'Are you gonna stand there gawping at me with your gob open?' he asked, reaching out his hand to her. 'Or are you gonna give us a kiss?'

Almost before Ginny realised what was happening, Ted had bent her back over the table, had pulled her skirt up over her thighs, her knickers down to her ankles and was pushing himself into her.

It was all over very quickly. Within minutes Ted was back on his chair and the only sign of anything having happened between them was a rip in Ginny's stocking and a flush covering her face and throat.

'You're looking good,' he said, running his fingers through his thick, dark quiff. 'All this austerity shit everyone's going on about obviously ain't affecting you.' He sniffed noisily. 'How about a drink then?'

Ginny, torn between feelings of near elation that her husband obviously still desired her and an absurd shyness after their moment of what she refused to acknowledge was a brief, brutal intimacy for Ted's purely physical relief, averted her eyes from his easy, direct gaze and turned to the kettle on the stove. 'I'll make a fresh pot,' she said in a girlish whisper.

'No. I mean a proper drink. Ain't Mum got no whisky?'

Ginny turned off the tap. 'Since you ain't been bringing her stuff home, she don't really keep anything in the house no more.'

Ted frowned. 'What d'you mean by that?'

'Nothing,' Ginny hurriedly assured him. 'I just meant that I think she drank it 'cos it was there.'

'Leave off. She used to knock the stuff back like it was water.'

'No, really. I reckon the only reason she goes down the Albert is for a bit of company. It's a terrible thing being lonely.' Ginny thought guiltily of how easily she had got into the routine of leaving Nellie alone each evening. 'To be honest, Ted, I feel a bit sorry for her.'

Ted snorted and shook his head. 'You always have to see the bloody good side of everyone, don't you? She drinks like a fish and you feel sorry for her.'

Ginny hoped he'd meant it as a compliment. Checking her hair in the glass by the sink, she grabbed her bag from the door handle and smiled broadly. 'Tell you what, I'll nip over the Albert and get us a bottle.'

Bob, the landlord of the Albert, folded his arms across his big barrel chest and whistled appreciatively. 'Ain't seen you for a while, darling, but just look at your hair and everything. You're looking a right little cracker. Here, come and have a butcher's at this little lady, Martha,' he called to his wife who was through in the other bar, serving. He leaned across the counter and winked. 'Tell us your secret before the old woman comes through and I'll see if it works on her.'

Ginny glowed with pleasure. 'I'm happy, Bob, that's all.'

'Are you, babe? Good. You deserve it. And I tell you what, I know you always had a lovely head of hair on you, but you look like a film star with it all blonded up like that. I'll have to get Martha to do hers that colour.'

'Do my what, what colour, you cheeky bugger?' Martha asked, giving Bob a flick with her glass cloth.

Not bothering to wait for her husband's answer, which Martha knew was bound to be saucy, she turned her attention to Ginny. 'Hello, love. Well just look at you all prettied up. You're a real sight for sore eyes.'

'Ta, Martha.' Ginny couldn't stop grinning.

'Come looking for Nellie, have you?' She turned to her husband. 'Don't think she's been in tonight, has she Bob?'

Ginny shook her head. 'No, she's round Florrie's. I was after some scotch actually. You ain't got a spare one to sell us, have you?'

While Bob went out the back to fetch the whisky, she chatted to Martha, who was as surprised as Bob had been by the transformation of Ginny from down-trodden drudge back to the vibrant young woman she had once been.

As Bob rang the one pound and fifteen shillings into the till, and Ginny practically skipped out of the pub, Martha stood next him with a worried frown clouding her face.

'What's that look for?' Bob asked. 'I know I only charged her—'

'I didn't expect you to make a mark-up on her, you great daft sod,' Martha said affectionately. 'I just hope she knows what she's doing, that's all.'

'What you on about?'

'Think about it, Bob. Nellie's out round Florrie's and that scotch ain't for Ginny, now is it? That conniving bastard, Ted bloody Martin, must be sniffing round again.'

Ginny poured Ted a generous measure and sat opposite him at the table, nervously nibbling her bottom lip. 'Ted, there's something I wanna tell you.'

He took a big gulp from his glass, swallowed, then drew in a sharp breath, stretching his lips tight across his teeth. 'Yeah?'

'It's about me job.' She paused, trying to gauge how he would react, whether his mood had suddenly changed in the way she knew from experience that it could. 'See, it's like this, I don't work at the factory no more.'

'I know, Mum told me.'

'But—'

Ted tossed back the rest of the scotch and held out his glass for a refill. 'She might be a wicked old fucker at times, but she ain't stupid.'

She unscrewed the cap and, with a shaking hand, poured the drink. 'So you know where I'm working?'

He nodded.

'Do you mind?' Another pause, then, in a rush, it all came out. 'Because if you do, I'd give it up like a shot. I'd give it up tomorrow. 'Cos I really want us to try and get our lives sorted out, Ted. And I'd do anything for the chance to make a go of it. Anything.'

For a moment Ted said nothing, he just gulped at his drink and looked fixedly at her, then he burst into loud, coarse laughter, tossing back his head as though she had just told him the funniest joke he had every heard.

Ginny stared back at him in uncomprehending bewilderment.

'Why would I care where you work?' he finally managed to ask, as his laughter subsided. 'Unless you wasn't earning much, o' course.'

'But—'

'But *what*?' His face creased into a contemptuous sneer. 'The only reason I'm here is 'cos I need some dough.'

'No.' She dropped her chin. 'You're just saying—'

He reached out and grabbed her face, sinking his fingers deep into her cheeks and jerking her head up so that she had to look at him.

Despite the pain, Ginny knew she mustn't let out the smallest whimper or let a single tear drop on to her cheek.

'Let me tell you, once and for all, you dozy cow, what the real world's about.'

Ginny didn't want to listen, didn't want to hear any of it, but she had little choice. She sat there, gripped by the cruelty of his hand and his words as he gave her a variously censored and exaggerated version of the life he lead when he wasn't with her. Censored to hide what he considered his failures and exaggerated to brag about his self-perceived successes. It was only as he got on to more recent times that his tone changed from one of sneering bravado to barely suppressed anger.

'So,' he murmured, finally releasing his grip on her and reaching for the bottle which was now almost half empty, 'there's been this silly tart what's been going out hoisting for me. But she's another fucking useless cow.' He was talking to Ginny as though she was some bloke in a pub he was complaining to about his missus not ironing his shirts the way he liked them. 'Know what she had the cheek to tell me tonight? She's going off with some posh old bastard – one of the prats what get a thrill from buying bent gear off us. Makes 'em feel like they're bastard gangsters. And her flat's been bought by some property bloke. I ain't even got that no more.'

Ginny, no longer even noticing the throbbing pain in her cheeks, couldn't stop herself from asking the question: 'Why did you have a woman stealing for you?'

Ted slowly raised one of his dark, sculpted eyebrows. 'I ain't been able to work, have I. I needed money.'

'You could have come to me.'

Ted shook his head in wonder at her stupidity. 'I have, ain't I? But anyway, I ain't talking about needing a couple o' bob. I'm talking proper money.' His voice was beginning to slur and he seemed to be having trouble focusing on her face. 'I nearly had it an' all. I had a blag all set up. Sweet as a nut. We was gonna turn over a bank in the Mile End Road. Had all the tools organised and everything. Sawn-off jobs that couldn't be traced. Right pukka.' He smacked the side of his fist on the table, making Ginny flinch. 'Then some bastard grassed us up. We had to call off the job and now we've all gotta keep our heads down.'

He poured himself another drink, spilling most of it on the table. 'Now I ain't got a pot.'

'They're always going on about needing workers in the papers and on the wireless lately,' she said warily, as

246

she screwed the lid back on the bottle for him. 'You could always try and get a regular sort of job.'

'What, like you? In some knocking shop?'

Ginny winced at the injustice of his words. She hadn't done anything wrong. All she was doing was trying to pay off some bills, make ends meet, keep his mother in food and earn a bit extra for some of the things that other people took for granted, that *she* had once taken for granted. Admittedly she was enjoying the job, but there was no getting away from the fact that she was working bloody long hours, which was a damned sight more than either Ted or Nellie had ever done.

Ted was staring into the middle distance. 'You know what it is, don't you?' he asked, his drunken speculation losing Ginny completely. 'It's since that bastard's had it in for me. If I ever get the chance to get my hands round that whoreson's throat . . .'

'Who? Who's got it in for you?'

'Him. The one who's been haunting me.'

'I don't understand.'

'The arsehole's ruined my business, ruined my life and *you* don't understand?'

Ginny looked blank.

'The bastard who grassed me to the law, you silly bitch.'

'What, over the bank job?'

He hesitated for a moment, as Ginny's words worked their way into his mind. 'Yeah,' he said with a nod. 'You're probably right. The same bloke. The one who stopped all the dockers trading with me, the one who—'

Now Ginny had tuned in to the corkscrew logic of his thinking, it was all she could do to stop herself laughing. 'You ain't talking about that feller from all that time back, surely? The one who had the police round here. I can't even remember his name it was so long ago.'

'Can't even remember his name?'

The low menace in his voice had Ginny wishing she had kept her mouth shut.

And as all his hatred and bile spewed out – as he slammed the truth about him and Dilys at her, and about Susan being his, and how he thought Ginny was just about the stupidest bitch he had ever laid eyes on, let alone fucked – Ginny wished she had never been born.

'Why Ted?' she whispered into her chest. 'Why?'

'Why not?'

She couldn't think of an answer.

'Be honest with yourself for once, instead of floating around like a bleed'n' idiot with your head in the clouds. You must have known.' He laughed cruelly. 'I mean, every other bugger seems to.'

Ted set about refilling his glass. 'You got any money?'

Ginny handed him her purse, turned her back on him and walked slowly from the room.

Upstairs, she packed her belongings into the suitcase that had once held packets of silk stockings, French perfume and chocolates. Things of which Dilys had no doubt had more than her share. Ginny vowed to herself that she too would have those things. But she would buy them for herself.

She'd been a mug for long enough. What did she have to lose?

Less than an hour later, Ginny walked into the club just as Carmen was fixing the cigarette tray around her neck.

'Innit your night off?'

'Yeah, it is,' Ginny said, striding past her without a glance. 'I've come in to see Leila.'

By the time Leila arrived, the club was about to close and the girls were almost bursting with curiosity.

What was going on? Why was Ginny sitting out the back with a face like a fiddle, bruises on her cheeks, a suitcase by her side and no explanation? That's what they wanted to know. But as they rushed to follow Leila into the dressing-room to find out, they were disappointed.

'Do me a tiny favour, girls,' she purred over her shoulder, 'get back to your customers and leave me alone with Ginny for a few moments.'

There was a general mutter of frustration.

'Please,' said Leila, her smile still in place, but her voice and eyes hardening.

The girls obeyed and Leila lowered herself elegantly on to one of the shabby little chairs. 'Now, what's all this about? Gloria said—'

'I want to do what they do,' Ginny interrupted her.

'Hostessing?' Leila suppressed a much broader smile. She'd been right about her all along. She could always tell, no matter what Shirley said.

Ginny nodded. 'I want to earn more money.'

'You'll certainly be able to do that.'

'And there's something else. I need somewhere to stay.'

'That shouldn't be a problem.' Leila draped her emerald-silk-clad arm around Ginny's trembling shoulder, her mind working overtime as she considered which of Saunders's properties might have a bedsit that wouldn't frighten her off completely. Ginny had something about her that men went for and Leila wasn't about to miss the opportunity of pleasing the governor by getting her to cash in on it.

'We'll find you somewhere. But you mustn't expect too much, you know, sweetie. Not at such short notice.'

'That's all right,' Ginny said flatly. 'I ain't used to much.'

Chapter 12

1952

Carmen sashayed into the dressing-room, a half-smoked cigarette dangling from her lips, her big brown eyes narrowed against the smoke. Apart from her hair, which was smoothed round big, fat rollers in an attempt to straighten its tight natural curl, she was made-up and dressed, ready for the evening's work ahead.

She tipped her head towards Ginny, who was sitting in the far corner of the dressing-room by the sink putting on her make-up. Rather than sharing one of the big communal looking-glasses that were propped up on the junk-covered tables, Ginny was doing her best to use a small handbag mirror.

'What's up with her?' Carmen asked Yvette.

Yvette flashed her eyes, shook her head and flapped her hand, in a pantomime signal for her not to ask, but Carmen was never one for subtlety.

'What's up with you then, Ginny girl?' she asked, flicking her cigarette into an already full ashtray. 'Penny for those dirty thoughts of yours.'

Ginny raised her eyes slowly; beneath them were dark mauve smudges like fading bruises, but they weren't marks of violence, they were marks of exhaustion and lack of sleep. 'Sorry, Carmen? What did you say?'

Carmen tutted amiably. 'I said, penny for them. You're miles away again.'

Ginny lowered her chin and returned to painting her face. 'I'm all right.'

Yvette glared at Carmen; she of all people should have

known what it was like to feel troubled, to want to hide away in a corner and be left alone.

Patty, who up until now hadn't said anything – she had been far too preoccupied constructing a fat, overspilling reefer – suddenly chipped in, in her increasingly London-tinged Irish brogue: 'It's about time you moved out of that room of your'n, Ginny. That dump's enough to get anyone down. And I should know. Didn't I stay there myself for a couple o' weeks? I nearly went barmy. And you've been there for what . . .? It must be getting on for eight months now.' She paused to lick the paper and to light the expertly rolled joint. 'That's what'll be upsetting you, living in that rat hole.' She paused and flashed a knowing look around the room. 'Or you've got yourself into a bit of debt maybe?'

Carmen took the cigarette from Patty and inhaled deeply. 'Well, it's either that.' She laughed. 'Or the fact that Elizabeth Taylor has gone and snapped up Michael Wilding. You've lost your chance there, darling.'

Ginny said nothing, but Patty wrinkled her nose and made a gagging sound. 'Michael Wilding? No thanks.'

Carmen handed back the cigarette. 'Not your type, eh, Patty.' Playfully, she flicked a clump of lipstick-stained cotton wool at Ginny's back. 'Hark at Miss Fussy Drawers, Gin. Making out he's not her type and we all know she'd go with Laurel and Hardy, the bloody pair of them at once, if they paid her well enough. She'd go with anyone.'

Patty leaned towards Carmen and hissed angrily, 'D'you mind. Unlike some people, I know where to draw the line.'

'Aw yeah?'

'Yeah. And I definitely wouldn't go with some of the old rough I've seen Ginny go with.'

'Shut up,' snapped Yvette; she could kill Carmen and Patty at times, they acted just like a pair of kids.

'What?' Patty was a picture of injured innocence. 'What have I done?'

'It's all right,' Ginny said, standing up, her mouth and eyes set hard behind her bright mask of cosmetics. 'Patty's right, I do go with blokes that most of you would run a mile from. But why should I worry about being fussy? What have I got to lose?'

She didn't wait for their reply.

It was barely half past one and Ginny was already leading her third customer up to one of the mercifully ill-lit rooms above the club. If the lights had been any brighter, the irrefutably sordid nature of the poky little cubby-holes, with their lumpy beds, and their faded and stained linen, would have been all too horribly apparent to anyone but the very drunkest or badly sighted of the customers that the girls took upstairs.

The customers were actually referred to as 'friends' within their hearing – what the girls called them in the privacy of the dressing-room would have appalled them. The girls' descriptions varied: according to how the customers had behaved; how far over the set rate their 'tip' had been; and – most importantly – how quickly they had managed to get it all over with. But customers is what they undoubtedly were, and the point in getting them upstairs and back down again as quickly as possible wasn't only because the girls found them distasteful, but so that they could get on with buying more rounds of the ludicrously over-priced drinks and gifts from the cigarette tray, or be sent off into the night, with reassuring murmurings about their virility and their ability to drive a woman to the heights of ecstasy, so that the girls could get on with targeting their next likely punter.

The girls earned less per trick if they took them upstairs rather than back to the flats they rented from the governor, but then they missed out on the commission from the extras and could only guarantee the one 'friend' for the night, so it was worth staying on the club premises. Plus, not only was working a foreigner – doing business on your own behalf without the governor's knowledge – strictly prohibited, but most of the girls felt safer using the upstairs, as, like the door from the street, they were watched over by an ever-changing series of minders. These were huge gorillas of men, who stood, arms folded, guarding the door to the narrow staircase that led to the rooms high up in the roof.

The minders safeguarded the girls and their customers from several potential hazards, ensuring that the men enjoyed their purchase for the evening in something like privacy and also ensuring that the club didn't attract too much attention. For while the downstairs operated quite legitimately as a licensed drinking club, upstairs was another matter and was completely illegal.

The first of the potential spoilers of the punters' fun – and the club's profit – was the local police. But because they were happy with their regular pay-off, they usually only bothered to mount the occasional, fairly half-hearted early-evening raid – at a time when no one of any importance was likely to be on the premises – more as a public demonstration of keeping the peace, than part of any genuine crusade to close what they all knew was a fully operational brothel.

Then there were the young thugs who, after watching one too many George Raft films, fancied themselves as budding gangsters and would see if extorting protection money was as easy as it looked at the pictures. They were something of a joke and were swotted away as easily as an annoying insect at a picnic.

There was, of course, the genuine article to be reckoned with: the real hard men. But they weren't a day-to-day concern. For the most part, everyone had their own patch in Soho – the English, the Greeks, the Irish, the Italians, the Chinese – and they tended to live in a sort of peaceful co-existence, where everyone knew their place in the pecking order of the criminal underworld. There was the occasional outbreak of a territorial skirmish, when one of the local firms or families decided to chance its arm and see if it could expand into someone else's manor. But those disputes were usually quickly, and often bloodily, resolved, satisfying everyone's sense of fair play and of honour. Lately, however, with the increasing numbers of Maltese arriving on the scene, there were worrying signs that the newcomers didn't intend to play by quite the same rules as the old firms.

But for now, the intruders who caused the most trouble for the club were the sightseers – who would never have set foot in the place had they even begun to suspect the charges; the do-gooders and the moralists – who wanted to clean up the area and save the girls and the customers from themselves and eternal damnation; and the wives.

The wives were a whole new breed of nuisance, who seemed permanently on the look-out for co-respondents to cite in the increasingly fashionable divorce courts. There, they were almost guaranteed deals designed to break their errant husbands, both in spirit and in pocket. Most men caught that way could only reminisce that that sort of thing would never have happened before the war when women knew their place.

The minder on the door tonight was Terry, a man with a neck wider than his head and fists like boiled hams. Usually silently inscrutable, he frowned as Ginny tottered past him on her high-heeled shoes, dragging a sweating, over-weight old man who looked barely conscious behind her.

'You all right?' Terry growled, his great bald head creasing like an ill-fitting overcoat. It took a lot to shock a man like him, but this pretty little blonde was going at it like some rough old street tom. Anyone could see she could make a much cushier living if she wanted to. There'd be plenty of blokes more than willing to have a doll like her to keep to himself – him included if he had the dough. But it was as though she just didn't care. And the old geezer she had in tow this time, well, it was enough to make Terry want to fetch up his tea.

Ginny stopped in her tracks and turned to face him. 'Why shouldn't I be all right?'

Terry shrugged and, returning the professional blankness to his gaze, opened the door and let Ginny and her 'friend' through to the upstairs.

As he stood stolidly on guard, Terry usually left the door slightly ajar so that he could hear the girls and the mug punters performing – he considered it one of his perks. But this time he made sure the door was shut tight. It made him shudder even to think of what was going on in there.

Less than two minutes later Ginny pushed past Terry with her hand over her mouth. Her hair wild and dishevelled, her lipstick smeared all over her face, her dress unbuttoned and hanging off her shoulders. And there was sick all down her front. Terry couldn't be sure if the vomit was hers or the customer's. Both maybe.

The next night, the other girls had already gone through to the club to size up the first of the customers, but Ginny was still in the dressing-room, sitting alone, looking at her painted mask of a face in one of the big shared

255

mirrors. She couldn't bring herself even to stand up, let alone shift herself out into the club to face yet another parade of men.

She traced a finger round her deep-carmine-tinted lips, then round the scarlet rouge highlighting her cheeks, and finally round the bold black lines defining her eyes. It was as though she was looking at a stranger; someone she knew nothing about. Someone she didn't recognise in any way at all. Someone her mum and dad would have been ashamed of.

She thought about what had become of Violet Varney . . .

Sticking her whole hand into the big jar of vanishing cream that the girls used to clean their faces, Ginny scooped out a great gobbet of the stuff. Ignoring the stray hairs and bits of cotton wool sticking out of it, she closed her eyes and plastered it all over her face. She would wipe it clean of every trace of paint and colour and walk out of the club. She didn't know what she would do then, but that didn't matter, she just knew she couldn't do this any more. Patty had been right about her debts, but she would find a way to pay back every penny. She would—

'Not ready yet?' someone cooed from behind her.

Ginny's eyes flashed open. Peering into the glass through the thick grease smeared over her lashes, she saw the reflection of Leila standing in the doorway with Shirley just behind her.

Leila's presence had Ginny's resolve collapsing into stammering guilt. 'I was just doing my face.' The part of her that had learned to please and appease people, regardless of her own feelings or wishes, could still instantaneously demolish any decision she had made, as surely as a bulldozer could clear a bomb-site.

'Don't get worked up, sweetie. I only want a little

word.' Leila turned to Shirley. 'How about waiting for me at the bar?' It was an order not a question.

'But, Leila—' Shirley began, not wanting to miss whatever it was that was about to take place.

'There are customers waiting,' Leila said evenly.

Shirley flared her top lip at Ginny's reflection, then flounced out. That little cow was just asking for her come-uppance and it looked as though it was about to happen. Shirley prided herself on having a nose for other people's misery and she could smell tragedy coming off Ginny as strongly as if someone had spilt a whole bottle of the stuff all over her. She was only disappointed that she wasn't able to witness it personally.

Leila, checking that Shirley had closed the door properly, said casually, 'You don't like doing this, do you?'

Ginny felt panic flood through her. Only a moment ago she had wanted to walk out of the club and never look back, but now it came to it, the question of what else she could do suddenly seemed a lot more important, the issue a lot more threatening. And where would she go? Even her rooms were tied to the job. And then there was the money . . .

'What makes you say that?' she asked, hurriedly wiping the cleanser from her face with a pad of rough cotton wool.

'No need to sound so worried. I'm not after getting you sacked.' Leila, raising her tight green shantung skirt above her knees, lowered herself on to the least unpleasant-looking of the chairs. 'Now, come on,' she encouraged Ginny, 'you can be honest with me, you know that.'

Ginny let the cream-covered pad drop from her hand and began speaking. At first she spoke to Leila, but soon it was as though Leila wasn't there and Ginny was speaking to herself.

She stared into the mirror, but she didn't see her smeared and make-up-streaked face, what she saw was her life spinning and reeling in front of her in a malevolent kaleidoscope of scenes and moments – like watching a film that was running at the wrong speed and in the wrong order.

'I'm doing something I don't understand. That I don't like. And I've got to leave. I know that. And I know all the other girls all say the same. The difference is, I mean it. But the trouble is, who'd want me when I've been leading a life like this? Where would I go? It was bad enough before. But now . . .'

A self-mocking smile lifted Ginny's lips, but her eyes remained unmoved.

'The girls talk about going to Australia, Canada, South Africa. Anywhere to get away and start a new life where no one knows about what they did. Somewhere they can become other people, turn themselves into someone else. Find a place where they don't ever have to . . .' Ginny sighed deeply. 'Where they just don't have to. That's all.'

She picked up a packet of cigarettes that was lying on the table and lit one. 'All those magic places they talk about where there's no more working until the early hours, no more fog, or cold, or bomb-sites. It all sounds like something out of a fairy story. But I knew someone once, she sent her kids to Southern Rhodesia. It was a woman from our street. I don't know how she did it. She didn't even know where the place was. It was in Africa somewhere I think. And it broke her heart, but she thought it was for the best. And at least she had her children and tried to do her best for them.'

Ginny took a long draw on her cigarette. She frowned as though trying to work out something important.

'There's something else I'm worried about. Someone who needs looking after,' she said eventually. 'What with all this polio about, I'll bet she's not even had the vaccination yet. Dilys would never think to get it done.'

Leila watched her for a moment, then said, 'Why don't you just remind this Dilys whoever she is? I'm sure she won't mind. But I wouldn't worry if I were you, it's only children they're worried about, isn't it?'

Ginny seemed flustered to hear another voice. She rubbed her hand roughly over her face, dragging the remnants of her mascara down over her cheeks. 'It's not for her,' she said absently. 'It's for her little girl. I used to mind her now and again.'

Leila said nothing; she was used to the girls having complicated lives. And Ginny having a child she 'used to mind' sounded to Leila like just another of the many ways the girls had of talking about their kids. They either wanted to keep their existence secret for some reason, or had somehow lost contact with them – whether by design, against their will, or even, most incredibly to her, just by carelessness. Leila sometimes thought she took better care of her crocodile handbags than some of the girls did of themselves and their offspring. But then she had never actually raised a child.

'And when you see what can happen to people.' Ginny was speaking again. 'It really makes you think.'

She stubbed out her cigarette and turned her head so that she was looking at Leila face to face. 'It's like when Pauline started drinking the real stuff in the club, instead of just tonic. She went downhill so quickly. It was tragic.'

Leila put on her professional, bright-but-sympathetic smile and leaned forward so that she could touch Ginny gently on the arm. 'You were very kind to Pauline when she had her operation,' she said, delicately skirting the use of the word abortion.

Ginny shrugged. 'I got rid of a baby myself once.'

Leila didn't show any sign of surprise. She just con-

259

tinued to touch her arm. 'A lot of girls make mistakes, Ginny.'

'No. It wasn't a mistake. Well, not in the way you think. Getting rid of it was the mistake.'

A single fat tear rolled on to Ginny's cheek and plopped on to her lap. She sniffed loudly and fumbled around clumsily with the Craven A packet on the table, trying and failing to get one out of the box. Leila took out her mother-of-pearl case and lighter, lit two gold-tipped black cigarettes and gave one to Ginny.

'But I was in such a state, you see,' Ginny explained to herself as much as to Leila. 'When there's hardship, people just can't manage. But they do what they think's best. Like poor Violet Varney.'

Leila didn't ask who Violet Varney might be, she just let Ginny continue.

'It's not fair. You see some of the big spenders coming into the club and you think, if I'd had just a little bit of the money they've got . . .' Her hand shook as she put the cigarette to her mouth. 'Yvette said that that bloke in here the other night, the one with the funny clothes, was a maharajah, all the way from India.'

'He was.'

'But I'll bet even he's got his own story. That he's either lonely, or miserable in some way. But hard times are easier to cope with when you've got a few bob. That's why I came here in the first place, to earn the money to get a better life for myself. A life I thought I deserved. Now look at me.'

A loud crack of thunder made Ginny jump.

'Just raining again,' soothed Leila in her warm, purring voice.

'Even this weather's getting me down,' Ginny sobbed, unable to hold back the flood of tears any longer.

'That's what I thought.' Leila handed her her lace-trimmed handkerchief. 'And that's why I want to put a proposition to you.'

Ginny shuddered as though someone was walking over her grave. 'How d'you mean?' she sniffed.

Leila twisted one long, slim leg elegantly around the other. 'I admire the way you dance with the customers, Ginny. And the way you speak when you're with them. You sound very classy. It impresses them.'

Ginny laughed mirthlessly. 'After nearly a year at this lark you learn how to act a part if you don't learn anything else. But I'd hardly call it classy.'

'No, I mean it. You have a way with you and you really can dance, you know.'

'I used to go dancing with my friend once upon a time. And even with my husband.' She shook her head in self-pity.

'You certainly know how to use your body.'

'You have to in this line of work.' Ginny's voice was thick with tears. She blew her nose loudly into Leila's delicate little hankie and flicked a cynical eyebrow.

'That's why I want to know if you'd like a part in the new show we're bringing in here.'

Ginny frowned briefly at the 'we' – nobody at the club was really sure why, but the governor never seemed to be around, while Leila appeared to have taken responsibility for all of the business side at Frith Street. There were rumours, of course: that he was inside, or that he was too busy with a whole lot of new interests, but nobody knew for sure. Whatever the reason, Ginny hadn't set eyes on him since she'd been there – well, not to her knowledge. In the dimly lit club, one man was very much like another.

'We have to keep up with the competition, you see.'

'What competition's that?' Ginny had lost track.

'The other clubs and theatres. The governor's keen we

261

should make the place look classy, so don't worry, it wouldn't involve you in anything nasty or unpleasant.'

Leila had actually mentioned the governor, but Ginny was too busy laughing, genuinely amused this time, to follow it up. 'Nothing nasty or unpleasant? After what I've been doing?'

Leila's tone hardened. 'You told me once you had dreams.'

'Yeah, so much for them. Look what's become of me.'

'Well I'm giving you a chance to make some of your dreams come true, a chance to be something special. A star in an artistic tableau.'

'What, standing naked in front of a room full of dirty old men, you mean?'

'Better than what happened last night, sweetie.'

Ginny hurriedly looked away.

'Terry told me.'

Ginny felt the tears pricking her eyes. She was so ashamed.

'Say yes, Ginny. For me. It'll be the best thing that's ever happened to you. I promise'.

'You have to keep *still* remember, Yvette. I told you, if you go wrong, just watch Ginny.'

Leila rolled her eyes and smacked her forehead with the flat of her hand. She must have told Yvette to stop quivering and wiggling about at least a hundred times during the past fortnight of rehearsals, and now here they were, in the middle of the final dress run through, due to open in a couple of hours and the girl still hadn't got it. She might be a gorgeous, redheaded beauty, but she certainly wasn't blessed with brains.

Leila tried again. '*Static* tableaux, sweetie, *static*. That's what it means. Remember? Staying still so we don't all get arrested? Now stop waggling those pretty little titties of yours all over the place and get on with it. You're meant to be a divine goddess offering herself up to Zeus, not a cheap chorus girl trying to pull a punter in the front row.'

Yvette narrowed her extravagantly made-up eyes and strode to the front of the stage that had been especially constructed at the end of the club, next to the dais where the three-piece band were positioned ready to play.

'I have never looked like a cheap chorus girl in my life!' she roared, the pink ostrich plumes on her head and the narrow, sequined straps that made up the rest of her goddess costume fluttering and glittering as she jabbed her finger at Leila. Then, grabbing her naked breasts in her hands, Yvette stuck her chin in the air and declared, 'And these titties are certainly not little!'

She spun round and glared at the drummer who had dared to mutter something about her bra size to the pianist. 'And you can shut your gob an' all, you fat old bugger. Just 'cos you've got bigger tits than I have!'

The drummer, who *was* a bit on the heavy side but didn't like to be reminded of the fact, threw down his sticks in protest. He knew it was a rather pathetic gesture, but he also knew it wasn't worth starting a row with Yvette; he'd seen her – under cover of the confusion of a police raid – floor a punter with a single left hook, just because she had taken exception to the way the man had smiled reassuringly at her. And she didn't look very happy now. In fact, Yvette looked ready to rip someone's head off.

Leila bit her lip, not knowing whether the sound that was bursting to come out of her mouth was a laugh at the absurdity of the situation, or a scream of despair over the possibility that she might have to cancel the opening night of a show that she had had advertised all over the West End. The governor would go mad.

The pianist, who was either bolder or less sensible than the drummer, grinned broadly at Yvette who still had her hands clasped to her bosom. 'Need any help holding them things, Yve? Not too heavy for you, are they?'

'That's it!' Yvette was steaming. She pulled off her head-dress and flung it to the floor. 'I've had enough. I'm off home. And don't expect me back.'

'But, sweetie,' Leila pleaded, 'if you walk out, the show can't go on.'

'Let Ginny do it by herself.'

'But it's all planned around the two of you. You know that. All the scenes are—'

'Tough.'

'Let me have a word?' Ginny asked, stepping forward.

Leila raised her hands in surrender. 'Sure, go ahead.'

Ginny picked up Yvette's feathers, took her gently by the arm and tried to lead her to the side of the stage.

Yvette pulled free and folded her arms firmly across her bosom. 'What?'

'Look, Yve, I know you've been here longer than me and you've seen girls come and go. In fact, I bet you've seen it all. But, please, listen to me for just a minute?'

Yvette shrugged carelessly. 'Go on.'

'I never in all my wildest dreams expected to wind up like this.' She raised her hand to silence Yvette who was about to interrupt. 'Please, I'm not judging anyone. I just meant that I was an ordinary little housewife whose life somehow went out of control. When I first came here, you were kind to me. You made me feel at home after my first night's work. And even though it was obvious I thought I was different from the rest of you, you knew I was gonna wind up doing what I've been doing the moment you saw me. Just like Leila did. And once I started . . .' She shook her head. 'Look, Yve, this is a chance for me to *stop* doing it. A chance for both of us. And remember it's us she picked, not the others.'

Yvette shrugged again. 'So?'

'Well, for a start, even though I'm nervous as hell, the money she's offering is bloody good and I couldn't half do with a few extra quid. Plus, if the choice is between earning my living flashing me knockers at the mugs out there, or letting them have it away with me night after night, then it's obvious the choice I'm gonna make. So how about you, Yve?'

'I don't take much notice of them to tell you the truth. I let me mind go blank. Just let them get on with it and wait till they finish.'

'Liar.' Ginny touched her gently on the cheek. 'Please, Yve. I can't go on brassing. I need this chance. And Leila said you can still do business as well, if you want. And the tips we'll get if we dance with them afterwards, can you imagine?'

Yvette sighed wearily. 'All right, but I'm telling you, if she tells me to stand still once more, I'm gonna chin the bitch.'

Ginny squeezed her hand. 'Thanks, Yve, really. You won't regret it, I promise.'

Plastering on a broad smile, Yvette took a deep breath, turned to face Leila, threw her arms into a dramatic pose and said sweetly. 'Is this better?'

'Much better, darling,' beamed Leila. 'The punters are going to love you.'

And the punters did. When the curtains closed after the final stirring scene – two shy maidens caught in the act of bathing by a river – the audience went wild.

And, to Leila's relief, the other girls liked it too. She had been afraid there might be some jealousy, or worse, that one of the screaming cat fights that had broken out

265

in the past over something as insignificant as a bottle of nail polish would erupt, but it all had worked out really well. Not only were the customers put in just the right frame of mind for going upstairs, but during the show they were so busy goggling at the stage that they were even more generous than usual – saying yes to almost any request for yet more drinks, or gifts from the cigarette girl.

Leila grabbed the only bottle of genuine champagne in the club, that she had told Gloria to cool for her behind the bar, and took it through to the dressing-room.

'You were wonderful! The governor's going to be thrilled with us.'

Yvette was about to question the 'us' when she spotted the champagne. 'I'm so pleased,' she said pleasantly.

Leila popped the cork with a theatrical flourish and poured three glasses. 'And you, Ginny? Are you pleased?'

Ginny, glowing with the adrenalin rush of performing in front of an appreciative audience, threw her arms round Leila and kissed her. 'I'm not only pleased, Leila. I can't tell you. I loved it. It was like being someone else. Like being a film star.'

Leila picked up one of the glasses and raised it in salute. 'I'm absolutely thrilled, Ginny. Thrilled to bits. And just wait till you hear what you're going to do next!'

Chapter 13

As Ginny sat at the mirror, fixing a sparkling rhinestone tiara in her hair, Leila bobbed down behind her and looked over Ginny's shoulder at their reflections.

'It's wonderful out there, darling,' she raved. 'Just wonderful. The club is simply full to bursting.' She took a box of Passing Clouds from her bag and offered the pink packet to Ginny.

Without a word, Ginny took one and waited for Leila to light it for her – at one time, such an exotic item as a deliberately flattened cigarette would have fascinated Ginny, but now it didn't merit the lifting of an eyebrow.

'How many of those *gentlemen* out there', Leila continued in a happy, encouraging trill, 'do you suppose have come up to the West End *supposedly* to buy Christmas presents for little wifey and the kiddiewinks, but have actually come here to see you instead?'

Ginny drew on her cigarette and shrugged. She couldn't give a bugger about lying husbands or their phoney Christmas shopping trips, all that interested her was trying to figure out why on earth she had ever let Leila talk her into doing this. The static tableaux were one thing – they were easy, just standing there like a statue, posing under the coloured lights, looking unseeingly into the middle distance as though you were a bit missing, while the band played a suitably cod-classical accompaniment. As Yvette always gleefully reminded her when they were counting their wages at the end of the week, it was actually *more* than easy, it was all a bit of a doddle, especially compared to hostessing. Admittedly they were stark naked up there on the stage – well as good as – but Ginny found it oddly soothing, pretending, as she stared at some imaginary vista, cloaked by the velvet darkness of the club, that she was all alone, that she was someone else, even somewhere else.

But this . . .

Ginny stared into the mirror at the exaggerated greasepaint mask she painted on nightly; the mask that the real Ginny hid behind as she posed in front of the punters. But a lot of good a bit of slap plastered across her chops would do her tonight.

Leila and her big ideas. Where did she think they were, the sodding Windmill or the bloody Moulin Rouge?

Ginny groaned and dipped her chin to her chest. Knowing that with the new act she was actually expected to look directly at the punters; to flirt with them with her eyes; to smile coyly but provocatively at them, as she wiggled, and strutted, and . . .

'Something wrong, sweetie?'

Ginny lifted her head and looked hard at the still beaming Leila. She had a way of sounding so innocent, so plausible, but there were times when Ginny could have sworn it was all an act. Times like now, for instance, when Ginny was so nervous she could barely stop trembling, yet Leila was yattering away as though it was something to look forward to, a real treat. But she must have known how Ginny was feeling. Just as she knew that she, Leila, was holding the trump card. Because, when it came down to it, it was this or hostessing. And if Ginny didn't want to do either, how else would she pay off her rent arrears? And rent arrears were certainly what she had.

Like all the other girls, Ginny was still living in a bedsit owned by the governor and had been only too pleased to accept Leila's kind offer of the occasional opportunity to put off paying for it for a week or two. Also like the other girls, Ginny had soon found herself with substantial debts.

She knew now that she shouldn't have delayed paying, but at the time it had seemed like a godsend. The trouble was, her money just seemed to go nowhere. After she'd sent her weekly envelopes – stuffed with half her wages between them – one to Dilys for her and Susan, and the other to Nellie, there was barely enough to live on, let alone to pay her bills. She had, once or twice, determined not to send them anything – Nellie and Dilys were probably both laughing at her anyway, while she ran up bigger and bigger debts – but just the thought of little Susan in that big old brown hand-me-down coat, and the guilt she felt at the state Nellie would probably be in without her help, had her sending off the envelopes by the next post.

She supposed it would have been different if Dilys had been a better mother, or if Nellie had had someone else she could depend on. But what was the point of supposing? All Ginny could hope was that Susan actually saw some of the money she sent to the prefab and that Nellie got hers before Ted had the chance to nick it.

If he was still around.

Ted. There was another worry. Had he thought to send his little daughter a birthday card last month? Ginny really hoped so.

Even though it still felt as though she was being slapped in the face just to think of Susan being Ted's child, Ginny couldn't stop caring about her. She loved her. It was as simple as that.

Ginny'd sent her a pretty lacy card and a baby doll in a cellophane-wrapped box, although she had no way of knowing if Dilys would even let Susan see it. Maybe Dilys had pretended that the gift was from her; knowing Dilys, she probably had. But, whatever happened, Ginny could only hope that Susan had had something on her birthday. And that she was happy.

Ginny shook her head, trying to clear the images from her mind of the smiling child she missed so much, took another drag on her cigarette, then ground it out with slow deliberation.

For the moment, she had more immediate things to concern her. 'Look, Leila,' she asked, twisting round to face the stylishly suited woman, 'are you honestly one hundred per cent sure about this? Are you positive I won't get in no trouble?'

Leila touched a gloved fingertip to Ginny's chin. 'I promise with all my heart. As long as you don't show anything actually moving, it's all completely legal. And let's face it, if *you* get in trouble, we all get in trouble.'

She had a way of making her words sound like a reassurance, but they could so easily have been interpreted as a threat.

Five minutes later, with Leila blowing her a final kiss of good luck from the wings, Ginny stood, quivering with fear, waiting for her cue.

And there it was: the band striking up the opening bars of the slow, sensual rumba she had rehearsed endlessly with them during the past nerve-racking weeks.

The curtains drew back to show Ginny, centre stage, lit by a single pink spotlight, with everything but her high-heel-shod legs hidden by two enormous pink feather fans.

As she took her first voluptuous steps to the left and let one of the fans drop a tantalising fraction, showing the merest hint of the creamy slope of the top of her breast, a loud cheer of approval went up and suddenly Ginny was no longer scared. Everything was going to be all right.

No, it was better than all right, it was wonderful.

Ginny was in a cocoon of soft feathers and sumptuous pink light, and lusciously flamboyant rhythms washed over her, urging her body to thrust and sway with the music. It was like being in a dream where there were no rent arrears, no worries and, best of all, no Ted Martin to hurt her.

As she gyrated behind, peeped over, and smiled coquettishly around, her provocatively swirling and dipping fans, she knew that the audience loved her.

Actually, not all of the audience was watching her. Carmen for one was too busy trying to get Patty's attention to care about what Ginny was up to.

When Patty failed to respond to Carmen's agitated waving and flapping, she reached across her punter – who was totally mesmerised by Ginny's bumps and grinds – and tapped her urgently on the arm.

'What?' Patty mouthed, angry at Carmen's interruption; she'd been enjoying a bit of peace, even letting her eyes close for a moment, while her punter goggled at the stage, his mouth half open like a drooling puppy.

'Look who's in tonight,' Carmen hissed, jerking her head towards the bar.

Patty lazily checked out the occupants of the tall bar-stools. Now her mark wasn't the only one with his mouth open.

She twisted back to Carmen. 'It's the governor!' she squeaked. 'So he *ain't* inside.' She dabbed at her hair to make sure it was tidy – although it would have taken a gale-force wind to have damaged Patty's teased and lacquered creation – and sat up straight, hitching her dress further up her thighs.

271

'Tits up and all, Carmen!' she giggled, sticking out her chest and adjusting her circle-stitched bra with a determined two-handed grab. 'You never know, he might take a shine to one of us and whisk us off into the night in that big fancy car of his.'

But despite Patty's and Carmen's best efforts, the governor was oblivious of their attractions; all he was interested in was Ginny's performance up on the stage.

As he sipped his drink and listened to Leila telling him about all the hard work she had put in rehearsing the fan dancer and the band so that the evening would be a success, he didn't take his gaze off Ginny for a single moment.

At the end of the number, the curtain dropped and the audience went wild. Their whoops, cheers and applause were so rapturous that even the resolutely morose Gloria, standing in his usually joy-free domain behind the bar, couldn't help but grin.

While Ginny further teased her audience by peeking around the edge of the curtain and flashing just a glimpse of her naked thigh – supposedly to acknowledge the appreciation, but actually because she was so high on the rush of performing that she didn't want it to end – the governor rose from his bar-stool and flicked a glance towards Johnno, his minder whom he had left over by the doorway.

Moving surprisingly swiftly for someone of his size, the huge man was almost immediately by his side, carrying his boss's Crombie and trilby hat with as much care as if he were a handmaiden offering up a delicate casket of precious jewels.

'Very impressive, Leila', the governor said, shrugging down into his overcoat. 'Very impressive indeed. As good as you said.'

'I'm glad you approve,' Leila said, smiling broadly in

an effort to cover her disappointment that he seemed to be preparing to leave without her. 'You're off now, are you?'

He nodded. 'Business before pleasure, you know me, girl.'

With that, he treated Leila to a friendly wink and left the club flanked by Johnno, his oversized bodyguard.

Shirley, who had spent the whole of Ginny's act with her eyes fixed firmly on Leila and the governor, was convinced she'd just witnessed something worth temporarily abandoning her punter for. And anyway, there was no risk of him going off with someone else, not tonight; there wasn't a spare girl left in the whole place. The titillation up on the stage had put them all very much in the mood and eager hands had grabbed for the nearest bit of female flesh to pull down on to their laps.

Shirley whispered something suitably lewd into her punter's ear – just to make sure she kept his interest – then sidled up to Leila, who was hovering by the bar staring into her glass of tonic water, trying to summon the enthusiasm to go and congratulate Ginny on the success of her solo début.

'It's enough to make a girl totally jealous, if you ask me, Leila,' Shirley rasped, her voice harsh with sly nastiness and insinuation. 'The way all the men in the place couldn't take their eyes off her. It was bad enough when she was just doing the tableaux with Yvette. But that fan dance. Well . . .'

Shirley paused, waiting for Leila's response. There was none, so Shirley continued dripping her poison. 'I don't think I've ever seen the governor so captivated by a girl before.'

Leila turned to Shirley and said very slowly and deliberately. 'I'd watch my mouth, if I were you Shirley.

Because no one likes a stirrer, especially a sad old stirrer who is coming very close to being a has-been.'

With that, Leila finished her drink, smiled sweetly at Gloria as she handed him her empty glass and swept off to the dressing-room to see Ginny.

Shirley was left standing at the bar, with Gloria staring at her with his usual mixture of undisguised contempt and camp disapproval.

'Don't say a fucking word, you skinny-arsed old queen,' hissed Shirley.

'A few days' time and it'll be Christmas. Can you believe it? I can't. Before we know where we are it'll be Easter again.' Carmen peered over the top of the late edition of the *Evening Standard* that she had been flicking through absent-mindedly, while she waited for the other girls to finish getting ready. 'What plans have you got for Christmas then, Gin?' she asked. 'Gonna give your feathers a few days off?'

Ginny said nothing.

'You must be due a break. You've been up on that stage every night for weeks, flapping them fans about *and* still doing the tableaux with Yvette. You must be knackered.'

Ginny, not wanting to become involved in any conversation that had anything to do with Christmas – and especially not one that was about families and Christmas – bent forward and started fiddling with the silver-sequined garter on her thigh.

'Well?' Carmen persisted.

'I don't know yet,' Ginny muttered.

Carmen, not sure she'd heard properly, but still sounding scandalised, had another stab at sorting out what Ginny actually meant. The fact that Ginny had never talked to Carmen about her family – and Carmen being a curious type at the best of times and bluntly nosy at the worst – naturally made her want to know more. And this seemed like the perfect opportunity. 'You don't what, Gin?'

Ginny sat up and snapped, 'I *said* I don't know yet.'

'Don't know?' Carmen was now clearly outraged and there was going to be no stopping her from saying so. 'But it's the twentieth of bloody December, girl. How can you not know? My mum would have me by the throat and be shaking me like a pepper-pot if I dared even think I didn't know what I'd be doing on Christmas day.'

Patty grinned. 'Sure don't we all know what you'll be doing at Christmas, Carmen? The same as every year. You'll be there with your mum, sitting in that big old church in Brixton, with your best hat perched on top o' your head, singing away like a beautiful brown skylark.'

Carmen rolled her eyes and groaned. 'Don't remind me, Pat. All Mum's sisters have invited themselves over to hers this year as well. Imagine it, all my aunties, all there snooping on me.'

She tossed the newspaper to the floor, stood up, stuck her fists into her waist and launched into an imitation of her Caribbean relatives. 'Why you not married yet, Carmen girl? I had ten kids by the time I was your age. There no nice boys where you work? No doctors?'

That last bit caught Yvette's attention. 'What you on about? Doctors?'

'Well, you don't think they know what I do for a living do you, Yve?' Carmen laughed self-mockingly. 'They all think I'm working at St Thomas's. A nurse on the night shift. You should hear the lies I tell.' She puffed out her cheeks and shrugged resignedly. 'But if I want to keep breathing, I've got no choice but to lie.'

'Least you haven't got to go all the way to bloody County Clare to see your family.' Patty sighed dramatically, handed Carmen the cigarette she had just finished rolling and flopped down on to one of the chairs. 'It'll be murder. And I bet I've told them more lies than you've told your lot. I'm working in an office, if you don't mind. Me!' She accepted the cigarette from Carmen and took a long drag, before handing it back to her. 'Still, I miss my little brothers and sisters. It'll be good to see them again. And it'll be cheaper than staying at home.'

'Broke again?' Carmen asked.

'What do you think?'

'But you've got no plans yet,' Yvette said, turning to Ginny.

'I'll probably be spending the day worrying if I can afford to put another shilling in the gas meter,' Ginny replied quietly.

'You're never still sending all your dough to that old cow of a mother-in-law of yours, are you?' Yvette exploded at full, shocked volume.

Ginny didn't answer, but it was obvious to Yvette, just from her expression, that Ginny was indeed still keeping Nellie.

'Now I understand why you've been so broke,' she went on. 'I wondered why you'd been holding on to your rent so often. I mean, it's not as though you've got kids to worry about. Not like some of us.'

Ginny had become close to Yvette in the eighteen months that she'd been working at the club, and enjoyed her company and her friendship, but she sometimes wished that her friend was a bit more subtle. *And* that she'd never mentioned Nellie to her. Yvette meant well, but it made Ginny feel vulnerable, having someone knowing things about her that, on reflection, she would really rather have kept private. She was only glad that she'd never blabbed about Susan.

Susan. The thought of what she might be doing on

Christmas morning had Ginny swallowing hard, gulping back the threat of tears. She knew from last year what hell it was, being all alone with too much time to think. Not having any money suddenly didn't seem so important . . .

'Here's someone who's not going to have to worry about having a spend-up over Christmas,' said Carmen, picking up the paper again and flipping it in half. 'Listen to this.'

She began reading out one of the news stories in a slow, halting monotone. 'Yesterday, in London's West End, three postmen were forced into an alley off Shaftesbury Avenue and attacked by armed thieves. The robbers got away with the van carrying registered mail worth over £200,000.'

'Two hundred grand!' Yvette gasped.

'And just around the corner!' Patty grabbed the paper from Carmen. 'Was anyone hurt? Fancy a terrible thing like that happening so close.'

A terrible thing. It was that all right. Patty's words made Ginny think about Ted and how he'd been so angry when they'd had to call off the armed robbery he'd been planning. From the way he'd reacted to being grassed it was more like he'd been stopped from doing an honest day's work, rather than prevented from committing a violent crime.

Ginny tugged at a loose platinum curl. How had he started thinking that way – that hurting people, stealing from them, was a reasonable thing to do? Surely he hadn't always been so callous. He couldn't have been. But was it possible for someone to change so much? Maybe he was desperate; but that was just finding an excuse. No matter how desperate or broke she was, Ginny knew she could never do anything to hurt anyone else.

Doing things that hurt herself, however . . . That was a different matter.

Ginny's increasingly disturbing thoughts were interrupted by one of the girls – a pale-skinned brunette, who had been sitting on the floor studiously painting her toenails. 'It's true what they're saying in the papers, you know,' she said, her words coming out in short grunting breaths as she bent forward to reach her smallest toe.

'What's that then, Betty?' asked Carmen.

'They've got to do something. 'Cos Britain's . . .' She paused. 'Hang on, how did they put it? *In the grip of a crime wave.* That's it. And it's really frightening.'

'Crime wave!' Carmen exploded. 'Are you having a joke, Bet? Most of our bloody customers are criminals. How else d'you think they can afford these bloody prices?'

'But I bet our customers don't all carry guns,' Betty replied sulkily, feeling that she'd made a fool of herself.

'Guns? Whatever are you talking about?' Leila stepped into the room looking a picture of shocked innocence, but from her tone it was clear that guns were now a closed subject.

Carmen hurriedly stubbed out her cigarette and slipped the butt into her handbag – Leila had already taken her to one side and explained very clearly the governor's views on girls using dope or alcohol while they were working and Carmen wasn't about to be caught out again.

If Leila noticed Carmen's sleight of hand she didn't make it obvious, instead she smiled coolly and clapped her hands like a headmistress calling her pupils to order. 'Don't look so miserable, sweeties. Show those teeth. Come on now, off you go. Mustn't keep them waiting.'

The girls jumped to their feet and began flapping around, hurriedly putting final touches to make-up and hair, straightening seams and slipping into elbow-length gloves. Leila turning up so early was a bit of a shock, as she didn't usually show till closing time and they were already nearly fifteen minutes behind their official schedule. Gloria must have been grassing on them again – getting on the telephone to Leila and telling tales on them like some runty little school sneak.

'By the way,' Leila purred, as the first of the girls reached the door, 'after you've all done your family duty on Christmas day, there's a party at my place.'

Patty groaned dismally.

'There's no need for that, Patty. There won't be any punters. It's strictly pleasure this time. A little treat to thank you for your hard work during the past year.' Leila didn't add that putting on a party for the hostesses was her rather sad alternative to an otherwise lonely Christmas night. 'So how about a thank you instead?'

'I wasn't complaining, Leila. It's just that I've promised my mum I'll go home to Ireland for a few days.'

Leila pinched Patty's cheek almost affectionately. 'Never mind. Another time, eh?'

Soon the girls had all drifted out into the club, and Leila and Ginny were left alone in the dressing-room.

If Ginny hadn't had been waiting to go on stage for her first number, she'd have joined them like a shot. Leila's unexpectedly early visit was making her feel nervous. 'Is anything wrong, Leila?'

Leila's smile barely stretched her lips. 'Of course not,' she reassured her.

'You don't wanna change the act again, or nothing?'

Leila shook her head. 'Don't be silly. It's a real success. Why would we want to change it?'

Ginny wasn't satisfied. 'So what's wrong? You don't usually come round before closing. Not unless something's up.'

279

'I just came in to see how you're getting on, that's all. And to tell you how pleased we are with the way the show's been going.'

Ginny frowned. Why would *we* want to change it? How pleased *we* are. What was this all about?

'So,' Leila continued, 'you're happy and we're happy. Good.'

Ginny relaxed a bit, but then, after a moment's thought, she continued. 'If you don't mind me saying, there is one thing *I'd* like to change.'

'Yes?'

'The money.' She took a deep breath. 'I could do with a bit more.'

'Could you?' Leila asked coolly. She wasn't sure if she liked the direction the conversation was taking, nor where it might lead.

'I want you to understand, I'm not being greedy. I've just gotta try and get myself out of all this debt. And most of the other girls are in the same boat.'

'Really?' Leila's lips compressed into thin, tight lines.

Ginny nibbled at the inside of her cheek. Had she said the wrong thing? It was so hard to know what was going through Leila's mind. Well, it was too late now.

'I know the fan dance has fetched in a lot of new punters.' Ginny tried a little laugh. 'I mean, this place must be a real gold-mine now.'

Leila blinked slowly. 'And is that your business?'

'Don't get me wrong, Leila, I wouldn't be saying anything, but like I say, it's not only me. I'm having a bad enough time, but some of the girls are in real trouble. They've been dumped by their blokes, left to bring up their kids all by themselves.' She had to make Leila see. 'How can they work if they're worried all the time? I reckon if they were treated right – paid more, I mean – it would be good for everyone.'

'You do, do you?'

Ginny nodded half-heartedly. Why had she started this? 'Well, I reckon if I had a club—'

'You? A club?' Leila snorted. 'You can't even open a second-rate spieler without the right sort of support. Money has to be paid. A lot of money. Money that would make your little debts seem quite ridiculous.'

'Look, Leila, I think you've got me wrong, I wasn't exactly serious—'

'It's probably just as well, seeing as you obviously don't know the first thing about it. Try and start up something without permission from the local firm, then you'd soon learn.'

Shirley appeared in the dressing-room doorway, smirking like a cat who'd just cornered a tasty-looking mouse. 'And you'd know, wouldn't you, Leila?'

'Shirley!' Leila fumbled around with her cigarette case and lighter, wondering how long Shirley had been standing there listening. 'I was just about to explain to Ginny that she should think herself lucky that she's working for a boss who actually understands the business side of things.'

'I hope you mean me,' said an amused male voice, from somewhere behind Shirley.

Shirley spun round. It was the governor. What was he doing here?

Ginny hastily snatched up her wrapper and pulled it round her – suddenly embarrassed about showing off her near-naked body – while Leila sprang to her feet, looking as though she'd been caught with her hand in the till.

The governor eased Shirley out of the way, stepped inside the dressing-room and lowered himself into one of the flimsy chairs more suited to a chorus girl's physique than to a man of his size.

'I was listening to what you was saying,' he said, lighting a cigar.

'I was only—' Leila began.

'Not you. Her.' He lifted his chin towards Ginny. 'Come out to the bar and have a drink with me.'

'But I've got to go on and do my fan dance,' Ginny stammered.

'I meant *afterwards*. Christ, I don't wanna stop you showing off that body of your'n and causing no riots, now do I, blondie?'

It was the first time Ginny had ever met the governor and she wanted to make a good impression on him; after all, he had the power to make or break her as far as the club was concerned – even more so than Leila. So, after finishing her set, Ginny rushed off the stage and began rummaging frantically through the clothes rail for an outfit likely to impress him.

She eventually decided on an almost modest, black moiré, ballerina-length cocktail dress with a broad patent belt to circle her narrow waist, and a plunging, sweetheart neckline – the feature that had earned it its place in the dressing-room wardrobe – that showed her breasts off to perfection.

By the time she eventually joined the governor at the bar, Ginny was panting like a highly strung thoroughbred straining at the starting line.

'Billy Saunders,' he introduced himself, rising to his feet and holding out a hand in friendly greeting.

Warily, Ginny smiled up at him and shook his hand – had she known of the connection between her husband and this big, attractive man, she would have been a lot more than wary, she would have been terrified.

'What can I get you?' asked Saunders.

'Am I allowed a proper drink?' Ginny asked quietly,

feeling that she needed something more than the usual tonic water to steady her nerves.

'When you're with me you're allowed whatever you fancy, blondie. But full marks for asking first. Shows you're using your loaf, that you ain't stupid.'

'Thanks. I'll have a Babycham then, please. And my name's Ginny, by the way.'

'And I'll have a glass of champagne.'

Ginny twisted round to see who had spoken; it was Leila, sitting stony-faced on the stool behind her.

'Don't mind if I join you, do you, Billy?' she asked.

Saunders laughed. 'Frightened you might miss something, Leila?'

'Don't be unpleasant, Billy,' she replied, forcing herself to show her teeth. 'I just thought you might enjoy the company, that's all.'

'You should know my routine by now, Leila. It's not company I'm after; I'm here on business. But I've got nothing to say that you can't hear.'

'Shall I go, then, Mr Saunders?' Ginny asked, not understanding what was going on.

'No, blondie, the business I had in mind is to do with you.'

'So, you reckon Yvette could do the dancing then? That she's up to it?'

Ginny nodded miserably. She had misunderstood Leila when she had said they were happy with the show – she'd never mentioned that they were happy with Ginny's part in it. Only the show. She was such a fool. Now here was Saunders taking her job away from her and she was helping him do it. 'Yvette could do it if she practises.'

'Good.' Saunders sniffed and tapped the ash from his cigar. 'And you'll be free to run the new club for me.'

Ginny turned round to look at Leila to wish her well – even if her own luck had just disappeared down the chute, she didn't wish Leila any ill will. But Leila wasn't sitting there any longer, she was disappearing into the dressing-room with Shirley close on her heels.

'I meant *you*, blondie.' Saunders grinned.

'Me?'

'Yeah. You're from the East End, ain't you?'

She nodded dumbly.

'I've been keeping an eye on you. The blokes like you. And you're bright. Bright as a button. But there's no old toffee with you, not like with some clever girls. And no slyness. That's rare in a bird.'

Ginny was too stunned to know whether he was paying her a compliment or insulting her.

'I've been developing me interests down your way for a few years now. I've already got one or two places up and running. All with women in charge. It was an idea I had and it seems to be working. It keeps the atmosphere calmer for some reason. Classier too.'

Ginny opened her mouth but Saunders raised his hands to silence her. 'Don't worry. You'd be the front, but there'd be plenty of back-up. Like Gloria's got muscle in this place and Leila to sort out the cash side for him.'

He paused to blow a plume of smoke in the air. 'Gloria's a right old Soho queen. Been knocking about this area for years. Knows everyone and anyone. But in the East End . . .' Saunders shrugged his massive shoulders. 'He'd be lost. Now this place I've got in mind for you . . .' He winked and grinned at her, showing even white teeth. 'You'll fit in just nice.'

Ginny knocked back the rest of her Babycham in a single swallow and slapped her glass down on the bar. 'Can I have another one d'you think, Mr Saunders?' she gasped through the bubbles. 'But before you say yes, I think you should know something. I reckon you must have heard what I said to Leila, back in the dressing-room. But I didn't mean I *really* wanted to run a club. I was sort of explaining . . .' She threw up her hands and shook her head. 'I just ain't up to a job like that.'

Saunders, obviously amused, grinned even more broadly. 'We'll see, blondie. We'll see.'

Back in the dressing-room, Leila was pretending to do one of her spot inventories of the clothes rail – the dresses had a habit of going missing and reappearing on the second-hand stall in Berwick Street market – but all she really wanted was to be left alone.

Shirley either didn't understand, or she didn't care. She was hovering over Leila like a hawk eyeing a vole. 'Didn't I tell you to keep a watch out for her, Leila. You know what the governor's like when he gets set on a girl.'

'Shirley—'

'But maybe you should be relieved rather than upset.'

Leila spun round to face her. 'Why would I be either of those things, Shirley?'

'Well, maybe Ginny in a manager's job rather than fan dancing would be a good thing. The governor would see her differently.' Shirley smiled slyly. 'Plus he wouldn't see quite so much of her, if you get my meaning.'

'I don't think I do get your meaning actually, Shirley, but maybe you can get mine. Things have become very slack lately. Girls are smoking dope and drinking while they're meant to be working.'

She leaned very close to Shirley and sniffed, her face showing her obvious distaste. 'Is that booze I can smell on your breath again, Shirley? Because if it is, I'd be very careful if I were you. It would be terrible, you losing your job at your age, now wouldn't it?'

Chapter 14

'Not the last one to leave *again*?' Gloria sighed melodramatically, wagged his finger angrily at Ginny, then switched off the overhead light in the dressing-room, plunging the place into semi-darkness. All that was left illuminating the cramped little room was an intermittent flashing from the red neon sign advertising the club across the street and a feeble glow from a string of fairy lights draped round the scrawny little Christmas tree that the girls – in a moment of seasonal sentimentality – had set up beside the cracked sink.

'Well?' Gloria demanded.

Instead of saying anything, Ginny just flopped down on to one of the rickety chairs and let her arms dangle carelessly by her sides.

'Come on, this isn't good enough. Will you please move yourself? Now.' Gloria flapped his hands about, as he lisped at her in his affected, slightly northern singsong of a voice. 'For Gawd's sake, girl, shift, will you?'

When Ginny showed no sign of moving, he minced across the room towards her, flicking disapprovingly at the shadowy, discarded heaps of clothing and shoes that formed a scented and stained obstacle course across his path.

'Well?' Gloria persisted, leaning over her, his fists stuck into his waist. 'Are you going home or what?'

With her eyes still directed at the floor, Ginny exhaled wearily and said in a tiny, pained whisper, 'D'you know, Gloria, I sometimes feel like this *is* my home.'

'This dump? Home?' Clearly horrified that anyone could even entertain such a ghastly thought, Gloria snapped upright and clenched his hands protectively across his skinny chest, as if warding off the contagion that might just cause him to start thinking the same way.

'It's like a palace compared to the pigsty of a room I'm meant to live in,' she said. 'And it's not so lonely.'

'What the hell are you going on about?'

'Even when this place is almost empty, I still get the feeling that there's a bit of life going on out there. Somewhere.'

'I really do not know what you're talking about, but I reckon you must be going a bit soft in the old head department, dearie.'

Lethargically, Ginny raised her eyes to meet his, although in the strange half-light she couldn't quite make out his features. 'Yes you do. You know exactly what I mean, Gloria.' She stabbed her thumb absent-mindedly over her shoulder in the direction of the window. 'There's the stall holders setting up before they go into the coffee shop for their breakfast; the milkman rattling around with his crates; the early papers being sorted out for the stands. People laughing and talking. It's a real little community out there. One people really belong to. Feel part of.'

'Not at nearly half past bloody three on a Christmas morning they don't, darling.'

Gloria might have sounded his usual dismissive self, but from the security of the shadows he was frowning with concern as he watched Ginny's troubled face glowing first red, then disappearing, then glowing red again, in the on-off light of the neon sign. He wouldn't have admitted it to anyone, but he felt genuinely moved by the anguish he heard in her voice. She was a sad one, all right, and an odd one too, there was no denying it.

While it was obvious to Gloria how most of the girls had wound up working the clubs – sometimes it was what they had been brought up to expect they would do; or they had run away from some man; or they'd been tempted by what they thought would be easy money; or any one of a hundred other all too inevitable reasons – Ginny ... He could never make up his mind which of the categories she fitted into – if she fitted any of them at all. Despite the way she drove men wild when she got up on that stage, swooping her fans and shaking herself about, Ginny was, at other times, very reserved, keeping herself to herself and just getting on with her job. She spoke to Yvette sometimes, but Gloria would never lower himself to ask that little madam what Ginny had to say about herself; it would have affected his authority and Lord knows he had little enough of that, what with the girls running around as if they owned the place.

Still, whatever he felt, or thought, or wondered, Gloria didn't intend letting Ginny cotton on to the fact that he was in the least bit concerned about her. She might just use it against him one day. Experience had shown him, very early on, that people were like that. You let them see a soft side and they pounced on you. They chewed you up and then spat you out. His long days and nights in Soho had taught him to be self-protective, and presenting himself to the world as a sour, spiteful old queen, rather than the rather contented old one that he actually was, was as good a protection as any.

'Come on, Ginny,' he whined impatiently, stamping his patent-clad foot, 'I've got to lock up. So stop being such a stroppy tart and get yourself shifted.'

Before Ginny had the chance to open her mouth in reply, a hand reached round the door and flicked on the lamp in the corner.

Feeling he might faint, Gloria covered his eyes, gasped

like a dying cod fish and flattened himself against the wall, uttering a silent prayer.

Ginny was more curious than scared. Shading her eyes from the light, she squinted across the room and made out the unmistakable silhouette of the governor filling the doorway.

'All right, Gloria?' Saunders enquired affably, as he threw his hat on to one of the tables, then folded his arms across his muscular chest and leaned against the door jamb.

'I said, are you all right?' Saunders repeated, clearly amused by Gloria's camp exhibition of fluttering and swooning.

'Never better, Mr Saunders,' he trilled, 'I'm just finishing off in here, then I'm off home. I told Ginny, didn't I? Five minutes, then we're off, I said. Both of us. Out of this place. Gone. And, aw yeah' – he paused to catch his breath, patting himself delicately on his chest – 'a very merry Christmas to you.'

Then, with a simpering approximation of a smile spreading unnaturally across his narrow lips, Gloria scuttled over to the door and waited politely for the governor to let him pass.

Saunders did so, and Gloria slipped out to the bar and began busying himself counting the bottles in a crate that just happened to be close to the dressing-room door.

Ginny stood up, ready to follow Gloria out of the room, but Saunders had positioned himself back against the doorpost, blocking her exit.

'I was waiting outside for you in the motor,' he said. 'I wondered where you'd got to when all the others left just now. Thought maybe you hadn't been in tonight for some reason.'

Ginny shrugged, unnerved by the directness of his gaze and unsure what she should say. 'I was in tonight,' she began hesitantly, 'but I stayed behind because I had a little bit of tidying up to do in here.'

She immediately realised how ridiculous she sounded. Not only was it obvious she was in tonight – she was bloody well standing there, wasn't she? – but seeing as they were surrounded by what looked like the tragic remains of a direct bomb hit on a make-up, clothing and fag-end factory, the idea that she was doing 'a little bit of tidying up' was an even more stupid thing to say.

Saunders laughed, a loud, booming sound that had Gloria straining his ears and moving as near as he dared to the still open dressing-room door – what the hell was going on in there?

'I think it's gonna need a bit more than a tidy up,' he heard Saunders say.

This time, Ginny too saw the funny side of what she'd said. 'Maybe a flame thrower might be the answer.'

Saunders laughed again and touched Ginny lightly on the shoulder, easing her down on to one of the chairs.

It had been a long time since a man had touched her so gently. She'd forgotten how it could feel . . .

She watched as he shifted his hat carefully to one side, perched himself on the edge of the debris-covered table and held out his hands in a sweeping gesture of what might have been pleasure, or could have been one of control. 'It's Christmas,' he said simply, taking out a packet of Players Navy Cut from his jacket pocket. 'Cigarette?'

Ginny nodded dumbly and took one. Why had she done that? Why hadn't she just shaken her head and left?

'So,' he said, squinting at her through the smoke he'd exhaled from his first deep lungful, 'what're you doing over the holiday?'

'I'm not sure if I'm doing anything,' she said automatically, although she knew exactly what she would be doing.

She would be alone in her bedsit; a place that, despite all her efforts to make it something like a proper home, would never be anything more than a disgusting little room, full of rusting, dripping pipes and wet, peeling wallpaper, three flights up from the shared lavatory that made her gag just to think about it.

She wondered if Saunders had any idea how awful the places were that he rented to the girls. Probably not. He seemed to have people to do just about everything else for him, so why would he bother himself visiting slums?

'You're having me on,' he said, interrupting her thoughts.

'Sorry?'

'Are you trying to tell me that a beautiful girl like you hasn't got a load of parties lined up?'

Ginny's cheeks flushed and she lowered her chin, hoping he hadn't noticed. It was ridiculous. She spent her working life showing off all she had and yet a single compliment from Saunders had her blushing like a virgin. It was something about him . . .

She peered up at him through her lashes and realised what it was. He was looking at her with the self-assured, direct gaze that was the prerogative of only the genuinely confident. A confidence that could come from a man's looks, his wealth, his authority, or, as in Saunders's case, she thought, from a combination of all those things.

'I've embarrassed you, darling. I'm sorry.' He smiled easily. 'But there's no shame in having no one to go to.'

Saunders's words jolted her. She turned away sharply. It was true, she had no one. They were gone, all of them. But she didn't want him to feel that she was . . . That she was what? The sad, pathetic figure that she actually was?

'I've had plenty of offers,' she said hurriedly.

Saunders raised a querying eyebrow.

'I mean, I've been invited to something tomorrow afternoon.' She paused. 'I mean *this* afternoon. So I have got things to do. I just don't feel like going.'

'Why not?'

'I feel a bit tired,' she said lamely. She could hardly have told him the truth – that she felt so depressed, all she was fit for was hiding under her bedclothes until the whole bloody holiday was over.

They sat there smoking in silence until Saunders eventually said, 'I'm on me own an' all, you know. Not always easy at these sort of times is it, when everyone's off with their families and there's no work to do 'cos no one's about? Life's always so busy; then . . . nothing. Still, you get used to it.' He laughed mirthlessly to himself, pressing his lips tightly together, as though recalling a painful memory.

'I nearly got married once,' he went on, with as little emotion as a man wondering whether he should wear his mac or his overcoat. 'But she went off with a bloody Yank. When I was away at sea serving me sodding country if you don't mind. Never had much inclination to settle down after that.'

Ginny's head jerked up. 'I thought you were, you know, with Leila.'

Saunders laughed again. 'Hark at me going on like a bloody old woman nattering over the fence. I must have had too much of the old giggle juice tonight. Or maybe it's Christmas getting to me, eh? But as for Leila . . .'

'Yeah?'

'Look, blondie, me and Leila go back a long way, but things change. Times change.' He levered himself away from the table and turned round to face the mirror. He studied his reflection as he carefully straightened his tie – a gesture clearly indicating that the subject was closed.

'I've bought the lease on them premises for the new club,' he said, turning round and standing over her like a great dark shadow. 'And seeing as you ain't got nothing to do while this place is closed, you can come and have a shufty at it. See what you think. We'll have a bite to eat afterwards.'

Ginny shrank back into her chair. She said nothing, just shook her head.

He looked at her for a long moment, then held up his hands in a gesture of surrender. 'All right. Bad time.'

Still she said nothing.

He winked, then turned away to pick up his hat. 'I'll catch up with you later on,' he said, his back still to her. 'When you're feeling a bit more chipper.'

With that he walked over to the door, paused briefly, looked over his shoulder and said, 'I've got a good feeling about this new year. I mean, *1953*, even sounds good, don't it?' He winked again. 'There's gonna be plenty of opportunities for anyone who's got the brains to see 'em. Opportunities like running a club for instance. Now that *is* a good opportunity. Especially for a woman.'

He touched the brim of his hat in salute, pulled the door shut quietly behind him and was gone.

Confused and exhausted, Ginny rose from her seat, her body as heavy as if it had been weighed down with bags of coal.

She flicked off the lamp by the door and returned the room to semi-darkness. But instead of going through to the club, she just stood there, staring at the flickering lights on the scrappy little tree, feeling as though her heart could break as easily as one of the gaudy lanterns that adorned its almost bare branches.

The sound of someone singing drifted up from the street below. It was a deep male voice that could – just could – have been Billy Saunders's, crooning the sweet opening bars of 'White Christmas'.

The sentimental lyrics were too much for Ginny. She buried her face in her hands and began to sob uncontrollably.

The door flew back on its hinges and Ginny felt arms wrap around her. She squirmed away in alarm, stumbling backwards across the litter-strewn room.

When Ginny regained her balance, she looked up and saw Gloria standing before her, his arms outstretched in a bizarre parody of a caring maiden aunt. 'Look,' he snapped petulantly, 'there's no need to look at me like that. I've come to sodding comfort you. Now, come here and tell me all about it.'

Ginny wouldn't have been more astonished if the skinny little man had just announced that he was leaving the club to go round the world with a troupe of travelling acrobats. She eyed him warily through her tears, wondering what new madness was happening to her now.

She swiped roughly at her wet cheeks with the back of her hand. 'What's going on? Why are you being nice to me?'

Gloria shook his head, pursed his lips and handed her a neatly washed and ironed handkerchief. He then held up one finger to silence her, told her to 'Hang on one minute!' in a soprano-pitched squeal and ducked back out into the club.

'I'll tell you why,' he carolled to her from the bar. 'Because, for one thing, I'm a fool to myself – and, if you ever tell *anyone* I've been nice to you, just remember, dearie, I'll scratch your eyes out.'

He reappeared in the doorway, brandishing a bottle of champagne and two glasses. 'And for another, I know that if I looked like a cross between Marilyn Monroe and Betty Grable I wouldn't be bloody well sitting by myself crying.' He pointed the bottle towards the sink and shot the cork across the room. 'I'd be wiggling me little botty all over flaming London, driving all the boys to distraction, and so would any of the other girls in this place. So, I know there must be something wrong. That's why we're gonna drink this champagne, wish ourselves a merry Christmas and forget all about the rotten bleeders who make us cry.'

Ginny sniffed inelegantly as she accepted the foaming glass he was handing her. 'Who's Marilyn Monroe?' she spluttered, choking on the heady mixture of tears and bubbles.

Gloria patted her back with slightly more force than was necessary. 'Some new, innocent-looking blonde I saw in one of the film mags the other day. Someone who can make a very good life for herself, I'm telling you. If she plays her cards right and takes the opportunities what come along for the likes of her.' He sipped daintily at his glass and smiled knowingly at her across the rim.

When Ginny said nothing, Gloria decided plain talking was the only way. 'Listen to me, little Ginny Martin. Saunders is a man with power. He's got that power because he's got a brain, and because he's scared of nothing and no one. And he's a right handsome bugger an' all, but that's another matter. Anyway, he can be a very good friend, but he can also be the very worst enemy you could ever imagine. And let's just say that he wants to be your friend, Ginny my love, and you should be very grateful. Very grateful indeed. 'Cos Mr Saunders looks after his friends.' He touched first one, then the other corner of his mouth with the tip of his little finger, as though wiping away unwanted crumbs. 'And he also looks after the friends of his friends.'

He tossed his head haughtily. 'So you see, I'm not all

heart, my girl. I know which side me bread's buttered. I look after you, and you ... Well, you know the rest.'

Ginny lowered her eyelids, blocking out the world. She felt as though she were an insignificant ball of fluff being swept into a corner by a very large broom.

'Don't you dare go falling asleep on me, girl!' Gloria shrieked, misunderstanding her closed eyes. 'There's me giving you the benefit and you go and start nodding off! Get some more of this champagne down you and we'll have a toast.'

Gloria topped up their drinks and raised his glass high in the air, the flickering light making the wine dance and sparkle like cut crystal. 'To all of Mr Saunders's friends. May they never be his enemies and may all our dreams come true.'

While Gloria sat in the dressing-room comforting Ginny with his unique blend of French wine, acid-tongued advice and self-seeking opportunism, Leila and the girls were downstairs on the pavement still waiting for a cab, shivering in the sleety drizzle and the bitter wind that was whipping round the corner of Frith Street, smacking their silky clothes around their legs like sails in a north-easterly.

'We'll never get enough cabs to take us lot,' Carmen wailed, shrugging down into her jacket. 'The drivers'll all be home in their beds, getting in what kip they can before their kids wake up and climb all over 'em, waving their Christmas stockings and chucking orange peel in the hearth, and—'

'What? Acting just like real people, you mean?' Yvette interrupted her, snarling through teeth clenched as much in anger as against the cold. 'I knew we should have ordered one earlier.'

'A cab'll come along, sweeties, you just see. And we'll all share if necessary.'

'One'll never take all of us,' complained Carmen.

'Want to bet?' Leila lifted her dress above her knee and winked. 'We have our ways, remember!'

As if on cue, a cab pulled up beside them, sending a muddy spray of icy water across the kerbside.

'Hello, darlings, home time, is it?' the cabbie asked. Unlike some drivers, he didn't mind the toms, they always seemed fair to him and usually gave him a reasonable sort of a tip. The only thing he drew the line at was if they wanted to go with a punter in the back of the cab. It wasn't that he would have objected, it was more to do with being scared of losing his badge if the Old Bill caught them at it. Never mind what his wife would do to him if she ever found out he'd let one get anywhere near his motor.

Yvette sidled up to the car. She was immediately in business mode, laying a black-gloved hand on the roof and flashing a dazzlingly sensual smile at the now slack-jawed driver.

While Yvette set about bamboozling the man into believing that what he most wanted in the world was to fit seven long-legged women into the back of his cab, Shirley was tapping Leila on the shoulder and dripping a cupful of her usual venom into her ear.

'Leila?' she whispered. 'Isn't that the governor over there? Just getting into his car over by the club?'

Leila didn't respond.

'I wonder if anyone else was up there?' Shirley went on, looking about her with exaggerated curiosity. 'Let's see. Milly went home with Gracie. And Lou went off with Mags, Maureen, and Iris . . .' She paused, placing a finger tip to her lips. 'Didn't Ginny stay behind? Wasn't she—'

Before Shirley could hiss another word, Leila sprang towards the taxi. She shoved Yvette to one side, wrenched open the cab door, leapt into the back seat and slammed the door firmly behind her.

She then wound the window, opened her mouth to say something, but changed her mind. After a moment's indecision, and deliberately avoiding meeting Shirley's gaze, she stuck her head out of the window and said with determined jollity, 'I'll see you all later then, sweeties. Now drive on please, cabbie, the ladies will be making their own arrangements.'

Yvette threw up her hands in despair. 'Now we'll never bloody well get home.' She spun round to confront Shirley. 'What the hell did you say to her?'

'Only the truth, darling. Only the truth.'

As the first flakes of snow began to fall in the biting early-morning air, the rest of the girls stood in puzzled silence, trying to figure out what was going on and looking wistfully after the taxi as it disappeared around the corner into Shaftesbuury Avenue.

Just a few hours later the snow had settled in a thick blanket over most of London, but its twinkling beauty held no attraction for Dilys.

On first waking, she had momentarily been captivated by the sight of the white mantle transforming even her miserable corner of Stepney into a place of almost ethereal muffled beauty, but then she remembered that Nellie Martin had stayed the night and was having dinner with them.

Ted's mum. The bloody bad penny that always turned up.

It was now barely half past eight on Christmas morning, but instead of being able to turn over for another few hours' sleep, Dilys was on duty in the prefab kitchen, with her back to the cooker, resentfully scoring the skin of a puny leg of pork, while Nellie sat alongside her, chain-smoking, drinking tea, finding fault and moaning.

It was only the fact that Dilys knew what would be in store for her if Ted turned up and she hadn't made at least a half-way decent dinner for the old trout that was preventing her from bending the leg of pork right over Nellie's curler-bristling head. Dilys had seen Nellie in action too often, twisting the truth until Ted was ready to throttle someone with his bare hands, to take the chance of upsetting her.

'This place's freezing. Can't you turn that gas fire in there up a bit?' Nellie sniped, interrupting Dilys's day-dream that had advanced to wringing the old cow's neck with the tea-towel.

'Actually,' Dilys said, wiping her perspiring forehead on the back of her hand, 'I'm a bit warm if you don't mind, Nellie. In fact, the heat from this oven's scorching me legs so bad that I don't know how much longer I can carry on. And if I pass out, we won't have no dinner.'

Nellie puffed out her cheeks and made irritating little puttering sounds through her pursed lips. 'I wouldn't say no to a little drop of something in me tea then,' she whined. 'Something to warm me through a bit like.'

'I'm sure Ted wouldn't mind if you had a drop of his scotch,' said Dilys pointedly, as she tipped a pile of salt on to the meat and rubbed it furiously into the latticework of cuts she had made.

She would have loved to have said no to the old dragon, but the chance that she might drink herself back to sleep was an opportunity she really couldn't afford to miss. 'Why don't you help yourself?'

Reluctantly, Nellie shifted herself just enough to reach the whisky bottle that stood on the side by the stove.

'Shame you don't talk much to them brothers o' your'n no more,' she said, topping up her cup until the liquor-laced tea sploshed over the side and into the saucer. 'Them wives of their'n have been filling that house with grub for weeks now. I've been watching 'em, going back and forward with bags bulging with gear. They'll be having a lovely do back in Bailey Street. Plenty of money them boys must be bringing in. Plenty.'

Dilys sank her teeth deeper into her lower lip and slapped the joint unceremoniously into a roasting tin. She wouldn't rise to her. She wouldn't.

But even if Dilys had been fool enough to say something, there'd have been little point because Nellie wasn't in the mood to listen to anyone. She was off and in full flight. And on her favourite subject – other people's mistreatment of her, a poor old girl that no one gave a bugger about.

'And that sodding Ginny. She's another one. After how good I was to that ungrateful bitch. What does she do? How does she repay me? Sends sodding gear round for that kid o' your'n that's how. And cuts me dead. Like a knife to my heart that was. How about me? That's what I say.' Nellie glugged back a mouthful of her tea.

'Mind you,' she went on, her devious mind on overtime, 'it must have saved you a few bob, her buying all them presents for the kid. You ain't had to buy a single thing for her, have you? Not a single, solitary thing. You dunno how lucky you are.' She swallowed another whisky-fortified mouthful. 'Maybe you should have spent the dough you saved on getting a bigger bit of pork.'

Dilys's blood boiled. Nellie knew they were lucky they had anything on the table at all, seeing as her darling Ted had, as usual, 'forgotten' that he had promised to bring in all the food from some bloke he'd met. In fact, if the butcher's stall up on the Waste hadn't had this pathetic bit of meat left last night, they'd have been having a tin of corned beef for their Christmas dinner.

As if reading Dilys's thoughts, Nellie's next target was her son. 'And then there's bloody Ted,' she exclaimed, throwing up her hands. 'Fancy him going amongst the missing again. Disappearing on Christmas Eve like that. Who'd believe it of your own flesh and blood? And without leaving his old mum so much as a sodding box of hankies. Don't no one think of buying nothing for an old woman at Christmas time no more? And you know what'll happen next, don't you? That kid of your'n'll be moaning and groaning.' Nellie screwed up her face into an ugly travesty of a hurt child. 'I want my daddy. Where's my daddy?'

Nellie's cruel impersonation could not have been further from the truth. Susan, a six-year-old who was already well used to her own company and to getting herself up and dressed every day, had been outside, solemnly and industriously constructing a snowman, since she had first opened her eyes to the strange early morning winter light over an hour ago.

Satisfied with her efforts, she was now ready to go in, and was fumbling with ice-numbed fingers for the doorkey she had worn around her neck on a piece of string since she had been barely four years old.

As she trotted into the kitchen, her eyes and face lit up with pleasure; when there were other adults around, her mummy was usually nicer to her than if they were alone. 'Hello, Nanny Nellie, I didn't know you was up yet. D'you wanna see what things I got in me stocking? And I can show you me snow—'

Nellie recoiled. 'Get off! You're all wet. And I told you before. I ain't your nanny.'

'But Mummy said—'

'And *I* said . . .' boomed Nellie.

With a wisdom far beyond her age, Susan dropped her chin and said very softly, 'I'm sorry.' Then she backed away and disappeared into the front room to play with the lovely china tea-set that Father Christmas had brought her.

'Queer sort of kid,' sneered Nellie. 'Too quiet for my liking.'

She lit herself another cigarette, again without offering one to Dilys. 'What a fine bloody day this is turning out to be.'

'And a happy sodding Christmas to you an' all,' Dilys muttered, slamming the dish into the oven and whacking shut the oven door, wishing with all her heart that she was anywhere in the whole wide world except in a poxy prefab in Stepney, and with anyone in the world but her bloke's bloody mother and her bloke's sodding kid.

She would have been unhappier still, had she known what Ted had been up to.

A couple of hours before Dilys had even opened her eyes, Ted had been following a heavy, mousey-haired woman up an unlit stairway.

'You can stay all night if you want,' she giggled over her shoulder. 'As a Christmas treat like.'

'What, the old man not docking till tomorrow?' Ted asked, grabbing a handful of her plump backside.

'Get off, you cheeky sod! And anyway, I ain't married, am I?'

She pushed open a door and they stepped into a pitch-dark room.

Ted began tapping around the wall, trying to find the switch to turn on the light.

'We don't want that on,' the woman breathed. 'Let's be romantic.'

She fiddled around until she found the switch to a frilly table lamp shaped like a crinoline lady on a swing. When she turned it on, the bulb was so dim, all it illuminated was a pale, red-tinted circle around its base.

Ted squinted in the gloom. Where the hell had he fetched up this time?

When he'd picked up the woman, in the dark side-street outside the spieler where he'd been playing cards and drinking, he didn't have a clue where he was. Hackney Wick way, he reckoned, but it could have been as far away as Stoke Newington. He'd been out pub-crawling till closing time and then doing the rounds of the tatty little unlicensed drinking and gambling clubs for hours. Anything to get away from bloody Dilys and his mother, moaning on about why he hadn't brought home the stuff they reckoned he should have done, because it was sodding Christmas Eve.

But after a while the Christmas spirit had caught up even with Ted, and he had been more than happy when this friendly sort had asked him up to her place to help celebrate the season of goodwill.

'How about a little bit of music?' she suggested, swinging her fleshy hips as she crossed to the corner of the room, where an old-fashioned wooden wireless set had pride of place on a little bamboo table.

Music? What was the silly tart going on about? He hadn't come here to have a poxy dance.

She found a station playing suitably festive music – a three-part women's harmony group singing 'I saw Mummy kissing Santa Claus'.

'I love this one, don't you?' she giggled. 'But it's a bit too loud. We don't want no distractions, do we?'

She twiddled with the volume control, lowering the sound until it was a barely audible background hum, then turned round and held out her arms to Ted. 'How about a kiss for me then, Santa?'

Ted moved towards her. This was more like it. But even though he was half plastered, Ted's instinct for trouble and self-preservation was still operating on full power. He stopped dead in his tracks.

'What's that noise?' he asked, visions of angry husbands, punched noses and pain filling his mind.

'It's only me little sister,' the woman said hurriedly. 'I wasn't planning on working tonight, not as it's Christmas like, so I said I'd mind her.'

Ted let the bit about 'working tonight' pass – he wasn't stupid, he'd realised straight away she was a tom and had already decided she wasn't going to be paid anyway – but he was more interested in the idea of a little sister.

'How old's she then, this little sister?'

'What?' The woman wasn't sure if he meant what she thought he did.

'Much younger than you, is she?' Ted leered. 'I get on well with young 'uns.'

He did mean what she'd thought.

'Leave off, she's just a kid.'

'Come on, it'll be a real Christmas party with the three of us.'

'Mum?' he heard a voice, thick with sleep, call from the doorway. 'Can I hear a man talking? What's going on?'

Ted grabbed hold of the woman's arm, his fingers digging into her flesh. 'What's she mean, *Mum*? You said she was your sister.'

With his other hand, Ted reached behind him and found the switch to the overhead light. 'Jesus!' he fumed. 'How old are you?'

'She's forty-nine,' the girl wailed, shielding her eyes with her arm against the sudden glare.

'Forty-nine?' Slowly, Ted shook his head. As he looked at the woman, his face contorted with revulsion, twisting into a mask of sickened contempt – not only at the woman but at himself for sinking so low. He saw in her all the women he hated. All the women who had caused his life to fail. All the women he wanted to get rid of. 'You're old enough to be my fucking mother!'

'Look, just get out,' the woman said, reaching out to snap off the light and returning the room to darkness – her irrational need to hide her raddled looks from the man who was not only insulting her, but was really hurting her arm, overcoming even her fear of him.

'You filthy, dirty whore.'

In a flash of explosive hatred, the madness inside Ted was unleashed.

With his teeth clenched as though they'd been bolted together, Ted pounced on the woman with the ferocity of a wildcat bringing down an antelope.

Try as she might, there was nothing the young girl could do to stop him, as he rained punches, slaps and kicks across her mother's twisting and writhing body.

When the girl returned to the room, still barefoot and in her night-dress, covered in snow and trembling with terror and the icy cold, with the only neighbour she had managed to awaken during the early hours of Christmas morning, she turned on the light and stared.

The shell of what had once been her mother lay in a bloody heap on the floor. An ugly, abandoned rag doll.

The young girl started screaming, screaming as though she would never stop.

Chapter 15

2 June 1953

Dilys was cheesed off.

As she sat at her dressing-table, her mouth set in a stern, straight line, her arms folded rigidly across her chest, staring gloomily into the mirror, she listened to the annoying cut-glass drawl of the radio commentator wittering on and on about: the huge crowds! the enthusiasm! the fun! and (considering the damp weather!) the general, all-round, bloody good time that every other bugger in the whole sodding world but her seemed to be having.

Hoo-bleeding-ray.

She hoped they choked on it.

Dilys had briefly entertained a vague hope that Ted would turn up at the last minute and announce that he was whisking her off to some exciting do or other that he'd got tickets for. But she hadn't seen hide nor hair of him for days – surprise – so that was off the menu.

It just wasn't fair; even Susan – a six-year-old – was out enjoying herself. All right, she'd only gone to the Coronation party in Bailey Street, but she was still out. Like every other bugger in the whole pissing country, according to laughing boy on the wireless.

And what was *she* doing? She was sitting here, with no one to answer to, free as a ruddy bird, but nowhere to bleeding well go.

She picked up her hairbrush and aimed it at the radio set. She missed.

It wasn't as though her brothers and their smarmy,

perfect little home-making wives hadn't invited her along to the Bailey Street party with Susan. They had. And Dilys had sort of said that she might be going. But when it came to it, she hadn't even bothered getting herself done up when she'd gone round there to drop Susan off a couple of hours ago. She just couldn't bear the thought of spending the whole day with that pair of self-satisfied bitches. She knew exactly what it would be like: bloody purgatory.

They would talk non-stop about how, after their father-in-law – *her* dad, mind – had died, they'd got *her* brothers to divide the old place in Bailey Street into two 'dear little flats', and how they now had plans to turn them into 'little palaces'.

Palaces! What was so bad about number 11 staying the way it was? That's what Dilys wanted to know. Maybe it had got a bit run down since her mum had got herself killed in that stupid accident, but the way that pair of dopey tarts carried on about having to rip out this, and panel over that, and cover every bloody surface in 'contemporary' bleeding fabrics and sheets of flipping Fablon, it made Dilys want to smack them round their smug, simpering faces.

Housework and home-making, it was all they ever talked about. And what was worse was the *way* they talked about it. They acted as though Dilys was a bit dim and needed helpful hints on the right way to run a home. As if she didn't have better things to do than sodding polishing and ironing.

She probably wouldn't have minded quite so much if they had been older than her, but both her sisters-in-law were only in their early twenties, a good five or six years younger than she was, yet they carried on like old women. Always fussing about in their frilly aprons, cooking and cleaning, and smiling and twittering away like a right pair of old trouts.

In fact, they reminded her of how Ginny used to be, back in her sainthood days. Killing themselves just to 'keep things nice'. It made Dilys shudder. Whatever her Micky and Sid had seen in them she couldn't begin to imagine.

At least Ginny had come to her senses and cleared off, once she'd got rid of the kid she was carrying. Dilys certainly didn't have the same hopes for her sisters-in-law. She could just see them once they started breeding. The thought was almost too horrible to contemplate.

There they'd be with their big, shiny, Silver Cross prams, suffocating under piles of hand-knitted, pearl-buttoned matinée jackets, struggling to get past the push-chairs and the rocking horses in the passage of number 11, a beaming baby covered in ribbons and lace under one arm and a bucket full of perfect, snowy white nappies under the other.

They were so stupid, they'd probably revel in the whole horrible business of motherhood and they'd make it a good excuse to spend even more of her brothers' wage packets. Not that they didn't already drain them every week as it was – the boys never had any money for her these days. Or time.

Dilys never saw them unless she went round there. And that wasn't very often, because having to watch those two witches keeping the boys just where they wanted them turned her guts.

Dilys propped her chin on her fists and puffed unhappily as she studied the faint lines that were beginning to form around her eyes and mouth, and the slight, but definitely visible, mauve smudges beneath her eyes. That's all bloody motherhood had done for her. Made her look old before her time.

Not for the first time, Dilys wished with all her heart that it had been her and not Ginny who'd gone to see Jeannie Thompson with her best yellow soap and her douching tubes. Getting herself knocked up by Ted had seemed such a good idea at the time. Where had it all gone wrong, she wondered? And, come to think of it, where had sodding Ted Martin gone an' all?

Dilys arched her back, so that she could reach into her pocket for her cigarettes.

Only two left? Wonderful! Now she was running out of fags on top of everything else. That was all she bloody well needed.

And there was hardly any milk.

She'd bet her sisters-in-law would never let themselves run short of fags. They'd never run short of anything. Not them.

She could just visualise the two polished and doilied sideboards, one in each of the flats in number eleven, and knew, as sure as night followed day, that there'd be a dinky little wineglass on each one, full of cigarettes for any 'guests' who happened to pop in from the street party, so that they could help themselves while they were sipping a drop of port or a gin and orange. And there'd be more milk in their cupboards than in a flaming dairy.

And a dairy was where they belonged, because that's what they were, a pair of right rotten cows.

Dilys's lip curled in contempt, as she flicked her spent match on to the dressing-table. She'd done the right thing staying away.

Then again, maybe she should just nip round there for a little while. It couldn't hurt just to show her face. And she could help herself to some of their fags, have a few drinks, something to eat maybe, and still be out of there all within the hour.

But, tempting as it was to see what she could mump

off them, there was no getting away from the fact that she bloody hated those two women.

With her resentment bubbling up to seething level, Dilys was now sure she had made the right decision about not going to Bailey Street. Fags or not, she had no intention of being within a mile of that pair if she could help it.

They could stick it. She'd find somewhere where she could have a laugh. Somewhere with a bit of life, where she'd be welcomed and appreciated, and not treated like the poor relation. Somewhere like the places Ted used to take her.

Bloody Ted.

She ground out her cigarette in the pickle jar lid on her dressing-table, snatched up her compact and began furiously powdering her cheeks.

She'd show Ted Martin she didn't need him to have a good time. She'd put on her war-paint and show the whole bleed'n' lot of them.

While Dilys was still dithering as to whether she should go for the Crushed Coral or the Peach Parfait lipstick, the Coronation do at Leila's flat was already well under way.

As with the one she'd put on for the girls at Christmas, Leila had ulterior motives for throwing a party for them. Again, she didn't want to be alone when everyone else would be celebrating, and doing business was out of the question. Men were expected to be at home with their families on such a special day, not out clubbing in the West End.

Inviting the girls round to the flat also presented Leila with an opportunity she couldn't resist. Having made damned sure that Ginny was coming this time – no excuses accepted – Leila was going to have another go at persuading her that taking the manageress's job in Billy's new club would be the best thing that could happen. And not only for Ginny.

During the past few months, Leila had become increasingly fixated on getting her to hang up her feathers and to leave the stage. The combination of Billy's – *her* Billy's – obvious admiration for Ginny's undeniable assets and Shirley's spiteful insinuations had convinced Leila that she had to get her working in a more sober role. She'd thought about trying to get her sacked, but she knew that was a non-starter – Ginny's act had become too much of a success and Billy had started seeing her almost as a talisman. Getting her promoted was the only way.

The trouble was, Leila wasn't having much success in persuading Ginny. She was reluctant even to consider the job.

That was why Leila was trying this new tack: she was going to give Ginny a taste of the good life and, when she compared the squalor of the sordid room in which she was living with the luxury of Leila's Mayfair flat, it might just get her thinking.

So the Coronation party had been planned, but Leila's scheme had almost fallen at the first fence.

The girls, like the majority of ordinary people in Britain, had initially been indifferent to the idea of even bothering to mark the event and were more interested in the possibility of just having the day off.

Who gave a toss about a church service with a load of toffs parading about in robes and silk stockings, was a typical comment. Especially when the average person in the street was busy coping with the day-to-day worries of overcrowded housing, the growing threat of their menfolk being shipped off to Korea and the ceaseless, grinding aggravation of the despised rationing system – *eight years* after the war had ended!

In fact, rather than being keen to throw parties to celebrate the crowning of one of their 'betters', the general mood was more conducive to throwing bricks.

But then something happened: the excitement began to gather, slowly at first, like a snowball, then it suddenly seemed that soon no one wanted to be left out of the merry-making.

In no time at all it was as though everyone had wanted to have a party all along. Community collections were swiftly organised to fund the festivities, tasks were, as always, delegated and commemorative plates, mugs and dishes were ordered. Some families were even able to boast that they'd bought a television set in honour of the big day. Although 'bought' was probably the wrong word as, unlike the little walnut number in Leila's sitting-room, most sets had been acquired with the spurious blessings of the never-never man.

Buying a television had actually been Leila's trump card in attracting the girls to her party, and it now had pride of place in the plushly carpeted room, where the girls were gathered, oohing and aahing in wonder and criticising the hairdos and hats of the female guests attending the ceremony.

Leila, as usual, was acting totally blasé. She left it to the others to behave as if they were a bunch of convent girls who'd been let out for the first time without the nuns, while she hovered at a discreetly refined distance.

'I can't get over it. It's so clear.' Ginny shook her head in amazement as she stared, transfixed, at the bulging glass of the nine-inch screen, not even put off by the fact that it was dwarfed by its massive wooden cabinet.

The picture itself wasn't actually up to much, it was grainy and flickery – nothing like the Technicolor wonders to be seen at the cinema – but as Ginny stood behind the enormous silk brocade sofa, peering over

Carmen's head at the grey and off-white moment of history being enacted in the cathedral before her, she was in no position to make rational judgements. Her critical faculties had been blown apart by her first sight of the eye-boggling marvel of Leila's sitting-room.

With her feet sinking into the soft wool rugs, Ginny felt like an actress in a glamorous motion picture about sophisticated couples leading their gorgeously urbane lives in Paris and Manhattan. It was so like a film set, in fact, that Ginny wouldn't have been at all surprised if Gene Kelly or Fred Astaire had come breezing into the room to whisk her away for a quick foxtrot across the parquet flooring in the hallway.

'Let me take that for you,' said Leila, easing Ginny's coat off her shoulders.

'What d'you think of the television then, Gin,' asked Carmen without taking her eyes from the set.

'It's just like you're there,' Ginny said, as she watched the tiny figures processing along the aisle.

'I know one or two people who *are* there, sweetie,' Leila whispered into her ear.

Ginny twisted round to face her. 'You don't mean . . .?' she breathed.

Leila put her finger to her lips and nodded.

'I feel like I'm dreaming.' Ginny turned her head so that she could take a full sweep of the room. 'Honestly, Leila, I've never seen such a lovely place in all my life. It's even better than that hotel you took me to that time.'

'You're very kind.' Leila smiled graciously and took Ginny's coat outside to hang it up.

'You should see the kitchen,' Carmen muttered from the sofa, her mouth stuffed full of canapés from one of the trays of food dotted around the room on the ivory and glass side tables. 'I saw it when I come here at Christmas. It's out of this world. There's all tiles on the walls, and a fridge and a food-mixing thing, and . . .' She shrugged. 'Everything.'

She tapped the arm of the sofa. 'Come on, Gin, park yourself next to me. Make yourself comfortable.'

Ginny couldn't bring herself to do it; perching on the pale beige arm was unthinkable. 'I'll be fine down here,' she said, lowering herself on to a squashy tan leather pouffe, tooled with patterns in red and gold.

Carmen, her gaze still fixed on the screen, held out one of the trays of food.

Ginny took a little square of melba toast spread with cream cheese and topped with a curl of smoked salmon.

'D'you reckon she'd let me have a look round later, Carmen?'

'Course she will. She gave Patty the full tour just before you arrived. She missed out at Christmas, like you. You ask her. Go on.'

When Leila returned, Ginny did exactly that and Leila happily obliged.

As they stepped into the hall – a wide oval, decorated in tastefully understated regency strips and with a classically inspired painting covering the whole of the high ceiling – Leila explained that two of the rooms in the flat were locked. They were what she called her workroom, and the maid's room – the maid's room! – but, if Ginny was interested, she was welcome to see everything else.

Leila had pitched it just right. Ginny was more than interested. She followed Leila around, her eyes taking in one wonder after another, walking as carefully and respectfully as if she were in a church, or the sort of art gallery where you knew without asking that the price of a single picture would be more than a lifetime's wages. And, with its sumptuous furnishings, its luxurious decoration and its up-to-the-minute gadgetry – there was even a telephone in the main bedroom! – it was actually more like an art gallery than anywhere Ginny had ever set foot in before.

That someone could live surrounded by such elegance and beauty was a revelation to Ginny. There were rooms everywhere and, to Ginny, every one of them was magnificent. It was all so bright and airy, and even though there were things – exquisite things – everywhere, there was still so much space and light, real room to breathe. And not a damp patch, or a rusting, dripping pipe in sight.

The thing that surprised Ginny most of all was that Shirley had her own room in the flat, with a full bedroom suite where she could keep her clothes and shoes and things. It wasn't that Shirley sometimes stayed overnight, Dilys had often bunked in with Ginny when she had been living at home with her mum and dad before she had married Ted – that's what friends did – but it was having a place that was big enough to keep a whole room for a friend, just in case she wanted to stay.

While Ginny stared about her in slack-jawed rapture, Leila chatted away, pointing out her favourite 'little pieces', as she called them: things of which she was particularly fond, or that had an amusing story behind them. Mostly they were gifts from men, but not one, Ginny noted, seemed to be a gift from Mr Saunders. Well, not that Leila mentioned. 'You like my little flat then, Ginny?' she asked as they came back to the hall.

'I think it's the most smashing place I've ever laid eyes on,' Ginny said, meaning every word, as she stared in awe, yet again, up at the painted ceiling. 'Gloria said you had a nice home, but this is . . . Well, it's . . .'

Leila noted that Gloria had been opening his big mouth. What was he after? But she'd worry about that later. Now she had to focus on Ginny. 'You could have a place like this yourself one day.'

'How?' Ginny asked with a little laugh, tearing her gaze away from the artist's vision of nymphs and goddesses. 'Rob a bank?'

'I'm serious. If you take this club manager's job, you'll be earning very good money, Ginny. Very good.'

Ginny's face clouded over. Not again. She'd been feeling so down it was all she could do to find the energy to turn up to do the show each night; how could anyone think she had what it took to do something as difficult as running a club? In fact, she had seriously thought that if it wasn't for the debts, and the weekly envelopes she sent to Susan and Nellie, she could have just given it all up and . . . That was the problem. And what?

She wouldn't even have a roof over her head. Not even a slum roof.

'Well, Ginny?'

'I can't.'

'Look at me, Ginny. And just listen to those girls in there.'

Ginny did as she was told and listened to the drunken chorus of laughter coming from the sitting-room.

'It's you Billy singled out for this job. Not them. And why? Because you're bright, you're able, you're from the area, and,' Leila added, suddenly distracted by a loose thread on her emerald-green sleeve, 'you look good. And let's face it, Billy's not asking you to run the Astor Club for him, now is he. It's only an East End drinking spot.'

They said nothing for a few moments, just stood there while the girls' giggles built to a crescendo of tipsy hilarity.

Leila took a deep breath and pulled her final rabbit from the hat. 'I've been very good to you, Ginny. And very patient. And I think you owe me a favour.'

Ginny couldn't look at her; she didn't want to hear what she was sure was coming next.

'As the governor's right-hand assistant, I was told to persuade you to take this job, Ginny,' she began, setting the foundation of her lie. 'And if you don't do this for me, I'm going to get the blame. I could lose everything I've worked for: my position in the business, my reputation, this flat. Do you want to be responsible for all those things happening to me?' Leila touched the back of her hand theatrically to her forehead.

'But Leila—'

'And I thought you were my friend.'

Ginny ran her fingers distractedly through her hair, as a fat tear brimmed over and plopped on to her cheek. 'I don't know why Mr Saunders thinks I can do it.'

Leila stretched her lips in a taut smile. 'Because he's got faith in you. He was only saying so the other day.' She then added with reckless impatience: 'In fact, it sometimes feels as though he speaks of nothing else *but* you.'

'But, Leila—'

'Look, I've put it to you straight, Ginny. You know the position now.'

'I'm sorry, I didn't mean to get you in trouble. I'm really sorry.' She shook her head at her own wickedness and sniffed loudly. 'All right if I use the—'

'The powder room? Of course. You go and get those tears mopped up.' Apart from an almost imperceptible fluttering of a nerve just below her left eye, Leila looked completely composed, but she could have smacked Ginny's face. What was wrong with her? Anyone else in her position would have jumped at a chance like this. Leila took a deep breath. She mustn't lose control. 'I'll be in the kitchen.'

While Leila and Ginny had been in the hall, Shirley was

pressed against the sitting-room door straining to hear their conversation. Now she'd heard Ginny go off to the lavatory, she dashed into the kitchen to find out the state of play from Leila.

'I wondered where you'd got to,' Shirley lied, as she hitched up the skin-tight skirt of her blue satin sheath dress and clambered unsteadily on to one of the spindly legged stools at the breakfast bar.

Leila could smell the gin on Shirley's breath from ten feet away.

'I was giving Ginny the guided tour,' she said wearily, taking a tray of ice from the refrigerator, cracking it against the stainless steel draining board and tipping it into a bowl.

'Hope you didn't let little Miss Butter-Wouldn't-Melt look in the workroom when you were showing her round,' Shirley snorted. 'You'd have scared the life out of her if she'd seen all the gear. Especially those new harnesses and whips you had delivered.'

Leila closed her eyes for a long moment. In a business where keeping your mouth shut was the first rule, Shirley's drinking was becoming a real problem. But she couldn't deal with her now.

'I like the girl,' she said lightly. 'And I was showing her my flat. Not interviewing her for a job.'

'Lucky you weren't, because let's face it, we're none of us getting any younger, are we? And having the likes of her working here, well, we wouldn't get a look in, would we?'

Leila poured herself a small gin, topped the tall glass with tonic almost to the brim and dropped in a single ice cube.

'Don't I get a drink?' Shirley asked petulantly.

'I think you've had enough.'

'Touchy!' Shirley grinned smugly. 'D'you know, she's

really getting to you, Leila. You want to get her off that stage in Frith Street before she really gets you going. You can't fool me, I know what it's all about: every time she flashes those tits of hers you never know who's going to be standing at the back of the club watching, and wanting her, do you? It must be driving you mad. But I can't say I blame you. I've seen the way Billy looks at her. And while I can't understand the attraction myself, whatever it is, she's got it. You want to get her all covered up in a frock, with her legs hidden behind a cash desk, as soon as you like.' Shirley laughed coarsely. 'And a pair of glasses wouldn't come amiss.'

Leila kept her back to Shirley, not trusting herself to face her. 'Have you finished?' she asked through gritted teeth.

'Don't blame me for the way she's making you feel, Leila. I mean, we all hate getting older. Even she must. I know she doesn't look it, but I reckon she must be, what? Late twenties? Maybe even a bit older. But she looks good. Very good. And you, Leila, you must be what? How old are you now?'

Leila spun round. 'That's it, Shirley. And this time I mean it. This is your last chance. Either you stop drinking and running off at the mouth, or I'm going to have to sack you.'

Shirley blinked. Sack? This wasn't going the way she'd intended at all. She had meant to carry on planting the idea that Leila should get rid of Ginny, not her.

'How could you sack me? Who'd help you out here with the private parties? None of the other girls have got half the brains or class I've got. None of them.'

'Brains? Class? I know you've been drinking, Shirley, but I didn't realise you'd completely lost your marbles.' Leila shook her head in disdain and turned away from her. She hated losing her temper, it was so undignified, but Shirley was really goading her. 'When did you last look at yourself?'

'This is all her fault. I told you, she's getting to you. You've got to stop her.'

Leila bent over the sink, trying to steady her breathing, her chest rising and falling as though she'd just completed the hundred-yard dash.

Shirley was relentless. 'And I don't know why you should pick on me anyway. How about Carmen and Patty smoking dope every night? You don't do anything about them.'

'They've stopped.' Leila's voice was unsteady, but quiet.

'Have they?'

Leila twisted round to face her again. 'Do you know, Shirley, you are really pushing your luck. I've told you before, there are very few things I hate more than a stirrer. But a big-mouthed, drunken stirrer is one of them. So just go in the other room, out of my sight, and keep that big mouth of yours shut for a while, because I'm going to be considering your future very carefully.'

Shirley did as she was told. Not because she thought she was in the wrong, but because she wanted to go in the other room anyway – she needed another drink. She scrambled gracelessly down from the stool, her skirt still tucked up around her thighs, and barged her way out of the kitchen.

As she flung the door back on its hinges, she almost knocked Ginny off her feet.

'Is Shirley all right?' Ginny asked, steadying herself against the wall and reaching out to stop the door slamming at the same time.

'Just a bit over-excited. Not everyday we have a coronation, is it?' Leila held up her glass. 'Drink?'

'I've already got one in the other room, thanks.'

Leila did her best to smile. But it wasn't easy. She really couldn't figure Ginny out at all. Any of the other girls would have accepted another drink without a second thought. Why should they worry about wasting other people's booze? But here was Ginny – an exotic dancer – acting as politely as if she were at a vicarage tea-party. It was like at the club, whenever men showed interest in her. There she was, up on the stage, stark naked apart from a few pink feathers, flirting and pouting with the best of them, but as soon as any of the punters made an approach – and there were always plenty – she shrank into herself and fled. Even though she'd brassed all that while.

Sexy without a sex life. It was a mystery to Leila. What did she want, a man with slippers and a pipe, reading the Sunday papers while she cooked the roast? She was such a complete contradiction. Every time Leila thought she had a handle on the girl, she immediately slipped out of her grasp, like a fish struggling to return to the river.

To make it worse, Leila couldn't even bring herself to dislike her. Not really. She was always so reasonable. So nice. So – apparently – genuine. Even if it was an act, and Leila knew all about acting, God alone knew how she managed to keep it up while working in the club every night. It was unnerving.

Much as Leila hated to admit that Shirley was right about anything, she was spot on about Ginny. She had to do something about her.

But what could she do? She'd tried her last trick and failed. She had to think. Had to be clear.

Playing for time, Leila offered Ginny a cigarette.

'Thanks.' Ginny bent forward to accept the light. 'Leila?'

'Mmmm?'

'I was thinking when I was in your, you know, your powder room, just now. And I've decided I'm fed up living in that hovel.'

Leila sighed inwardly. More complaints about the room. If she heard one more word about the slot-meter gas fire giving out less heat than a forty-watt bulb she'd scream. Ginny didn't have a clue, that was her trouble. If she did, she'd count herself lucky that the rent collectors – Saunder's real ones, that is, the hard men with the coshes – didn't visit her the way they did some of the other tenants. And she'd take the sodding job like a shot.

'It was very short notice, Ginny.'

'I know. And I didn't mean to be ungrateful, but I want something better out of life.' She paused. 'And I really didn't mean to get you in no bother.'

Leila closed her eyes. 'I don't suppose you did,' she said flatly.

'So d'you honestly think I could do it? And d'you really promise it would be more money?'

Leila's eyes flicked open again. 'Sorry?'

'Run the club. D'you really think I could do it?'

'Of course you can do it, sweetie!'

'But I never meant—'

'Look, just give it a go. What have you got to lose?'

Leila stood in the doorway of the sitting-room, a chilled bottle of champagne in each hand, trilling a loud, 'Da-daaaa!' like a conjurer's assistant – she had, after all, just pulled off a successful illusion. But her intended big entrance fell flat on its face. The historic events were still flickering away on the screen in the corner, but the sound had been turned down and nobody was paying any attention to it. Instead, they were all slumped back in their seats, with faces like kites.

'What on earth's going on?' Leila asked, scanning the

room for Shirley, who, no doubt, had been spreading more of her poison. 'It's more like a funeral than a party.'

But Shirley was sitting perfectly quietly at the far end of the room nursing another large drink.

Carmen peered over the back of the sofa. 'We were just talking, Leila,' she said, flapping her hand in the direction of the television. 'Seeing all this going on: all the fuss there's been in the papers and on the newsreels. It makes you sick when you think about them girls what have been mullered and how hardly anything's been said about them.'

'D'you know what makes me sick?' Patty chipped in. 'If he'd been doing in nice little housewives, or shop girls, it'd be all over the papers and everyone'd be demanding something was done about it. But they don't give a fuck about us working girls.'

'Patty!' Leila's face was like stone. She didn't allow the girls to use such language. 'I think you've said enough.'

'I'm sorry, Leila, but it's like we don't count for nothing. I get so wild thinking about the way we get treated.'

Leila took a deep breath and pinned on a smile. 'Well, I'm doing the treating today. So let's all get fresh glasses and have a toast, because we girls now have a reason to celebrate. Ginny, would you, please?'

Ginny went around the room with the tray of champagne goblets Leila had given her to bring in from the kitchen.

A once more serene vision in emerald green, Leila stepped into the centre of the room, leading Ginny by the hand. 'Not only are we drinking to this new Elizabethan Age, and to the success of Hillary and Sherpa Tensing—'

'Whoever he is when he's at home,' said Patty gloomily.

'Thank you, Patty,' Leila replied graciously. 'But we now have cause for a more personal celebration.'

Having finished handing round the glasses, Ginny stood by Leila's side.

'I know you've all heard the talk about Ginny being offered a manager's job. Well, I'd like you to be the first to know that it's true and, what's more, she's decided to take it.'

'I said I'd discuss it with Mr Saunders,' Ginny whispered under her breath, nervously twisting the stem of her glass between her fingers.

'It's the same thing, darling,' Leila whispered back, while flashing one of her most dazzling smiles. 'Now, let's drink to the future. I'm sure it's going to be wonderful for us all!'

Everyone in the room raised their glass. Everyone, that is, except Shirley.

She sat alone at the far end of the room, the smell of booze that she carried with her now nothing compared to the hatred that was oozing from her very pores. Leila had it in for her and it was all Ginny's fault. Shirley'd known she'd be trouble the first time she'd set eyes on her.

The girls crowded round with kisses and congratulations. It was fine by them if Ginny got promoted. They certainly wouldn't have wanted the responsibility of running a club, but there might be a few bob for them somewhere in this new deal. And maybe a little nightly spot taking over the fan dancing wouldn't be such a hardship either.

Shirley watched Ginny and Leila smiling at the girls as though they were a pair of princesses acknowledging the dues of their sycophantic courtiers. And she hated the pair of them.

*

Afraid that Ginny might get stroppy, or nervous, and change her mind about the job, Leila was on the telephone first thing in the morning, organising a get-together between Ginny and Billy Saunders. It was arranged that they would meet on the corner of Bethnal Green Road and Club Row at one o'clock the next day and Saunders would take her to see the building.

Ginny *was* nervous, but she still turned up; in fact, she arrived nearly half an hour early. She'd dressed in a simple navy costume she'd borrowed from Yvette – the plunging neckline hidden by a matching chiffon scarf; styled her platinum curls into a discreet French pleat; and topped off her outfit with a neat pill-box hat – courtesy of Carmen's going-to-church-with-her-mum wardrobe – that had a cute little spotted veil that stopped just above her mouth. She looked more like a guest at a society wedding than a fan dancer going to meet a night-club owner in the East End. The effect was intentional.

Even though Saunders had seen her performing, part of Ginny wanted to give a good impression, to look business-like and refined; to show that there was more to her than blonde hair and a body. But another part of her said she must be stark, raving barmy, and that she should get on the first bus back to Bailey Street and throw herself on the mercy of Ted and Nellie.

Ted and Nellie. The thought of those two brought her back to her senses immediately and to the reality of her situation. She couldn't let Leila get in trouble, just because she was a coward. She had to do this.

So she waited and, as she stood there smoking one cigarette after another, she went through all the advice she had been given by Gloria, her surprise champion, about what she should and shouldn't do. Gloria was right, she knew that, this was a real chance and she mustn't mess it up.

When Saunders eventually arrived at a few minutes past one, in his big, chauffeur-driven car, it had started to rain. But Ginny didn't mind, she had her umbrella, and anyway, she had other things on her mind more important than a summer shower. She had been practising what she was going to say and she knew she had to get it out before she lost her nerve completely.

Before Saunders had a chance to say hello, she took a deep breath and she was off, counting the points on her navy-gloved fingers.

'So I get a rent-free flat. Not a room. And it won't be shared. And it'll be near the job. I won't have fares or nothing to pay—'

Saunders grinned. 'Blimey, you been practising?'

Ginny fiddled with her umbrella, anything to avoid his gaze. 'I just want to get things straight. To know where I stand.'

'Good. Me too. So let's get under that umbrella of your'n and go and have a look at this gaff. And I can tell you all about it.'

Saunders told the driver to stay with the car and held out his arm to Ginny.

She paused for a moment before taking it, then allowed him to lead her through the still bomb-damaged and debris-littered streets. They walked past soot-blackened, semi-collapsed buildings with boarded-up windows and doors, deeper into a part of the East End that even hardened locals thought twice about venturing into without good reason. It was an area that had so far been neglected in the efforts to return London to its pre-war greatness; City offices and middle-class housing obviously coming first in the order of things.

As they walked, Saunders spoke. 'Well, there'll be no rent to pay. The flat's got about four rooms altogether. I think that's right. And it's all yours. So there'll be no sharing. Unless you decide otherwise, of course. And, as it's right over the shop, I don't reckon it could be no nearer.'

Ginny felt herself relax. It was strange; Saunders was a big, handsome, forbidding man, but on the few occasions she had spoken to him, he always gave her that rare feeling that she had known him for years. It was a feeling she enjoyed, it made her comfortable, put her at her ease. Sensations which Ginny had experienced all too rarely.

Suddenly Saunders stopped. They were at the top of a little unnamed alley off Virginia Road, just at the back of where the old Columbia Market stood.

'Any other questions?' he asked.

'Yeah. The big one really. Why me? I know you said you like women running the places, but there's lots of others—'

'Look, Leila said you're kosher. You've got a brain, you learn quick and you don't ask stupid questions. And', he looked her up and down, 'you look good. With or without your clothes. Now, anything else?'

She shook her head; her face burning behind her veil.

'Right. So that's that. But now I've got a question.' He gave her a cigarette. 'Like I said, Leila reckons you're kosher, but is there anything I should know? Anything that could cause me problems?'

'What sort of thing?'

'Let's just say that you'd know if there *was* anything I should be worried about.'

Ginny shrugged. 'Well, in that case, no.'

'Good.' Her jerked his head towards the alley. 'It's down here.'

Gingerly, she followed him along the rubbish-strewn cobbles.

'Here we are.'

She held her umbrella to one side to get a good look. 'This?' she gasped, staring up at the decrepit four-storey Georgian building.

'Granted it needs a bit of work.'

Saunders pulled open the rusting iron gate – a new-looking padlock dangled from one of the railings as though someone had just unlocked it – took the flight of wide stone steps two at a time, shoved open the solid wooden door and stood aside so that Ginny could go in ahead of him.

Surprisingly, there were electric lights blazing everywhere.

Ginny stood her umbrella against the door jamb and stepped inside. She saw a spacious entrance hall, with a wide central staircase and heavily panelled doors leading off both sides. And it was absolutely filthy, derelict almost.

Disappointment flooded through her. She'd thought this was a chance to better herself at last, but she couldn't work here. She was going to have to let Leila down after all.

'What d'you think?'

She looked about her, considering what to say. 'You got this lease before Christmas? What, six months ago?'

'That's right.'

'And you ain't thought about making any changes?' Unless this is your idea of decoration, she thought to herself, as she pictured the squalid tenement where she lived.

Saunders rubbed his hand over his chin. 'You know what it's like. I've been busy. I've been setting up over Virginia Water way. Very exclusive it is. Tell you what, you'll have to come over there one day and have a butcher's.' He grinned wickedly. 'You'd have a right laugh watching all them stockbroker types. They love mixing with the stars, don't they. And with the villains. Then they get a thrill reading all about it next day in the Sunday papers, knowing they've been there. And they can lie to their mates on the golf course that they know Diana Dors and that.'

'I don't know if I could live with this wallpaper,' she said, carefully avoiding responding to his invitation. It was probably one of those suggestions made out of politeness rather than a genuine offer, and she didn't want to make herself look any more stupid than she did already. Fancy her thinking that anyone would want her to run even a half-way decent sort of place. 'Mind you,' she sighed to herself, 'it'd take my mind off the floor. My feet are sticking to it like it's been covered with glue.'

Something darted across the filthy black-and-white tiles.

Ginny grabbed Saunders's arm. 'What the hell was that?'

'Er ... A cat?'

She pulled herself together and stepped away from him. 'Funny-looking cat.'

'Look, I don't intend leaving it like this, do I? I've already got blokes in here looking the place over for me.'

The sudden irritation in his voice immediately had Ginny on guard. He was a big, powerful man and she was alone with him.

'Mr Saunders, I didn't mean—'

'Well, it is a dump,' he said flexing his shoulders. 'And the name's Billy.'

'It's not a dump exactly—'

'Look, I'll be honest with you, blondie. I ain't done nothing yet, 'cos I was waiting for you to do it up how you fancied. Give it the woman's touch, like. That's why I had 'em come in and set up all these lights, so you could see what you reckoned.'

She frowned in bewilderment. 'You've been waiting for *me*?'

'Yeah.'

'But how did you know I'd take the job?'

He grinned. 'How could you resist me?'

She hurriedly turned her head and peered at the wall as though she were studying it. He wanted to see what she reckoned? Was she going mad? 'I reckon, it's . . . er, got, you know, plenty of, what's is name, potential,' she stammered.

'I hope so, darling.'

'And . . .' she blustered, 'yeah. I'll bet it's got a great big cellar.'

'I think it has.'

'Well,' she went on, her words now coming out at a nervous gallop, 'we could have a lovely room down there. A cellar club. Right continental that'd be. Just like you see at the pictures.' Ginny strode over to one of the grimy but elegantly proportioned Georgian windows and stared wildly at the faded tapestry pelmet dangling drunkenly from a tarnished brass rod. 'I could be like Calamity Jane. You know when she put them little curtains in that shabby old log cabin to make it all pretty, and—'

'I'm sorry. You've lost me, darling.'

That stopped her burbling. She spun round. 'What, you haven't seen it?' She saw the blank look on his face. 'It's a film.'

'I don't get no time for films.'

'So you've never heard "Whipcrackaway" or "Secret Love"?'

He shook his head.

'You do know Doris Day?'

He thought for a moment. 'Don't think I've had the pleasure.'

330

'She's American.'

'I don't get the time to meet everyone what comes in the clubs.'

'You must know her.' Ginny, stunned that anyone could even claim not to know about Doris Day, started singing, 'Once, I had a secret love. The way that dreamers often do . . .' and immediately wished she hadn't. She couldn't imagine what had come over her. 'Now d'you know her?' she asked sheepishly.

'Sorry.'

Just as Ginny was beginning to think that she'd ruined everything by showing she really was mad, and that she might as well go over to the window and throw herself out on to the spiked railings below, one of the doors opened and two men joined them in the entrance hall.

'Afternoon, guv,' one of them said.

'Where's George?' Saunders asked.

'In the music room, for a change.'

Saunders shook his head as though that was just the answer he had hoped not to hear. He went over to another of the doors, banged on it with his fist and hollered, 'Georgie, get out here. You spend more time in that lav than a flaming plumber.'

The door opened and a short, thin man appeared. He had a newspaper tucked under his arm and was concentrating on buttoning his trouser fly.

'Yes, Mr Saunders?' he said, looking up. When he saw Ginny he cringed and covered his front with the newspaper. 'Didn't know there were ladies present.'

'This, believe it or not, is our architect.' Saunders rolled his eyes. 'I was just telling Miss Martin here how, with her help, we're going to transform this place into something special. And I want you to tell her about the structural plans you've drawn up.'

'How d'you do,' Ginny said with a smile. She was

going to add that it was Mrs, not Miss, Martin, but for some reason changed her mind.

By the end of September, the club had indeed been transformed. Staff had been engaged, bars had been stocked and in the cellar there was now a gaming room boasting the most modern of equipment. All that was left to do was for Ginny to move into the flat and the place would be ready to open.

There had been a moment, when Saunders had explained that the gambling would be what he called 'a bit on the informal side', when Ginny had paused to wonder exactly what she was getting herself into, but Leila had turned up to reassure her that all the clubs had gambling. And as they were only talking about a few hands of Kaluki and *chemin de fer*, and one simple little roulette wheel, there was nothing to worry about.

That conversation had been over a week ago and, although Leila seemed a bit strange – sort of distracted for some reason – Ginny had been persuaded. Now she had other things on her mind. If she was about to move in, she was going to make sure that her flat above the club was really as spotless as it looked. She had had enough of living in a slum and the image of the 'cat' running across the black-and-white tiles three floors below was still too vivid to be ignored. So she'd kitted herself out in a pair of slacks and a shirt, tucked her hair up into a scarf and was concentrating on giving the freshly laid lino a final going over with a bucket of Izal-laced hot water.

The sound of someone opening her new front door startled her. She looked over her shoulder, scrubbing brush still in hand, to see Saunders in the doorway, obviously amused by the sight of Ginny on her hands and knees, covered in suds.

'Leila said you was a hard grafter. But I'm well impressed. Didn't they do it out right for you?'

'Yeah, but I just wanted to make sure it was really clean.'

Saunders pushed himself away from the door frame and walked in, his nostrils twitching at the disinfectant. 'I've brought a few things round for you.'

Ginny stood up, brushing a stray curl from her forehead with the back of her hand. 'But you've already done so much. There's the kitchen . . .' she jerked her thumb over her shoulder towards the newly decorated room with its fitted Formica-covered cupboards and work tops. 'And all the wallpapering and the lino . . .'

Saunders shrugged and smiled. 'You can't get by without some decent furniture or a bit of carpet.' He stuck his head out on to the landing and called down the stairs. 'Up here, Jim.'

A man and a young lad came puffing up the stairs, carrying a double bed between them.

'Miss Martin'll tell you where to put it,' Saunders said, flattening himself against the wall so that they could get into the flat. 'And you can take all the old gear back down to the truck.'

Ginny's excitement grew as she watched the old stuff disappear and the 'few things' that Saunders had bought begin to fill the flat.

There was a wardrobe, a kidney-shaped dressing-table and a velvet-upholstered headboard with tassels to go with the bed; a light oak dining-table and six chairs, with a matching bookcase – Saunders said he figured Ginny was the type who probably read a bit – occasional tables with splayed spindly metal legs with balls for feet; an equally modern three-piece suite in the latest 'contemporary' style; brightly coloured rugs with vibrant, abstract patterns all over them; standard lamps and bedside lights; and even one of the very latest wood and gilt cocktail cabinets.

'Go on then,' he said to the now dumbfounded Ginny. 'Open it.'

She lifted the mirror-lined lid and gasped as it began to play a tune. 'It's playing "Secret Love"!'

'Thought that'd tickle you,' he said. 'Better than that old Utility gear you had up here?'

'I don't know what—' she began, but was interrupted by Jim staggering backwards into the room clutching one end of a television set.

'Where d'you want this, Miss Martin?' his young helper puffed from behind the other end.

Stunned by this final addition to her good fortune, Ginny could only point to the corner of the room, the place where Leila had hers.

With the television in place, Saunders slipped Jim and the lad some money and told them they could go.

As Jim closed the door behind them, with a muttered 'All the best in your new home, Miss Martin', Saunders turned to her and smiled. 'And that goes for me an' all, Miss Martin,' he said, bending forward and kissing her on the cheek. 'I know we're gonna have a very profitable future together, you and me, 'cos I trust you, Ginny. D'you know that? There's no edge to you. What you see is what you get.'

He grinned, looking like an oversized, handsome schoolboy. 'And let's face it, I've seen quite a lot of you, one way or another.

Ginny blushed.

'That gets me, d'you know that?' He shook his head in amusement. 'You've been up on that stage, flashing it all about, yet you still blush. I love it. You can't lie if you blush. Shows you're an honest bird. And there ain't too many of them about.'

Chapter 16

Ginny stepped into the middle of the big room that took up the whole of the second floor of the now completely refurbished building and did a neat little pirouette. 'What d'you think then, Flora? Will I do for opening night?'

Flora, a heavily built, completely bald-headed Scotsman in his mid-fifties, put the glass he'd been polishing down on the bar and smiled admiringly. 'You look just the business, Miss Martin. Just the business. Black's always very tasteful.'

She smoothed down the skirt of the figure-hugging barathea dress and walked slowly across to him. Leaning on the serpentine maple-wood bar top, she asked, 'You don't think these shoes are a bit much?'

Flora craned his neck to get a good look over the counter. 'They're perfect,' he said, scrutinising the black patent four-inch stilettos that Ginny had bought on nervous impulse just that afternoon. 'Very stylish.'

'I couldn't agree more.' Billy Saunders handed his overcoat and hat to his minder and strolled across to them. 'You look just right, girl. A million dollars.'

Saunders sat on one of the high stools with his back to the bar and surveyed the room. 'Just like this place. Georgie was very impressed with your ideas you know, Ginny. That spot-lighting over the dance floor . . . Great idea. And d'you know what else? He reckons it was the way you talked to that bloke they sent round that got us the full late-night supper licence. You've done a good job, girl. A real good job.'

Ginny lowered her chin to avoid meeting his eyes. Even though she'd done her very best, had worked her socks off to make it all work, she still found it hard, after the years of being abused by Ted, to accept compliments of any kind without a certain amount of foreboding. Always, a nagging little voice in her head had her flinching as it told her to wait for the raised fist that would surely follow what had to be the mockery of false praise.

If her eyes had been raised, however, she would have seen wordless signals being exchanged between Saunders and Flora; signals that might have given her different pause for thought.

Ginny had taken Flora on as her chief barman on Gloria's recommendation, but what she didn't know was that although he was indeed a friend of Gloria's – a very close friend, as it happened, whom he'd met in a notorious Turkish baths in Jermyn Street – it was Saunders who had told Gloria to recommend him to Ginny. Saunders's intention was that she employed someone who knew how to mix a cocktail without using a pennyworth more bitters than was absolutely necessary, but also that that someone had no doubts as to his loyalties. And Flora, like Gloria, owed Saunders enough favours to be sure that there was no doubt as to where his allegiance should lie.

It wasn't that Saunders was overly suspicious, but he had spent a lot of money opening the club and he wanted someone on the inside who would keep an eye out for Ginny – as well as on her – to make sure she was up to running the place, superficially at least. Furthermore, Saunders wanted someone who'd keep an eye on everyone else who worked there.

For while Ginny believed she had been given a free

hand with the club, Saunders was still a businessman and intended to be very much in control of the place.

There was the booze, the gambling, the girls, not to mention the band and the cabaret, and all the cleaners, moppers and washers-up in the kitchens. All of them had the potential for fiddling and conniving. Saunders had seen every stroke known to man being pulled in his time – in fact, he had pulled more than a few himself – and someone as powerful as he just wouldn't tolerate the liberty of having some two-bob hoodlum getting away with making anything out of him on the side; even a single brass farthing would have hurt.

Ginny looked at her watch. 'Quarter past eight. Only fifteen minutes to go.'

She turned to Saunders, nibbling her lip. 'D'you think many people are gonna turn up, Billy? I mean, this is Shoreditch. Who's going—'

'Many people gonna turn up?' Saunders interrupted her with a grin. 'You listen to me, darling. Tonight's little party is gonna be the biggest do of the year. After what I've told them about you, how could they resist? They've been fighting to get an invite to this opening bash. You mark my words, girl, Ginny's is gonna be a real success.'

'Ginny's,' she breathed, looking about her as though she could hardly believe she was there. 'Having a whole club named after me. It's such a big responsibility. Let's just hope you're right.'

And he was. By nine o'clock the club was heaving and the tills were ringing like church bells on Easter Sunday. Every inch of the building, barring the fourth floor where Ginny had her private apartment, had been transformed into profit-making space.

A stage had been built, with a separate area sectioned off for a three-piece band, big enough to take the cabaret turns without wasting too much floor area; there were tables for diners to eat fancy suppers at equally fancy prices; an 'intimate' little dance floor – again small enough not to waste space – and plenty of room left where the customers could knock back over-priced drinks into the early hours, while they watched the shows with a pretty girl on their knee, or went down to the discreet room in the cellar for a hand or two of cards, or a few spins of the wheel.

Saunders was sitting in one of the booths on the second floor, watching Ginny working the big main room, meeting and greeting her customers, when Leila made her entry in a shimmer of emerald-green chiffon.

'All right, girl?' Saunders called, beckoning to her.

As Leila eased herself into the booth beside him, Saunders gestured to Flora to have some drinks sent over.

'Just thought I'd pop in to wish Ginny well,' Leila smiled, allowing her fox furs to drop from her shoulders. 'Tell me, how's the little sweetheart managing?'

'You can see for yourself, girl. First class,' he said, acknowledging the arrival of their drinks by leaning back to give the young waiter room to set down the glasses. 'I've gotta hand it to you,' he went on. 'You put me on to a good 'un. Look at her. She's working this room like a real pro.'

'I'm glad you approve, Billy.' Leila sipped her drink, studying him surreptitiously across the rim of her glass, wondering how much of what she had on her mind she dared actually say. Deciding she had nothing much to lose, Leila began hesitantly: 'I hear you've no girls working here.'

Billy frowned. 'No girls? What're you talking about, woman? This place is packed with pretty girls. All hand-picked by Ginny.'

Leila hesitated, using the ritual of lighting a cigarette

338

to give herself a bit of thinking time. 'Yes ...' she said slowly, '... but what I meant was', she leaned forward and said softly, 'the girls are saying there's no *upstairs.*'

Saunders grinned. 'What? There's no toms working here you mean?'

She sat back primly in her seat. 'Exactly.'

'Well, I have to say I wasn't bonkers about the idea at first, and I still ain't, to tell you the truth. I mean, I don't have to tell you, Leila, it's a very nice little earner. One of the best there is, if you run it right. But Ginny was mad keen to make a go of the business without the whoring. Said she wanted to keep it refined like.'

Leila said nothing, she just sat there with the bitter taste of bile rising in her throat, knowing and hating the fact that Billy would never give her such leeway – wouldn't even give her a club to run, because she'd made herself sodding indispensable. He thought she already had *enough to do* ... She sucked hard on her cigarette. Now here was Ginny – the dowdy little frump *she* had dragged out of her mean little life – deciding that working girls weren't fit to do business in her *precious fucking club.* Working girls like *her.*

She continued to nod and even managed a smile as Billy carried on talking, but inside, Leila was trembling, furious at being driven even to thinking such foul language. And what was worse was that it was all her own fault. Why hadn't she just left her in the gutter where she belonged?

'And so she persuaded me to let her run it without the toms, just for a month's trial like,' he explained. 'Then I'll have a look at her profits, and if she's doing okay I'll let her carry on a bit longer.'

He laughed loudly, as though suddenly getting the punch line of a joke. 'Fancy me having a club with no whores. It ain't natural, is it, girl? Still, I reckon I can trust her to have a go. And you know how important trusting someone is to me. It's what I like, trust. Always have done.'

He took a swallow of his drink and lifted his chin to indicate Ginny who was standing by one of the tables. 'Just look at her operating.'

Leila looked. Ginny was smiling down at a customer with a hideously raised chiv scar right across his already ugly mug, but from her expression, anyone would have thought him the most handsome man in the room.

'Just clock the way them blokes on the next table are looking at her. She's really got something, but it's like she don't even realise it. When she used to stand up on that stage . . .' He shook his head in wonder. 'I'm telling you, there's just something about her. And you'd never believe she'd ever worked as a tom, would you? She looks too good, if you know what I mean. She ain't got that hard sort of look about her.'

Leila couldn't find the words inside her to reply, so she just nodded, staring at Ginny, the apparent receptacle of all feminine virtue, as she left the customer's table and turned towards them.

Leila could have spat: Saunders was waving to her to join them.

Ginny, smiling with delight at seeing Leila, waved back and made her way over to them, accepting more praise and congratulations with every step she took on her four-inch spiked heels.

Flushed with admiration and compliments, Ginny finally arrived at the booth. Saunders stood up, took her hand in his and pressed it to his lips. 'You're doing good, girl, very good.'

Ginny, beaming with pleasure, bent forward and kissed Leila on the cheek. 'I'm so pleased you could come.'

All Leila could offer by way of a greeting was a weak stretching of her lips across her teeth into something approximating a smile.

Ginny sat down next to Saunders with a satisfied sigh. 'D'you know, Leila,' she said, 'I don't think I've ever been so happy. And I want you to know how grateful I am, because it's you I've got to thank for all this. If it wasn't for you I'd ... Well, never mind all that, I just wanna say thanks.'

In her head, Leila responded to Ginny's gratitude by telling her that the trouble with dreams coming true was that they usually – no, *inevitably* – turned into nightmares. That, unfortunately, was the cruel way of the world, as she would find out all too soon. But she actually said nothing; she just carried on flashing her tight-lipped smile and gripping the stem of her glass as though it were trying to escape.

Before Ginny had the chance to settle into her seat, Saunders was on his feet again. 'You'll have to excuse me, Leila, but I'd better go and say hello to some of these people.' He finished off his drink and checked the knot of his tie. 'And you, Ginny, you'd better come an' all, they'll want to say they've met the governor.' He held out his hand to her. 'Come on.'

Ginny shrugged with mock helplessness at Leila, as she allowed Saunders to lead her away.

Leila lit yet another cigarette. She didn't particularly want it, but nor did she want to be seen sitting alone doing nothing, or worse, to sit there watching Billy and Ginny parading around the room laughing and joking like an over-excited courting couple out on a first date.

'Penny for them?' someone asked her – or rather slurred at her in a drunken drawl – as Leila tossed her lighter back into her bag.

Leila looked up. It was Shirley. Her hair was tousled, her cheeks flushed and her eyes bloodshot and puffy.

'Shirley! What the hell are you doing here?' Leila demanded, making sure, despite her anger, that she kept her voice low; Leila was nothing if not professional. 'You know it's Sally's night off. I told you. You were to stay at the flat and take the calls.'

'Didn't want to miss the party, did I?' Shirley mumbled. 'Glad I didn't. S'lovely party.' She smirked lazily. 'And I've been watching Billy. Real gentleman. Treating her like a proper lady. Kissing her hand like that. Nice.'

'You're drunk.'

'And you're jealous.' Shirley grinned, flashing one of her badly pencilled eyebrows and clutching the side of the table to steady herself. 'Like I said before, it's your fault. You've let her . . .' She paused to gather her thoughts, to find the right words. 'Get away with it. That's what you've done. I told you all along.'

'Shirley—'

'And do you know what?' Shirley dropped inelegantly on to the bench seat in the booth so that she was facing Leila. 'The whisper is, she's not letting the girls here do any business. Well,' she wagged her finger in Leila's face, 'I reckon that's crap. I don't believe it. She's doing a foreigner. Letting them all work without telling Billy. I guarantee it. She'll be raking it in. And he won't even care. She's got him bamboozled. Miss Innocent Bloody—'

'Shirley. I think you've said enough. If you knew how ridiculous you sounded.'

'Ridiculous? Me? You're the one who's letting her get away with all this. You and Billy had something special. Now look at him. The way he's looking at her. Hanging around her like a dog after a bitch on heat. It's so obvious, it's staring you right in the bloody face.' She slapped the

342

table with the flat of her hand, knocking Leila's drink flying. The young waiter was immediately there, mopping up.

Shirley giggled girlishly until he left, then, after another struggle to recollect her train of thought, she continued her drunken monologue. 'Anyone can see she's letting him have it to keep him sweet. But you've got to hand it to her, she's not got a bad price for it. A whole fucking club.'

Leila sprang to her feet and wrenched Shirley from the bench, signalling with her eyes to the ever-vigilant Flora that she needed help.

'That is it, Shirley,' Leila whispered into her ear as she and Flora escorted her off the premises. 'That's the final straw. You are out.'

'Who is it? Is that you, Flora?' Ginny squinted at her watch through sleep-blurred eyes. Half past ten. She groaned wearily. She hadn't got to bed until five o'clock.

The knocking continued.

'Hold on.'

She pulled on her wrapper and dragged herself through the flat to the front door.

'Billy. I wasn't expecting—'

'Never mind who you was expecting.' He scowled at her. 'What did I tell you?'

'Listen. D'you know what time I—'

'No. You listen. I told you. Use that spyhole. And always put the chain on. You never know who might be about.'

Pleased with his concern, but embarrassed by her own foolishness – Billy had warned her over and over again about security – Ginny stood there like a child being chastised by a displeased parent. It wouldn't have been

343

so bad if she'd been dressed properly and had done her hair. She must look a real sight.

'Well? Can I come in?'

Ginny stepped aside. 'Sorry. Of course. Come in.'

'Get your clothes on. I've got something to show you.'

'Can I just make some tea first?'

'No. Go and get dressed.'

Ginny nodded. 'All right.' She went back into the bedroom, shut the door and started to sort herself out. What should she put on? A dress? Slacks? A skirt and blouse? A skirt. Yes. But which—

'How many sugars?' she heard him call from the kitchen.

Ginny mugged at herself in the dressing-table mirror. Billy Saunders was in the kitchen. Making her a cup of tea . . . 'Er none thanks,' she called back. 'Just a splash of milk.'

Whatever next?

'It's just a little something. To say thank you. You've done a good job.'

'Where is it?' She stood on the steps of the club, glancing up and down the alleyway, completely at a loss to know what she was supposed to be looking at.

'There.'

'What? The car?'

'Yeah.' Saunders handed her a key hanging from a silver fob engraved with her name.

She twisted round to look at him. 'For me? Really?'

'Don't get too excited,' he said, leading her down the steps to where the car was parked at the kerb. 'It's only a little Anglia.'

'I know.' Ginny touched a tentative finger to the shiny turquoise bonnet. 'It's the new one. I've seen it in all the magazines.'

'Can you drive?'

She thought of the times Ted had made her drive them home when he'd been too drunk even to hold the steering wheel. 'A bit.'

'Well, get in, and we'll soon have you racing about like Fangio.'

'Fangio?' she gasped, as she slipped into the driver's seat, her skirt riding up high around her legs. 'I feel more like Kay Kendall. You know, in *Genevieve*.' She laughed happily, running her hands round and round the steering wheel. 'Sorry, I forgot. You don't know much about the flicks do you?'

'I could, if the right person wanted to teach me.' He reached across the few inches that separated them and let his hand rest on her thigh.

Ginny felt his heat like a brand on her flesh. She had begun to long for that touch, but didn't want to make a fool of herself by misinterpreting its intention. 'I thought this was meant to be a business arrangement.' Her voice sounded odd. Sort of breathless.

Billy laughed easily and held up his hands in a gesture of surrender. 'Fair enough. I ain't never had to force meself on a bird yet.'

Ginny swallowed hard. He'd called her that before. In the same sort of tone. Was that all she was to him? Just some bird?

What else could she expect, taking off her clothes and going with all those men? And she a married woman. Even if she had let Billy believe she was single.

'You're a strange one, Ginny, d'you know that?' He half turned his body so that he was leaning back against the car door, folded his arms and studied her through narrowed eyes.

To avoid his gaze, and to hide her flushed cheeks, Ginny stared out of the window. Did he see her any differently from the way Ted had done? A bit of decoration to be used when he felt like it.

Ted.

Ginny was surprised to realise she hadn't really thought about him for weeks. The timid little thing who used to jump like a scared rabbit every time she heard a sudden noise, fearing it might be him, was gradually fading away. She no longer looked nervously over her shoulder at every single shadow, scared out of her wits that he might be standing there, asking for a bed for the night, because Nellie had locked the door on him. Or because Dilys was fed up with his womanising and – as she could now get by very nicely without him what with the extra money Ginny was sending for her and Susan – she'd thrown him out on his ear.

'Want a fag?'

Ginny looked round, as though she was surprised to see Saunders sitting there.

'Sorry. I was miles away.'

'I could see.'

As he lit her cigarette, Ginny was still thinking about Susan and Ted: how she still missed Susan with all her heart, but how all she felt for Ted was contempt. Then Billy's hand brushed against hers and the confused feelings of desire and a still lingering self-doubt flooded through her again.

'You okay?' Saunders asked. 'I ain't upset you, have I?'

She shook her head. 'No, I'm fine.'

And it was more or less true. She wasn't completely fine, maybe, but almost.

She didn't have Ted hanging around her neck, and she was actually having fun for a change, the sort of fun that made her feel like a woman again. She'd missed that feeling.

It was as though the excitement of the past weeks had

begun to waken her from a long sleep, just as London itself was waking. She was leaving the drab blacks and greys of the bomb-sites behind and was embracing a world of brilliant Technicolor, a new way of life, where there was plenty for everyone and people were smiling again. Just as they did in the films.

And in the films, didn't the hero always win the girl?

Ginny took a deep breath, slowly raised her head and looked directly into Billy's eyes. If he really did think of her as just another bird, she was about to make a very big mistake.

'You know what you said about not having to force yourself on me, Billy?'

'Look, I didn't mean—'

'It's all right, I just want you to know that I don't intend putting up a fight.'

Billy grinned happily as he reached across and opened the car door for her. 'Well in that case, we'd better go back inside then, hadn't we? There ain't much room in these little motors for what I've got in mind.'

It was a Saturday afternoon in October and the autumn chill was really beginning to set in, but as Ginny walked along the wide London street, all she noticed was the beauty of the afternoon sun shining through the golden leaves of the plane trees. There was a spring in her step and she felt glad to be alive, as she headed for the private hotel, just around the corner from Claridge's, where she was meeting Leila for afternoon tea.

Not only was the club showing a healthy profit after being open for only a month – without her having to open any rooms 'upstairs' – but, what was more, she was in love.

As Ginny paused at the hotel reception, Leila, who was already seated at their table, watched as she handed over a pile of bags and parcels, all bearing the names of exclusive shops, for safe keeping.

'Bond Street, eh, sweetie?' Leila said, as Ginny joined her. 'You've learned well.'

'It's only what you taught me, Leila.' Ginny kissed Leila's offered cheek and sat down opposite her, moving the red-shaded lamp and the extravagant flower display to one side so they could see one another.

'A few months ago, you wouldn't have dared touch that vase in case someone told you off.'

Ginny rolled her eyes. 'I wasn't that bad.'

'Weren't you?'

A formally dressed waiter appeared by their side.

'Would you order, Leila?'

Leila did so.

Once the waiter was out of earshot, Ginny leaned across the table and whispered, 'I still struggle with the way I talk sometimes, but I'm getting better.'

She took a gold case from her handbag and offered Leila a cigarette. 'It is all down to you, Leila. Honestly. You gave me the confidence to do things. It's like when Billy told me to treat myself to something.' She jerked her thumb over her shoulder towards the reception desk. 'I didn't argue, I just gave them shops a right caning.'

Leila took a deep lungful of smoke.

'And I reckon it's down to you that I'm finding Ginny's so easy to run an' all. Hard work. But there's plenty of people helping me. You know, it still tickles me, having the place called after me.' She smiled happily. 'I miss Soho, of course, and the girls, but I'm really happy being in charge.'

Leila smiled back at her. Much as she would have liked to knock Ginny down to size, telling her that she was no more running the place than the meanest lavatory cleaner, Leila would never break Billy's trust. It wasn't only loyalty that made her keep her mouth shut, she knew a side of Saunders that Ginny probably hadn't even imagined. 'I'm pleased for you, darling,' she said. 'Now, tell me all about it.'

As the waiter set their lavish tea before them, Ginny launched into an excited description of her life at the club, any shyness about her speech completely forgotten.

'You should see the sort of people we get, Leila. Really surprising. I mean, it's in the middle of the East End, but I'm playing hostess to all sorts of customers. They're from "right across the social spectrum", Billy says.'

As she poured tea into the delicate china cups, Leila had to stop herself from yelling out loud: *Billy says*, what do you know about what Billy says?

'They're out slumming, if you ask me. But wherever they come from, I'll tell you this, all the customers have got money, whether they've earned it from some posh job in the City, been born to it, or robbed it from a bank. Mind you, from some of the things you hear them saying, I don't know that there's a lot of difference between some of the so-called honest ones and the crooks.'

Ginny took a gulp of tea and a bite from one of the tiny crustless sandwiches. 'You'd have been proud of me the other night, Leila. I'm not the soft touch I used to be.'

'I can see that,' she answered quietly.

'See, when I realised one of the girls was working a spinner—'

Leila's eyebrows shot up. 'A spinner?'

'Fixing the roulette wheel.'

'I know what it means, I'm just surprised that you're familiar with the term.'

'I'm familiar with all sorts now, Leila.'

'I'll bet you are.'

'Well, I told Billy straight away and he chucked her

right out and the bloke she was working with. Right out of the door they went.'

While Ginny continued with her tales about running the club, Leila sat listening with increasing bewilderment at just how in control Ginny seemed to be.

'It's from what I saw in Frith Street, I suppose,' Ginny went on. 'That's how I know how to attract the customers. That "artistic" stuff we used to do in the tableaux, that's all old hat. People want something modern, contemporary. You should see the girl I've got doing a routine to "Diamonds Are A Girl's Best Friend". Billy said it makes my fan dance look like an evening with the Girl Guides!'

'Is Billy at the club very often?'

'Yeah. Most of the time.'

'Really?'

'Mmmmm. He seems impressed with what I'm doing.'

Leila busied herself pouring more tea. No wonder she hadn't seen him for nearly a month.

'I nearly forgot.' Ginny took another swallow of tea. 'He asked me to say hello. Said he hadn't seen much of you lately.'

Leila shook her head, making the feather trim on her hat shimmer in the lamplight. 'Not for a week or two.'

'How about Shirley? Any word on her?'

'She could be on the streets for all I know.' Leila did her best to smile brightly, although the effort was nearly killing her. What she really wanted to do was scream at Ginny that she was a stupid little tart who was getting involved way over her head, and if she had any sense she'd get back where she came from and get her bloody claws out of Billy Saunders.

But Leila had never been one to display her emotions.

Ginny emptied her cup and picked up the teapot for a refill. It was empty.

'Shall I order some more?' Leila asked, a study in graciousness.

Ginny wrinkled her nose and looked at her watch. 'No thanks, Leila. It's nearly half four already.'

'You're going?'

'Yeah. I don't like being away from the club for too long.' She pulled on her gloves and grinned happily. 'I take my responsibilities very seriously, you know. I want Billy to feel he can trust me.'

'But when I told the girls from Frith Street we were meeting up they said they'd see us in the Three Greyhounds in Greek Street.' Leila paused, checking the desperation that was creeping into her tone. 'So we can all have a natter and a drink together.'

'Sorry, Leila. Better not. But don't let me stop you going to have one with them.' Ginny stood up, took a large white five-pound note from her purse and put it on the table. 'And treat the girls for me, eh?'

With that, Ginny pecked Leila on the cheek and left, pausing in the doorway to look over her shoulder and waggle her fingers in a gesture of farewell, then she wiggled her way out to reception on her now customary stiletto heels to collect her shopping.

Leila didn't need to look round to check, she just knew that every man in the room had his gaze fixed on Ginny's backside.

Later that evening, as Ginny was putting the final touches to her hair, Dilys was standing in her bedroom in Stepney looking at her watch for the tenth time in so many minutes.

'That's it,' she snapped, throwing up her hands. 'Half past seven. I'm off. I've waited long enough for you, Ted bloody Martin. In fact, I've given you more chances than I've got lipsticks and that's saying something.'

She pulled her coat from where she'd chucked it over the back of her chair the night before, slipped it round her shoulders and ducked down for a final glimpse in the dressing-table mirror.

As she looked in the glass, she saw the reflection of Susan standing behind her in the doorway.

'What d'you want?' Dilys asked, wiping away a smudge of lipstick from the corner of her mouth with the tip of her little finger.

Susan gnawed the skin around her thumb-nail, unsure how much she dared say, but her empty stomach overcame her fear. 'I'm hungry,' she said quietly.

'I told you, there's stuff in the maid-saver.'

'There's not, Mum. I looked.'

Dilys sighed wearily, twisted round and snatched her handbag off the bed. 'Here,' she said, rummaging in her bag. 'Go and get yourself a bag of chips. And don't leave the lights burning when you go to bed. I ain't made of money.'

With that, Dilys threw some coppers on to the eiderdown and flounced out of the room without so much as a goodbye, let alone a good-night kiss, for her little girl.

While Dilys was out doing her now familiar Saturday night round of pubs, looking for men willing to treat her – not a difficult task as she had vamping down to a fine art – Shirley was sitting on her foul-smelling bed in the little room in Berwick Street she was renting from the most unpleasant Greek woman she had met in her entire life, wondering what on earth she was going to do next.

When Leila had first thrown her out, Shirley had found the room straight away and things hadn't seemed too bad. She had only ever had to deal with the landlady's husband and he had been a right mug; not worrying if she was late with the rent and even occasionally letting her off an entire week at a time, so long as she gave him a free seeing to now and again. But then he had gone back to Crete on some sort of family business, and Shirley had been left dealing with his monster of a wife.

As soon as the woman had realised that Shirley didn't work in the market, as her husband had claimed, but was on the game and using the room as her 'lumber', she had put up the rent, demanded a share of Shirley's weekly takings and now, worst of all, was insisting that Shirley should be *nice*, as she put it, to her elderly father as he was missing his wife who was back home in Crete.

When the landlady had said what she expected her to do if she wanted to keep a roof over her head, and for absolutely no money, Shirley had laughed, thinking she was having a joke. But the woman had just stared at her with her sunken, piggy little eyes and cursed at her in Greek.

Shirley cursed back in English. She wouldn't take that sort of crap from a runty little middle-aged woman.

But runty or not, the landlady had meant business and had cracked Shirley – smack! – right round the side of the head with a pair of brass knuckles that Shirley hadn't even suspected she was wearing.

Shirley stumbled backwards across the room, clutching her ear as blood dripped between her fingers.

She had only gone round there to pay the rent and the woman had come up with this bloody nightmare of an idea. It wasn't as though Shirley had never done an old man before, she had, plenty of times, but at least there had always been money involved. And this one looked as though he was on his last legs. His face was all yellow and shrivelled with age, and his wrists were so thin they looked as though they might snap at any minute. It would be like going with a corpse.

As Shirley pressed herself against the wall, staring at

him, as he sat dwarfed by the carver chair in the woman's kitchen, she knew she wasn't going to go through with it. It wasn't just the thought that the effort of getting him on to the bed would probably be more excitement than he could take – let alone what the act itself would do to him – it was the thought that the woman would be taking her for a mug, and before Shirley knew what she was doing, she'd have all the old cow's uncles and cousins queuing up for a free go as well.

So, here she was in her room, with a half-empty bottle of gin and the few clothes that Leila had let her keep stuffed into a brown paper carrier, knowing that she had had enough, that this wasn't the life she deserved. But what next?

She couldn't think straight. All that filled her head – apart from the pain from the blow and a raging hangover – was the knowledge that this was Ginny's fault. She hated the bitch. Hated her more than that Greek cow downstairs and her disgusting father; more than Leila for throwing her out; more than anything in the whole fucking world.

Slowly a smile began to form on Shirley's lips.

Ginny had caused her all this trouble, so it was only fair that she should get some too. Shirley would get her own back. She would get revenge.

Her smile broadened.

All the girls knew that *Miss* Martin was actually a married woman who had an old man tucked away somewhere. Just as they all knew that for some reason she never wanted him mentioned.

Shirley would go and find Ginny's husband.

And Ted was surprisingly easy to find. All Shirley had had to do was nip round to Frith Street, blow all but her last ten shillings on a nice little treat for Carmen and offer it to her in exchange for a favour.

Carmen, stupid as ever when promised some free dope, had immediately agreed to find out from Yvette where Ginny used to live and her husband's name.

Ginny hadn't been wrong when she'd worried that she'd told Yvette just a little too much, because although, unlike Shirley, she had no malice in her, Yvette did lack an ability to think things through.

A couple of hours later Carmen turned up in the Moka Bar with the information and Shirley handed over what she claimed was a really potent strain of gear she had bought from Italian Tony in Brewer Street.

Shirley had then only to visit a few pubs and buy a couple of drinks, to find herself steaming along the right track in the direction of a dismal boozers' pub near the Rotherhithe tunnel.

'Hello. Ted is it? Ted Martin?'

At the sound of a woman's voice, and a cultured sort of a voice at that, Ted looked up.

Shirley could see he was obviously half cut, but she was more interested in how good-looking he was. From the amount of drink that Carmen had reported he was supposed to put away each night, Shirley had expected someone looking more like the landlady's shrivelled old dad than this handsome, slightly stockier version of James Mason.

She smiled seductively. This was going to be more fun than she'd hoped.

'Who wants to know.'

'I'm Shirley. A friend of your wife's. Now how about buying me a drink and I'll tell you some things that might well be of interest.'

'If you're gonna tell me she's working as a hostess, I

know. I know all about her whoring. And I don't care. All women are the same.'

Shirley noted he didn't seem to know anything about the club. It wouldn't hurt to keep back a little information. You never knew when you might need a bargaining tool.

This time, as she smiled she leaned forward, making sure that he could get a good look down her dress. 'All women aren't the same, Ted,' she purred.

'No. I can see that. And I like the look of what I see an' all, darling.'

'And I like the look of you too.' She leaned closer and breathed into his ear. 'I'm not wearing any knickers. Fancy coming outside?'

She let Ted lead her from the warm fug of the bar out into the cold night air, and round the corner to where the railway arches formed a dark, dank maze behind the pub.

Without saying a word, Ted slammed her against the dripping wall, shoved up her skirt, tore open his fly and thrust straight into her.

'Like it a bit rough, do you?' Shirley giggled.

Chapter 17

1954

'Sorry to bother you, guv, but I reckon you ought to give your eyes a chance on this one.' Flora straightened up from his subservient pose over Saunders's table and looked warily about him.

Saunders nodded his apologies to the two men and women at his table and stood up. 'This had better be good, Flora.'

'It's ...' He hesitated. 'You'd better see for yourself.' Flora lead his boss over to one of the tall, small-paned windows at the far end of the room. 'Take a butcher's out there.'

Saunders lifted the fine lace curtain and squinted out into the darkness. Down below, in the dim glow of the wrought-iron street lamp, he saw the unmistakable outline of two squad cars and a matching pair of Black Marias blocking the end of the alley. Their lights were off and there was no sign of anyone inside them, not even the drivers.

Saunders snorted, shaking his head contemptuously. 'Hurry-up wagons? Are they sure?'

'Johnno gave me the whisper they were out there,' Flora said under his breath. 'I thought you'd better know.'

'Yeah, all right, Flora, get back to the bar, eh? I'll see to this.'

Flora backed away from his boss's side. He was immediately replaced by Ginny. Having seen the unprecedented spectacle of Flora leaving his precious bar to the mercies of his two underlings, she too wanted to see what was so fascinating in the street below.

'It's the law,' she gasped, leaping back from the window, with the net draped limply over her head.

Saunders flicked the curtain from Ginny's hair, took her firmly by the shoulders and steered her back towards the bar. 'Keep it down, girl, we don't want no one panicking, or we'll have the customers getting upset.'

'But—'

'But nothing. It's only the Old Bill sprinkling a bit of frightening powder around the place.'

'But you said the police had—'

'You just ignore it. Carry on as usual. I'll nip down in a minute and see to 'em.'

'How—'

'Look, I've already straightened their governor out. He's getting more than a fair wage off me.' He shrugged. 'But they'll be after a few quid for themselves. It's the way the world turns, innit? A bit of bunce and everyone's happy.'

Ginny reluctantly allowed him to help her up on to one of the bar-stools. 'So why are they—'

Again he interrupted her. 'They're just flexing their muscles. Right, Flora?'

'He's right, Miss Martin.' Flora, now comfortably back in his rightful place, had relaxed. He nodded calmly. 'They like to put on a bit of a show, don't they. They'll be lurking out there until someone goes down and gives them a nice little drink, then they'll stick it in their bin and disappear like nothing's happened. Then go and bother someone else.'

Saunders lowered his head and kissed Ginny gently on the forehead.

She smiled up at him. It wasn't often he made any

358

public show of affection, but that kiss – maybe it was just a peck – he'd given her right there, in front of everyone.

He chucked her playfully under the chin and was just about to signal to Johnno to join him, when an almighty crash, followed by the sound of wood shattering and splintering, reverberated up from the hall below.

Saunders twisted away from Ginny as though an electric charge had pulsed through his body. 'What the fuck was that?' he yelled, barrelling across to the double doors that opened on to the main staircase.

As he flew down to the entrance hall, four minders tight on his tail, the whole club was erupting around him.

Someone in one of the downstairs rooms shouted, 'It's a raid!' and it was as though someone had fired a starting pistol. Men in evening dress were scrambling over tables, sending chairs and glasses flying, not caring whom they knocked out of their way as they raced towards the emergency doors and the fire escape at the back of the building. Police raids were all very well when you heard of one of your pals in the City being arrested in an illegal casino or a bawdy house, but they weren't the sort of thing you wanted to happen to you. And the girls were just as frenzied, screaming and scrapping as they chased after the men, not from fear of being left behind to the mercy of the law, but of losing out on their promised tips for the evening.

Reaching the bottom of the stairs, Saunders saw a young-looking plain-clothes man he'd never seen before, calmly stepping over the wreckage of what had once been a painstakingly restored Georgian front door. He was flanked by six more mature uniformed men – all of whom Saunders knew very well.

As Saunders stood there, panting from the exertion, trying to understand what was going on, his bewildered gaze passed from one officer to the next. The older men's faces were glowing as red as the sunset on the hand-painted mural that covered the wall behind them, but the younger man, apparently in charge of the operation, seemed entirely, and arrogantly, unmoved by the situation.

Saunders took another look at the shattered wood-work, *his* shattered woodwork, snatched up one of the heavy, mahogany hall chairs and lunged with it at the plain-clothes man. If his minders hadn't stepped in to restrain him, Saunders might well have found himself on a charge of attempted murder; this particular policeman happened to be a stickler for the letter of the law.

'Temper, temper, sir,' said the young officer, seemingly unmoved by the situation.

'Who the hell d'you think you are?' Saunders snarled, his anger giving him the strength to shake himself free from his minders' vice-like grip. 'Fabian of the fucking Yard?'

'Detective Sergeant Chisholm, actually.'

'Billy?' Ginny asked from half-way down the stairs. 'What's going on?'

Without taking his eyes off him, Saunders barked out his orders at Ginny, while stabbing his finger into the face of the now smiling DS Chisholm. 'Get upstairs, Ginny. Now. And get Millson on the blower. This *little boy* has got some explaining to do.'

Within half an hour, Saunders was sitting at a table with Detective Inspector Douglas Millson in the second-floor bar of the club.

Apart from the minders and Flora, who were all down-stairs doing their best to patch up the front door, and

Ginny, who was behind the bar pouring the drinks, the place was now empty.

'I couldn't believe it, Doug, I'm telling you. That wet-behind-the-ears little bastard was actually threatening me. Saying he was gonna send the zombies round with the kiddie wagon. The silly bleeder was even going on about white slavery. White slavery?'

Ginny put two triple scotches on the table. 'Zombies?' she asked quietly.

'WPCs,' Millson explained with a weary sigh. 'They go out looking for under-age tarts. Then they round 'em up and send 'em off to the kids' home.' He spread his hands in bewilderment. 'What's wrong with the bloke? I know you don't have no shit like that in here.' He grimaced as he realised what he'd said and bobbed his head in apology in Ginny's direction. 'Excuse my French.'

Saunders tossed back his drink as though it were buttermilk. 'Everyone knows this place is kosher. Except for the spieler downstairs, of course. And everyone gets more than his fair cut outta that.' He shook his head. 'I don't understand. What's his problem? I mean, she won't even tolerate me showing a few blue films in a private room. Will you, girl? That's how straight this place is.' He held up his glass for Ginny to refill it. 'I'm telling you, Doug, what with this and with all these other blokes causing trouble, I'm gonna get out of this lark as soon as I can. But in the meantime, just get him off my back, will you?'

Douglas Millson raised his glass and winked. 'As good as done, Billy. As good as done.'

The next morning Saunders woke up early.

As had become almost his routine, he hadn't bothered to go home to his own flat, but had stayed the night in

Ginny's bed. 'I've made us a cup o' tea,' he said, clanking the spoon in the saucer so that she'd wake up.

Ginny levered herself up on to her elbows, squinting against the bright April sunshine that was flooding the room with its golden light. 'What time is it?'

'Nearly nine.'

'Billy!' She flopped back on the pillows.

He sat down on the edge of the bed. 'Come on, drink this and you'll feel better.'

She dragged herself up into a sitting position and leaned back against the padded velvet headboard. With her eyes tightly closed, she held out her hand for the cup.

'Spit it out. What's worrying you?' she said, after she'd taken a mouthful of tea. 'Is it that business last night that's getting you all worked up?'

'You know me too well, Ginny,' he said, touching her tangled blonde curls. 'But it's not just that.'

Her eyes flicked open. 'So, what is it?'

'It's the whole business of security. How could that have happened last night? I'm paying through the nose and then some little runt—'

'Calm down, Billy, you sorted it all out with Millson, didn't you?'

'Yeah, but that ain't the half of it. There's more of them Maltese moving into Shoreditch every day. Coming over here on them assisted passages, and—'

'I'm sorry, Billy, but I won't listen to you talking like that.' Ginny slapped her cup down on to the bedside table, not caring that she spilled the tea in the saucer. 'I've made myself clear with all the staff and I want you to be clear too. I won't have no colour bar in this club. I treat people the way I find them.'

'And so do I. But we ain't talking about some Maltese geezer coming in for a few drinks and a bit of a cuddle

362

with one of the girls. We're talking about gangs of 'em. All trying to muscle in on other people's territory. On *my* territory.'

'How d'you mean?'

'Millson put me straight last night. They're setting up a nice little network for 'emselves round these parts. A bit of gambling here. A drinking club there. Whores all over the place. They're getting more and more confident. Too confident. And I don't like it. It's attracting too much attention. That's why that young copper was round here sticking his beak in. He wants to earn himself a few points, get a chance of promotion under his belt, so he come where the action is.'

'But surely—'

'But, nothing. It's all getting silly. Out of control. This turf's gonna be carved up like bleed'n' allotments the way this mob's carrying on. At least around Soho you know where you are with the likes of Albert Dimes and Jack Spot. But these little bastards . . .'

Saunders stood up and began pacing around the room. 'I'm glad I listened to you about not running toms from this gaff. You was right about that. Even if it was for the wrong reason. At least that's one bit of aggravation I ain't got to worry about: Maltese ponces fighting me over territory.'

He pulled on the navy silk dressing-gown that Ginny had bought him – a gift that was as much a wordless confirmation that she wanted him to stay with her, as it was an actual Christmas present – and lit himself a cigarette.

'This is all getting to be too much bother.' He walked over to the window and stared down at the alley below, inhaling deeply on his cigarette. 'After the war, even *during* the bloody war, it used to be so easy. All the competition you had was the tuppenny-ha'penny spivs running their black-market scams out of the docks and maybe keeping a few pathetic old toms they could scare into working for them. They acted like tough men, but they was never no real trouble. They still ain't, their sort. You only have to shout boo! and they're running away with their tails between their legs. But these new blokes. Some of 'em sound right nutters.'

Ginny swung her legs from under the covers and went to stand next to him. 'So you meant it then, Billy, what you said to Millson yesterday.'

He turned round to face her. 'Meant what, babe?'

'That you wanna get out of this business.'

'Yeah, I meant it all right. I've been doing a lot of thinking, figuring ways of getting out of the clubs.' Saunders stretched his arms wide. 'Look at me, I'm forty-five years old. I don't wanna spend the rest of me life living off tithes from poxy little dice games, worrying about bar staff fiddling the tills and whether some Maltese slag's gonna chuck a petrol bomb through me window 'cos he fancies taking me clubs over.'

Ginny frowned. 'So what do you want to do?'

'I'm gonna expand the property side.'

Ginny sat down on the dressing-table stool and stared into her lap. 'I see,' she said quietly, then considered for a moment before continuing. 'Look, Billy, I know this is just a business to you, and you probably think I'm a right naive so-and-so at times, but this is the way I earn my living now. So if you are gonna close the club, could you give me a bit of notice, so's I can sort something out for myself?'

Saunders stubbed out his cigarette and pulled her to him. 'That's what I like about you. You're a good girl caught up in a rotten world. But you're decent. There's no edge to you. You say what you think. Not like the rest of them.' He stroked her hair off her face and smiled tenderly down at her. 'I'll make sure you're looked after, Ginny. Whatever happens, you're my girl now.'

She reached up and took his face in her hands and kissed him softly on the mouth.

He twisted round, threw himself on to the bed and pulled her down on top of him.

'I reckon I could eat a bit of breakfast after that,' Billy grinned, slapping Ginny playfully on her backside. He rolled away from her and grabbed his discarded dressing-gown from the floor. 'Get me energy back.'

'What d'you fancy?' Ginny asked, pulling the covers up to her chin and flapping her lashes at him.

'You can get that idea right out of your head!' He pulled the covers off her again and tossed them on to the floor, leaving her lying there naked. 'Mind you,' he said slowly, 'on second thoughts . . .'

He had just thrown his dressing-gown back on the floor, when a loud bashing started on the repaired front door.

'What the bloody hell . . .' He looked at the bedside clock. 'Half ten. Why don't Flora get it?' He dragged his dressing-gown back on.

'You'd better get something on and all, Gin,' he said over his shoulder as he strode out to the flat door. 'Who knows who it'll be this time?'

'Flora! You there?' he hollered down the stairs.

'Yes, guv,' Ginny heard him shout back.

'Then why ain't you getting it?'

'I am, I'm going.'

'If you need me, gimme a shout. I'm just gonna get me strides on.'

Before Saunders had the chance even to locate his trousers, let alone put them on, Flora, puffing like a steam engine, was calling to him from the flat doorway. 'Sorry, guv, I couldn't stop her. It's that Shirley Truman, she says she's gotta see you. I told her—'

Shirley didn't give Flora the chance to explain what he had told her. She shoved him out of the way and stumbled into the flat, rushing angrily from room to room until she found Ginny and Saunders.

They stared at the wild-haired, scruffy-looking, middle-aged woman who stood before them, hardly able to believe that it was Shirley. She had never been exactly beautiful, but she had always been elegantly dressed and well-presented, even when she'd had a few. That had been her big attraction for the type of punters who got a thrill from doing something naughty with a girl who could play it a bit on the posh side.

'Shirley,' Ginny said, when she'd managed to get over the shock, 'it's not even opening time.'

'Don't you start preaching to me,' sneered Shirley. She staggered sideways, hitting her shin hard against the dressing-table. 'Shit!'

Overcoming her disgust, Ginny held out her hand to steady her. 'We were just going to have some coffee. Come through to the kitchen and join us.'

'Come and join us?' Shirley threw back her head and laughed wildly. 'You've got a bit above yourself haven't you, *Miss* Martin?'

'Can I do anything?' Flora called from the flat door, scared that he was going to be blamed for letting Shirley up the stairs, but even more scared that he might be expected to deal with the drunken woman who had just knocked the wind right out of him.

'No, you're all right, Flora.' Saunders called back. 'We can manage.'

'You won't blame me for being pissed when you know what I've been through these last few months.' With a shaking hand, Shirley put down her coffee cup, sniffed loudly and pulled open her blouse, showing the small red scars dotted all over her torso. 'Cigarette burns,' she said, tucking her blouse back in. 'There're more, all over me. And I got this, this morning.' She turned her head to one side and lifted her hair away from her face.

In the bright spring sunshine slanting through the window, Ginny saw a row of raw, ugly gashes pitting Shirley's cheek.

Shirley brushed her hair forward with her fingers to cover the marks again. 'Know how that happened?'

Ginny shook her head.

'Fish hooks.'

'What?'

'Bastards who want to act the big man,' Saunders broke in, 'to keep a girl in order. They sew them on to their sleeves. And then a gentle stroke across a girl's cheek . . . Well, you figure out the rest.'

Ginny covered her mouth with her hands. 'That's *disgusting*.'

'Too right, it's disgusting,' Saunders agreed. 'You can't imagine the sort of slag who'd do that, can you?'

Ginny poured more coffee into Shirley's cup. 'But why did you stay with him?'

'Why did you?'

'Sorry?'

'You honestly don't know who I'm talking about, do you?' Shirley turned to Saunders. 'So I don't suppose you do either.' She helped herself to one of Saunders's cigarettes. 'I've been seeing her husband.'

Ginny shook her head. 'No.'

'Oh yes, Ginny. And d'you know what? If I hadn't been bringing in plenty of wages brassing for him, I reckon I'd be dead by now. Because he likes things rough, your husband. And I've just about had enough of it.'

Shirley leaned back and blew a plume of smoke into the air. 'Is that why he never topped you, Ginny, because you were earning him plenty?'

'Would someone mind telling me—'

A sly smile lit up Shirley's face. 'Silly me, I forgot. You didn't know she was married, did you, Billy? I wonder what else you don't know about little Miss Perfect.'

Ginny stood up and grabbed Shirley by the arm. 'Look, Shirley, I wanna talk to Billy. Go downstairs and Flora will make sure you get some breakfast to sober you up. And tell him to give you a tenner out of the till an' all.'

Billy shook his head. 'No. You leave her. She can get something to eat in a minute. I've got a few questions I wanna—'

'Don't listen to her, Billy. Please. It's over. It's been over for years. Why drag up old—'

'Oh yes? It's over, is it?' Shirley leaned across the table and stared into Ginny's face, as she sat there like a rabbit trapped in a car's headlights. 'That's not the way he tells it. He said he threw you out, that you begged him to have you back. But he wouldn't because you were such a trollop.' She chuckled horribly, a low, guttural sound in the back of her throat. 'He's a right one, you know, Billy. Women go mad for him, even though he uses them. Been pimping for years, he has. Pimped for you, did he, Ginny? Were you already on the game when you met Leila and me? I bet you were. I always knew there was something about you. Something not quite true to form. *Did* he pimp for you? Or did he get you to do it for free for his friends? He likes that sometimes. Likes to watch. Bit funny, isn't he, your husband? Mind you, I bet he loves your little Miss Innocent act. That sort of thing would really get him going.'

She took another leisurely drag on her cigarette. 'When did you last see him? Recently, was it?'

Saunders stood up, not caring that his dressing-gown was flapping open. 'Get out, Shirley.'

Shirley looked at him and laughed. 'There's one born every minute, they say, and you must be one of them. Mind you,' she said, lowering her eyes until her gaze rested on his groin, 'I can see what Ginny sees in you.'

'I'm gonna get dressed,' he said quietly, 'and when I come out of that bedroom, you'd better be gone, Shirley. Or you'll be sorry.' He looked at Ginny and went to say something, but changed his mind.

He pressed his lips together, shook his head and strode over to the bedroom door. 'I'm getting out of here,' he said, without turning round, 'and I don't wanna hear another word from you, Ginny. Not another single word.'

Ginny ran to him, but he slammed the bedroom door in her face. 'If there's one thing I can't stand,' he shouted, 'it's being taken for a fucking mug.'

'Let me in, Billy, please,' she sobbed.

'Leave it, Ginny. Just leave it. Keep your old toffee for the punters.'

Ginny slid down the door and collapsed on to the carpet in a crumpled heap.

'You know when they say that things are "nothing personal"?' Shirley asked, as she hauled herself to her feet. 'Well, this was completely personal. From the day I met you you've made my life a misery, now I hope you're as miserable as I am. Cheerio, Ginny. I won't wish you good luck.'

'Thanks for coming, Leila.' Ginny stepped back and let her into the flat. 'I know we've not spoken for a while, but I—'

'It's okay. No need to be embarrassed, sweetie, it's easy enough to lose touch when you're busy.'

Leila followed Ginny into the sitting-room, pulling off

her gloves and tucking them into her handbag. 'It's such a wonderful evening,' she said, walking over to the window and looking out. 'Nearly half past seven and it's still so warm. Summer's really here at last.'

She turned and faced Ginny, her professional smile lifting her lips, but not reaching her eyes. 'And this is a lovely flat.'

'I know I should have asked you over before,' Ginny began. 'I feel terrible. You've not even been back to the club since opening night, have you?'

Leila laughed mirthlessly. 'What a night that was.'

Ginny gestured for her to sit down on one of the armchairs that stood either side of the tiled fireplace. 'That was the night you told Shirley to get out, wasn't it?'

Leila shook her head. 'Don't remind me. It's been eight months and I've not heard a word. She might have sent a note of apology. No class, some people.' She took out her cigarettes and offered one to Ginny. 'Still, all that's water under the bridge. Let's get down to present-day business. Nice as it is to see you, Ginny, why the sudden invitation?'

Ginny reached across and lit Leila's cigarette with the heavy chromium table lighter that stood on the coffee table between them. 'You heard about me and Billy breaking up?'

'I heard.'

'Did Billy tell you?'

Leila thought for a moment. 'Yes.'

'So you've seen him?'

Leila lifted her hands. 'Now and again.'

'How is he?'

'Is that why you asked me over. To find out how he is?'

'Sort of.' Ginny shrugged. 'So, how is he?'

Leila didn't reply immediately; she took her time tapping the end of her cigarette into one of the pair of tall chromium ashtrays that matched the table lighter. 'Look, why don't you just tell me what's on your mind, Ginny? Where all this is leading.'

Ginny stood up. 'Would you like some coffee? Tea? Something stronger?'

'A gin and tonic would be nice.'

Ginny dipped her chin. 'This isn't easy for me, Leila,' she said, going over to the cocktail cabinet.

'I can tell.'

As Ginny opened the lid, and the twinkling music box rendition of 'Secret Love' began to play, tears blurred her eyes. She swiped at them with the back of her hand and got on with pouring the drinks.

'I wanted to find out if it really was over between me and Billy,' she said, setting the glasses down on the table.

Leila shifted uncomfortably. 'Why ask me?'

It was as though Ginny hadn't heard her question. 'You know, Leila,' she went on, staring down into her, 'I really thought Billy cared about me. But then Shirley turned up.'

Leila frowned. Shirley?

'She said these terrible things about me. Made Billy think I'd been putting on an act. That I'd been having him over. That I was . . .' Ginny sniffed miserably. 'Never mind what she made him think. Maybe she's right in some ways. But I don't understand how . . .' She rubbed her hands over her face and took a deep breath. 'How one minute, he could act as though he really wanted to be with me, then to turn against me like that. I've tried talking to him, to explain. But he won't see me, won't even speak on the phone. He's not been near the place for over two months.' She raised her head and looked at Leila. 'That's why I had to talk to you. To see if there was a way I could get in touch with him. To pass a message on. Anything. You've always been close. He'd listen to you.'

Leila said nothing; she just sipped her drink.

'Leila, please, tell me, has Billy got someone else? Is that why you're not saying anything?'

Leila opened her eyes wide and sighed loudly. 'You might as well know, Ginny. Me and Billy. We're sort of together again.'

'You and Billy?'

'Like I say, it's just sort of. And I expect there are probably one or two others in the picture. Because, let's face it, he's not exactly the faithful type, now is he?'

'He was when we were together.'

Leila smiled stiffly. 'Was he, darling? Are you sure?'

Ginny didn't answer. 'Is he happy?'

'He doesn't really say.' Leila picked up her bag and stood up. 'Look, I don't want to be rude, but I must go, I've got an appointment at nine and it's not polite keeping people waiting, now is it.'

'Will you tell him I was asking after him? And I'd love to, you know, hear how he is.'

'Of course I will.'

'Thanks for coming, Leila. Thanks for everything,' Ginny said quietly. 'Especially for being so honest.'

'Any time, sweetie. Any time.'

As Leila stepped out into the early June sunshine, she drew in a deep lungful of air. Now Ginny was out of the picture, maybe she really did have a chance of getting back with Billy again. She just hoped he never got to hear about the little white lie she'd told that they already were.

It was true then, he really didn't want her any more. Ginny lay on her bed, staring up at the ceiling, tears spilling down her cheeks and running into her ears. She'd waited a whole fortnight for him to call, but she'd heard nothing.

And she'd loved him so much – she still loved him – but he had chosen to believe a drunken tart, hadn't even given her the chance to explain.

She rolled on to her side and stared at the wall. It was all her fault, she should never have . . .

Never have what? Let someone into her life again? Let herself become involved? Lie?

No, none of those things. Even lying wasn't as stupid as letting herself believe she could ever be happy again.

But it was no good going over it all again – that was all she had done for two long weeks. It was too late for that now. This was the way Billy wanted things and she had no choice. All she could do was get on with her life.

But how could she carry on without the man she loved?

She buried her face in the pillow and sobbed herself to sleep like an abandoned child.

An hour later, Ginny was wrenched awake by the telephone ringing on her bedside table.

She was alert immediately and snatched up the receiver. 'Billy?'

'No, Miss Martin, it's Flora. Just to let you know we've been open a wee while now and the customers are asking for you.'

'Okay, Flora, I'll be down.'

Ginny dragged herself from her bed, had a bath, did her hair, put on her make-up and her slinkiest black satin sheath dress and, less than an hour after Flora had phoned, she was walking into the second-floor bar with her chin in the air and her eyes as dry as if they had never seen a tear.

'You look magnificent, Miss Martin,' Flora cooed. 'The best I've seen you look in weeks.'

'Thanks,' she said flatly. 'Is Simon Parker in tonight?'

Flora wrapped his pudgy fingers round his chin. 'Parker?'

'The journalist.'

'Aw, him. The very nice-looking blond?'

'That's the one.'

'His name's Simon, is it?' Flora flapped his glass cloth in the general direction of the stage. 'He's up the other end. I've been watching him hanging on to every word that big-mouthed git, Welsh Davey, has been spouting. One of the waiters – young Alan – was earwigging earlier. He said Welsh Davey was going on about how there's not a bank vault in the whole country that he can't blow. And he said the reporter was lapping it up. Probably thinks there's a story in it.' Flora leaned across the bar and said in low-voiced confidence, 'But I hope he doesn't write it; it's all rubbish.'

'Everyone knows Welsh Davey's a liar, Flora.'

'I don't think that young newspaper feller does. From the look of him, he thinks Davey's the source of all flaming wisdom.'

Ginny did her best to produce a thin smile. 'I'll sort him out. If anyone wants me, I'll be over at Mr Parker's table.'

'I envy you, Miss Martin.' Flora rolled his eyes heavenwards. 'I only wish I could say the same.'

Ginny tapped Simon Parker on the shoulder. 'Still interested in talking to the "lady club boss"?'

Parker stood up, a delighted smile lighting up his boyishly handsome face. 'You've changed your mind. You're going to let me do your story.'

She shook her head. 'No, I just want to talk to you.'

She turned to stare into Welsh Davey's shifty eyes. 'There's someone over at the bar been asking for you, Davey. Said something about ... What was it? Some banking business or something? Or maybe it was about a load of old toffee. Or maybe it was just about settling up your bar bill.'

Welsh Davey finished his drink, stood up and treated Ginny to a sarcastic smirk. 'Very funny,' he said, before leaving her alone with the reporter.

'What was that about?' Simon asked.

'Just a private joke.'

'You're not laughing.'

'I don't really feel much like laughing at the moment.'

'What's wrong?'

'It's a long story. Some other time, eh?'

'Okay. So what was it you wanted to talk about?'

Ginny ran her fingers through her hair, stared down at her feet, then finally blurted out, 'I've got a bit of free time and I was wondering if that offer of a date was still on.'

Chapter 18

Ginny threw the full-skirted floral-print dress, and its matching net petticoats, on to the bed. They landed on top of the pile of clothes she had already discarded as being totally unsuitable for a day out in the country. 'Whatever d'you think you're up to?' she asked herself as she opened her wardrobe yet again. 'You've got nothing in common with the likes of Simon Parker. You're only doing this because—'

Her voice trailed off, as her attention was suddenly caught by a squash of unopened parcels and bags that had been shoved right to the back of the top shelf. She didn't need to think what they were, she knew exactly: they were the spoils of her last shopping spree, the things she had bought the day before Billy had walked out on her. She gnawed anxiously at her bottom lip as she felt her eyes begin to sting.

Blinking back the tears, Ginny reached up and pulled down the bags.

She went through them, one by one, having a struggle to remember where she'd bought what, but always remembering exactly why she'd bought every single thing. Each item would have been fully approved of by Billy. Either because they were fashionable, or because they were what he called classy looking. And, inevitably, each had been more expensive than anything she would have chosen – had she not been trying to please him.

From amongst the hoard, Ginny dug out a pair of cavalry-twill slacks, which she couldn't even recall trying on, let alone buying, and a pale-blue angora twin set that she remembered all too well. She could just see the assistant holding the cardigan up to her: cooing and smiling, saying how lovely she would look in it, assuring her how the colour would set off the blue of her eyes and how it would complement her blonde hair.

What a load of shit. She knew the moment she walked out of any one of those snooty shops that all the assistants would be talking about her behind her back, speculating on how she had so much to spend. And they probably wouldn't be far wrong.

Ginny stared into the dressing-table mirror and sighed, brushing the soft, fluffy sweater against her cheek. She might as well look the part for a day out, even if she didn't feel like it.

By ten thirty, Ginny was ready and on her way downstairs to meet Simon Parker; just as they had agreed over a week ago. As she went to open the front door, she hesitated and peered through the side lights. There was nothing surprising to see, only Simon, standing next to a sleek, dark-green car, checking his watch.

Ginny covered her face with her hands. For Christ's sake, what was she doing? She should have telephoned the newspaper office yesterday evening – as she had almost done at least a dozen times – and told him she couldn't go out with him after all. Anyone could tell him she was far too busy. She had responsibilities, a club to run. All sorts of things to do with her time.

But she hadn't called him. Instead, here she was, acting as though she'd nothing better to do than go running off to the country with the first handsome man who'd asked her for a date since Billy had left her.

She was behaving like an adolescent kid. And all because she'd been hurt again. But that was no excuse.

She was a grown woman. She should be used to pain by now.

She would find Flora and get him to make up some story – that wasn't exactly adult of her, but she saw no need to be rude to Simon. It wasn't his fault she was an idiot. Flora could go out and tell him she was ill or something. She stepped back from the door and turned on her heel to go and find him.

She didn't have to go far; Flora was coming down the stairs towards her. 'Look at you!' he trilled, slapping the side of his face with the stubby fingers on one hand and thrusting a wicker hamper at her with the other. 'Ava Gardner in a blonde wig. No. No, wait.' He put his head on one side. 'It's not Ava Gardner, is it? Wait, it's coming to me. I know! You're Grace Kelly's double! That's what you are. All you need's a row of pearls and you could pass for her twin sister.'

Ginny waited for him to finish, then held up the basket. 'What's this?'

'I got the kitchen to knock you up a few bits for the journey. A nice wee picnic. Some ham, sausage rolls, a few pies, a bit of salad stuff, and I've set aside a couple of bottles of something special to wash it all down. I've even had a Thermos of coffee made up, in case it turns nippy later on.'

'It was a kind thought, Flora, thank you. But I'm not going.'

'Oh yes, you are, Miss Martin.' Flora backed away from the hamper she was trying to return to him. 'As if I'd let you throw away the chance of spending the day in the country with that gorgeous hunk of manhood. Have you seen him? He's been waiting outside for you since ten o'clock, poor lamb. Now come on, it's just what you need, a day out. Something to bring a bit of sunshine into your life and to put the roses back into those pretty cheeks of yours.'

'The sun isn't shining, Flora,' she said lifelessly.

'What a sourpuss! You see, you'll have a lovely day. And don't tell me you don't deserve it. You've been working that hard lately.'

Flora guided Ginny forward and, with all the skill of a collie herding a recalcitrant sheep, pulled open the door, eased her outside and down the steps to where Simon was standing, smiling fit to burst.

'And don't let me see either of you *near* this place till six o'clock at the earliest,' he said, taking the hamper from Ginny and handing it to Simon. 'Now go on, have a lovely day, and I don't want a single crust left in that basket when you get back.'

Ginny climbed into the car without a word, while Flora took Simon inside to collect the bottles and flask.

'You will try and keep her out for a good few hours, won't you?' Flora said with a sad shake of his head, as he loaded Simon up with the drinks. 'Honestly, she's been that overworked, it's about time she had a little bit of a treat. You'll have to get her to relax, if you know what I mean.' He winked extravagantly. 'I know she'd be very grateful, so it'll certainly be worth the effort.'

Flora stood and waved until the car had pulled out of the alley, then he went back inside the club and picked up the telephone. 'Gloria? It's me, I've—' He tutted irritably. 'It's Flora, you silly tart, who'd you think it is, Liberace and his magic flaming fingers? Anyway, I've got rid of the ice maiden at last, thank God, so the poker game's on. Any more of her moaning and I'd be slitting my sodding throat. What?' He listened impatiently. 'Yes, of course I've fixed it all up this end. We've got the whole place to ourselves for a good seven hours. You let everyone know, and by the time they get here Casino Floriana will be open for business.'

After they had left the East End far behind and the broad South London streets had narrowed into the hilly, winding lanes of Kent, the sun made an appearance from behind the bank of clouds that was at last breaking up in the soft, late-morning breeze.

Without taking his eyes from the road, Simon handed Ginny a pair of diamanté-studded, butterfly-wing sunglasses. 'Try these for size.'

'I'm all right, thanks,' she said, balancing them on the polished walnut dashboard in front of her.

'I thought they'd make you smile.'

'Look, Simon, I don't mean to be miserable, but I don't feel much like smiling. Okay?'

'Do you know that apart from the dismal-sounding hello that you just about managed to bark at me earlier, those are the first words you've uttered since you got in the car?'

'I'm sorry.'

'You haven't even mentioned what you think of the motor,' he said, reaching out of the window and giving the car roof an affectionate pat.

'It's very nice.'

'*Nice*? This is more than nice. This, Ginny, is a Jaguar. It was meant to impress you.' He flicked his eyes sideways and flashed her his cheeky boyish grin. 'My father's Jaguar, admittedly, but it's still a Jag. I keep telling him he's too old to drive it and he should give it to me. But he won't listen. What do you think? Should he give it to me? He can certainly afford to.'

'It's up to him.'

'I suppose it is.'

They drove on in a silence broken only by Simon's

shouted 'thank you' to a roadside AA man who saluted them, and his occasional strange pronouncements on interesting features he spotted in the passing landscape. Then, without warning, he stopped the car in a layby next to a five-bar gate.

'Look, Ginny, I could talk for a living if I had to, but even I can't spin out a phoney commentary on oast-houses and hop gardens and cherry orchards for more than an hour. It's wearing me ragged. You're going to have to help me a bit. Even if it's only to note what a good-looking sort of a devil you think I am.'

Ginny stared down at her hands. 'Okay. Where are we going?' she asked eventually.

Simon looked about him. 'We're sort of here, really. I thought we might get out and enjoy the fresh air. There's a river over there. What do you think?'

'Fine,' she said flatly.

'And if we're lucky, we might see the eclipse. This is a special day, you know, Ginny. One for the old headlines.' He pointed at the windscreen, as though composing the front page of a newspaper. '*Wednesday, 30 June 1954. Solar eclipse over Britain. Ginny Martin amazed!*' He put his head on one side. 'Well? Will you be amazed? Are you looking forward to witnessing this extraordinary event?'

'I did see something about it.'

'Did you? Where?' he asked, trying to encourage her. 'In my paper, I hope.'

'No. On the television.'

'I've been thinking about getting one of those. Do you think I should?'

'If you want one.'

Simon nodded briskly. 'Right, tell you what, let's have that picnic.'

Simon ferried the picnic hamper, Thermos flask and

bottles, a fringed tartan travelling rug and a black leather case that he tucked carefully under his arm, to the far side of the field. There, he set out the rug on the river bank, in the shade of a massive chestnut tree. He then went back to the Jaguar for Ginny, who had shown no interest in even getting out of the car, never mind any enthusiasm for a nature ramble through a wheat field.

Gently, Simon pushed her down on to the rug. 'You have a choice,' he said, filling two glasses with deep-red wine. 'While we dine on these fine morsels, so kindly supplied by Flora, you can either listen to me telling you all about myself – how I'm going to get the biggest series of scoops ever known in Fleet Street and how my great success will mean that they'll have to make me an editor before I'm thirty-five. *Or* I'll play you my clarinet.' He held up the black leather case. 'And that will show you why, instead of editing *The Times*, I might become the best jazz clarinettist who's ever been born this side of New Orleans.' He pulled a face. 'Although, even I have to admit I just *might* need a tiny bit more practice on the old licorice stick before that happens. But with my good looks, maybe they won't notice the duff notes.'

'You really reckon yourself, don't you?' Ginny said, wondering why she'd let Flora bamboozle her into this.

He looked up from ferreting through the hamper. 'Me?' He sounded shocked.

'Yeah. You.' She could have added, just like almost every other man I've ever met in my life, but she didn't have the energy for a row. Instead she took a gulp of her drink.

'Well, I know I used to get upset when I was a child and the other kids at school called me big-head,' he said, topping up Ginny's glass. 'But d'you know what my mother always said?'

'Surprise me.'

'She'd say, don't let them upset you, son. You just go down to the fruit and vegetable shop and get me fourteen pounds of potatoes in your cap.'

Ginny stared at him blankly. 'Very funny.'

'If I'm such a comedian, then how come you look so sad?' He found a pork pie in the basket and took a large bite, giving her the chance to say something, but all she did was sip fitfully at her drink.

'Is it something I've said, Ginny? It wasn't meant to be like this, you know. We were meant to have a lovely day. And you were meant to—'

'Simon, I'm sorry,' she broke in. 'It's not you. It's just that . . . I've not had much to be happy about lately.'

He aimed the half-eaten pork pie into the middle of the river, sending up a gentle plop into the still midday air. 'But you've got so much. You've got the club, and you're—'

'I know. I'm luckier than most people. In lots of ways. But that doesn't mean . . . Aw, I don't know.'

Simon pulled up a blade of grass and sucked it between his teeth. 'Tell me about your dreams, Ginny,' he said in a mock Viennese accent.

'How do you know I've got dreams?'

'We all have dreams,' he said continuing his bad impersonation of Dr Freud. 'Whether it's buying a television. Owning a car like my father's. Or being the editor of a Fleet Street newspaper.' He rolled on to his stomach and touched her on the tip of her nose with the grass. 'I bet I can guess one of your dreams,' he went on in his own voice, scratching his chin thoughtfully and staring at her through narrowed eyes. 'I know. You dream of having a plush flat in Eaton Square and a pair of matching French poodles trotting by your side when you go promenading in the afternoon sunshine.'

'You're wrong.'

'How? Come on. Tell me.'

'You're not really interested.'

He sat up, refilled her glass to the brim once again and laid his hand on his heart. 'I am absolutely riveted.'

Ginny, feeling heady from the combination of drink and her choice of clothes in the sultry June heat, leaned back against the tree-trunk and closed her eyes. 'There's this bus. The number 15. It goes along the Barking Road, up through Aldgate, along to Bank, then the Strand, then Oxford Street—'

'So, I was right,' he crowed triumphantly. 'East End to West End.'

'No.' She opened her eyes and looked at him stretched out on the rug next to her. 'What I imagine is staying on the bus, and it takes me right out into the countryside. You know, like going on a Green Line. And I go to a place, well, it's like this, really. Lovely fields and a river. But then I go round this corner and there's a massive, great big house. Just like Tara in *Gone With the Wind* . . .' She swallowed the rest of her wine and held out her glass for more. 'Hark at me, going on, you must think I'm a right fool. Trouble is, you're too easy to talk to.'

'It's my job, getting people to feel at ease and talk. But I don't think you're a fool, I think you're wonderful. Hey! You nearly smiled then.'

He reached out and touched her cheek. 'There, I knew you could do it.'

He pulled himself up so that he was kneeling in front of her. 'You really are wonderful, you know, Ginny. Truly beautiful.'

Slowly he folded his arms around her, touched his mouth to hers and pulled her down on to the rug. 'You must be so hot in those things,' he breathed into her ear.

Within moments, as a skylark trilled high above them and the moon continued on its inevitable journey that would plunge the brilliance of the glorious summer's day into darkness, Ginny lay naked beneath Simon's urgently thrusting body.

It was nearly a quarter to seven; too early, really, to leave for Piccadilly, but Dilys didn't want to hang around in case Ted turned up and spoilt her plans. And anyway, it'd be no hardship waiting a while for Chuck, he was more than worth it.

She pulled up her skirt to check her suspenders and, as she smoothed her stocking-tops she eyed her thighs appreciatively. 'You're amazing, Dilys girl, d'you know that?' she said out loud to herself. 'Look at them legs. No one would ever believe you was a mother – thank Gawd.'

She straightened up and hollered towards the open bedroom door, 'Susan. Get that letter from behind the clock.'

Susan did as she was told, then hovered uncertainly in the doorway. Her mother's room was strictly off limits, unless she had been specifically told otherwise.

'Bring it here then,' Dilys snapped impatiently. 'I ain't got bloody rubber arms.'

Susan stepped cautiously into the room, knowing from experience that she was more likely to get a swipe round the ear than a thank you for her efforts.

Dilys ripped open the envelope and pulled out the contents: two sheets of folded paper and two five-pound notes.

Kissing the money before stuffing it into her handbag, Dilys tossed the rest on to the bed without a second glance. 'If Ted turns up,' she said, as she took a final glimpse in the mirror, 'tell him I've had to go round to see your Uncle Sid about buying you some new shoes 'cos I'm broke again. If he gives you anything, put it on the mantelpiece.'

Then, without another word, Dilys left her child alone in the prefab and went outside to run the gauntlet of her neighbours – Milly Barrington and her troop of apron-wearing harpies.

'There'll be murders if he comes home and catches her going out looking like that,' offered one of the chorus, in a voice pitched deliberately loud enough for Dilys to hear.

'Leave off,' Milly corrected her at the same volume. 'What would he care if she went out in her drawers? He's never there.'

'Probably got some other old bag tucked away,' chipped in one of the others. 'His sort have always got their feet under someone's table.'

'I've heard he still lives with his mum,' Milly said with a sneer. 'Fancy, a man of his age! Over Grove Road way somewhere, they reckon. Near the Roman.'

'With his mum!'

'That's what I heard.' Milly craned her neck to watch, as Dilys dodged across the street in front of a motor bike and side-car that had to swerve to avoid her. 'You know I'd lay money that kid's not his,' she shouted by way of a final parting shot as Dilys disappeared round the corner to find a cab – with ten pounds spare cash in her pocket she could afford such luxuries.

As she watched her mother from the prefab window, Susan heard Milly Barrington shouting that Ted wasn't her father and knew she was wrong. Her mum was always going on at her about it and saying how it was her fault that Ted hung around the place all the time.

Susan didn't really mind Ted. He wasn't like most of her little friends' dads, but when he was there he was quite nice to her and even brought her presents sometimes, ones that he made sure her mum let her keep. But for now, Susan was more interested in her aunt than her father.

Having dodged back into her mum's room, Susan retrieved the envelope and paper from the bed and settled herself down on the half-moon rug in the front room, where she was slowly working her way through the latest letter from her 'Auntie' Ginny.

She smiled happily to herself as she read the kind, loving words and wished, as always, that she could see her auntie again – or at least know a place where she could write back to her. It would have been hard, writing a whole letter, but Susan would have tried her very best.

There was something that Milly Barrington *had* been right about: Dilys really had no need to worry about Ted turning up. Although he wasn't at his mother's.

In fact, Ted hadn't seen Nellie for weeks; he was too scared he'd be spotted by Dilys's brothers to venture anywhere near Bailey Street. Dilys had been spinning the boys some sort of a line about how hard done by she and Susan were and the last time he'd gone to see his mum they'd threatened to knock nine kinds of bells out of him until he'd handed over every last penny he had on him to buy new summer dresses for the kid, *and* a pair of shoes for sodding Dilys.

He'd had one good hiding off them – when the silly cow had finally admitted that he was the kid's father – and he certainly didn't fancy another. They were a right handy pair of buggers. He'd tried talking his way out of it, explaining that he'd already given Dilys money for the self-same things only the week before, that the kid had dresses coming out of her flaming earholes and that Dilys had enough shoes to open a stall, but they wouldn't listen to him. They'd just kept on and on about what an arsehole he was. If it hadn't been for their big-gobbed wives dragging them indoors – because they hadn't wanted to be shown up by their husbands indulging in something as common as a street fight – Ted would probably have come off even worse than he had.

But, all that aside, Ted was the first to admit he didn't exactly look after Dilys – she didn't deserve looking after – but he always made sure the kid wanted for nothing. Well, most of the time he did.

Anyway, rather than risk another beating, Ted kept well away from that pair of nutters, dividing his time between ducking and diving in any pub where he thought he could pull a scam and with Shirley in her pigsty of a room in Soho.

That particular evening, Ted had just left the Three Greyhounds in Greek Street, after selling a slow-talking yokel type – up in London on business for the day – a camera he had earlier 'found' in the nearby Coach and Horses. He was now letting himself into Shirley's room, more than pleased to be fifty bob richer for absolutely no effort whatsoever. But his smile soon faded when he saw Shirley lounging on the bed flicking listlessly through a magazine.

'Why ain't you out working?'

'I'm tired,' she answered, flipping over the page.

'Pissed again, you mean.'

'And where would I get the money to spend on booze? You steal every single penny I earn.' She tossed the magazine aside and leapt to her feet. 'We don't all run—' She shut her mouth as though it were a spring-loaded trap. Christ! She'd nearly let the cat out of the bag about Ginny's.

'We don't all run what?'

'Nothing.'

Ted swung back his fist and smashed it into her stomach. 'That'll teach you to be lippy.'

Doubled over with pain and gasping to catch her breath, something in Shirley snapped. Sod it, why not? She'd tell the rotten bastard. And maybe it'd get him off her back.

'You think you're so clever, hitting and punching, and doing poxy little deals, but you haven't got a clue.' Still winded, she grasped hold of the bed head to steady herself. 'You don't even know about your own wife.'

'What about her?'

'She's earning a fortune, that's what. You're sleeping in this rat hole and she's running a club.'

'She's what?'

'You heard.'

Ted eyed her suspiciously, he trusted no one, but especially not toms. She was talking shit as usual. Fantasising. Like they all did. 'Why didn't you tell me before?'

Shirley shook her head and laughed wildly. 'If you can believe it, just for a while – a very short while, mind – I actually didn't want you leaving me to go back to her. Then, when I couldn't give a damn who you were with, it was too late. If you'd have found out I'd known, but hadn't told you, you'd have gone raving mad.'

He was right, she was making it up. She was rambling like a lunatic. 'Where is it then, this club?'

'How would I know?' Shirley lied. 'You'll have to ask around.'

'So how come you know about it?'

'I bumped into one of the girls. From the club. She told me,' she improvised, then added hurriedly, 'but I didn't bother with the address. I mean, I'm hardly going to go round and visit her, now am I?'

Ted was torn. Should he waste precious time beating Shirley until her teeth rattled, or should he set off straight away to find his wife instead? He could certainly do with a few quid, and if Ginny *was* running a club she must be worth a fortune. And he'd be entitled to his share. He was her husband, after all.

But then again, Shirley was really getting on his nerves . . .

Simon pulled the car into the kerb outside the club. 'Before you get out, Ginny, there's something—'

'Look, Simon, I thought I made myself clear, I need time to think. I don't wanna talk, all right?' Talk? She couldn't even look at him, she was so angry with herself at what she'd let him do. Maybe it was revenge, a way of getting back at Billy Saunders for leaving her. But whatever the reason, she'd let it happen and wished with all her heart that she hadn't, because, much as it hurt, she was still in love with Billy.

'Please, Ginny—'

'I'll talk to you later.' She grabbed hold of the door handle, but Simon stopped her getting out.

'I've gotta open the club.'

'Ginny, please, I know I don't know the form about these things, but I'd like to give you a little present.'

'Don't, Simon. Please.'

'I want to.'

With his free hand, he reached inside his sports jacket and took out his wallet. 'What's the rate?' he asked.

'I don't understand.'

'When Welsh Davey told me about you and the girls, he never mentioned how much—'

'He what!' Ginny stared at him. 'Everybody knows what a bloody liar that bastard is.' She shook her head in disbelief. 'I never had you down as an idiot, Simon.'

'I'm sorry, Ginny. I didn't—'

'Leave it, Simon. Do us both a favour.'

'But I swear—'

'I mean it, Simon. Please. Just leave it.'

'Does this mean you won't see me again?'

'Just go.'

She grabbed hold of the car doorhandle, but again he stopped her. 'No, I won't. Not like this. I've been clumsy and stupid, and I've insulted you. Promise me you'll see me again, Ginny. Please.'

'Simon—'

'But I've got to see you. And it isn't just about what happened back there. I told you, Ginny. I think you're the most wonderful . . .' He looked away as his eyes filled with tears. 'Please,' he begged. 'Give me another chance.'

A shudder racked through Ginny's body. She had to get away. 'Call me in a few days.'

As Ginny climbed up the steps of the club, she too began to cry. Was this what it had finally come to? Was it true what they said? No matter how you told yourself you'd got out of it, it was still obvious to everyone what you really were. Once a brass, always a brass.

She shoved open the door and let the hamper fall from her hand on to the tiled floor.

If whoring was all she was fit for she might as well do it right this time. Not like she did in Frith Street. She'd put a proper price on herself. Simon seemed a decent enough bloke and it looked like he had a few quid. Maybe when Billy got rid of the clubs, Simon could be her solution. He could give her a decent life; the kind of life she'd dreamed of . . .

What was the point in kidding herself? Dreams always came to nothing. Just like every other even half-way reasonable thing that ever happened to her, Simon would be snatched away, and she'd be left alone and lonely.

But then again, what did she have to lose? Certainly

not her self-respect; that had been lost long ago – on the day she had been stupid enough to get involved with Ted Martin.

Chapter 19

Ted was sitting in the prefab, staring unseeingly into the middle distance, drumming his fingers tunelessly against the side of his chair. He'd kill her when she came in. He'd fucking kill her.

At the sound of a key in the front door he leapt to his feet. As Dilys stepped inside he grabbed her by the arm. She tried to shake free of him, but he held her fast.

'I've been waiting for you for three days.' Ted spat the words at her through his teeth, his lips hardly moving. 'Where the fuck have you been?'

'Not that it's anything to do with you, but I've been out.'

'Out?' he asked incredulously. 'But it's Saturday. You ain't been here since Wednesday. How can you be *out* for three days?'

Dilys raised a cynical eyebrow. 'I'd have thought that was a question you of all people could answer.'

'That kid in there,' he went on, his face right up close to hers, 'she could've been dead. And d'you know something else? Her bed was that disgusting I had to go and get her new sheets. *New sheets.*'

Dilys laughed scornfully. 'Why're you so worried about her all of a sudden? What, turned into some sort of wonderful father, have you? Funny though, you waiting till she's seven and a half years old before you come over all concerned.'

'You bitch.'

'Look, let's forget all the old fanny, Ted. What're you after?'

Ted wanted to hit her, to knock the smug look right off her face, but he had to play it clever, there was something he wanted even more – information. He let her go. 'I wanna know where Ginny is.'

Dilys laughed again. 'So, you've heard at last, have you? I wondered how long it'd take.'

Her mocking tone was too much for Ted; he raised his hand ready to knock the laughter out of her. But instead of cringing in fear as she usually did, Dilys turned her back on him and walked casually to the door.

She stopped, looked over her shoulder at him and said very calmly, 'I wouldn't do that if I was you, Ted.' Then she yelled in a terrified voice, 'Chuck! Quick! Help me!'

Almost before Ted had a chance to realise what was going on, he had been pushed backwards into the sitting-room and was pinned up against the wall, with a hand gripped so tightly round his throat that he could barely breathe.

'Has he upset you, honey?' asked his captor in a deceptively gentle American accent, as he stared menacingly into Ted's face.

'No, Chuck. You're all right. A coward like him could never hurt me. He just frightened me, that's all.'

Dilys stepped forward and looked Ted directly in the eye. 'Let me introduce you to my fiancé, Mr Chuck O'Grady. Handsome, ain't he? And don't you just love his uniform? He's in the American Air Force, ain't you, Chuck? And d'you know what, Ted, he's got mates what're even bigger'n him.' She giggled girlishly and squeezed Chuck's massive arm. 'Can you believe it?'

'What shall I do with him, sweetpea?'

Ted's eyes bulged.

'I reckon you should let him go, then we can get going

and all. I did intend sorting out a few things first, but seeing as Ted's here now, I think we can leave it to him.'

Slowly Chuck released his grip and Ted started coughing and spluttering, and clasping at his throat.

Dilys ignored the display; she just turned on her heel, took Chuck's arm and walked with him out to the front door.

Ted wasn't going to let her get away with it. He levered himself away from the wall and, finding the breath from somewhere, bellowed after them, 'She's got a kid in here, you know.'

Dilys patted Chuck's arm. 'Ignore him, love, he's barmy. Believe it or not, he's my best friend's husband. It's his little girl I told you about, the one I was minding, remember?'

Chuck nodded. 'Poor kid. Do they still neglect her?'

'Yeah. And just 'cos I have her sometimes, to give her a treat like, he thinks he can hang about the place an' all. Bloody cheek, innit?' Dilys paused on the doorstep and looked back into the prefab. 'Don't expect me back, Ted,' she shouted.

Ted was out to the door in a flash. 'But how about Ginny? How about Susan?'

Dilys smiled sweetly at her fiancé and kissed him on the end of his nose. 'You go over to the cab and wait for me, Chuck. I'll be one minute.'

'Are you sure you'll be okay?'

'I'll be fine; go on.'

She waited for Chuck to get inside the taxi, gave him a reassuring wave, then spun round to face Ted. 'As for Ginny, you can go and ask any one of them old toms she knocks around with. I'm sure they'll be only too pleased to help you out if you bung 'em a few bob. And as for Susan, I was gonna take her round your mum's and leave her there, that's why I come back here. I reckoned I ought to do something with her. But she's your bloody kid an' all. So if you're so worried, you sort her out.'

She turned away, stuck her chin in the air and began walking over to the taxi, but she hesitated. 'By the way, Ted,' she said, peering haughtily over her shoulder at him, 'I've told the council I don't need the prefab no more, 'cos I'm going to live with Chuck. We're getting married, see. This afternoon, as a matter of fact. Romantic, ain't it? So don't think you can kip here, will you?'

She took a single step, then stopped again. 'Aw, and another thing, that money you had hidden in the back of the maid-saver, don't bother looking for it. I've got it, 'cos I reckon you owe me, Ted Martin.'

'*I know, Mum, I know.*' Ted ran his fingers distractedly through his Brylcreemed hair. 'But I only need you to let us sleep here for a few days, just till I get something proper sorted out.'

Susan didn't know why her dad was bothering. She had taken one look at Nellie, who was standing in the kitchen of number 18 Bailey Street with her arms folded belligerently across her aproned chest as though she were guarding the place from invaders, and had known she wasn't wanted here, just as she didn't seem to be wanted anywhere. And she was tired and hungry. But then she was nearly always tired and hungry.

'Why can't she stay over the road with her uncles and them two stuck-up tarts?'

''Cos Dilys has rowed with them and they don't wanna know,' he improvised, covering up the fact he wouldn't dare go anywhere near the Chivers brothers – well, not without a sawn-off shotgun in one hand and a pickaxe handle in the other, he wouldn't. 'Mum, please. Do us this one favour. Like I say, this bit of business tonight, I won't be no time at all.'

'Leave off, Ted,' snorted Nellie. 'As if I can trust you to go out on a Saturday night and only be gone a few hours. I've heard all that old toffee before, remember. No time at all you say, then you disappear for days on end.'

'Mum, believe me. I promise on my baby's life I'll be back here before you know it. And I'll see you all right for your trouble. You know that.'

Softening slightly at the idea of being paid, Nellie jerked her head sideways at the stove. 'Well, I ain't doing no cooking or nothing. If you want grub you can go and get some pie and mash if they're still open, or some fish and taters.'

'You're a diamond, Mum, thanks.' Ted pulled out one of his mother's kitchen chairs and pushed Susan down on to it. 'You sit there and I'll go and get something for us all to eat.'

Nellie glared spitefully at Susan as they both listened to Ted running down the passage. 'And you can bring me in a quart of light ale from the Albert while you're at it,' she hollered after him.

Ted was in so much of a rush to get out again that he didn't even stop to wash his hands and face after he had eaten, and he still had grease from the cod and chips around his mouth when he stormed into Shirley's room.

'Look, Shirley, I've had enough old shit today to last me a lifetime, so just save all the crap for the punters. This is me you're talking to, not some ham bone up from the country. I need to know where that club is. Now are you gonna tell me, or—'

'Or what?' Shirley blew a slow stream of smoke into the air above her head, propped her cigarette on the mantelpiece and carried on ironing her dress on the makeshift board she had propped across her sink.

'Don't try and be clever with me, Shirley, I'm warning you. I ain't very happy at the minute, so you just tell me where I can find Ginny—'

'I'll tell you something, Ted,' she butted in again, 'that Maltese bloke's been round here looking for you.'

'How d'you mean, looking for me?'

'That so-called fixed fight you told him to put that big stake on – remember?' She flipped the dress over so that she could iron the back. 'It turned out it wasn't fixed at all. It went against you, Ted. And let's just say your Maltese friend isn't very happy. He wants money off you, he said. A lot of money. And he wants it soon.' She picked up her cigarette and took another puff.

'Did you tell him where he could find me?'

'As if I'd do that.'

Ted spun her round and jabbed his finger into her face. 'You'd better not have, Shirley, but you better *had* tell me where that club is.' He smacked the cigarette out of her hand. 'Now!'

'Why should I do anything to help you?'

'Because if you don't, I'm gonna rip that wrinkled old head o' your'n right off your fucking shoulders.'

Shirley tried backing away from him, but there wasn't anywhere to escape to in the cramped, sordid little room. 'All right, Ted, I was only joking. You know me, always having a laugh. The club's in Shoreditch. In fact, I've got one of her cards right here in my purse.'

Ginny took a deep breath, then made her way downstairs to the main bar. It was only four days since Simon had taken her to the country. Only four days since they'd . . . Well, since they'd *done it*. And she had been stupid enough to call him and invite him to her big, jolly, full-of-fun end-of-rationing party. And here she was, going down to meet him, or rather to face him. She must be mad. But it had seemed like a good idea. After all, Simon was going to be her saviour when Billy sold the clubs.

She sighed loudly to herself. She could only give it a try. Maybe he'd turn out to be different from the others.

Maybe.

It was barely half past nine and the club was already full, with most of the customers crowded into the second-floor bar, craning their necks to get a view of the big attraction on the stage.

Ginny had had a real brazier set up, right in the centre and, as had been stated on the invitations, all the guests were being encouraged to burn their now useless ration books in a celebration of the good times to come. And the biggest joke of the evening – one that had everyone laughing every time they heard it – was that no one in the club had ever had to worry abut rationing anyway. But what the hell, any excuse for a party!

Someone touched Ginny on the arm and she turned round, flashing her full professional smile.

It was Simon. 'Hello, Ginny,' he said warily. 'I'm really glad you asked me to come along tonight.'

Ginny nodded. 'It'll make a good story, won't it? I hope you've brought a photographer.'

'I didn't mean that. I meant I'm glad we're talking.'

Ginny kept up the smile. 'So am I.'

'And are *we* talking?' asked a woman's voice.

Ginny turned round again. This time she was met with the unmistakable sight of Leila, clad in her trade mark emerald green. She had her head on one side and was holding out her arms in a gesture of reconciliation.

'Simon, would you go and tell Flora to take a bottle of champagne over to my booth?'

'How many glasses?' he asked cagily.

'Just two for now. For me and Leila. But get yourself a drink and give us ten minutes alone, then come and join us, eh?'

'I'm surprised Billy's not here at a big do like this, sweetie. All these contacts to be made and faces to acknowledge.'

Ginny busied herself pouring the drinks, deliberately avoiding Leila's gaze. 'He never comes round when the club's open any more. He does turn up some nights, to go over the takings and the books and things. But only when he's checked with Flora that he's not going to bump into me.'

'I've not seem much of him lately either.' Leila was smiling, but the quaver in her voice betrayed her. 'I thought he might pop in here this evening. He must be celebrating somewhere. Everyone is.'

'D'you know, I wondered the self-same thing,' said Ginny raising her glass to Leila. 'If he might show up here, I mean. But according to Johnno, he went over to see how Belle's getting on at the Old Compton Street club.'

Leila nodded. 'Belle's place. Right. So that's who he's seeing now.'

Neither of them knew what else to say. Ginny tried to ease the silence by offering Leila a cigarette, but it didn't help much, especially as they were surrounded by laughter.

It was with relief that Ginny spotted Yvette standing in the doorway, scanning the room. 'Yvette!' she called, beckoning to her. 'What a lovely surprise! Look, Leila's here as well.'

But as Yvette fought her way across to them, Ginny could see from her face that the surprise wasn't going to be quite as lovely as she'd thought.

'Whatever's wrong?' Ginny helped her into the booth and waved for one of the waiters to come over, but Simon, who had been hovering around waiting for the ten minutes to be up, beat him to it. 'Get us a large brandy, will you, Simon?'

'I can't believe it,' Yvette sniffed, her hand trembling as she tried to light a cigarette.

Ginny took it from her. 'Here, let me.'

'Take a deep breath, sweetie,' Leila said, stroking her hand.

'I've been everywhere looking for you, Leila. I didn't know what to do. I just got in a cab and went round all the clubs.'

Simon appeared with the brandy.

'Come on, Yve,' Ginny soothed her, 'drink this.'

She half emptied the glass in a single gulp, not even noticing the burning in her throat. 'Shirley's been murdered.'

'She's what?' Ginny gasped.

Yvette stared down at the table top. 'She was smashed over the head. Earlier tonight some time. In that poxy little room of her'n in Dean Street. The girl across the landing found her. She saw all this blood. It was on the stairs, when she was going down to start working for the night.' Yvette swallowed more of the brandy. 'They reckon the bastard done her in with her own iron.'

'Who? Who did it?' Leila could hardly speak.

Yvette swiped at her tears with the back of her hand, rubbing tracks of mascara down her cheeks. 'There's all sorts of rumours going round. But it couldn't have been a thief, like some of them are saying. The poor cow didn't have a pot to piss in, everyone knew that.'

Leila hastily looked away.

'I tried to tell the law when they turned up it must have been a punter.' Yvette buried her face in her hands and sobbed. 'Not that they're bothered. Once they saw she was a working girl, they didn't wanna know. But I tried, Gin, I tried telling 'em. She was so broke she was going with anyone. She must have picked up some nutcase, and . . .' Yvette shook her head. She couldn't go on.

Ginny stood up again. She went to the bar and spoke to Flora. 'Get rid of everyone, please. Quick as you can. I'll explain later.'

Within minutes, Yvette and Leila had been put into the back of a taxi instructed to take them to Leila's flat, and the club – apart from Ginny, Flora and three of the minders who'd stayed behind to deal with any late-comers – was cleared.

Over two hours later, Ginny was still sitting up at the bar, drinking her way to the bottom of a pot of tea that Flora had fetched from the kitchens. She couldn't bear the thought of going up to bed; there were too many bad thoughts spinning and churning around in her mind.

'I'm telling you, she'll let me in,' she and Flora heard someone shouting from downstairs.

'Ginny. It's me, Simon. Tell these chaps it's okay.'

'Excuse me, Flora.' Ginny set her cup in her saucer and climbed down from the bar-stool. 'I'll only be a minute.'

At the bottom of the stairs, Ginny saw Simon struggling with one of the minders. 'The party's over, Simon. Go home.'

'Look, Ginny, I know you must be angry, me running out like that, but my first reaction was to get the story. To get the scoop.'

'Simon, I don't wanna row with you, but—'

'Can't I come upstairs for a while? To talk?' He smiled winningly. 'I'll even play my clarinet for you if you like.

That'll make you laugh. I've got it out in the car. I'll go and—'

'Simon. Stop. Please.'

'Ginny, if I don't take chances like this. If I don't make my name and become a rich and famous editor' – his smile graduated to his cheeky grin – 'how can I ever buy you your Tara?'

'Simon. Not now.' Ginny turned and went back upstairs, leaving the minders to see him out.

It was almost half past two in the early hours of Sunday morning and Ted was downstairs in the kitchen of number 18, listening to the sound of Nellie snoring up above him. He was wondering how, at nearly thirty-five years old, he had come to this. He was living back home with his mum, but scared to be seen out in the street; stuck with a kid to look after; no money to speak of, but with a wife who was running a club and probably had plenty; knowing there was some Maltese arsehole after his blood; and enough tea inside him to float a sodding battleship.

He was just deciding whether he should go out into the yard again, to check whether the bonfire he'd started had at last reduced his gore-stained clothes to unrecognisable ashes, or whether he should make himself another cup of tea first, when he heard what was for him the familiar sound of a jemmy working away at the woodwork round the front door.

Shit! Dilys's brothers must have spotted him. And presumably they were hoping to give him a surprise.

Ted switched off the lights and crept upstairs to where Susan was sleeping in the front room. He lifted the corner of the curtain and peered down.

But it wasn't Sid and Micky; it was the Maltese bastard and two of his trained gorillas.

That big-mouthed whore, Shirley, must have blabbed after all.

Ted clapped his hand over his sleeping child's mouth. Her eyes flicked open in alarm. 'It's all right, it's only me,' he whispered into her ear. 'We've gotta go. Get your coat on as quick and quiet as you can and follow me on tiptoe down to the backyard. All right?'

Susan nodded in wide-eyed silence.

As they clambered over the back wall, Ted could hear Nellie screaming blue murder and the unmistakable sound of her enamel chamber pot finding its mark, as the Maltese apparently found his mother's bedroom.

'Ain't you gonna ask me in?'

'Ted, it's three o'clock in the morning. You turn up here when I ain't seen you for—'

'Don't clubs stay open till late no more, then?'

'Not tonight,' said Ginny, wishing she's never insisted that Flora and the minders took the rest of the night off. 'I've had some bad news.' She didn't bother wasting her breath telling him what had happened to Shirley, he probably wouldn't even care, knowing the way he'd treated the poor cow, or worse, he'd say she'd had it coming to her. That's what everyone seemed to say when a tom got murdered.

Ginny was just about to slam the door in his face when Ted played his blinder. 'At least let the little 'un in for a minute, Gin. To have a drink or something.'

'What little 'un?'

Ted jabbed his thumb over his shoulder at the waiting cab. 'Susan. My little Susan.'

Ginny pulled her dressing-gown round her and ran barefoot down the steps to the taxi. She wrenched open the door and held out her arms to the pale-faced child.

'Oi, before you take her, that'll be fifty-two and six, if you don't mind.'

Even Susan, huddled in the corner of the back seat of the taxi like a scared rabbit, couldn't distract Ginny from the shock of the fare. '*How much*?'

'Don't blame me, darling. It's that bloke o' your'n. He's a bit strange if you ask me. Had me driving all round the back doubles, going round in circles and back again, like he was on a treasure trail or something.' He leaned towards her. 'Not trying to give someone the slip or nothing, is he?'

Ginny sighed resignedly. Ted Martin was back.

'I've settled her down in the spare room, she's whacked out.'

'Lovely. And thanks, Gin, I always said you was one in a million.'

'Save it, Ted, I don't fall for that old madam no more. Now, how did you know where to find me?'

'I heard on the grapevine, didn't I, babe.'

'You do know you wouldn't have even got a foot through that door if it wasn't for Susan?'

'I know,' he said honestly – that having been the only reason he had brought the child with him in the first place. He knew she was Ginny's weak spot.

'What I don't understand is why she's with you.'

'Gin, you wouldn't believe it, darling. Dilys just walked out and left the poor little thing to look after herself. Can you imagine? She's been begging scraps from neighbours. Laying in a filthy rotten bed. You wouldn't believe the half of it.'

'But I've been sending money to Dilys regular, so she could buy stuff for Susan.'

'Have you? That was kind.' That conniving bitch, Dilys, had never mentioned no money to him.

'And to Nellie. Why didn't she make sure—'

'Me mother's dead.'

'Nellie's dead?'

Ted rolled his eyes towards heaven. 'Yeah, Gawd rest her soul. That's why we came here. I wouldn't let that kid stay in that prefab a minute longer and there was no one else I could turn to.'

'Where are you living then?'

He didn't hesitate. 'A poxy little bedsitter in Notting Hill Gate.'

'Notting Hill? If these are more of your rotten lies, Ted Martin, I'll —'

'I swear on my mother's . . . On my life. That's why we're here. Susan can't stay over there with me. It's terrible, Gin. Honest, you should see it. There's all these fights between the local yobbos and them West Indian gangs.' Ted was getting into his stride and was rather pleased with his imaginative choice of fictitious address. 'How could I take her over there? Poor little kid. Plus she needs a woman's touch. You know, she's nearly eight now. A proper little lady.'

'There's no need for all your old flannel, Ted. Susan can stay here while you sort yourself out.'

'I don't reckon I should leave her though, Gin. She'll be scared without her dad. It's bad enough losing her mum like this. And what with her old granny going an' all . . .'

Ginny sighed wearily. 'All right, Ted, save it. You can stay. But just for a few nights. And I really mean it.'

'I knew I could depend on you, babe.' He reached out and touched her shoulder.

'Aw no,' she said, pulling her dressing-gown tight to her throat. 'Don't even think about it.'

'But, darling—'

'And don't you darling me neither. D'you think I'm

stupid? What d'you want me to do? Stand here like a punch-bag, waiting till the mood takes you, then let you take swings at me all night?'

'But d'you think I'd have bothered hitting you, if I hadn't cared about you?'

'*Do what*?'

'And if you hadn't cared about me, you wouldn't have married me, now would you?'

'You live in a sodding dream world.'

'Anyway, I've changed.' He held out his arms. 'Look at me. Here I am with me little kiddie—'

'Bollocks, Ted, I've heard it all before. And I saw what you did to Shirley.'

He was suddenly alert. How could she know? 'What're you talking about?'

'What you did to her face with them fish hooks. That was disgusting.'

She didn't know. Thank Christ for that.

'And if you wanna stay, you can sleep in the sitting-room. I'll fetch you some blankets and a pillow.'

'You're still a tight-arsed bitch,' he muttered.

'What was that?'

'Nothing. Well, actually, I did say something. I said, I really have changed. You just see if I ain't.'

A whole week went by before Simon dared show his face at the club again; now it was Saturday morning and he had thought of a way to try and make amends, or at least to try and get himself back into Ginny's good books. He was surprised by how important her approval was to him, but he couldn't make up his mind whether it was the thought of getting a brilliant story about the lady club boss – that he could probably syndicate worldwide if he played it right – or whether he had actually fallen for her. It wouldn't be the first time he'd fallen so quickly for someone. But there was something special about Ginny . . .

'I don't know that it's a good idea,' said Flora, when Simon asked if he could go up to see her.

'It's okay,' he replied, running up the stairs. 'It's a surprise.'

'It'll be that all right, dearie,' Flora said, shaking his head at the terrible waste when you had such a good-looking hunk preferring the ladies.

Simon was only half-way up the stairs, but was already calling out to her. 'Ginny. It's only me. Simon. Flora let me in. Hurry up and get your coat on. We're going out for the day.' He reached the top of the stairs. 'To the beach,' he went on, pushing open the door and walking into the flat. 'I'm going to cheer you up if it's—'

He stopped dead in his tracks. There was a man, sitting on the sofa in his trousers and vest, with his heavily greased dark hair sticking up all over the place, as if he had been sleeping. He was eating toast.

'Hello,' Simon said politely. 'Who are you?'

'I think I should be asking you that, mate. But for your information, I'm Ginny's old man. Now piss off out of it.'

Simon left, slamming the door behind him.

'Ted,' Ginny called from the bathroom. 'Who was that?'

'No one.'

A fortnight passed and Ted was still camping out in Ginny's sitting-room. She wasn't surprised, really. Nor was she surprised that Ted's claim that he had changed had been just another of his lies. Nothing about Ted had changed at all.

Not only did she discover from Susan that Nellie was very much alive and still living in Bailey Street, but she found out from Flora that Ted was at his old game of stealing money from her. Flora had actually caught him with his hand in the till and he'd still tried to wriggle out of it. Ginny had done her best to keep calm, for Susan's sake, and she had managed quite well, but then late one night, after the club had closed and Ginny was sitting in her booth entering different versions of the night's takings in the two sets of ledgers, one of the girls came stumbling into the bar. She looked a complete mess and was crying hysterically.

'So he's been taking money off you?'

The girl was still weeping uncontrollably and Ginny was having trouble making sense of her story. 'He made me,' she gulped.

'Made you what?'

'Said if I didn't go with the customers . . .' She shook her head wildly. 'I didn't want to. He made me. I can't keep quiet no more.'

'Try and tell me.'

'I know he's your husband, Miss Martin, but . . .' She staggered to her feet and pulled open her blouse.

Ginny's hand flew to her mouth. The girl's chest was criss-crossed with bloody knife slashes.

Ginny left the girl sobbing in the booth, while she instructed Flora to telephone a doctor she knew who had gambling debts with her big enough to ensure that he would do her a favour and keep his mouth shut. Then she took Johnno, the minder she trusted most of all – even unsupervised with the takings – upstairs with her and told Ted to get out.

Ted didn't need to be told twice, not with Johnno there. But he was determined to be as spiteful and awkward as he could get away with. 'Susan,' he shouted. 'Get up. We're leaving.'

Ginny shook her head. 'You bastard.'

The door to the spare room opened and Susan came

out, wearing one of the nighties that Ginny had bought her. She was hollow-eyed with sleep and fear. 'I don't wanna go,' she whispered, her bottom lip trembling with the effort of holding back her tears.

'You're not going anywhere, dolly face. Come on, come and give us a cuddle, you'll be all right with your Auntie Gin. Daddy's the one who's gotta go away for a little while. He's just going downstairs with Johnno, aren't you, Ted? So go and give him a kiss and he can get off.'

Susan kissed Ted's unshaven cheek, then fled back to Ginny's side. She watched warily as Johnno and her dad left the flat.

Ginny took her back to her bed and tucked her in with her teddy bear. 'If you want me, I'll just be in the other room sorting out a couple of things. All right?'

Susan nodded.

Ginny kissed her on the cheek, turned on the squirrel-shaped night light that stood on the bedside table – another of the many things she had bought for Susan during the past weeks – and sat with her until her eyes finally closed.

Then she went back into the sitting-room, bundled up the blankets off the sofa and threw them in the kitchen ready for the laundry. At least the place didn't have to look like a refugee camp any longer, nor did it have to stink of Ted Martin.

She had no fear that he'd be back, he was too much of a coward for that, but he was such a spiteful bastard, he might just try and get Susan away from her. And she couldn't bear that. She'd have to work something out; find a way to keep her safe. She couldn't let her go again. She just couldn't.

She went over to the cocktail cabinet to pour herself a drink, but, remembering the music box rendition of 'Secret Love', she stopped. She didn't want Susan being disturbed again, the poor little thing had been through more than enough already.

Ginny dropped wearily on to the sofa. But, exhausted as she was, she vowed she wouldn't go to sleep until she had worked out a way to keep the child she loved.

She felt as though her head was ready to split with the effort of going round and round the same useless ideas, then, quite suddenly, it came to her. Ted had let slip that Dilys had married some American soldier, whom she'd kidded about Susan not being hers. If she got in touch with her somehow – it couldn't be that difficult – Dilys would have no choice. Her name – the only name, the father being *unknown* – would be on the birth certificate. If Dilys wanted to keep up her little pretence she would have to give Ginny guardianship, or she would spill the beans so fast, Dilys wouldn't know what had hit her.

She'd done it. She'd found a way. Now Susan could stay with her for ever.

Chapter 20

April 1955

It had been another long day. Ginny had originally intended to get herself into a routine of getting up to see Susan off to school, then having another couple of hours' sleep, but once she was up it seemed slatternly to go back to bed, especially with the bright spring mornings. Feeling a bit tired was nothing, compared with the happiness, love and pride she felt as she looked down at the peacefully sleeping child, barely recognisable as the pale-faced waif who had turned up at the club in the early hours of the morning over nine months before.

The morning after Johnno had thrown Ted out, Ginny had gone to Bailey Street to see Dilys's brothers, Sid and Micky, full of foreboding at what they would have to say about her suggestion that Susan should stay with her at the club. It had been quite a while since she'd seen them, but when Ted had stayed, he'd told her plenty about the women they'd married and they sounded terrifying.

But she had had no need to worry. They – or rather the wives – had seemed only too pleased that they weren't about to have a seven-year-old cuckoo forced into their cosy little nests and soon persuaded their husbands that Ginny caring for Susan would be best all round for everyone. Then Ginny had crossed the street and popped in to see Nellie. It was an odd sensation going into number 11 again after all that time, but it had to be done. She had to warn Nellie that if her son came anywhere near Ginny's club she would have the law on him.

Nellie had been her usual aggressive self, but Ginny had remained calm and just told her to remind Ted that she had enough high-ranking policemen amongst her customers to make his life very uncomfortable. And if Nellie forgot to give Ginny's message to her son, she might just find that her weekly envelope started getting forgotten as well.

She had then spoken to a solicitor – another regular at Ginny's – and had asked him about tracing Dilys.

With all that organised, and Susan enrolled in the local school, the only worry Ginny had was what she would do if Billy Saunders did eventually get rid of the clubs. She would need to find a new job and a new home, and now there were two of them it wouldn't be quite so easy.

Nor would it be easy meeting up with Billy Saunders again. She'd heard the odd word of gossip about him, but she hadn't set eyes on him in a long time. She couldn't, though, put it off any longer, she really would have to find out what he intended doing about his businesses.

She'd make a cup of tea, have a glance through the paper and get herself off to bed. Then, in the morning, after she'd got Susan off to school, she'd organise a meeting with Billy to get things settled once and for all.

She'd only intended a quick flick through the news while she drank her tea, but when she read the headline – *Ruth Ellis charged with murder* – and saw that the story had been written by Simon Parker, Ginny put her untouched tea down on the side table and read every word.

To begin with, she had been half smiling with embarrassment at her own foolishness, remembering how she had actually considered Simon as her potential saviour, but by the time she had finished any trace of amusement had vanished.

413

Simon was a good sort of bloke and she hoped he was doing well, but had he been the most wonderful man in the world, Ginny still wouldn't have been able to do what it seemed that Ruth Ellis had done.

Ginny studied the photograph of her in the paper. It showed a woman, not particularly exceptional, but attractive, with hair dyed as blonde as her own; and she wondered whatever had made her do it. What had made her put a man before her children? What had made her decide that that man, any man, was so important?

She folded the paper and picked up her tea. It was stone cold. How long had she been sitting there? She looked at her watch.

Ten to four?

Johnno should have been round to pick up the takings nearly an hour ago. Where the hell had he got to? It wasn't like him to let her down.

She yawned loudly. She might as well make a fresh cup of tea while she was waiting.

She had just set the water to boil when she heard the welcome sound of footsteps on the stairs. 'Come in, Johnno,' she called from the kitchen, getting out another cup. 'You must have heard me put the kettle—'

Her words froze on her lips and the cup fell from her hand and went spinning across the tiled floor. Standing in the kitchen doorway was Ted, looking and stinking like a meths drinker who'd just been thrown off a bench on the Embankment.

He lifted his food and stamped on the spinning cup, shattering it into a myriad pieces.

'How did you get in?'

Ted winked and stumbled into the room. 'Fire escape and a bit of force, darling,' he slurred. 'You wanna get that checked. You never know who might find their way up your stairs.'

'What d'you want?'

'I've decided,' he said, waving his arms wildly about him. 'If you ain't gonna give me a fair share of this gaff, then you ain't gonna have the kid. I'm taking her with me.'

'If you go anywhere near that child,' she said, putting herself determinedly between Ted and the door, 'I swear I'll—'

She put up her arms to protect herself, but she was too late. Ted caught her a sharp crack to the side of her face, splitting open her cheek like a gaping mouth. She screwed up her eyes in pain, but didn't utter a sound.

Don't let her wake up. Please, don't let her wake up, Ginny prayed in her head.

He pulled back his fist for a second shot, but lost his balance and staggered backwards, then, trying to steady himself, tripped forward and crashed into the table.

Ginny's mind was racing in spite of the blow. If she could get him downstairs, away from the flat, away from Susan, Johnno would be here soon.

'Look Ted, I'm sorry. I'm being selfish, you are her father after all. And it's not fair, me keeping her all to myself. Tell you what, let's go down and discuss it over a drink.'

Unable to resist the offer of another drink, Ted followed her out of the flat and down the stairs.

The second-floor bar was in darkness. Ginny turned on the red-shaded lamp in her booth. 'Make yourself comfortable, Ted, and I'll fetch a bottle over. Scotch all right?'

Ted's angry sneer distorted his once handsome face into a brutal mask of hatred. 'Here's you living like Lady fucking Docker, while I'm on me uppers.'

Ginny swallowed hard, willing Johnno to hurry up. 'I won't be a minute.'

She flicked the switch that illuminated the bar, found a bottle of whisky, then hesitated over whether to take one or two glasses. Ted was just as capable of belting her for not wanting to drink with him as for having some of the scotch that he could have drunk.

She decided on two and put them on a tray with a jug of water. If he wanted her to drink she would at least keep a clear head by watering it down. She had to keep control until Johnno arrived.

'Here you are.'

'What's that noise?' Ted frowned. 'It's someone letting themselves in. You'd better not have no bloke shacked up here with you.' He made as if to stand up.

'No, Ted, of course I haven't. I'm your wife.'

There was the sound of the door being closed.

'Well who is it?'

'It'll be the bloke come to do the bottling up for me.'

'At this time of the morning?'

'He works nights. Does a double shift.' Christ she was talking crap. She just hoped he was drunk enough not to notice. Anything to give Johnno time to get up the stairs.

'Go and get rid of him.'

'Okay. But you stay here.'

Ginny fled from the room, terrified that Ted would go back up to the flat.

'Johnno,' she whispered as she ran down the pitch-dark stairs. 'Please. Keep your voice down. Please. It's import—'

Suddenly she felt a pair of large arms grab hold of her. It was all she could do not to scream.

'What's up?' a man's voice asked.

'Billy?' she gasped. 'Is that you?'

'Yeah. What we whispering for?'

'I didn't expect—'

'Johnno's old woman's gone into labour and he's having to mind the other kids and—'

'That don't matter—'

'I left it late so's you'd be in bed. He should have phoned, but he probably—'

'Look, Billy, please, you've gotta help me.'

Ginny stood behind Billy as he turned on the main overhead lights that lit up the whole second floor for the cleaners.

Ted shielded his eyes. 'What the fuck are you up to, you stupid tart. Turn them lights off.'

Billy stared in disbelief. 'Ted Martin? *Ted Martin*? One of the stupid little two-bob snakes what's been trying to have one over on me over the years? *He's* your old man? This piece of—' He turned to look at Ginny. 'What's happened to your face?'

'Billy? Billy Saunders?' Ted was on his feet, barrelling across the room straight for him. 'You bastard!'

'Billy, mind out!' Ginny yelled, pushing him sideways.

The chair that Ted had thrown at Billy's head missed him and hit Ginny instead, sending her tumbling backwards towards the stairs. She grabbed hold of the banister and fell, screaming in agony as her arm was nearly jerked from its socket.

Billy ran to help her.

'No. I'm all right,' she gasped. 'Just stop him getting upstairs. Please, there's a kid up there. Don't let him hurt her.'

Ted was already half-way up the stairs to the flat. Billy lunged at him at full stretch and just managed to get hold of the back of his jacket. He pulled him backwards and the pair of them fell in a heap on to the landing. By the time Ginny got to them they were up on their feet again, punching and kicking at each other like savages.

Ginny wanted to get past, to get up to Susan, but she was too scared to go near them, they were completely out of control.

Suddenly, Billy was staggering backwards holding his arm and blood was pouring down his sleeve.

'Billy?'

'Mind, Gin, the bastard's got a knife.'

Ted started laughing, then turned round to run up the stairs.

She wasn't sure where she got the courage from, but Ginny launched herself at Ted and started smacking him round the back of the head. 'Keep away from her,' she sobbed. 'Keep away.'

Ted laughed louder and turned round, shaking her like an Alsatian trying to rid itself of a troublesome terrier. 'Piss off.'

Ginny, her eyes wide with fury, sank her teeth deep into his hand. He dropped the knife and she snatched it up and stuck it straight into the side of his neck.

The next thing Ginny knew, she was standing looking down at Ted, who was stretched out on the landing with his head twisted round like a broken doll and his eyes staring up at the ceiling.

Billy took her by the shoulders, rolled Ted out of the way with his foot and eased her towards the stairs. 'Go up to the flat. I'll be up in a minute.'

As soon as he saw her close the flat door behind her, Billy ran back down to the second floor and grabbed the telephone from behind the bar. 'Yeah, Johnno, I know it's hard, but I need you here. I need someone I can trust.' He pulled out his cigarette case. 'I need you to clear something up for me. Right away.' He flicked his lighter and inhaled deeply. 'Yeah. That's right. It's some rubbish. I want it out of Ginny's way. It's not too bulky but you might wanna bring one of the chaps with you. Someone we both like, if you see what I mean. I'll get straight on the blower to Leila. She'll get someone round yours to mind the kids.'

As Johnno put the phone down he rubbed his hands over his unshaven face. This was all he needed. He'd promised Chrissie faithfully he'd stay with the kids while she was in the hospital. And after all the rucks they'd had lately she'd said this was his last chance. He was just about fed up being at everyone's beck and call. He earned good money but he never had the chance to bloody spend any of it. And if Chrissie knew that her nippers had been minded by one of Leila's toms she'd kill him stone dead. But he couldn't say no to Billy. He'd just have to get it done as quick as he could and get back home before the kids woke up and saw that it wasn't their daddy who was looking after them.

'Are you all right, girl?'

Ginny nodded, her hand was trembling so badly she could hardly hold her cigarette.

'I'll make you a cup o' tea, yeah?'

'But how about—'

'Don't worry. Someone's sorting it out.'

Billy went into the kitchen and made the tea. When he brought it through to the sitting-room Ginny's shoulders were heaving as she wept silently into her hands. He put the tray down and knelt beside her. 'Don't cry, girl, it's gonna be all right.'

As she dropped her hands to look at him, Billy winced at the sight of the bloody gash across her cheek. 'That slag did that, didn't he?'

She turned her head away. 'What am I gonna do, Bill? This is all such a mess. There's a little girl asleep in there and—'

'Who is she, this kid?'

'Her mother was the person I used to think was my best friend. She's not around any more, so I took her in.'

'How about the father?'

She lifted her chin and looked into his eyes. 'I just killed him.'

The next evening Ginny was in too much of a state to go downstairs to the club, but Billy insisted they should open as usual, keep everything as normal as possible – he would see to things, make sure everything was all right, while she got some rest. There were a few eyebrows raised amongst the staff when Billy emerged from the flat upstairs, but they all knew better than to ask any awkward questions.

It was nearly half past nine and Ginny, her nerves twanging like badly tuned harp strings, had just been in to check on Susan yet again, when there was an urgent knocking on the flat door.

As she carefully closed Susan's door, Ginny's stomach was turning back flips and she ran through all the possibilities of who it might be. She had to remember what Billy had said about keeping up a calm appearance. She managed to call lightly, 'Okay, I'm coming,' and walked unsteadily out to the door that she had double-locked and chained for the first time since she had moved in.

She didn't know whether to be relieved or even more worried when she saw that her visitor was Leila. What did she want? They'd not said a word to one another since the night Shirley had been killed.

'I'd like to talk to you, Ginny,' Leila said very formally. 'May I come in?'

Ginny stepped back and ushered her through into the sitting-room. 'Course. But I'd appreciate you keeping your voice down. As I'm sure you've heard, I've got a little girl living with me now.'

Leila draped herself across the sofa and allowed her fox furs to fall from her shoulders. 'That's not the only thing I've heard.'

'No?' Ginny automatically covered the gash on her face with her hand. Surely Leila hadn't found out about last night. Her other hand shook as she offered Leila the cigarette box from the coffee table.

Leila took her time lighting and inhaling, then with her eyes fixed on Ginny's she said, 'You know what people are like. How they talk.'

Ginny said nothing.

'Billy stayed here last night, didn't he?'

Was that it? Was that all she knew? 'He's downstairs now, if that's what you mean,' said Ginny warily. 'I didn't feel too well today and he said he'd keep an eye on things.'

'I can see from that cut on your face that something's wrong.'

'That's nothing to do with Billy.'

'I didn't think it was.' Leila pinned on her professional smile. 'And it's no concern of mine. But you don't have to lie to me, Ginny. And before you ask, no he doesn't know I'm up here, I slipped past him. Regular little spy, aren't I?'

'Leila, I don't know—'

'Look, darling, it's no secret that Billy and I haven't exactly been what they call an item for quite a while now. But when he's just messing around with different girls – Belle one week, Sylvia another – I know I still have a chance.' She tapped the ashes from her cigarette and studied the little grey mound in the chromium ashtray as though it were an item of great fascination, then she raised her eyes and laughed mirthlessly. 'I'm having a bit of trouble saying this, sweetie. Bit embarrassing, if you know what I mean. You see, until you

421

came along I was always the one Billy came back to. The trouble is, he likes you, Ginny, he likes you a lot.'

Ginny's head was thumping. She really didn't need this. Not now. She stood up. 'Leila. Please, I—'

'Just hear me out.' Now Leila was on her feet too. 'All I want to say is, it's up to you what happens next. You're the one with all the cards. But if you don't really want him, then please tell him, Ginny.' Leila looked away. 'You can't imagine how much I hate being reduced to this.'

'Sit down, Leila,' Ginny said wearily. 'I'll get us a drink.'

She went over to the cocktail cabinet and lifted the lid; the mechanical opening bars of 'Secret Love' came plinking out, as loud in Ginny's head as a round of church bells. 'Bugger! I forgot.' She snapped down the lid and paused, listening for any sound of Susan stirring. 'I'll go in the kitchen and get us—'

'I'd rather you stayed here,' said a man's voice.

Ginny and Leila both twisted round to see a youngish man standing behind the sofa.

Shit! She must have forgotten to lock the door when she'd let Leila in.

'Remember me?' he asked.

She shook her head.

'Try,' he persisted.

She really didn't remember him and she was too pre-occupied with trying to remember all the other things that Billy had told her she should do – apart from locking the door and not letting anyone into the flat – to bother playing guessing games with some punter who'd somehow found his way upstairs. She just knew he was about to beg her for a loan so he could play *just one more game* of chemmy, or to have an extension on his bar tab. She'd heard it all before.

'Look, if you—' she began, but then she saw the two

policemen blocking the doorway behind him and a sickening realisation flooded over her.

Of course she remembered him. He was a copper. He was Detective Sergeant Chisholm, the cocky young plainclothes officer who'd raided the club; the one who had threatened all sorts – until Billy had got Doug Millson round to sort him out.

'Leila,' she said calmly, 'would you mind going down and telling Billy, please.'

Leila went to stand up, but Chisholm shook his head. 'You'd only be wasting your time, Miss Harvey,' he said, using Leila's name as though they were old acquaintances. 'Saunders knows I'm up here. Two DCs are keeping him company downstairs and I don't think he should be disturbed. He wanted to have a word with DI Millson on the phone. But I told him, like I told you, he'd only be wasting his time.' He sighed contentedly. 'There's no wriggling out of it this time you see, Mrs Martin. We've got everything we need. It's as simple as that.'

Ginny's mouth was so dry she could barely speak. 'What d'you want?' she croaked.

'Well, I'm not here for a cut of the gambling, or for free drinks, or even a free fuck for that matter. I leave that sort of thing to my older colleagues. I'm here to tell you that the body of Ted Martin, your husband, was found washed up in the tide on the Essex marshes earlier today. And from the rocks in his pockets it seemed that someone was trying to conceal it. Not very well, as it happened. Rather a rushed job I'd say. Or maybe an amateur's attempt.'

Leila's eyes widened just a fraction, but she didn't utter a word.

'We found something else in his pocket,' Chisholm continued, digging inside his jacket and pulling out a clear cellophane envelope. 'This.'

Ginny wouldn't look at it, whatever it was. She shook her head. 'I've been separated from my husband for years.'

Chisholm took a step forward. 'I've just noticed your face, Mrs Martin. 'How did you get that injury?'

'I fell.'

'Your husband had quite a reputation for smacking women around, didn't he?'

'Did he? I don't know. I've not seen him for I can't remember how long. And—'

'Do you recognise this, Mrs Martin?'

Chisholm held up the clear packet so that she had no choice but to look at it.

'What ' Ginny swallowed hard. 'What is it?'

'It's a business card. It was found tucked inside the torn lining of his jacket pocket. It's a bit soggy from the river water, of course, but it's quite obvious what it is if you look. It's your card, Mrs Martin.'

Ginny dropped down on to the sofa next to Leila, the taste of bile bitter in her throat.

'I think we'd better continue this conversation down at the station, don't you, Mrs Martin.'

'But there's a little girl—'

'Don't worry, Ginny,' Leila said. 'I'll look after her.'

'Oh dear, oh dear, Chisholm, you have been a bit previous, haven't you?'

Chisholm was standing – standing! – stony-faced in front of DI Millson's desk, while Millson, and Saunders, and Saunders's fancy, over-priced West End brief sat looking at him as though he was something they'd just stepped in.

'You've held Mrs Martin in custody all night, haven't you?'

'Yes, sir. I—'

'Keep your trap shut, Chisholm. If you listened a bit more you might learn something.'

Chisholm's jaw was rigid with anger. How dare that bent bastard Millson tell him what to do?

'Mr Saunders here has been, let us say, keeping company with Mrs Martin and she had not been out of his sight for three whole days. Gentleman that he is, Mr Saunders would like this to be kept quiet, of course, to protect the lady's reputation.'

Billy Saunders grinned happily at the now puce-faced Chisholm. 'If you wanna do a proper bit of detective work, son,' he beamed, 'I can help you. Would you like that?'

Chisholm managed a brief nod. He wanted to smash the bastard's face in.

'You take yourself down the docks. Anyone'll do. The Royal, the Albert ... And talk to some of them fellers down there. The ones in the bonded warehouses all knew Ted Martin. They're the ones who reckon their stock keeps "disappearing". They were business associates of his, you might say. I wonder if he owed any of them any money? You could ask 'em, couldn't you? But you'll have to watch yourself, son, they're hard men down there.'

Saunders leaned back in his seat and pulled his cigarettes out of his pocket. 'Tell you what, when you've finished down there, you can try talking to some of the girls round Soho. Ask them about him. They'll be able to tell you all about his nasty little ways and what a no-good slag he was. There must be plenty of toms and their ponces who had the right needle with that piece o' shit.'

Chisholm stared determinedly in front of him. 'Can I go now, sir?'

Saunders knew full well he was talking to Millson, but he couldn't resist. 'Course you can, son,' Saunders said.

'And mind how you go. Some of them brasses can be right hard nuts.'

As Chisholm left Millson's office, Saunders's laughter followed him like a bad smell.

'Don't you say a single word,' Chisholm barked at an open-mouthed WPC who just happened to be walking past.

Within ten minutes, Billy had shown his appreciation to Millson with a bundle of used notes, had paid his brief for his very expensive time – which hadn't actually been required, but Saunders always liked to be prepared – and was now helping a deathly pale Ginny into the back of a cab.

He told the driver where to take them and slid the glass screen shut. 'Are you all right, girl?'

She shook her head and stared down at the floor. 'I can't take any more of this, Billy. I can't. I just don't know what to do. I wanted to tell them it was me. But I was so scared for Susan, I—'

Billy folded his arms around her and she buried her head in his shoulder.

'Ssssh, girl, don't get all upset, I'm here now and I'm gonna look after you.'

Chapter 21

July 1957

Ginny leaned back in the blue-and-white-striped deck-chair, stretched out her bare, tanned legs and pressed her toes into the soft, cool grass. Maybe, when your life was so good, it wasn't right to ask for more, but it wasn't as though she was asking for herself. And it wasn't as though she was asking for that much – just for Dilys to mention Susan in her letters. Then at least Ginny could show them to her. That would be something, some sort of contact with her mother. But no; not a word in any of them about anything other than how wonderfully Dilys was doing in America. It was as though her daughter had never existed.

Ginny sighed and let the single sheet of airmail paper, and the two brightly coloured snapshots showing Dilys and a tall, handsome man holding a baby in his arms, fall into her lap. She would put this latest one with all the rest and maybe, when Susan was older, she would let her see them and try to help her understand.

In the meantime she would write back to Dilys asking her, yet again, please to jot down just a few extra lines for Susan. Anything would do.

Perhaps it was silly bothering, especially as Susan was so happy. She knew she was wanted, treasured and loved. That she was Ginny's very special girl.

But was that enough? Ginny sighed again. Love was powerful all right, but could it ever take away the pain of rejection completely? She could only hope so.

'Mrs Saunders.'

At the sound of the woman's voice Ginny looked up,

squinting into the bright sunlight at the neatly uniformed maid standing a respectful distance to the side of her chair.

'Have I got to collect Susan already, Janette?' Ginny asked with a concerned frown. She put her watch to her ear to check it was still working.

'No, ma'am, that's not for over an hour. And Mrs Taylor said she'd be dropping her off, if you remember.'

Ginny relaxed. 'Of course.'

'You have a visitor.'

Janette's formality drove Ginny mad. 'Who is it?'

Instead of acting with her usual efficient primness, the maid pursed her lips and waggled her head with displeasure.

'Is something wrong?'

'She wouldn't say who she was, Mrs Saunders. Said it was to be a surprise. I didn't know what to do.'

Ginny smiled thinly. It would be one of the local worthies after a donation for some charity or other, thinking she was being a real wag by aggravating the staff. She still hadn't got used to the way of things in her new neighbourhood; in fact, it was like living in a foreign country at times.

'It's okay, Janette. Don't worry. Just bring her out, please.'

As the maid returned across the sweeping lawns with the surprise visitor in tow, Ginny leapt to her feet. 'Leila!' she yelled, running towards her with outstretched arms.

'Sweetie, you recognised me!'

'How could I fail to, with that bloody emerald-green frock coming across the grass?'

Ginny saw the shocked expression on Janette's face but she didn't care. 'It was like you was in flipping camouflage, girl!'

*

428

Ginny filled Leila's cup, sat back in her deckchair and took in a deep lungful of flower-scented air. 'I might not be Grace Kelly, like Flora used to reckon, but sitting here drinking tea in the garden with my old mate, well, this'll do me.'

'Less of the old thank you, Ginny – but we're still friends, are we?'

Ginny smiled and tutted loudly. 'Of course we are.'

Leila avoided her gaze, picking at an imaginary thread on her skirt. 'And you're happy are you?'

'Yeah, I reckon I am.'

Leila lifted her chin and Ginny winked at her across the rim of her cup. 'D'you know, Leila, there were plenty of times when I never believed that poor little Ginny Martin would ever make it. But just look at me now, eh?' She cocked her head on one side. 'And how about you? How are you doing? 'Cos pleased as I am to see you, I'm dying to know why you've turned up out of the blue like this.'

Leila didn't answer her question; she took her time breathing out a long plume of lavender smoke, then said: 'Strange, isn't it? Who knows what'll become of any of us? What'll happen in our lives. The twists and turns.'

'Well, you know what they say, Leila.' Ginny held her hands to her heart, stared dramatically towards the horizon and gasped in her best southern belle's drawl, 'Tomorrow is another day.'

Leila clapped her thigh. 'God! I remember that. It's from that old film.' She flapped her hand. 'Don't tell me. You used to drive us all crazy going on about it. And that woman in it. The one with all the dreams . . .'

Slightly shamefaced, Ginny grinned. '*Gone With the Wind*. Scarlett O'Hara. And they were *my* dreams too, if you don't mind.'

Leila shook her head and smiled, remembering. 'That brings back some memories.'

'I still dream, you know. When I'm sleeping, I mean. All about this place I knew a long, long time ago.'

'What place was that?'

'The street where I used to live. I see the rooms in that house as plain as day. It's a strange feeling. And all the neighbours, I see them too. There were some really decent people there once, back in the old days. And some right old cows.'

'You get those everywhere.' Leila laughed.

'It's all been knocked down now. Nothing left but a big patch of bare earth. Slum clearance, they reckon.' She paused. 'You know, it never seemed like a slum. Not back then. Still, things have to change, I suppose. And now they're talking about putting up one of them big blocks of flats. Well, that's what I heard.'

'And is Billy still in the property business?' Leila asked casually, suddenly fascinated, apparently, by the ash on the end of her cigarette.

'Yeah. And he's doing very well.'

She nodded. 'So I can see. This place is fantastic.'

'Not bad, is it?' Ginny looked about her, taking in the solidly respectable seven-bedroomed red-brick house, set in its four landscaped acres. 'And very well thought of he is nowadays. Works with this bloke. Peter. And talking about slums, that's what they do. They buy up slum property; terrible old places, all over London. Then, when the tenants move out, Billy's firm does them up.'

Leila's eyebrow rose very slightly. She knew all about the slum landlords and their scams: acquiring occupied properties on the cheap, then terrorising the tenants until they got out. In fact, she'd put on enough private parties for them during the last few years to be able to write a book about them and their influential friends. But she said nothing. She'd never been able to figure out whether Ginny really didn't know what was going on half the time, or whether she just chose not to see what was right in front of her.

Well, it wasn't any of Leila's business. Not any more.

She closed her eyes for a brief moment, then, flashing her lips-only smile she said, 'This really is a glorious garden, Ginny. And I'd love to see around the house.'

'You're on, girl, but the guided tour'll cost you half a crown.'

'I'll pay willingly, darling, and I'll bet it's every bit as wonderful as . . . What was Scarlett's place called again?'

'Tara,' Ginny replied without a second's hesitation.

'That's it. Tara. I should have remembered.' She tapped her chin with an exquisitely manicured fingertip. 'Well, Ginny, my love, it looks as though you've got your Tara at last.'

'And it's just right for a family.'

Leila stared at Ginny's flat stomach and frowned. 'You mean you're . . .'

Ginny shook her head – more to dispel the visions of Jeannie Thompson and her best yellow soap than by way of an answer. 'No, I'm not pregnant,' she said evenly. 'I'd like to be, but it just hasn't happened. Anyway, I've got my daughter. We adopted Susan.'

'Susan? Not that lovely little girl you were caring for?'

'That's my Susan. You'll be able to see her later, when she gets home from her riding lesson.'

'You're a lucky woman, Ginny.' Leila's voice caught as she spoke.

'I know. And when you think how things could have turned out. When you think of Shirley and some of the others.' She took a moment to top up their cups. 'Poor Shirley, eh?'

Leila showed no sign of what her thoughts were about

Shirley, she just took a dainty sip of her tea. 'So, where's Billy?' she asked as matter-of-factly as she could.

'Out wheeling and dealing as usual. Entertaining some bloke. A politician, if you must know! They'll be in some club somewhere I suppose.'

This time Leila raised both eyebrows and made sure that Ginny saw her questioning expression.

'Don't look at me like that. It's probably some very respectable gentlemen's club for all I know. But to be honest, I don't have anything to do with the business side of things any more. I've got all I want right here.'

'I think you have.'

'Tell me, Leila. It's something I've always wondered. Why did you help me out that time? Looking after Susan when the law took me away.'

Leila hesitated before she spoke, then, staring down into her cup, she said: 'I had a child myself once. A little girl. She must be, what, twenty-two. Almost twenty-three.' She held up her hand. 'And before you say anything, I was a child myself when I had her.'

They laughed uneasily, as old wounds opened for both of them.

'The trouble is, she's ashamed of me. Won't even see me.' Leila raised her head and looked at Ginny. 'She was adopted. By a very nice couple. Friends of the doctor who delivered her. Actually, he was the same doctor who made me pregnant in the first place.' She pinned her smile back on. 'Aren't some men absolute shits?'

'I'm so sorry, Leila. I didn't know.'

'Don't worry, no one does. I don't even know why I brought it up.' She gave Ginny a cigarette and lit it for her. 'And anyway,' she went on, screwing up her eyes against the smoke as she lit one for herself, 'that was then. At the time it was all I could do to get by from day to day. You know, just clinging to the wreckage and hoping for the best. But things got easier. Over the years.' She laughed carelessly. 'Well, when I saw your face as that little creep said he was taking you down to the police station, I had to stay with her, didn't I? How could I have done otherwise?'

'But you were so upset with me.' She considered before adding: 'You know, about Billy. You could have got one of the others to stay over.'

'Ginny,' Leila said, her chin jutting, 'there was a child involved. I'm not a monster.'

'I'm sorry, I never ...' Ginny looked at her, at her expertly made-up face and her elegantly dressed hair. It was like talking to a lovely mask. 'There's so much we don't know about one another. I'm really glad you came today and that we're talking like this at last. Tell me, Leila, how are you? How are you really?'

'Rather well, actually. I've found myself a decent chap at last.'

'You haven't!'

'Thank you!'

'I didn't mean—'

'How about some more of that lovely tea?' Leila said a little too brightly. 'Pour me some, will you?' She held out her cup. 'He's a reporter actually. His name's Simon.'

Ginny nearly dropped the teapot. 'Not Simon Parker?'

'The very one.' She allowed a genuine, if self-deprecating, smile to curve her lips. 'That's one of the reasons I came to see you, I suppose. To brag.'

'So what were the other reasons?'

'Only one. To come and see you.' Leila should have said: to come and see if you and Billy really look like staying together before I finally throw in my lot with Simon. But she didn't.

'Come on, how did you and Simon get together?'

433

'When Billy was selling up and he gave me the pick of the clubs—'

'Did he? I didn't know that,' Ginny broke in, then added hastily: 'But like I said, I don't have anything to do with the businesses now.'

With a shameful kind of pleasure Leila noted the edge that had crept into Ginny's voice. 'I suppose he thought he owed me something for all those years. I was very loyal.' She gave a little shrug. 'Well, I chose Ginny's. But don't even think of asking why, I'd be much too embarrassed to answer.'

'Leila—'

'Don't worry, water under the bridge, and before you ask, no it isn't called Ginny's any more. It's called Leila's. Far more classy.' She chuckled lazily. 'Anyway, Simon turned up one night. He was looking for you, but he found me instead. We got talking and I asked him if he still wanted a story. He did. And did I have a story to tell.'

'You didn't tell him everything?'

Leila looked horrified. 'Edited highlights, darling! Edited highlights! But it still took months to get through it all and he was absolutely riveted. He treated events like . . . like . . . let me see . . . I know, like Johnno being killed, as if they were crossword clues.' She stared directly into Ginny's eyes. 'Do you know he simply refused to believe it was a hit-and-run accident?'

'I often wondered if that was anything to do with the Maltese gangs,' Ginny said quietly.

Leila leaned back in her deckchair. 'He never came up with that theory,' she said with a shake of her head. 'But it's possible, I suppose. Although Simon always thought Johnno was being paid off by someone close to home. For some mistake he'd made. Maybe—'

'Whatever it was,' Ginny cut in, 'I know it was really sad, happening just two days after his wife had her baby.'

Leila did her professional smile again. 'Perhaps he'll get to the bottom of it one day.'

'Isn't he too busy playing that clarinet of his?'

'Don't!'

'Is he just as bad?'

'Let's just say he'll never be a Benny Goodman.'

They laughed, slightly more easily this time, and sat for a while in almost companionable silence.

'He decided not to publish my story in the end.'

'Why not?'

'He fell in love with me instead. Wanted to keep me all to himself. That's why he proposed.'

'Leila!'

'I know.' She took a long draw on her cigarette. 'I didn't really take him seriously for a while. Plus I suppose there were things I had to be sure about.' She paused as though she were thinking something through. 'It took me a while, but I eventually said yes to him. Last weekend, actually.' She held out her left hand and flashed a large, square-cut diamond solitaire.

'So that's an *engagement* ring?'

'It is. Can you imagine, darling? Me, about to become a respectable married woman, marrying a man who is about to be made editor of the *Evening News*?'

'Leila, that's wonderful.'

'It's a start. But he's still got his eye on *The Times*, of course.'

'No, I meant about you getting married.'

'It is a bit of a turn-up, isn't it? And do you know, I've decided that on the big day I'm actually taking off the emerald green for once and I'm going to—'

The droning of a low-flying aeroplane drowned out the rest of Leila's words.

435

'Bloody row,' Ginny shouted, shielding her eyes against the sun, as she sought out the culprit. 'Who'd's he think . . .' But then her tone changed from one of protest to one of amazement. 'Well, will you look at that?'

Ginny pointed at the clear blue summer sky, where the plane was now flying up and away in a wide swoop, high above their heads. Behind it snapped a long white banner, whipping and flapping in its trail. The inscription on it read: *You never had it so good, love Mac X.*

Ginny clapped her hands with delight. 'I reckon he's right there, you know, Leila.' She grinned, raising her teacup by way of a toast. 'We really haven't had it so good, have we? All our dreams really have come true.'

Leila looked at Ginny and was about to say something, but changed her mind. Instead, she too lifted her cup in salute and smiled. 'Let's hope so, sweetie, let's hope so . . .'

GILDA O'NEILL

The Lights of London

The lights of London seem bright to Kitty Miller, but their sparkle soon fades when she finds herself alone and destitute, at the mercy of those who inhabit the fog-bound streets and alleyways of the East End.

Rescued by the feisty young prostitute, Tibs Tyler, who takes her under her wing, Kitty's real adventures in London begin. For she and Tibs must earn a living – but Kitty, who has run away, knows nothing of surviving on the streets. It falls on Tibs to find food and shelter for her new companion, in a city in which the gulf between rich and poor is ever wider.

When Tibs and Kitty stumble across one of the new music halls opening up across London, a music hall in desperate need of some good acts, their luck begins to change. Can they persuade the owner to try them on stage? Attracted by the possibility of a night away from the streets, they bluff their way into the show.

But as they throw themselves into singing and dancing, Tibs must always keep one eye out for a sinister figure from her past, Albert. He wants his girls earning money for him alone – and doesn't care who he hurts in the process. And Tibs has someone she must protect at all costs . . .

KATIE FLYNN

Strawberry Fields

Liverpool: Christmas Day 1924. When twelve-year-old Sara Cordwainer, the unloved child of rich and fashionable parents, sees a ragged girl with a baby in her arms outside her church, she stops to talk to her, pressing her collection money into the girl's icy hand. But from this generous act comes a tragedy which will haunt her for years.

The day Sara meets Brogan O'Brady, a young Irishman working in England, she feels she has found a friend at last. She does not hesitate to confide in him, but Brogan has a secret which he dares tell no one, not even Sara.

And in a Dublin slum, Brogan's little sister Polly is growing up. Polly, the only girl in a family of boys, knows herself to be much loved and valued, but it is not until Sara begins to work at the Salvation Army children's home, Strawberry Fields, that the two girls meet — and Brogan's secret is told at last . . .

Saga titles available

☐ A Liverpool Lass	Katie Flynn	£6.99
☐ The Girl from Penny Lane	Katie Flynn	£6.99
☐ Liverpool Taffy	Katie Flynn	£6.99
☐ The Mersey Girls	Katie Flynn	£6.99
☐ Strawberry Fields	Katie Flynn	£6.99
☐ Georgia	Lesley Pearse	£6.99
☐ Tara	Lesley Pearse	£6.99
☐ Charity	Lesley Pearse	£6.99
☐ Ellie	Lesley Pearse	£5.99
☐ Camellia	Lesley Pearse	£5.99
☐ The Blue and Distant Hills	Judith Saxton	£5.99
☐ Someone Special	Judith Saxton	£5.99
☐ Harvest Moon	Judith Saxton	£5.99
☐ Family Feeling	Judith Saxton	£5.99

ALL ARROW BOOKS ARE AVAILABLE THROUGH MAIL ORDER OR FROM YOUR LOCAL BOOKSHOP AND NEWSAGENT.

PLEASE SEND CHEQUE/EUROCHEQUE/POSTAL ORDER (STERLING ONLY) ACCESS, VISA, MASTERCARD, DINERS CARD, SWITCH OR AMEX.

☐☐☐☐☐☐☐☐☐☐☐☐☐☐☐☐

EXPIRY DATE .... SIGNATURE ....

PLEASE ALLOW 75 PENCE PER BOOK FOR POST AND PACKING U.K.

OVERSEAS CUSTOMERS PLEASE ALLOW £1.00 PER COPY FOR POST AND PACKING.

ALL ORDERS TO:

ARROW BOOKS, BOOKS BY POST, TBS LIMITED, THE BOOK SERVICE, COLCHESTER ROAD, FRATING GREEN, COLCHESTER, ESSEX CO7 7DW.

NAME...

ADDRESS ....

....

Please allow 28 days for delivery. Please tick box if you do not wish to receive any additional information ☐

Prices and availability subject to change without notice.